PRIVATE
Pilot

KAREN DEEN

PRIVATE PILOT
Copyright © 2020 by Karen Deen

Published by Karen Deen
Formatted by Opium House Creatives
Edited by Contagious Edits
Cover Design by Opium House Creatives

ABOUT THE AUTHOR

Karen Deen has been a lover of romance novels and happily-ever-after stories for as long as she can remember. Reaching a point in her life where she wanted to explore her own dreams, Karen decided now was the time to finally write some of her own stories. For years, all of her characters have been forming story lines in her head, just waiting for the right time to bust free.

In 2016, Karen put pen to paper for the first time, with Zach and Emily being the first characters fighting to have their story written. From that first word, she hasn't been able to stop. Publishing Love's Wall (her first novel in the Time to Love Series) in 2017 has ignited her passion to continue writing and bring more of her characters to life.

Karen is married to her loving husband and high school sweetheart. Together, they live the crazy life of parents to three children. She is balancing her life between a career as an accountant by day and writer of romance novels by night. Living in the beautiful coastal town of Kiama, Australia, Karen loves to enjoy time with her family and friends in her beautiful surroundings.

CONTACT

For all the news on upcoming books, visit Karen at:
www.karendeen.com.au
Karen@karendeen.com.au
Facebook: Karen Deen Author
Instagram: karendeen_author

Dedication

For my hubby who stands beside me
while I'm chasing my dream.
So grateful for you in my life xx

PRIVATE *Pilot*

1

Mason

Another day — another case of blue balls.

My job's dangerous to my health but not as much as my boss is.

Fuck, that woman is going to kill me.

At times, the pain she causes is not pleasant. Just thinking about her is already making my balls twitch.

That ass, the way it sways as she ascends the stairs. Long legs and perfect calves. All leading down to those fuck-me heels. Brightly colored that draw my eyes every single time!

One day maybe she'll notice the way I look at her. Until then, I live with the pain.

Climbing out of my Jeep, George is walking around the front of my plane.

"Morning, Captain"

"Hey, George. Got my baby ready for the day?" I walk into the hangar, looking up at the love of my life. Meredith, my *Dassault Falcon 8X* private jet. Technically she's not mine, but she may as well be. No matter how much I fly her, she still brings me joy every single time.

"She's all fueled, checked, and ready for you." George stands, wiping his greasy hands on a rag. He is my main aircraft maintenance technician. I trust him with my baby, which means I trust him with my life and those of my passengers.

"Thanks, man. What would I do without you?" I walk towards the stairs to head on board and start my preflight checks, hearing him chuckling behind me.

"Same thing I always tell you. You'd be on your knees begging for forgiveness from the boss lady because she can't fly across the country to bust someone's balls today."

Laughing to myself, that's a vision I don't want to picture for too long.

Placing my bag in my locker, I enter the cockpit, my office. The moment I sit on my chair in here, closing my eyes and taking a deep breath, I feel home. Where I belong. This has become a ritual for every flight. Get myself in-tune with Meredith, working in sync, nothing a problem.

Preflight checks done, my copilot Aaron and flight crew Holly are on board and settled. George is hooking up Meredith to the towing vehicle and pulling us out to the tarmac to wait for the boss to arrive. There is one thing I never have to worry about. She's always on time.

"Wonder who we have on board today for the flight to Florida, besides the boss? Hope she doesn't have that dickhead assistant Tyson. I'm close to reminding him with my fists that we don't take orders from him." Aaron looks at me, more serious than I would like to think he is.

"Calm down, man. I agree with you, but he works for the boss, so if she says he can tell us to jump, we say how high," I reply while signaling to George from the cockpit that he can unhitch the plane. "Remember, they are always right, and we are here to do our job." Aaron grumbles as he gets on with it.

Looking up, I see the car in the distance crossing the tarmac. Making its way towards the plane, as usual.

"Go time, people." I exit the cabin down the staircase. As the captain, it's my role to welcome all passengers on to my plane. Part of the reason I love my job is the personal service we give. I tried my hand at being a commercial pilot of a larger plane but realized this is more my style.

The car pulls to a stop. Black with dark tinted windows, it doesn't allow me to see our passengers for today.

My eyes are pinned on the rear passenger door. Waiting like always. Standing with my hands behind my back, feet slightly apart.

I've never lost my military training. It's embedded in me no matter how hard I try to shake it off.

My body is racing waiting to see her. Time to breathe deeply and maintain my role.

What feels like ten minutes passes and finally the driver exits the car, opening her door. Today's shoes are bright yellow.

Her fuck-me heels show her confidence and power.

Well, that's what I'm thinking in my head.

Shoes with attitude, her signature look.

Never black. Always a loud color, yet she is far from loud.

Even standing, she's still partly hidden behind the car door, yet I can see her face. Just her face and never her eyes. Not until she is in the confines of the plane. Sunglasses hide her from the world.

I often wonder where she's looking. At me?

Smoothing her clothes down and looking so perfect, she steps out, walking straight to the plane.

"Hello, Ms. Ellen."

She offers a gentle controlled nod, acknowledging me as she passes.

My view from behind as she ascends the stairs spikes my breathing. That ass is one I'd very much like to be acquainted with. More than just admiring it from afar.

Yet, she has a secret flirt with me just to make sure I notice her. I'm sure she knows exactly what she's doing as she sways her hips.

My hands hold tight as I pound into her. These are fantasies I can't be having.

She's my boss and totally off limits.

High-powered CEO Paige Ellen. Totally out of my league.

Never a thing out of place, the master of her domain.

The star of all my dreams since my first day on the job.

I hear a throat clear from behind me. Before I even turn, I know who it is.

Tyson.

Paige's assistant. Grade-A jerk.

What's his fucking problem?

If I say anything, he'll just go running to Paige, saying I was mean to him. He's that kid at school who sucked up to the teacher and then tattled on everyone, so it made him look good. The kind of kid who got picked on because he was such a nerd.

Slowly, I turn back to face him, pulling my shoulders back, that little bit more imposing.

"Sorry, Tyson, I didn't see you there. I was just making sure Ms. Ellen made it safely up the stairs in those heels." I step to the side.

"I'm sure you were. It's Mr. Burke to you. Don't know how many times I need to remind you. Just concentrate on your job flying this plane and I will do my job of looking after Ms. Ellen in every way she needs. Understood?" His attempt to puff out his chest and assert his authority just makes me laugh. I try to hold it in, but as he starts up the stairs, I'm sure he hears my mumbles under my breath and the snickering that goes with it.

Paige's driver, Bent, is beside me with her day bag for the trip, a smirk on his face.

"One day someone is going to tell that guy what we're all thinking." He hands the bag over to Aaron who is now standing next to me.

"Please let it be me. Please, Mason, I'm itching to knock him down a peg or two." Aaron pretends to throw a few air punches like a child.

"I'm first, but something tells me if he steps out of line, the boss will put him in his place, quicker than we can punch. That woman knows how to take care of herself. She eats men like him and you for breakfast." Bent and I laugh at the look of annoyance on Aaron's face. Shaking hands, Bent and I get on with our work for the day.

After loading everything on board and signaling for the cabin to be secured, I smile at Paige.

"Enjoy the flight, Ms. Ellen, and let Holly know if there's anything we can get you to make it more comfortable. We should be in Florida in just over two hours, in plenty of time for your meeting. Tyson, is there anything that I can help you with as the captain of the plane?" He wants to shoot daggers through me for my sarcasm.

Looking up from her laptop that she's already got open on the table in front of her, Paige finally shows me her eyes for the first time today. A tiny twinkle in her eyes at my comment, but then it's gone.

"Thank you, Captain White," is all she says. Holding the look between us that little bit longer than usual, she seems a little sad today. Maybe I'm just imagining things, but I'm not seeing that hard edge that's normally there.

I want to ask her but doubt she'll answer. I've been working for her for around six months now, yet it hasn't gone much beyond the polite greetings and silent flirts. Instead I just look away and leave her to the work in front of her, and I return to the cockpit to get us up in the air.

"Boss lady all belted in, ready for take-off." Aaron looks across as I tighten my harness. I glare at him, and he gets the message.

"Chicago Midway International Tower, this is Lima Delta Foxtrot 215 requesting permission to take off on runway zero-seven on route to Orlando executive Airport Florida. Over." I flick switches and buttons to get the engines started, waiting for the reply.

"Roger Lima Delta Foxtrot 215. You are clear for takeoff on runway zero-seven. Over."

"Roger CMI tower. Approaching runway now, ready for takeoff. Over." While I'm liaising with the tower for permission, Aaron has done the cabin cross check to make sure all doors are secure and passengers' seatbelts on.

"Roger Lima Delta Foxtrot 215, clear for takeoff. Over and out."

Stilling my breathing and focusing my thoughts on nothing else other than getting this plane in the air, I push forward on the throttle and we start the high-speed acceleration down the runway. Counting in my head until I know I've hit the right marker. I pull back hard on my steering to hoist the nose up into the air and we are heading into the sky.

That adrenaline rush of takeoff never gets old.

Settling into the flight as we climb to our cruising altitude, the weather is good, and everything is happening as it should be.

"This is Captain White advising you are now free to move around the cabin. We are currently cruising at forty thousand feet and expect clear weather this morning all the way to Orlando. Our estimated time for landing is nine twenty-five this morning. Sit back, relax, and enjoy your flight."

I activate the autopilot switch for this part of the flight. Leaning back and stretching my arms above my shoulders, I release the nervous energy that always builds during takeoff. The moment I get complacent about flying is the moment I need to stop. I learned a long time ago that you need your wits about you at all times in the air. Even on the simplest of flights there can always be a problem that can make things turn to shit in a matter of seconds.

"Got any plans today while we're on the ground?" Aaron questions.

"No, I'm just going to hang out on the plane and watch a movie. Had a big day yesterday with the boys. Grayson took us back to the track and we got to race each other again. Speeding around a track in a Nascar takes a very close second to flying for the rush. You should try it." Unbuckling my harness, I stand. "All yours for a few minutes, I need to take a leak."

He nods as I pass him to exit the cockpit. Holly is just outside the door preparing breakfast for Paige and Tyson.

She smiles at me while I ease past her in the small galley. Stepping into the main cabin, I notice Paige with her head stuck in her laptop, busy typing away, her nails clicking on the keys at an amazing speed. Tyson is not in his seat which is unusual. I stand leaning against the wall watching her, wondering if she ever stops. What does a relaxing day mean in her world? I'm not sure she even knows what a day off work even means. We've regularly flown on Sundays so she's ready for a meeting early Monday morning. Worse still, she's often flown and had meetings on weekends. Of course, I'm not complaining because the payment for my services is greater on a Sunday. Not like I'm knocking the extra money.

Tate, Grayson, and Lex—my buddies—are always ribbing me when I fly weekends with her. Plenty of Mile-High Club jokes, parking my jet in her hangar, asking what the runway looks like, and other ridiculous but funny comments. You can always rely on Tate to put a shade of dirty in anything innocent.

Paige hasn't noticed me watching her yet. Her fingers stop and hover over the keyboard, like she's thinking. Her chest heaves like she's trying to hold something in and not let it out.

A single tear escapes, sliding down her cheek. Just one. Like she won't give herself permission to let any more release. If there is one thing I can't take, it's to see a woman cry. Yet Paige and her single tear has me moving before I even realize what I'm doing. I kneel beside her chair with my handkerchief, and she startles.

"Captain White, where…" She stammers a little in a voice far softer than I've ever heard from her before.

"Mason, please call me Mason. Sorry to disturb you." Offering up my handkerchief, she shakes her head and turns away from me for a moment to wipe the stray tear away.

"Can I help you with anything? I saw you had dust in your eye."
I place my hand on hers, giving her an out to explain the tear. She
jerks her head back towards me and pulls her hand away from me. I
leave the handkerchief for her on the armrest anyway.

"I'm fine. Thank you for asking. Just very busy preparing for the
meeting." Her voice is cold and hard again. Like the wall she let slip
for that small moment is back firmly in place.

"Which she would be able to do if you would stop annoying her,
Captain White. If you're back here, then who's in charge of the
plane?" Fucking Tyson. I just want to stand up and deck that asshole.

"Tyson!" Paige glares at him, which makes me grin like a
Cheshire cat. Her sharp tongue has him stand still.

"Obviously, unlike you, Tyson, I can manage to fly a jet, take care
of Ms. Ellen in all areas she needs a skilled man, and have time to
take a leak. Don't fret, little boy. Captain White will keep you safe
and get you back on the ground so you can go back to your secretary
duties." Standing now eye level with him, I see his anger rising. For
the first time, I hear a little snicker coming from beside me. It was so
quiet I doubt Tyson heard it. Maybe it was just meant for my ears
only.

"That's Mr. Burke!" It's like he's so close to exploding, and I can't
help myself.

"No worries, *Tyson*." I pat him on the shoulder and turn back to
Paige. "Excuse me, Ms. Ellen, I really need to use the bathroom."

"Paige." She smirks. "Of course, please move, Tyson, so the good
Captain Mason can get past. He has an important job to do so he can
get back to the *cock*pit." She waves her hands at him to accentuate her
point. The way she emphasizes cock has me wanting to do more than
take a leak with my cock.

"Thank you, Paige. Don't forget I'm here if you need my help
with anything at all. I'm a man who aims to please." With that, I
smirk at Tyson and push past him on the way to the bathroom. Seeing
his face turn a bright shade of red with frustration makes my day.

"Thanks, Mason. I'm sure you do try to. I'd be interested to know
your success rate, though." She ends the discussion as her fingernails
start hitting those keys again. Was that a subtle invitation to show
her, or just her pure ball-breaking sarcasm?

The boss lady's back, and Paige is neatly tucking herself back
away where she's hiding.

I need to find a way to get to know the real Paige.

Paige

No grown woman I know is on the phone at this hour of the morning to their father.

What a way to start a day.

I'd prefer some hot guy telling me the dirty things he would do to me if we were in the same room.

My father's voice snaps me out of that fantasy!

"Yes, Daddy, I understand. I just think I should cancel Orlando and send Brian. You need me here." Pacing my bedroom at five-thirty am, I should've hung up by now. Or declined the call in the first place.

"You might be the CEO of the company, Paige, but I am still your father. You will go to Orlando and visit me when you return. You don't cancel an appointment, it's bad manners. You should know that. You never cancel unless someone is dead." I roll my eyes at his stern voice coming through the phone. Well, that can certainly be arranged, Daddy dearest. One day he will remember I'm an adult.

"Yes, Daddy, I might be the CEO, but I am also your daughter and the only family you have. If you aren't well, then I should be looking after you. Brian is perfectly capable of handling the meeting." I can't tell if he is coughing or scoffing at letting Brian fly to Florida. "It's okay to let the vice president take on some of my work. That's what he's there for. Otherwise, I'm wasting the exorbitant salary I'm paying him."

"Don't worry about me, Paige. The company is always your top priority. It should come before everything, including yourself. Now get on that plane and secure the contract. There is a reason I put you in charge. You are my little firecracker. No one takes advantage of my girl."

"Of course, Daddy, you're right." I grit my teeth. "I'll be back by late afternoon and will call around then and check on you. I'm assuming Beth is there looking after you?" My father's housekeeper has been working for us since before I was born. She's like a grandmother to me, practically raised me while Dad was off building an empire for me to take over.

"Yes, she just brought me in a hot cup of tea. Now go and sort out this meeting and let me know what happens. Love you, my firecracker."

"Love you too, Daddy." Ending the call, I stand glancing out at the skyline of Chicago, watching the city slowly waking up to Monday, the start of another crazy week.

Time to get on the treadmill and start the day while listening to the morning news, catching up with the world from overnight. It's been the same routine since I was about sixteen. I always knew I would take over the company from Dad when he was ready. He had been planning that since the day I was first in his arms.

The day he finally stepped down as CEO, I got the speech – or should I say lecture – from him on what is expected of me.

"You're in charge now. Trust no one."
"Be the tiger, the corporate leader."
"Paige Ellen, the CEO they're scared of but aspire to be!"

That was ten years ago, after his mini stroke and he was told he needed to retire. Limit his stress, otherwise he's in danger of a another one which might not be so minor. I was twenty-nine at the time and had been more than ready to take on the world.

Only one thing was stopping me.

A father who retired but was still standing in my office every day checking up on me.

Driving me crazy!

It's hard to finally run things my way with someone still looking over my shoulder and stamping his feet every time he didn't agree with the decision I was making. This little firecracker was about ready to explode.

Finally, I was given a reprieve when his longtime friend, who's my godfather, told him to get out of my way. Franco's the only one who could get away with it. Dad grumbled and sulked for a few months but finally took notice and left me to run the company on my own.

Ellen Corporation continues to have amazing growth and is a leader in the communications industry. Currently we hold a supply contract for the United States Government defense services. It took two years of hard negotiating to land it. Now, my goal is to hold onto it, with the aim to secure more.

I'm greedy like that. When I want something, I'll do whatever it takes to get it.

Within the law, of course.

I'm not one to play dirty in the corporate world. To me that just shows you aren't a skilled businessperson if you need to resort to bribes or under-the-table deals. Work hard and win it on your own merit is the way my dad always taught me.

Sweat pouring off me from running, I hit the shower. Smoothing my soap over my lower body, I'm reminded of how long it's been since it's been touched by anyone but me.

It's a sacrifice I've made. There is no time for anyone else in my life.

As my father reminded me this morning, the company is the most important thing in my life. Something I accepted a long time ago.

I grew up with just my father and Beth. My mother dumped me on the doorstep of Jonathon Ellen's home one night with a note saying she couldn't look after me and hoped that someone could give me a better life. My father had never married and had no intention of having any children. But Beth tells the story of the moment he picked me up out of the basket on that cold night, he fell in love with me and there was no way he was giving me up. Having plenty of money to make sure the adoption process was easy, I became Paige Ellen, the adored daughter of Jonathan Ellen, within days.

He did try to find my mother, but she didn't want to be found. With absolutely no clues to trace, it made it impossible to pursue.

I often wonder about her.

What she's like, why she gave me up, and why did she pick my dad's doorstep of all the ones in that street? Was there some connection to my father, or was it just the universe playing a part in the whole story? Either way, I was blessed in my life, and I hope she is happy wherever she may be now.

Showered, hair and make-up done, I slip into a grey tailored dress that sits just above the knees, acceptable for a boardroom. My matching suit jacket secures at the single button on my waist. I'm sure people wonder where I come from. My father is just five-foot-two, fair skin and heavy-set. While I'm olive skinned and with a very slight build, standing at just under six feet. So, once I slip into my yellow heels for the day, I stand close to six-foot-two.

Many men find this intimidating. I learned very early on in my career never to show fear. Walk into any boardroom or office as if you own the space. Even if you are shaking like crazy on the inside. You will either intimidate them or they will respect you and communicate on an even level.

Unfortunately, the business world still has a bias towards men in the top positions of companies. So, any women who run companies are usually known as bitches with balls or ball-breakers. I don't know why it always relates to men's balls, but maybe that just shows how pathetic the ones who say it are.

Bent, my driver, is waiting patiently with the car when I walk from the foyer of my building. He learned early, I'm punctual and never like to be kept waiting. Time is money in my business.

"Morning, Ms. Ellen, Tyson is in the car waiting." He dips his hat, opening the door for me.

"Thank you, Bent." He smiles as I slide into the car. "Morning, Tyson." I straighten my skirt and place my bag on the seat next to me. He hands me my organic espresso coffee. I can't start the day without it. The first day Tyson worked for me he turned up with a cappuccino which I took one sip of and spat it out.

I'm a coffee snob.

It needs to be from Starbucks, only beans that are organically grown and ethically sourced. Strong and piping hot. Otherwise, I won't drink it. More of us need to make a stand in this world about how our fellow humans are treated in less-fortunate countries. These large corporations that use adults and children in poorer countries and pay them very little are criminals. They make huge profits on abusing people's basic right to a fair wage. I'm very conscious in my business to make sure we never do this. When I purchase products in all aspects of my life, I try to support companies that use fair trade with wages for raw materials. Like coffee beans.

"Morning, Ms. Ellen. I have forwarded the meeting agenda with the changes you asked for to your email and all the contracts are in the drive, ready for the last adjustments of negotiations that occur during the meeting. The jet is on standby and ready to go." I've got to give it to Tyson; he's efficient and knows what I expect from him. As soon as I'm in the car, we're working. There is no idle chat.

"Thank you. I saw them early this morning. Everything looks in order. I want you to know that my father isn't feeling well this morning, so if he or Beth call at any time during the meeting, I am to be interrupted straight away." I have my first sip of coffee for the morning, turning to look out the window.

I hear him reply behind me, but I'm not really paying attention. Every time my father gets ill lately, I realize he's not getting any younger. He is now eighty-one and ageing by the day. The sense of how alone I am in this world is really weighing heavily on me this morning. If something were to happen to him, then it's just me.

No parents, siblings, relatives — or friends, for that matter. I have plenty of acquaintances, but let's be honest, they're just business contacts, not one of them I could call a friend to rely on. Growing up, I had a few girlfriends at school, but we drifted apart when they became the society wives of the men they married. They can't understand why I haven't found a man, married, and let him run the company while I stay at home and procreate the perfect little children that society thinks I should produce.

My father brought me up to be a strong independent woman, and that's who I am.

Just as we're driving across the tarmac towards my jet, the tone of my phone breaks me out of my thoughts. Looking down, I notice Beth's name on my screen. Sliding to answer immediately, my heart skips a little with fear that something has happened.

"Beth, is my father okay?" I blurt out. Blunter than I meant.

"Yes, dear. Sorry to panic you. I was just calling to put your mind at ease before you fly. He is doing fine and resting after his breakfast. It is just a little cold this time, and I will have the doctor call on him later today just to be sure." Her voice has the soothing effect that she knows I need.

"Thank you, Beth. I appreciate the call." The stubborn old bugger never tells me the truth, especially if he thinks that it will affect the company. I could throttle him at times.

"Can you message me after the doctor leaves, please?" I sound more like the woman she raised, now that I've taken the sharpness out of my voice.

"Of course, sweetie. We both know how painful he is. That's why I call with the facts and not that garbage he tries to tell you. Have a safe flight, and I will see you later this afternoon. Will you be here for dinner? I'll make your favorite, chicken and vegetable soup and fresh-baked bread." In that moment I remember I'm not entirely alone. I have this sweet old lady as my family. For how long I don't know, but I cherish every day I still have them both.

"That sounds amazing, Beth. Looking forward to it." I want to have her tell my father to behave or I'll scold him later, and then tell her I love her. But with Tyson and Bent in the car I don't.

"Love you, sweetie. Now go and be amazing and I'll look after the grump upstairs."

"Thanks, Beth, talk soon." She knows what I'm thinking without me even saying it. With that I hang up and just sit for a few seconds collecting myself. I never let people see me vulnerable.

Deep breath.

"Thank you, Bent," I let my driver know I'm ready to exit the car.

Standing and straightening my clothes, I look out and there he is.

My Private Pilot.

Captain Mason White.

So tall with those broad shoulders. Strong arms that are always ridged and behind his back. Legs slightly apart. Almost standing to attention in his tightfitting pilot's uniform.

Fuck, he has those damn aviator glasses on again.

Why do they make me feel weak at the knees, when no man has ever made me feel that before?

He reminds me of my teenage Tom Cruise crush, Maverick from Top Gun.

I can't let him know that he has any effect on me. Then he smiles that smug cocky grin, and I'm done. If I am ever going to break my no-man streak, he's top of the list. I know I won't, yet sometimes a girl deserves dreams. Naughty ones…very naughty!

Locking down my thoughts, I strut my stuff past Mason, acknowledge him with a nod, and head straight up the steps. Knowing he's checking out my ass gives me a tingle where I shouldn't be tingling.

Distraction, I need to look busy.

As he enters the cabin, I direct my eyes down and work.

13

Be the firecracker. That's my life and I'm damn good at it!

2

Paige

Crossing my legs is doing nothing to quiet the tingling Mason stirs in me every time I see him. Squeezing that little bit harder should stop me having to head to the bathroom to take the edge off this ache.

"Is there anything I can get you before we take off, Ms. Ellen?" Holly sweetly asks. "The captain is about to put the seatbelt sign up so I just thought I would check."

"No, thank you," I answer, trying to appear calm and not give away my dilemma. My brain is also still buzzing from my coffee, and I never drink alcohol before a meeting, so I'm all good.

"I'll have a chai latte and my fruit," Tyson demands from her. He's such a dick. Lucky his skills are top-rate, otherwise I'd have booted him long ago. I glare at him, which is enough for him to realize his mistake.

"Of course, only if it isn't too much trouble." He then tries to cover up his arrogance.

"Oh, that might have to wait until we're in the air now. Seatbelts fastened, please." With that, Holly turns quickly and walks away. Good for her. Don't take crap from anyone.

There is something about taking off in a plane that just doesn't sit well with me. As often as I fly, you would think I'd be used to it by now, but it still makes me apprehensive. Feeling the acceleration as we race down the runway, I lay my head back on the seat and close my eyes. The only problem with that is it causes my mind to wander. Thinking of my father and worrying about him. As much as he's a pain, he's mine. The one person who stepped in thirty-nine years ago when no one else would. My protector.

I hear the wheels come up under the plane with the familiar thump underneath me and open my eyes to look out the window. The ground is fast disappearing under us. Clouds start to envelop the plane. It's like you slip into this different world when you're up here. It's just white and blue as far as I can see. A kind of peace I very rarely find on the ground.

I hear Mason's smooth deep voice over the intercom pulling me out of my thoughts. Tyson releases his seatbelt and moves towards the bathroom.

Suddenly I'm alone.

Everything I've been thinking about my sick father surprisingly creeps up on me. I try to start work by drafting points for the meeting, but it's overwhelming and I can't hold it back. I fight to stop it.

A single tear escapes.

I never cry.

Ever. I'm tougher than that.

I feel his electrifying presence before I see him. I jump at the sight of him handing me a crisp white handkerchief. I'm stumbling trying to talk, mumbling his name. His body being so close makes my body tingle. His eyes are a beautiful brown shade that are totally focused on me right now. I wasn't expecting him to see me, or even care that something isn't right for me. I don't get close to people, yet here he is. He offers up his handkerchief again. Mortified he's seen my tear, I shake my head and look away. Quickly wiping the lone tear gone.

"I saw you have dust in your eye," he says, touching my hand. Panicking at the intimate touch, I pull back quickly. I can't be vulnerable, *trust no one*, my father's words echo in my head.

Be strong.

Mason is starting to test that strength. I mean, when was the last time a man had a crisp white handkerchief and was down on one knee offering it to me. Seriously, do these types of gentlemen even exist?

"I'm fine. Thank you for asking. Just very busy preparing for the meeting."

Noise of the bathroom door opening signals we are no longer alone.

"Which she would be able to do if you would stop annoying her, Captain White. If you're back here, then who's in charge of the plane?"

Oh my god I can't believe Tyson just said that. This is starting to become a problem. Mason is quick with his reply that puts him right in his place.

I love a strong man who doesn't back down!

Again, calling him Tyson just to rile him. I can't help but laugh. It takes my mind off my sadness and gives me a reason to smile for a short while.

Time to break this little party up. To be honest, I'd feel more confident too if the pilot was actually at the controls and not in the bathroom.

Mason's words are spinning in my head *'Obviously, unlike you, Tyson, I can manage to fly a jet, take care of Ms. Ellen in all areas she needs a skilled man, and have time to take a leak. Don't fret, little boy '* Oh, how my mind is thinking of the ways he can take care of me. They're definitely not PG-rated. Damn. I need to shut this down.

What's wrong with me?

I'm his boss, for god's sake.

"Thanks, Mason." Ending it, I put my head down to continue with my work. I indicate to Tyson, grow up and do your job. The door to the bathroom closes and Tyson flops into his seat with his arms crossed. Looking like a sulking five-year-old. I don't have time for this shit from him. Ignoring him, I'm back in the zone of what I need for the meeting with the potential new supplier.

Tapping away on my laptop, I have the notes of the last meeting playing through my earphones. It stops me having to talk to anyone. The last price negotiation point we finished off on was five cents per part. I think I can get it to four cents but will take four point five. That extra cent reduction would save me one-point-three million dollars.

Today's important. I have them on the ropes and need to nail them down and secure it in writing. The two salesmen I've been dealing with are useless. I'm meeting with the president and vice president of the company as well as the salesmen. It makes me laugh that it takes four men to negotiate against me. Better bring their A-game. Otherwise, as painful as it is, I'll walk away and find another company who is willing to supply me the same part at the price I need.

Like I said, I know what I want and won't stop until I get it.

The next two hours pass quickly, and before I know it, we're on the ground and taxiing to the ground staff. Packing my briefcase, I'm ready and in the zone. Let's get this meeting done and over with. Holly unlocks the cabin door as we stand waiting to disembark. Mason, exiting the cockpit with his flight manifest, stops to let me past.

"Hope your meeting is successful today, Paige. Behave yourself, Tyson, and be a good little boy for the boss." He gives me a wink, and I hear a groan from behind me. I just keep walking, slipping my sunglasses on but with a smile plastered across my face. Listening to him provoke Tyson, I can't help but melt a little more for this guy. Why does he have to be funny as well as so irresistibly hot.

After we're in the town car and heading into the city, Tyson finally gets the courage to say what he's thinking.

"Why do you let him speak to me like that and call you Paige? I've worked for you a lot longer than him, and I'm not allowed to call you by your first name." I haven't noticed before, but Tyson can be such a child. He doesn't like it when he's not the center of attention.

"Firstly, when you speak to him, you need to show him the respect he deserves as the captain of my jet. Our lives are in his hands. Secondly, my choice, end of story." I give him the look that lets him know not to question me.

"Now, don't you think we have more important things to be thinking about with this meeting starting in twenty minutes? Seriously, what's gotten into you?" I stare him down, and when he has no comeback, he just puts his head down and starts checking his phone for emails.

Maybe Mason's right when he calls him a little boy.

By the time we get to the office building, Tyson seems to have gotten over his tantrum and is back to being my PA. We're shown into the boardroom that's full of suits sitting back drinking their coffee, trying to appear relaxed; It's game time.

"Ms. Ellen, lovely to see you again. May I introduce our president, Morris Gaven, and vice president, Evan Tosca." They both stand and straighten their ties and jackets. Stretching up tall to try to look intimidating. Pfft, good try, fellas.

I reach out to shake their hands. It's always interesting in these situations. Men never know what's the right thing to do. Should they offer their hands to shake with a woman or not. So, I take the indecision out of it for them.

My handshake is firm and short. Letting them know right from the start I mean business.

"Nice to meet you, gentlemen. Let's get started so I don't take up too much of your time today. I know you're all very busy, and time is money." With that I take a seat, pull out my folder, and stare them down.

Game on, gentlemen.

I can see they're already on the defense and thinking I'm a hard-ass bitch. I don't wait for them to get organized. I launch straight into my discussion, bringing them up to speed with where their current deal is at and what I want.

"So, as you can see, we are ready to sign a contract today if we can agree on the price of four cents per part for a two-year deal." Eyeing each of them, they're sweating. Talking in hushed voices to each other. Pointing to things on the papers in front of them.

"Ms. Ellen, as you would appreciate, we are very interested to do business with your company. However, we can't possibly sign a contract that we'll lose money on," President Morris tries to sound confident.

"We need to keep our investors happy. Oh, and of course we don't want people to lose jobs." There it is. The guilt trip thrown in at the last minute. It annoys the fuck out of me that the first thing they worry about are their investors and not the people who keep them in a job. The hardworking people who keep this company running.

"Here's the thing, gentlemen. The exposure and credibility you will receive just from being listed as a supplier to Ellen Corporation is worth gold for your marketing department. You should be factoring it into your advertising budget reduction. However, I'm a reasonable person. My final offer for this deal is four-point-five cents per part for twelve months with a clause to review at the end of that time. What do you say to that?" The two salespeople are fidgeting with their pens and shuffling papers. The two executives whisper to each other while they're madly punching numbers into the calculator. I sit back in my chair sipping water very calmly from my glass. Giving off the body language that I'm not nervous as hell on the inside. This deal has taken six months of work, and it could all be for nothing if they back out now. I decide it's time to give them a push.

"Sorry, gentlemen, but I'm going to need an answer. I have a flight that leaves shortly which I can't miss. If you aren't able to meet this deal, unfortunately, I'll have to look for other suppliers."

Bam, and the firecracker has lit the fuse for the final bang.

"You drive a very hard bargain, Ms. Ellen, but we want to secure this partnership between our companies. You have a deal."

Boom! In the bag, baby.

I stand very smoothly and hold my hand across the table to shake the president's hand and seal the deal. My father always told me a handshake on a deal is as good as a contract.

"I look forward to doing business with you, gentlemen. Tyson has the paperwork ready, so if we can just get it signed. Then I can make my plane and let you get on with the rest of your day." I never let up on the negotiating until the contract is signed and sealed. So, the tigress is still in the building. "Excuse me, I'll just visit the bathroom while you get it sorted." Not waiting for an answer, I walk towards the bathroom at the end of the room. Once inside, I stand in front of the mirror, taking a much-needed breath and letting my shoulders relax a moment.

"You did it again, Paige. Daddy's little girl. Just like he taught you." Talking to myself, I try to feel proud of what I just achieved, but for some reason it's not doing it for me today.

Freshening up, I head back into the boardroom, looking at four men who are a little defeated but resigned to the fact they got the best deal they could. Poor things, they never stood a chance really.

Signing on the dotted line, we make small talk for five minutes at the most, about how thrilled we are to be working together. I tell them my legal team will be in touch, and we're in the back of the town car before we know it.

"That went well, congratulations, Paige," Tyson says as we pull away from the curb.

What the fuck. Not this again!

Just when I want to relax, I've got to keep my bitch face on.

"Thank you, Tyson, and it's Ms. Ellen to you," I curtly reply and pick up my phone to make a call but decide to put the nail in the coffin first.

"Please message Mason and let him know we're finished and will be there shortly." The pout on his face tells me he's pissed off and not sure how to tackle this. I pay him no attention and press dial on Beth's number.

After checking in on my father, who's still feeling the same as this morning, we are back at the airport ready for boarding. I notice Mason is out checking the plane is ready for the flight home. I've watched him do it a thousand times, yet today he just looks that little more interesting. I sit for a moment in the air conditioning and behind the tinted windows of the car. Enjoying my view.

Tight ass, broad shoulders.

A shirt that looks like it molds round his arms. His sleeves rolled up showing his forearms. I wish I was closer to get a better look. Those glasses make me tingle every time. No man is hotter than Mason in uniform with those damn aviator sunglasses.

This perving gives me more of a buzz than closing the deal. Something is very wrong with me today. The thrill of the chase always gets me excited. Today, not so much. Maybe that's the problem. I'm bored with the same old games. Same old people.

Maybe there's a new player. A new game.

I just can't do a thing about chasing him.

Exiting the car, I choose to stand and stare a little longer. Feeling my eyes on his back, he turns and throws a saucy grin and a wink at me as he walks to the stairs ready to greet me.

Mason

I don't know what's happened with Paige while she was gone, but the woman who hops out of the car and heads into the plane has the most gorgeous smile on her face for a change.

Her dickwad assistant on the other hand looks like someone has taken his ice cream away from him and smudged it in the dirt.

Part of me feels anxious that another man is responsible for that smile. I want to be the one who puts that glow on her cheeks and a grin that comes from great mind-numbing sex.

Man, now I need to think of something to take my mind off fucking Paige. Why do I torture myself?

Finishing my safety checks, I return to the cabin and inform them we have a ten-minute wait before we are scheduled to depart. Holly takes over and prepares drinks and food to keep them happy. I didn't tell them the wait is because my stupid co-pilot went for a quickie with his Florida fly-in fly-out girl. Idiot thinks he's some highflyer who can have a woman in every city. I thought that only happened in movies, but apparently Aaron takes it to a new level. I tried to warn him this wouldn't be a long meeting. Calling him back to the plane, I gave him ten minutes and said obviously he only needs one to get his rocks off and the other nine minutes are to get his ass on the jet, or I fly without him. Legally I can't, but at times it's tempting.

With two minutes to spare, he's scrambling into the cockpit. I hear him telling some load of crap to our passengers about him just getting the clearance we need. Whatever he feels he needs to do to cover his ass with the boss. I wonder if she sees straight through his macho like we do.

"One day you're going to get yourself in serious trouble that no amount of bullshitting can get you out of. Now buckle up, we need to be taxiing in one minute. I hope she was worth it." I start the engines and start signaling the ground crew that we're ready.

"Fuck, you have no idea. Of all the women, Chilly is the wildest. The things she can do with her tongue…" Aaron is about to give me a detailed description.

"Stop right there. I don't want to hear it and neither does the control tower that I'm about to radio." We both laugh and get on with the job of getting Meredith off the ground and on her flight home nice and smoothly.

The storm activity on the flight back to Chicago stops me leaving the cabin. Then we have the good old Chicago winds to battle as we land. I can't say it's a smooth flight, but we do our best to take out the rough patches. By the time I've filled out my flight log and collected my things, Paige is just about to leave the cabin.

"Thank you, Mason, for taking care of my needs today." Giving me a sly smile, she drops the white handkerchief I left on her seat this morning. Stepping forward to pick it up, she beats me to it. Bending over so her ass ends up in my face, her fingers reach it.

Any closer, I'll be leaving my bite mark on her ass cheek.

Standing so close and back at eye level, she is staring me down. Fuck, this woman is hot. Her perfume is enveloping me and branding itself in my memory.

"My pleasure as always. I like to leave lasting memories." My eyes drop to the handkerchief in her hand.

"Yes, so I see. I like to be self-sufficient, taking care of my own needs. Good day, Captain White." With that she turns and is out the door, the noise of her heels going down the steps driving me crazy. I want this woman, in so many more ways than just talking. Another cold shower tonight for me.

Before my day's finished, I clean the jet, helping George to get her back in the hangar and lock her up tight for today. Heading to the gym for a workout before dinner, I send a message to the boys to see who's around and wants to join me.

No reply from Tate means he's in surgery, and I remember Lex is in court on some big case today. Gray is in and will meet me there. I'm surprised I'm able to pry him away from Tilly, his new fiancée. They've been inseparable since they finally did the deed. Well, the second time, I should say. The first time she ran off and left him hanging. Luckily, he finally caught her. Who would have thought Doc Gray would be the first to fall and fall hard!

I swipe my member card. Jenny, one of the personal trainers, is on the front desk.

"Hi, Mason, Gray's already in the weight room."

Chucking my bag in a locker, I head over to lover boy who is loading up the weights ready for our workout. He's fooling himself if he thinks he can lift that amount straight off the bat.

"A bit ambitious today, aren't we?" Slapping him on the shoulder, I walk past him to grab the rest of the gear we need.

"Hello to you too, Mason. My fiancée tells me I have an ego problem. Are you trying to tell me she might be right?" He chuckles as he tightens the weights on.

"No, I'd say she's spot on. Both you and Tate have a god complex, but we love you anyway." He rolls his eyes and lies down ready to start.

"Don't ever repeat that in front of Tilly. I know you're just jealous of how perfect I am, but can you keep it to yourself? Now get over here and watch the man in action and do your job." He takes hold of the bar, ready to lift while I spot him.

"Well, then you having a fiancée is a problem. There is no way we can take you being any cockier than you already are." We both start laughing.

This is what our life is like. I have the three best friends a guy can have. We don't take life too seriously, but I know when life gets tough, they're there. They proved that when I came home from war and while I was posted in Afghanistan. The ridiculous pictures, emails, and care packages I would receive from them had me being known as the laughingstock of the base. Yet I knew everyone couldn't wait for the next one to arrive because lord knows we needed some comic relief while we were there. The package that had the blowup Suzy sex doll in it with a big tube of lube and a packet of condoms in the extra-small size had every soldier in the camp wanting to see my girlfriend. Of course, until the Major found out, and said it wasn't appropriate with the women on base. He was probably right, but it was fun while it lasted.

"Nothing on this earth will make me give Tilly up." He gets the words out with some difficulty as he's trying so hard to bench press the weight and not admit defeat. Watching his arms shake and the sweat start beading on his brow tells me he's not giving up, just to prove his point. The last heave brings a loud grunt from Grayson as he grins with satisfaction at proving me wrong.

"That sounded pretty definite, man." I pass him his hand towel to wipe his sweaty hands and line up for another lift.

"She's the one, Mas, I just had to convince her of that. I'm going to marry that girl. That I can promise." Wow, that's a big statement from Grayson who's never wanted to commit to any one woman.

"What's made you change your tune? You were going to be the eternal bachelor, the man who would just spend time with a lady when it fit in with his schedule. Now you're talking the old ball and chain. What the hell happened to you? Did she drug your drink or something?"

He grits his teeth through the next lift before he can answer me. "Tilly. It's that simple. She made me want more." He glares up at me and then sits up on the weight bench.

"Yeah, we get that. She has you by the balls, and you're like a puppy dog who can't get enough of the pussy cat he's made friends with."

24

He swings his hand trying to slap my arm. "You seem to be asking other questions without coming right out with it. Have you got something you want to talk about?" I stand, changing the weights and trying not to make eye contact.

"Mason, I've known you a long time. I know when you're hiding. Spit it out, man, what's going on?" He's now standing in front of me, arms crossed over his chest. Looking like the big-brother stance.

"Man, Tilly is right, you do have a big ego, which obviously compensates for something else."

"Forget the distraction tactic, spill your guts, Mas. Otherwise I call Tate and Lex and we all end up in your apartment tonight. Your choice. You know what happens when the interrogation starts. No one wants to be pinned down while Tate farts on your face. That's a fate worse than death." He's not giving in.

"That's a bit drastic, calling in the big guns. We aren't twenty anymore." He smiles stupidly at me. "Okay, I'll talk rather than be put through the Tate torture chamber." Until this moment, I hadn't realized how much this has been playing on my mind.

"I've got this little problem. Well, actually he isn't little, he's huge, especially with the problem." That sounded much better in my head.

"What the hell are you talking about?" Grayson looks with confusion.

"Okay, plain and simple for the dummies in the room. I have a thing for my boss Paige. Every time I'm near her, my cock is rock solid and I'm thinking very unprofessional thoughts about what her and my cock could be doing together. I feel like a schoolboy with a crush on the teacher. It's ridiculous. Don't you dare tell Tate, or I will never hear the end of this." I did not expect to be blurting that out this afternoon when I decided to come to the gym.

"Now, was that so hard to say, young Mason?"

"Fuck off. If you're going to be like that, I'm out of here," I grumble.

"What a great idea. Why didn't you just say you need a drinking buddy? Let's get out of here and go grab a beer. Sounds more fun than this." I laugh at him as we collect our towels and drink bottles.

"You're just trying to get out of looking like a loser, because you can't lift as much as I can. Put your stuff down and help me put all these weights away, and then beers sound great." We're out of the gym and in the bar down the road within ten minutes.

"Now tell Doctor Gray all about the things that ail you, young Mason." I pick up pretzels out of the bowl and throw them at him. "No seriously, tell me what's going on with Paige."

Running my hand through my hair, I take a deep breath before I start to tell him what's on my mind.

"You know I have trouble sleeping most nights. The visions and sounds that haunt my head keep me awake or in a restless state." He nods his head at me, knowing exactly what I mean. I've never hidden my PTSD from any of the boys. Mine is minor compared to others that suffer, but it's a badge I carry every day, even if at times I wish I could just take it off.

"Yeah, well those thoughts and nightmares have been getting less intense, and for the last month have disappeared totally. It's all because of Paige. Sexy, hot as fuck, Paige Ellen, my super uptight boss." The vision of her bent over in front of me today is right there tempting me.

"I lie down at night and start thinking about her. What she was wearing that day. The way she moves, the vision of her ass climbing the steps onto the plane. But the most stupid part of it all was, up until today, we haven't said more than two words to each other in a conversation. Well, not in words. We practically eye-fuck each other every time. Yet she invades my head and I want to know so much. Learn about her life, her work, what makes her tick. Do I sound crazy?" Gulping another mouthful of beer, I'm not sure I'm ready for the answer. Grayson sits there quietly with a smirk on his face.

"What? Say something?" He starts laughing and puts down his drink. He holds out his hand towards me to take mine and starts shaking it.

"Welcome to the club, Mason. The one you join but can never leave. She has you under the spell. She may not know it yet, but she is about to be hit by the Mason charm. Time to weave your web and catch your girl, bud."

"You're crazy. Paige is so far out of my league. Plus, she's my boss. I'm just the guy who flies her plane from A to B, and then gets her back from B to A so she can keep her fast-paced life moving forward." Listening to myself, I sound pathetic.

"Why does it matter if she's your boss? It's not like you signed a contract to say you couldn't take her on a date, did you?"

"No, don't be stupid. But even you know that it's not a good idea to play and work in the same place. You learned the hard way. I don't want to get caught in the same problem. Anyway, we aren't even friends, so how am I going to get her on a date? Just walk up to her in front of her assistant and the crew and say *'Paige, you are one hot chick. Will you come out on a date with me? Oh, and by the way, I want into your pants more than I want to breathe when you tease me with those fuck-me heels every day.'* I'm sure she'd just look right through me and wonder who's even talking."

"Seriously! Are you listening to the crap coming out of your mouth? What are you, fifteen years old? Just ask her out for a drink. When the assistant isn't around if you're scared of him. Surely, he needs to leave her side at some stage. You're ex-Army, man, surely you can create a plan to win her over."

"I know how to follow a target and take a hostage. Does that count?" He laughs at me.

"No, you dickhead, that's called stalking and kidnapping in the States, and the only one you'll be sharing a bed with will be your big burly cellmate. Doubt he'll look like Paige. Lex will help pick out your perfect match, when he dumps your sorry ass in the courts for being so stupid." Now we're both chuckling together. This is what I need, a good belly laugh.

Grayson has no idea of what Paige is like. Neither do I, but I want to find out. Perhaps it's that simple, just ask her out. I do tend to overthink things. Since coming home from the war, I'm always trying to think of every scenario. I tend to look for the things that can go wrong rather than the things that could work. Looks like tonight I'll be working out how I can convince Paige it's a good idea to have dinner with me.

"What's the worst that can happen, she says no?" Gray says with a shrug. I wish that was it.

"No, the worst thing that could happen is her firing my sorry ass and then I don't get to see her again." Although I already know in my head that's a risk I'm prepared to take.

"Or the best thing that can happen is you end up fucking each other senseless, you stop suffering sore dick-itis, and your tiny balls stop being blue. Is it worth the chance?"

"Fuck yeah!"

This next flight could be a little more interesting than normal.

3

Paige

The last three days have been exhausting. After getting home from Orlando, I thought this week was going to be a normal one. Stupid me.

My father's simple cold is getting worse and has him bedridden. Beth keeps assuring me he's fine, and she has it under control, but it doesn't stop me from worrying.

By day, I'm running the company, and by night, I'm staying at his home. Sitting by his bed talking about my day, working while he sleeps and then reading to him before I go to sleep. My dad is a lover of classical literature. Tonight's read is *The Great Gatsby*. It doesn't escape me that our roles have reversed. The memories of all the years of my father reading to me on the precious nights he was home in time for bedtime, or on a weekend curled up on his knee in his leather chair as he read me some of the children's classics like *Huckleberry Finn*.

To the rest of the world, my father is a hard but fair man. Never cross him, you only get one chance.

To me, he's different. Sure, he's hard and fair with me, but so loving too. He gave me the world and never expected anything in return. Built his business empire for me to take over. I never doubted my future role. Sometimes I lie in bed wondering what he'd have done if I had turned my back and chosen another career away from the company and business world. Would he have accepted it and supported me in my chosen life? Or would he have turned his back and our relationship would never have been the same again?

I might be a strong, kick-ass woman, but to be honest, I would never have been strong enough to disappoint my father.

He gave me a life, and this is my repayment for his love.

His soft snore lets me know he's finally drifted off to sleep. I put the bookmark in on the last page I read. I could never be one of those people who folds over the corner of the page. My father would kill me. Books are to be treasured. They're pages full of an author's soul. The words they blend together, taking us on a journey. My love of reading came from my father, and although the only paperbacks I read these days are the ones in my father's house, I still have a library in my apartment full of loved books from my favorite authors. It's a random mix, but they have a story to tell of a time in my life.

Placing the book on the bedside table, I slowly edge out of the seat to leave the room when my phone vibrates in my pocket with a call. Answering in a whisper from the corner of the room, Brian, my vice president, is checking in to see if I want him to take the meeting in Washington DC tomorrow. He was previously my father's right-hand man, so he knows what I'm dealing with; he's also worried about an old friend.

"Thanks, Brian. I'm just not sure that I should be that far from my father at the moment. He's not well. Maybe we should think about you heading to Washington." My voice is low and barely above a whisper.

"Not dying, you go to meeting. Don't cancel," I hear mumbled from behind me. Stubborn old bastard. I thought he was asleep.

"I heard him. When will he ever finally stop trying to have his say?" Brian starts laughing as I glare at my father, eyes barely open looking at me.

"When he's dead! Which will be soon if he doesn't butt out." My words bring a grin to his face, and his eyes drop closed again, knowing he's won. Brian laughs hard. "Guess I'm on my way to Washington tomorrow as planned. I'll talk to you in the morning."

I get ready to end the call, but at the last minute I need to say this: "Brian, thanks for caring and understanding. I know you can run this company just as well as me. It's not that he doesn't trust you. It's more about pushing me. You are a good and loyal man. Thank you."

There's a pause on the other end of the phone. "Thank you, Paige. It means the world. Get some sleep. Tomorrow will be a big day with those government pencil pushers. Goodnight." Brian is close to retirement age. He'll never have the top job, but he's happy where he is and is a valued employee.

"Goodnight, Brian." I end the call and walk over to my sleeping father, who's getting a nice loud snore happening. Taking the blanket, I pull it up to his chin, making sure he's covered and comfortable. Kissing him on the forehead, he doesn't even stir.

My childhood bedroom is long gone, in its place is one fit for a queen. The room is all styled with rich cream furnishings and a hint of pink and rose gold. There is a small bookcase full of all my favorite childhood books. *'Just in case you get bored,'* Daddy would say. Not a day in my life have I been bored.

I email my group message confirming the flight details as per the schedule for the morning. I'm shocked to see a reply from Mason pop up in my inbox.

Captain Mason White

Good evening, Paige,
Thank you, we are all ready for the morning flight. I hope you've had a good week. I was surprised we didn't have a midweek flight. Hope you're okay?
Mason

—

Ms. Paige Ellen – CEO Ellen Corporation

Good evening, Mason,
Thank you for your concern. My Father has been ill, and I tried to stay close by. So please note that you will need to be on standby at all times when we are away, in case we need to fly home in an emergency. I will try to keep tomorrow's flight to DC short.
Paige

—

Captain Mason White

I'm sorry to hear that, Paige. I hope he starts to feel better soon. It will take the worry off you. I'm happy to be on standby for you at any time.
Besides your dad being unwell, how has your week been?
Mason

I stare at the reply email, unsure how to handle the question. No one has ever really asked me that, except my father or Beth. How did we go from an email confirming a flight to asking how my week has been? I'll just keep it simple.

Ms. Paige Ellen – CEO Ellen Corporation

Mason,
My week has been a busy working week as usual.
Paige

Yes, that's it, hit send. Short and sharp reply. It's a little inappropriate for him to be asking such personal questions.
Shit, he's replied again.

Captain Mason White – CEO Ellen Corporation

Come on, Paige, surely you have a life outside of work. I'll be more specific with my question this time. What have you been up to besides work this week, that you have enjoyed?
Mason

My hands start typing straight away, and I hit send without thinking. Fuck, I shouldn't have sent that.

Ms. Paige Ellen – CEO Ellen Corporation

I don't have a life besides work, not that it's any of your business!
Ms. Ellen

He was just being friendly, and I had to reply like the snarky bitch that I am. Now nothing. My emails have gone quiet.

Should I apologize?

No, that'll make me look weak.

I tell myself that I shouldn't be thinking anything about Mason. I'm sure I've wrecked any chance of that now anyway.

That's it, stop waiting for a reply. Just go to the bathroom and to sleep. I'll deal with another sulking man tomorrow morning. He'll look at me like the hard-ass bitch I am. I should be used to it by now.

Spitting out the mouthful of water from brushing my teeth, I hear my computer chime with another email. The toothbrush hits the sink with a clatter as I run across the room, jumping onto my bed to get to my computer. Only to have my hopes sink when I see it's just from Tyson. I'm sure that man never sleeps either.

Tyson Burke - PA to Ms. Ellen - Ellen Corporation

Dear Ms. Ellen,
I am feeling very unwell this evening and am unsure if I will be able to make the flight in the morning. I don't know if it's a twenty-four-hour stomach virus or food poisoning. Would you like me to organize Laura to fill my role, so you have someone with you?

My sincere apologies, but I am concerned I may pass the virus to you and put your father at risk.

Tyson Burke

Today is just getting better by the minute. Luckily, it's almost eleven pm so there's not much time for anything more to go wrong.

Ms. Paige Ellen - CEO Ellen Corporation

Dear Tyson,
I'm sorry to hear you are unwell. Thank you for thinking of my father and yes, I would prefer you stay home. Don't worry about Laura, I will manage on my own. It's just a simple meeting to discuss any changes needed in the program for the next year. I will record it so you can type it up at a later date.

Ms. Ellen

As I hit send, my phone starts ringing. Damn Tyson is obviously too impatient to wait for my reply. I freeze when I look down at the name on the screen.

Captain Mason White – Pilot.

Shit, what does he want?
Fuck, how did he even get my number?
It stops ringing.
Good, now I don't have to worry about what he wants. My palms are sweaty, my thoughts scattered. You idiot, of course he has your number, you're his boss and he is your personal jet's pilot.
Tomorrow is going to be awkward.
My phone chimes now with a text message.

Mason: Answer your phone, Paige. I'm just going to keep calling.

Paige: I'm asleep

Mason: Yeah right, that's why you're replying.

Paige: You woke me up.

Mason: Liar

The phone starts ringing.
"How dare you call me a liar! You don't even know me!" I blurt out, and then I feel panic, realizing he's gotten what he's after. I answered the stupid phone.
"Now see, that's the purpose of the phone call. Let's get to know each other a little. I mean, it would be tragic for you to go a whole week with no life outside of work to talk about when you're asked by someone. Now you can say I caught up with a friend for a chat. It was pleasant."
"I don't have friends," I snap back.

"Now that's where you're wrong. I thought we were friends," he replies with a little bit of cockiness in his voice.

"What makes you think that?" I ask.

"Well, we are on first-name basis, and usually that's reserved for friends, isn't it?" I don't know how to answer that. "Come on, Paige, relax. Are you always this highly strung?" His voice sounds so smooth. I want to answer no, but the truth is, I don't know how to be anything but high-strung. That's how I live my life and it keeps me successful.

"Do you want the truth?" I mumble.

"Of course, friends don't lie to each other." Why is it every time he speaks tonight, I just keep blurting out words that I should be keeping to myself.

"My whole life is permanently high-strung. I don't know any other way. It's the world I was raised in and it's my normal. You probably think I'm a high powered bitch like all the rest of them do." I plunk my head on my pillow, pulling the blankets up over me to find comfort. Mason is exposing a part of me that I never let anyone see…my vulnerability. I don't know how. I cut men off at the knees with my intimidating looks and sharp tongue, yet he talks, and I answer without hesitation.

"Why would I think that, Paige? Like you said, we don't know each other. The only Paige I know is the beautiful lady who travels with me on my jet many times a week. She's pleasant when she speaks to me – although it's not often. Up until earlier this week I wasn't even sure she knew I existed. Although I have a sneaking suspicion her ass sway as she walks up the stairs is a little put on just for my viewing pleasure. Actually, even if it's not, can you humor my ego and tell me it's for me anyway?"

I can't help but laugh now. Not just a little giggle but a good laugh that you feel all over.

"Now that sounds much better, like a Paige I'd really like to be friends with and get to know more." Mason keeps talking, I think, to make sure I don't hang up on him.

"You are very sure of yourself, aren't you? What if I said the ass sway was for Tyson?" I'm trying to control myself and keep a calm voice waiting for his reaction.

"You crush my soul. I thought I had a chance against the little whiner, but now you've confirmed I should just pack up my toys and go home." Everything he says is so lighthearted. He doesn't seem to take anything seriously.

"Well, don't panic just yet. You can leave your toys in the playground and keep playing for a little while still. I can one hundred percent confirm that I would not be wiggling my ass for Tyson. Ever!"

"Awesome, I knew it was all for me." I imagine him fist-pumping the air.

"I never said that." He groans out loud into the phone. "Who sounds like the little schoolboy now?"

"That would be me. The man whose ego has just been crushed. Can we talk about something else while I just sit here in my corner and sulk?" There's an awkward silence for a moment.

"Mason, why did you call me? I mean the real reason. You have never replied to any email before and then you just randomly call me." There's a reason I'm no good at this. I'm too direct. If I want to know something, I ask it. No beating around the bush.

"Okay, like you said, do you want the truth?" he asks a little reluctantly.

"I'll answer just like you did, friends don't tell lies, so yes, I want the truth." I turn onto my side in bed and look out to the night sky, waiting for his answer.

"I want to ask you out for a drink and dinner, but I knew you would turn me down if I just walked up to you on the jet and said *'Hey can I take you for a drink and dinner,'* not to mention what your little boy Tyson would say or do. I've been trying to work out a way to get to know you. When your email popped up tonight, I decided, now or never, it's worth a shot." His voice has a hint of nervousness in it. Which surprises me. I's hard not to picture him the confident guy I see. Then again, people say that about me, I'm sure.

"Why did you assume I'd say no?"

"Because you don't know me, apart from being your pilot, plus you're my boss. You're always so busy. At least I got to talk to you tonight, make you laugh a little. Get you to admit your fine ass sways for me. Night made, really. Plus, I was worried about you on Monday, you looked sad." The last part shocks me. I don't think I've ever had anyone worry about me.

Blankets tighten in my fist because I know I'm about to do something really stupid and totally out of character for me.

36

"Ask me now," I murmur.

"Pardon?" Mason asks.

"Ask me now," I say with more confidence.

"Paige, I hope you aren't playing with me. You've already crushed my ego once tonight. But okay, here goes. Could I take you out for a drink and dinner one night soon?"

My head says you're crazy, but my stomach says it's about time you do something crazy in your life for a change.

"I think I would like that, Mason. It sounds like it might be fun." We both start to laugh. "You know we sound like teenagers, right? Totally pathetic." I'm giggling. Yes, actually giggling. I don't think I've done that since I was a teenager.

"Speak for yourself. I'm here acting like a sophisticated gentleman asking a beautiful lady on a date." He then starts to laugh a deep, manly laugh. With that rasp to it that is certainly sexy.

While I wait for him to stop laughing, it hits me that twice he's made the comment that I'm beautiful. This guy is smooth. Smooth normally means dangerous.

"Not sure I agreed to a date. I thought you asked me for a drink and dinner?" I need to put him back to the place where he is not too overconfident as to what this is. "Remember, friends having a drink."

"Okay, Paige, if that's the way you want to play it, yes, friends having a drink. At least I got you to acknowledge we're friends now. I get points for that." I could lie here and listen to his voice all night. I know I need to cut this off, though.

"You're quite the negotiator. I'll have you know you are up against a woman whose life centers around negotiating to get what she wants from people, without them even realizing it. So, I'll give you this point, just don't expect another one anytime soon." I feel back to myself. This is a language I speak. I know how to keep ahead.

"I would love to see you in action in the boardroom. I have a feeling you would take no prisoners and win the war, all the time looking sexy as hell while you do it."

I sigh, contemplating that he sees me just like everyone else does. I'm not sure why it worries me that he does. Do I want him to know the real me? That would make it hard to keep him at a distance if I do.

"Yeah, that's me. Anyway, we have a flight in the morning. You need sleep so you can concentrate. I don't want you falling asleep on me."

"There is one thing you can count on, Paige. I will NEVER put your safety at risk. Ever. I have gone days without sleep and flown dangerous missions behind enemy lines and never made a mistake. I don't count on starting now. I will always keep you safe." His voice sounds stern and a little offended.

"I didn't mean to upset you, Mason. I know you're good at your job, otherwise I wouldn't have hired you. I just mean, we both need sleep," I try to soften things.

"Sorry, I get carried away sometimes. You're right, though, we both should get to sleep. I will see you in the morning. I enjoyed talking to you. I hope we can do it more now that we're besties." He sounds like he's smiling as he says it.

"You don't give up, do you. Besties might be pushing it. I'll see you tomorrow, Mason. Goodnight." As he replies with goodnight and we hang up, I lie looking up at the ceiling with a smile plastered to my face. Many nights I stare at the ceiling of my bedroom trying to solve the problems of the world. Tonight, I'm just wondering what the hell I just did by agreeing to meet Mason for a drink. My heart is beating a little faster than normal. I'm not sure how easily I'll get some sleep. Maybe I'll just get some work done until I feel sleepy. At least I won't be wasting time or be thinking about Mason.

Well, maybe.

Not sure he'll be that easy to get out of my head now.

~

"Thank you, Bent." I slide out and stand next to the car. I go through my usual routine of smoothing my outfit, before starting the walk to the steps of the plane. I'm surprised to see only Mason standing waiting for me, without his copilot. Last night I thought of about ten different scenarios of how today will play out.

Standing to attention with his glasses on is definitely one thing that ran through my head when I pictured this morning.

"Captain White." I nod as I get closer. The same way I would normally acknowledge him.

"So that's how we're playing it this morning. I thought we agreed it's Mason." He smiles, not moving from his military stance.

"Okay, Captain Mason, is that better?" I snigger as I keep walking straight up the stairs. My hips swaying way more than they usually do and in slower motion.

With Bent still standing at the car and George almost next to him, all I can hear is a quiet groan from the captain this time. With no Tyson following behind me, he knows it's all for him. I shouldn't be teasing, but he deserves it for his brazenness this morning.

Taking my seat in the jet, I start unloading my bag with all my electronics needed for the trip. He's coming through the door much quicker than normal.

"Bent tells me your little boy Tyson is sick this morning so he's not flying with us. Such a shame."

"Don't be awful, Mason. Tyson is a very valuable person on my team. His level of skill in organization and efficiency is one I appreciate." I won't let him become unprofessional just because we've moved to a different level.

"Maybe so, but he needs an attitude adjustment. Anyway, how are you this morning, and how is your father feeling?" I can't quite work out what it is between Mason and Tyson, but I know there is definitely trouble and no love lost between them.

"He was still sleeping when I left, however Beth has the doctor coming by again this morning. She'll keep me informed. Thank you for asking." I open up my laptop, knowing I have plenty of work to get done this morning before we touch down. Mason takes the hint.

"We are on schedule for the flight, and with the tail winds we should have you in Washington in plenty of time. I will leave you to your work and get us moving. Enjoy the flight." Turning to walk away, he stops just before the door to the cockpit, looking over his shoulder. "Don't worry, Paige, I had plenty of sleep, even if one of my besties kept me up chatting on the phone until late. I'm good to go for this flight." Winking at me with his signature grin, he disappears into the cockpit. That man is trouble, I can already tell.

The rest of the flight runs smoothly, and Mason pops out to chat when he supposedly needs to use the bathroom. I have to remind him, when he's heading back to the cockpit after talking to me, that he hadn't even made it to the bathroom. The thing is, the more time I spend talking to Mason, the easier it is. It seems we can talk about random things. Today he wanted to know, if I was eating ice cream what flavor I'd choose. When I told him I don't eat it, he was horrified. Then we took ten minutes debating the pros and cons of ice cream as opposed to frozen yogurt. Where that conversation even came from, I have no idea.

Touching down in Washington, my phone chimes as we're pulling to a stop on the tarmac. A message from Beth letting me know my father has woken up a bit brighter this morning, and the doctor is happy with his progress. A sense of relief washes over me. He's not out of the woods yet, but every bit of improvement is a welcome sign.

Exiting the plane, Mason calls out to me to wait as he runs down the stairs after me.

"Paige, I just wanted to catch you and let you know I've told the crew they're all to stay with the plane today in case we need to depart in a hurry. You have my number, just message me and I'll have the plane ready and standing by as you arrive." Is this the professional Captain White doing his job, or the sweet Mason who is making sure I don't worry so much during my meeting?

"Thank you, Mason. I appreciate that. I expect the meeting will run for around two hours unless something out of the ordinary comes up. I will skip the lunch today and will message when I'm on my way back." Nodding for the driver to open the door, Mason grabs my arm which startles me, and I stagger a little.

"Paige, you need to eat. I'll have Holly prepare lunch ready for you when you get back." He looks at me with a 'don't argue' face.

What the fuck!

"Mason." I glare at him, and he pulls his hand back. "I am a grown woman who looks after herself. Thank you." I don't give him another word and take my seat in the car and signal for the driver to close the door.

Leaving him standing there looking like he wants to rip the door open and have his say. Not a chance. No man tells me what to do. My father marginally gets away with it, but no other man will ever control me.

The government officials I'm on my way to meet better be careful. I'm ready to tear someone's head off now.

Mason's just lucky it wasn't his.

40

He needs to learn right from the start if he wants to be friends with me, he knows his place. The moment he steps over it, he's gone. It's probably why I don't have friends. Like my father, I don't have patience for bullshit. One strike, and you're out.

The skies are gray and overcast as the car heads toward the city for my thirty-minute trip. I'm checking and replying to emails. My inbox is never empty, and as fast as I clear them, they pour in from the top. There are a few from Tyson that he's forwarded to me that are relevant to the meeting. Skimming through them, I notice that some of the numbers don't seem right. I disregard them, knowing Tyson's off his game being unwell. Logging into my personal files, I quickly gain the information I need and slot it into the report. I don't want to let Tyson know he made a mistake. He doesn't have to be working when he's sick; obviously he's trying to look after me, which I appreciate.

"Sorry, Ms. Ellen, there seems to be an accident ahead, we'll have to take an alternate route which will take a bit longer than anticipated. I will do my best to have you there on time." It's not his fault, but I can't afford for today to stretch out too long. I want to be back in the air by early afternoon, heading back to Chicago, just in case.

"Thank you, I appreciate your help. These things happen." I shoot an email off to the meeting attendees advising that I may be late. I'm sure they're used to the crazy traffic around Capitol Hill.

I live a fast-paced life, and Chicago's a busy city, but I know I wouldn't want to live here. Even I feel like I'm suffocating with all the security and chaos that is Washington. Too many people, too much crazy.

Sometimes I dream, one day I'll retire to a country property with rolling green hills. No houses for as far as I can see. Horses in the corrals. A big wide porch wrapping around the house. A porch swing and lots of books in my library, to get lost in while on my swing. Summer nights sipping a glass of wine, listening to the sounds of the evening. Winter spent in front of an open wood fire, curled up on a fluffy rug with a dog that just wants to be loved. I have no idea where this dream comes from because I've never even visited a place like this. My whole life's been in big cities. It just keeps popping into my head at times.

The universe is trying to tell me something, otherwise it wouldn't keep coming back to me. I'm just not sure I know what.

4

Mason

That woman is so fucking stubborn!

Ugh!

I'm just trying to make sure she's looked after. No wonder she thinks people call her a bitch with balls. That's because she acts like it at times.

I'm the boss on my plane!

Holly will have lunch and wine ready for her when she returns whether she likes it or not.

If she refuses, I'll tell her I'm not flying the jet until she starts eating. She might think she is the master negotiator, but she can't get around me. My years in the army have taught me many skills, including covert operations. Getting to where you need to be by stealth.

She won't even see me coming for her.

By the time I'm finished, she'll be in my arms, letting me take care of her. She's a challenge, but this is a war I'm happy to take on. Just like Grayson said. Time for my Mason charm to weave its way into her life.

Walking back on the plane, I hear Aaron making arrangements to leave for a short time to meet up with a lady.

I see red!

"Not a chance, dickhead! I told you we're not leaving the plane today. Understand?" He picked the wrong day to push my buttons.

"Whoa there, Captain, cool your jets. Didn't realize it was that important. What's got you all wound up like you're about to explode?" He's trying to be funny, but it's not helping.

"You! Why would I tell you earlier if it wasn't important? You can be so fucking stupid sometimes, I even wonder how you passed your pilot's exam. So put your dick back in your pants or go and choke it yourself for all I care. Just do not leave this aircraft. Got it?" My emotions are getting to the point I want to hit something. I don't know what's come over me. I haven't lost my temper like this in a long time.

Damn you, Paige. If this's what a woman does to me, I'm not sure I want to go down this road.

I need to cool off. Away from the crew. I'm usually carefree Mason, nothing ever gets me worked up. Walking into the bedroom at the back of the plane, I close the door and just sit on the bed and take a deep breath. Holding it in for a few seconds, slowly letting it go. A few more and my brain is finally calming down.

I drop my head into my hands, eyes closed. What the hell just happened? I need to get a grip on such a knee-jerk reaction to something so trivial. Paige will think I'm a jerk.

I look around the room, having never really paid much attention to it before. It's just the bedroom of the jet, yet now I'm sitting on Paige's bed that she sleeps in on long flights. I smooth my hand over the pillow. The same place she lays her head when she's taking time out from the world.

Picturing her dark hair fanned out on the crisp white linen.

I'm thinking things I shouldn't be.

Especially about the woman who's my boss.

Does she sleep here naked? Her flawless tits peeking out of the sheets. What's she thinking as her skin touches the cold sheets? Is she thinking about me flying up front and keeping her safe while she rests her weary body?

Shit! I need to get out of here.

I'm sounding like some dirty pervert or a stalker. I'm neither, but I need to stop these thoughts in her bedroom while she's not even here. That's just sleezy.

Doing some checks on the plane sounds like a far better option to blow off steam. Kicking the tires a few times I'll feel better. Well,

Aaron might appreciate it anyway, because at least I'm not kicking the crap out of him.

Standing at the rear of the jet, I hear steps behind me. I know by the sound of the heels it's Holly.

"You okay, Mason?" Her sweet voice makes me take a deep breath before I answer. She doesn't deserve my gruffness. She's only in her mid-twenties and has been working on planes for two years. She's lucky enough to be working a private jet this early in her career. Right time at the right place when one of the hostesses quit over an argument with a client. She was outfitted and thrown into the job with a ten-minute induction, straight out of her interview. Luckily it was only a short flight, and the client just wanted alcohol and lots of it. He was half drunk by the time we landed, and we didn't have any passengers on the return trip. She's been part of my crew ever since.

"Hey, Holly. Yeah, thanks. Just not enough sleep last night. Aaron's pushing my buttons by thinking with his dick instead of his brain."

She starts laughing. "When is he ever going to think with his brain before his dick? In case you haven't noticed, the guy is led around by his head and it's not the one that contains the brain. Not going to change anytime soon. Now, can I get you something to eat? I'm heading into the terminal to get some snacks. You know company policy, can't eat the stock on the plane." She rolls her eyes because we both know that no one sticks to that.

"On a chocolate binge again?" Placing my arm around her shoulder, I start walking with her towards the terminal doors. "Grab me a decent coffee, plus one for the testosterone boy on the plane, please."

"You trying to tell me I make crappy coffee?" Pretending to be offended, she jabs me in the side with her elbow.

"Nope, they just make it better. My treat." Passing her money, I'm heading back to apologize to Aaron. He might need to pull his head in a little, but he also didn't deserve the way I spoke to him.

~

After good coffee and chocolate have soothed our souls, we're watching an Avengers movie. Aaron won the rock-paper-scissors contest, so we're suffering through his choice. Although it's better than what Holly would choose. I don't know how many love stories she's tried to tell me are comedies.

I thought I would have heard from Paige by now. She told me several times that she was keeping this meeting to a minimum so she could get back home. Wanting to check on her, especially since she's on her own, isn't worth the grilling when she returns. Doubt my message would be appreciated the way it's intended. Instead, I head into the cockpit to check on the current weather conditions for the flight home. The grey skies here aren't looking fantastic. I want to make sure there are no delays.

The weather is starting to close in around Washington. A thunderstorm is predicted. I start to prepare my flight path, trying to avoid flying through it. My phone finally chimes with a message.

Paige: Meeting finished. In the car on the way to the airport. Please be prepared for takeoff as soon as I arrive.

Mason: Thank you. We are ready and waiting. Hope the meeting went well.

I wait to see the dots replying. Nothing appears. After a few minutes, I give up waiting and get back to work. Her message is all business, so I need to be the same.

"Okay, time to move. Boss is on her way back and wants to take off as soon as she arrives. To be honest, so do I, weather isn't going to be much fun. Holly, can you make sure she eats something once we're in the air? I know she will have skipped lunch. Aaron, I'm doing the preflight checks. Can you radio the tower and file our flight plan, please? I've made some notes on the screen about the storm cell we're trying to fly around. Our time for takeoff is in approximately thirty minutes. Get a booking for a runway. Back shortly."

"Yes, Captain," they both echo behind me as I head outside to talk to the ground staff and do my checks. The time for lying around and relaxing is over, it's work time now. I know that as much as we joke around, we're a tight crew, and when I say it's time, they never hesitate to switch on straight away.

I'm in my position at the bottom of the stairs waiting when her car pulls up, just as the rain starts. The driver steps out, but I've beaten him to the side of the car with an umbrella. I reach my hand to her as he opens the door to help her out. She grabs her bag and quickly stands with me, trying to hide from the rain.

Her closeness is intoxicating.

Her perfume is a soft sweet fragrance. Her hand's trembling a little in mine. I'd like to think it's from my touch, but I can tell by her face it's not. Something isn't right. This woman's life is like a roller coaster.

I lean in to whisper in her ear, and she gasps as I get closer. "Are you alright?" My lips are so close to her ear, I want to take it and bite down. Fuck, how I want to but can't.

A breathy, "Mmm," is all I get from her. Remembering where we are, I back away and concentrate on getting her out of the rain. Then I need to get the jet in the air and head home before this storm really breaks. Perhaps then I can find out what's going on.

"Thank you, Mason." Paige steps out from the umbrella into the cabin, and Holly pulls the cabin door closed behind me, securing it.

"All part of the service. Now let's get you home to your father and sunny Chicago." This brings a faint smile to her face which is enough for the moment.

Securing my harness and radioing the tower, we start taxiing out to the runway.

"Thank goodness the boss made it back when she did. This storm cell on the radar looks like it's going to get nasty in the next hour. I'll be happy to be well out of it by then. Let's get Meredith up in the air, Captain."

"That's the plan," I reply to Aaron as I push forward on the throttle and we start the adrenaline rush of takeoff for the second time today. The first twenty minutes of the flight are a little hairy with the storm. Nothing I'm not used to, though. I've flown in far worse conditions. As we're sitting at cruising altitude now and with clear sky in front of us, I want to check on Paige.

"Can you take control for five minutes? I just want to check on the boss. Something wasn't right when she came on board."

Aaron gives me a smug look. "Sure, Captain. Take as long as you need. I've got this." He switches control to himself.

47

"You can wipe that look off your face too," I comment as I unharness.

"What look? The one that says you have a thing for the boss lady?" He laughs as I glare at him.

"Yeah, that bullshit look. I'm just doing my job and checking on my passenger. Not everything is about sex, like in your world." I'm not good at lying so I exit the cabin so he can't see my face.

Holly is just coming back from the cabin with an empty plate. That makes me happy. At least she's eaten something. Probably not much, but I'm not going to push it. Entering the cabin, I see Paige with a glass of wine in her hand just staring out the window. She's zoned out which is not like her. Normally, no matter what, she's working while we fly, unless she's sleeping. So I don't startle her again, I clear my throat as I walk to gain her attention.

"Hope the turbulence wasn't too bad. We tried to fly around the storm but were just on the edge of it." I take a seat opposite her.

"Thank you, it wasn't too bad. I've had worse. It happens when you fly so often." Her finger is doing circles around the rim of the glass.

"Paige."

She looks up from where she was concentrating on her wine glass. "Hmm." Her response is very vague.

"Are you okay? Did something happen at your meeting or is it your father?" Her face turns to look out the window again before she takes a deep breath.

"Thank you for asking. I'm fine. There are just some things I was told in the meeting that I wasn't expecting. To be honest, I was totally blindsided, which doesn't happen often. Just means I've got some serious work to sort it out. Nothing I can't handle. That's what I do, I handle it all." Although she usually manages to keep her expression stone-faced without giving away her emotions, this last week I've seen her struggling to hold her composure. Not the same Paige I've worked for over the last six months.

"Can I help in any way?" I place my hand over her free one on the armrest. This time she doesn't pull away. She sits silently. This is how I know something big has happened.

"Not unless you're a super spy," she mumbles before taking a sip of wine.

"What's that supposed to mean? Are you in danger, Paige?" I start to sit up straighter and my voice gets more serious.

"No, no. I was just being silly. Ignore me. It's just been a long week. I might just take a nap before we reach Chicago." She places her glass on the table and pulls her hand away from me, reclining her chair a little. It's my cue to leave her alone. I'm not convinced everything's fine.

The word *fine* is such an ambiguous word. It's the word people use when they're trying to convince you that everything's okay, yet they don't have the energy or emotional strength to find the word, such as great or perfect. Or when they're afraid to say how bad they feel in case it opens up the emotions that they're trying to hold together. Instead, to the world they are just... fine.

Well, I know one thing. I'm not letting Paige be just fine on her own. Whatever's worrying her, I'll be helping to make it right.

"That's a good idea. A nap will help you feel better and clear your mind." I reach into one of the cupboards to retrieve a blanket and lay it over her.

"Wow, the captain of the plane and the hostess with the most-est. You really can multitask. Impressive."

"You would be surprised at all the things I excel at with my multitasking skills. Now rest and I'll make sure Holly doesn't disturb your beauty sleep until we're ready to land. Not that you need beauty sleep." I wink at her and return to the cockpit.

Ignoring Aaron's smartass comments as I'm returning, we continue the flight without any more problems and land perfectly back in Chicago. Paige has a habit of taking off before I finish in the cockpit. I plan on calling her later to check everything's okay. She's probably lucky I don't know where she lives, otherwise, I'd be turning up on her doorstop.

I need a drink, and it better be strong. Before I jump into my Jeep Cherokee to head home, I put out the message to the boys, our group message aptly named "crazy fam."

Mason: Drinks/dinner -Timothy O'Toole's Pub - 7 pm.
   Be there - No excuses!

Putting my phone in the tray ready to ignore it, I crank up the music to take my mind off the shit day it's been. "Ride it" by Regard starts radiating through the speakers.

Time to belt out a karaoke session. It's the only place I'll sing, on my own in the car or the shower. Except for that one time when the boys and I all went out to celebrate me arriving home from deployment in Afghanistan. We were that drunk, we ended up in some bar downtown, singing karaoke at three am. I don't remember one part of that night, but the video evidence on Tate's phone can't be denied. As usual he was the ringleader, and it involved a few females too. You can hear him on the video on a microphone telling the single girls in the bar, I'm a returned soldier who's needing some sex to make me forget the bad memories. I cringed so hard when I heard it. No amount of sex can wipe away images of war. Thank goodness Gray drunk dialed his dad. He turned up, herded us all into a taxi. Took us back to Gray's apartment and dumped us on a bed fully clothed. The next day was ugly, I remember that headache. That memory won't leave me in a hurry either.

Pulling into my underground carpark, I'm checking out every corner of the space. My training is still there. Always be aware of my surroundings. Keep your wits about you at all times. It's part of my problem. My brain won't switch off. It's too busy processing information. My counselor tells me I need to remember I'm no longer in the army or in a combat role.

Yeah, easier said than done!

Once you train your senses to be on alert twenty-four seven, it's hard to come back from that. I think that's why I've become an adrenaline junkie. It fuels my brain that's already living on the peak of activity every day.

Bingo! Three replies from Tate, Lex, and Gray. Just what the doctor ordered. Well, at least two of them are doctors. Lex is just the painfully cautious lawyer who continually worries about the stupid shit we do.

Grayson and Tate both work out of Mercy Hospital. Gray is an Obstetrics/Gynecologist and Tate's a neurosurgeon. Which is scary that they let that man touch people's brains. The guy I know is the biggest idiot, treats life like one big party. Yet they tell me in surgery he's the best there is in the city. He's pretty impressive, not that I ever tell him that. When we were all at Brother Rice High School for boys,

I always knew Gray wanted to be a Gyno, looking after women to honor his mom, but Tate surprised us all. Even his parents, who assumed he would be a trust fund baby and living off them for the rest of his playboy life. He proved us all wrong. For the thousands of lives he's saved, I'm sure they're happy he proved the world wrong.

After a shower and some internet surfing, I'm waiting for Gray to pick me up. He's on call, so he's the designated driver tonight. The only issue being if he gets called to the hospital, we're on our own. That's always a dangerous thing, to be left with Tate and no exit plan. Thank god for Uber, otherwise tonight could be a messy one. That's not guaranteeing it won't be anyway.

The ride to the pub is silent because Gray's on the phone to the hospital, discussing a patient that has gone into labor. Looks like he'll be with us for only a short while tonight. Long enough for dinner, then we'll be waving him goodbye. Nothing unusual for us. He's still on the phone as we pull up. I leave him to it and head in to get a drink. Spotting Tate and Lex already at the bar, I head straight to them, and the moment my ass hits the seat I signal the waiter, Johnny, for my usual beer. Gray won't be drinking so he can order his own when he finally gets in here.

"Where's lover boy?" Tate laughs as he wipes the beer froth of his lips with his tongue.

"On the phone, talking about some woman's body parts I have no interest in ever knowing about. If I didn't need a beer before the drive here, I certainly do now. No one should know that much about a woman's pussy unless he is fucking it," I grumble as Tate and Lex both spit their beer out on the bar.

"For fuck's sake, you three. Can you drink the beer and not spit it all over my bar like camels?" Johnny starts wiping down the bar in front of us.

"Oh, come on, Johnny, then you wouldn't have a reason to wipe the bar. Isn't that what bartenders do all night, just constantly wipe down the bar with some rag just so they look busy?" Lex is not the joker in the group, but when he comes out with them, they're usually gold. This one earns him a flick in the chest with said rag, which has him squealing like a pig and Johnny getting the last laugh. This is just what I need tonight. My boys, beers, food, and good laughs. Life's little pleasures.

"Sorry, man. Couldn't ignore that call. A high-risk pregnancy, so need to be ready to go shortly. Lex, Tate." Gray slaps me on the back of the shoulder and gives the man-nod to acknowledge the others.

"We should order food then. I'm starving anyway." Tate grabs the menu. I'm not sure what for. He orders the same thing every time.

"When are you not hungry, Tate?" Gray teases. "You must have one hell of a workout every day, so you don't look the size of a house."

He sniggers at Gray. "Maybe not every day, but I certainly enjoy one hell of a workout. I make sure of it," Tate boasts.

Johnny stands in front of us, ensuring we don't dirty his bar again.

"Such a cocky bastard. Not sure why you need to give your hand a daily workout. Good luck to you, with those blisters. You should see a doctor. Let's get food so it shuts him up for a while. Four rib baskets, thanks Johnny. Not sure why you even bother giving us menus." I laugh handing the menus back. From the look on the boys' faces, everyone's happy and settling in while we wait for the food.

"How's your court case going, Lex. You seem stressed the last few weeks. Still battling that chick who gives you grief in the court room?"

He groans and runs his hand through his hair. "Jacinta Nordick is going to be the death of me. I just wish we could be on the same team some days. She is the best fucking attorney I've come up against, so this is like battling myself. Have you ever tried to play with yourself?" We all roar at that comment. That's not something you say in front of a group of guys.

"Well, apparently Tate does almost every day," Gray pipes up and high-fives me.

"Oh, you are all so fucking funny. I can tell you, the last time I had to jerk myself off wasn't even in this decade," Tate replies.

"Tate, you are so full of shit you should've been a lawyer. Anyway, back to the bane of my existence this week in the court room. Being opposing council against Jacinta is the worst challenge. I keep analyzing the facts and thinking about how I would fight the case with her evidence. Then counter her arguments with my own. The jury's gone into recess, and it could be a few days before they come up with the verdict. I'm just sitting back now and waiting for the result. So frigging annoying."

Gray just rolls his eyes at him. "Sounds like a good day."

"You think it's annoying to you," Tate starts in, "imagine what it feels like waiting when you're the person who's charged with the crime. For your client, it's the difference between jail or freedom. Pretty sure it's just a tad more stressful for them." Lex picks up his glass of beer and chugs it down. I'm not sure he's happy with that comment from Tate. All our jobs carry their own type of stress. We've all noticed that it seems to be weighing Lex down lately.

"Tate, you can be such a prick sometimes," I say. "If it wasn't for Lex, the client wouldn't even have a chance. Let's get off work. No one wants to be thinking about that on a Friday night. Well, except lover boy here who's off to spend the night with some woman who isn't his fiancée. Who would have thought Doctor Dreamy would cheat on his Tilly?" That earns me a whack around the back of the head from Gray but breaks the moment and moves the conversation to the game that's on the television. It's a replay of a game from last year's NFL season. A game we all lost money on at the time. It starts the debate up again about the shit referee decisions that cost us the game.

Ribs are eaten and everyone's comfortable with our third beer for the night. Gray left as soon as he ate and told me to call him tomorrow about our discussion last week. I was grateful he didn't blurt it out in front of the boys. I'm not in the mood for the crap that'll get started if they find out I'm interested in my boss. I don't even know why I keep referring to her as that. It's not like it's an issue, and maybe I'm the only one that's worried about it.

Finishing my beer, I know it's time to call it quits for me. I want to be sober enough to call Paige when I get back to my apartment. I don't want it to be too late either. She might be asleep, and I'll feel terrible if I disturb her.

Pulling my wallet out to pay my tab, my phone starts ringing on the bar. Paige's name lights up. Tate goes to open his mouth, and I immediately hold my hand up in front of his face to make it clear I don't want to hear a word from him.

"Hey, Paige, how are you?" My heart beats a little faster. She's reached out to me this time. I'm getting somewhere. Unless she's calling to tell me we need to fly tomorrow. The word *boss* springs back into my head.

"Mason, I'm scared." She slurs her words and I know she's very drunk. Immediately my body's on alert and I'm already heading for the door. Waving over my shoulder to let the boys know I'm out.

"Paige, where are you? I need you to tell me where you are, and I'm on my way." My arm is up flagging down a cab while I'm trying to get her to answer.

"I'm at home." It's a little softer, and I'm worried she's about to pass out.

"Okay, are you safe?" I climb in the cab and give the driver a signal to wait. She doesn't answer. "Paige, honey, I need you to tell me where you live."

Then she giggles. "Shhhhh, it's a secret. I live in a building." Oh, fuck this.

"That's nice, Paige, I promise I'll keep your secret. What's the building called?"

"It's the nice one, you know, near the park." Now I'm getting mad.

"Paige. What's your address? Tell me right now!" My army voice is yelling down the phone. One I hate to use now.

She rattles it off perfectly like she's replying to a policeman.

"Good girl, now I'm on my way so make sure you stay awake to let me in. I'm not far away."

"You're bossy. Oh, wait, I'm the boss." Her giggle starts again, and I know I'm not getting any more sense out of her. I need to keep her conscious, so I do the one thing I know most drunk people are good at. I get her singing.

"What's your favorite song, Paige, can you sing it to me?" I know I'll regret this so pull my phone away from my ear a little.

"That's easy. *Eye of the Tiger*. I'm the besterest singer. Ready?"

No, but I'll suffer anyway.

"Sure, baby, let me hear it, nice and loud. Show me your tiger."

As my eardrums are crying in pain and my head is spinning, I wonder what the hell's going on. She might've pushed me away today but tonight, she has no choice. She'll be telling me, one way or another.

5

Mason

Thank god I've arrived at her building and I don't have to listen to this singing anymore. Man, I thought my voice was bad.

I think this is the one thing that Paige is not even close to perfect at!

"Paige, honey. I need you to stop singing for a minute and buzz me into your building. Can you hear the door chimes in the background from me pushing the button?" I'm trying to get her attention.

"*It's the eye of the tiger, it's the thrill of the fight,*" she keeps singing off-key.

"Paige!" I yell into the phone.

"Ow, that hurt my ear. You're too noisy." Still slurring. "What, Mr. Bossypants?"

I'm groaning and trying to keep my cool.

"The button that opens the front door, push it." I'm constantly pushing the buzzer in and out, and I can hear it going off in her apartment.

"It's noisy too. Can you make it stop? It's hurting my head."

"It'll stop when you push the button to open the door," I grumble like I'm talking to a two-year-old.

"Okay, okay, stop yelling at me." She has no idea what it's like if I yell. This volume's nothing. Finally, the door release activates. Pulling it open, I storm to the elevator.

"What floor are you, Paige?"

"The top one, silly. With the big bath and lots of bubbles. I like bubbles. Bubbles are fun. Phew, fly little bubadubles." Her little giggle kills me, but not as much of the vision I now have that she's naked in a bubble bath.

She's walked around in the apartment wet, no clothes on, just to buzz me in. This vision is one I hope to repeat with me in the room very soon.

"Are you drunk in the bath, Paige?" Pushing the penthouse button, I curse because I need a security number or pass.

"You're drunk, Mr. Hotty. The bubbles are drunk, they don't fly straight. Not like my private pilot, he always flies me straight. He keeps me safe." Fuck. What's going on?

"Yes, he does. Now tell me the elevator code. What are the numbers?" There's a silent pause.

"I can't 'member how to count. Can you count, Captain Yummy?" Jesus, I'm getting nowhere fast. Except hot and horny if she keeps pulling out her pet names for me. Are they what she uses when she's getting herself off at night?

Fuck. Concentrate, idiot, otherwise you'll lose her.

"Paige. What's your dad's date of birth?" A stab in the dark but let's see if it works

"Twelve, twelve, thirty-nine. He's old, my dad. Very old." She keeps rambling while I push the numbers in and strike a winner. Now moving upwards towards the penthouse, I try to work out how I'll handle drunk, wet, and naked Paige.

It's like a dream come true. Her naked and in a bubble bath. But seeing her for the first time away from work, naked and drunk is not how I imagined our first date.

The elevator slowly stops then opens straight into the apartment. *Holy fucking hell.*

I know she's wealthy, but this is past my expectations. I don't have time to take it all in while I'm trying to work out where her voice is coming from. Two sets of stairs lead up to the second level. Jogging up one set, I'm wandering along the hallway with several doors. Pushing a few open, they're bedrooms, so hopefully I'm on the right side of the apartment. I get to the end, but nothing.

I'm not even listening to what she's saying, but she's still talking which is all I need. Now heading up the opposite flight of stairs, there are only two doors. Pushing open one it looks like a television room.

I'm now faintly hearing her voice. Slowly opening the next door, it leads into her bedroom, I'm guessing.

The bed's huge and everything in here is very feminine. Lots of those damn throw pillows on the bed. I can't understand why women insist on that many. They're a pain in the ass to take off and put back on every morning. There's a door to my left that I hear her voice coming from. The wet footprints in the carpet also give it away.

"Paige, I am outside your bathroom door. I'm going to open it so don't get scared, okay?"

"No, you're not. No boys come to my house to visit me. My dad said no boys allowed. No kissing, no fucking. No touching boys. It sucks." Damn my cock's already straining hard in my jeans.

"That's okay because I'm a man, no boys here. I'm opening the door now, so you'll see I'm not lying. Remember, Paige, I said friends don't lie to each other." Slowly I turn the knob.

In a whisper she replies, "I don't have any friends. Friends are pains."

Well, if that doesn't stop me in my tracks for a moment. That's not the first time she's said that. How can such a wealthy, high-powered woman not have any friends? I think it's just drunken self-pity, because it's hard to believe it's true.

I push the door open, and there she is. Lying back in a bath big enough to be a pool. Bubbles overflow onto the floor. I'm relieved that they're so thick they're covering her body. All I can see is her bare shoulders and head, with her hand holding her phone to her ear. Her hair is pulled into a messy bun on top of her head, which reveals her long slender neck. She's staring at me like she's not sure if I'm really here.

"A wet dream?" Paige mumbles, and I couldn't agree more.

"Hi there." Still she doesn't move, her eyes are just fixed on me. "I told you I wasn't lying. I was behind the door, just like I said." She just nods her head a little.

"Looks like you've been having a little party for one in here tonight." Sitting on the side of the bath is an empty bottle of wine, plus a half-empty bottle of scotch. I hope like hell she didn't open that tonight. Otherwise we'll be on the way to the hospital when this all hits her system.

"Nope, no party," she mumbles. I shake my head at her.

"Okay, hun, I beg to differ. Now let's get you out of the bath and somewhere safe. Probably not the best idea to be drinking in here. Put your phone down first. We don't want that going for a swim." She slowly puts the phone down where her empty glass and the bottles sit. Looking around for a towel to wrap her up in, I find exactly what I expect. Thick and fluffy, soft, white towels.

"I'm going to keep my back turned while you stand up and wrap this around you. I don't want you to try to step out until I help you. Okay?" I'm guessing my arrival is sobering her up a little because the reply has the first little hint of snark in it.

"I'm not a child, you know." Well, that's debatable tonight.

"Mhmm, so you say." I hear the water moving and hold out the towel behind me, until it's snatched from my hand.

"See…" I turn as soon as I hear her voice start to rise and become a squeal. I catch her in my arms. This is bad. Very, very bad. I need to show the restraint of a gentleman here.

Looking down at her face. So soft and supple, looking scared and sad. I wonder if she's ever had anyone to lean on before. Why did she call me when she hardly knows me? Right this moment she looks so exposed, and that's not just because she's standing in front of me naked. There's a real sense of despair about her tonight.

I want to take her face in my hands and kiss those sad lips until she smiles again. That's stepping over the line I need to maintain, though.

"What did I say? You don't listen very well, do you? Now let's get you into bed so you can sleep off the massive hangover that's coming in the morning." There's no point even trying to find out tonight what's going on. No sense has been spoken since she called me. Except how sexy she thinks my ass is.

Still silent like she doesn't know what to say, Paige lets me lead her into her bedroom. I pull back her covers and sit her down, then lower her head on the pillow. Lifting her long legs up and onto the mattress, I place the covers over her.

"Now take the towel out for me, and I'll hang it up." Her eyes are getting heavy as soon as her head is placed on the pillow. She manages to get the towel off, but it isn't graceful. Using the bed covers, I shield her and myself. My cock can't take much more.

"I want you to sleep and we can talk in the morning. Okay?" I smooth her loose hair off her face as she snuggles down into the pillow.

"I'm scared. Don't know why they…" Her voice drifts off as her drunken sleep claims her.

As much as I'm worried, I know tonight she's okay. Tomorrow we tackle this together.

"You're safe with me. I'll protect you always." Taking the last glimpse at her, looking so gorgeous while she's unraveled and free, I walk out the door. I need to call the guys and explain why I rushed out and then find some coffee in the kitchen. It's going to be a long night. Sleep will be light and short. I know now that my body is already on high alert.

Tomorrow is going to be an interesting day.

Paige

"Shit." I can't even lift my head off the pillow without it hurting like hell.

What truck hit me?

Slowly opening my eyes to small slits and noticing familiar surroundings, I'm a little relieved. I have no idea what's going on. Trying to remember last night, I come up completely blank. The more I try, the worse the pain in my head gets.

Oops, here we go. I jump up and run to the bathroom to throw up.

Ugh. I sit here for a moment, emptying my stomach of every bit that's in there. My head's spinning, and my mouth feels like it's been eating sandpaper and rotten meat. I need to get up off the floor and try to clean myself up and squeeze a whole tube of toothpaste into my mouth to get rid of that taste.

Slowly standing, I see the wine and scotch bottle on side of the bath, with the water still in the tub. Oh god, I must have had a good time in the tub last night. No wonder I'm feeling like shit, seeing how much I drank. I stagger into the shower and turn it on the massage setting. I let the hot water drain over my body and my back feel the pressure of the jets. A faint memory is hovering in my head of wanting a glass of wine and a bath to try to relax after what had been a really fucked-up day.

Mason being a dick, the meeting totally blindsiding me, and then my dad worsening again after the recent improvement. No wonder I drank hard. Needing to pull myself together, I take deep breaths. I need to get over to my father's and check on him. Thank god I have a driver. I'm not sure I'd be safe behind the wheel today. Just walking will be hard enough.

After washing my hair, myself, and brushing my teeth three times, I'm dressed in jeans and a tank top heading downstairs. I need to make an extra-strong black coffee to take some heavy-duty painkillers. Padding barefoot along the hallway, soft carpet between my toes, I can hear noise and someone in the apartment. Freezing, my heart is almost stopped. I feel for my phone that I normally have in my pocket, but I haven't even noticed it anywhere this morning.

Fuck. Who the fuck is in my house? No one gets up here without the code or a security card.

Okay, breathe, it has to be someone I know. Maybe the cleaners came on a different day for a change. It can't be my father because he's in bed.

Then I hear a terrible rendition of *Old Town Road* by a male voice that sounds familiar. I can't work it out. I tiptoe to the top of the stairs, peek over the edge. The singing gets louder as I get closer. It's coming from the kitchen. Plus, the smell of food and oh god, strong coffee. I see the corner of a shoulder and arm. A maroon shirt, sleeves rolled up, and a strong arm reaching for a plate from the cupboard. Then it happens.

He steps into my view. With his back to me. A slight turn.

Holy shit!

Mason.

What the hell is my private pilot doing in my kitchen? I'm rubbing my temples, trying to push my memory. How did he get in here? What did I do last night?

Oh god! I was naked in my bed?

Shit. Shit. Shit.

Surely, I would know if I slept with him. Wouldn't I? Oh man, I can't remember a thing after arriving home and getting into the tub.

Trying to lean farther over to look down the stairs to see him, I end up overbalancing. I'm stumbling down the staircase. I land awkwardly at the bottom before I know it. Not the gracious entrance I would have liked. Standing, trying to straighten myself out, Mason just looks across at me and starts laughing.

"Nice trip? Did you send me a postcard and buy me the shirt?" He's smiling as he's trying to stop laughing hard at me.

Embarrassed, my words come out, not as calm as they should, "What the hell are you doing in my house?" Hands on my hips, I glare at him waiting for an answer.

"Sounds like someone woke up grumpy this morning. A bit of a hangover headache, have we?"

Ugh, he's so annoying. "Can you answer my question? How did you get in here?" He starts walking towards me, and I back away a little.

"You let me in. Don't you remember?" His eyes are fixed on me like he's trying to read me. "Oh, this is hilarious, you have no idea what happened last night, do you?" Turning back to the kitchen, his laugh is loud and deep as he opens the oven and takes out some muffins that have been baking.

"Mason, don't be a jerk. Tell me why you're in my kitchen cooking, and I have no idea how you got here. Just humor me and fill in the blanks." I'm trying to ask calmly, but on the inside, I'm freaking the hell out.

"Sit, here's your coffee and a muffin to line your stomach, which I'm imagining's not the best this morning. Then we can talk."

My patience is short this morning. "Mason!" I scold. "I'm freaking out here." He points to the stool at the kitchen island. "Alright, I'm sitting, you better start talking." He places coffee and food in front of me along with some pain meds. Man, this guy's too good.

"Thank you," I grumble.

"You're welcome." He sits beside me. I glare at him and if looks could start a fire, he would be burning red hot right now.

"Okay, okay. You called me last night, very drunk. Told me you were scared, but I couldn't get out of you why. I managed to get your address from you while you were busy singing *Eye of the Tiger* to me."

I can feel my face turning red. "You're making that up. I don't sing."

"You're right, you don't. I'm not sure what you were doing could be classed as singing. My ears are still hurting." He smiles his cocky grin.

"Well, what I was just listening to is certainly the worst singing I've ever heard." There, smarty pants, take that. Oh my god, what am I, five?

"Touché, Paige. I'll have to agree with that. Now, I need you to tell me what's going on. Why are you scared to the point you got so drunk last night you called me?" He turns sideways on his stool; he looks straight at me, not letting me ignore him. I can't tell him what's going on. I need to keep that to myself and find a way to sort it out.

"I don't even remember calling you. Sorry, I don't know what I was rambling about." I try to break off some of the muffin to eat so I don't have to talk.

"I call bullshit. Your body language is telling me something completely different. When I put you to bed, you told me again that you're scared. You can trust me with whatever it is."

For some reason, the feelings in my gut tell me I can, however my head is telling me that I need to keep my mouth shut.

"I don't know what to tell you." Then my brain realizes what he just said.

"Wait." *Oh no.*

"What?"

No, no, no!

"You put me to bed?" Bastard's just smiling at me. "Did you undress me? I woke up naked!"

His eyes light up like he's hiding something. "You really don't remember what happened between us last night?" Oh god. My head drops into my hands. What did I do? Don't get me wrong, there is a big part of me that would very much like to sleep with Mason, but at least I would like to remember every enjoyable moment.

"No," I hesitate to say.

"Well, when you tell me why you're scared, I'll tell you what happened last night." Straightening on his seat, he tries to intimidate me in a nice way.

"That's blackmail! Just tell me now! I'm done playing games." I stand up, starting to get pissed off. This is my home. I'm calling the shots.

"Well, that makes two of us, Paige. You were scared enough that you called me. A person you barely know, let me into your building, gave me the security code, and didn't freak out one bit when I walked into your bathroom where you were in a bubble bath naked. I'll do everything I can to make you tell me what the hell is going on. I want to help you. I'm not just some useless employee. I'm a trained soldier who knows far more about danger than I would like to. However, these skills will be what can keep you safe when you need me to." He stands up straight in front of me, breathing hard, chest puffed out, and shoulders back.

Looking hot as hell. My emotions are so scrambled and mixing with anger. I know I'll regret this later. Losing control, I slam my mouth on his, doing what I've been longing to do for the last six months.

There's no hesitation from Mason. His hands go straight to the back of my head, grabbing at my hair and trapping me right where he wants me.

His lips are rough and strong, overtaking the kiss and seizing control from me. Where I'm kissing with all the ferocity that I'm feeling, Mason's now slowing it down. Kissing me softly and deeply. The warmth from his lips is spreading through my body like nothing I've ever felt before.

Fuck!

What am I doing! This can't happen.

For so many reasons, this can't happen. I'm pulling back quickly, and although he's fighting a little with his hands in my hair, he reluctantly lets me go.

"I'm so stupid," I say as I step farther away from him. "This can't happen. You need to leave. Please, you need to go now." Both my arms wrap around my body, and I'm starting to shiver all over.

"Paige, calm down. I'm not going anywhere. We need to talk about this. About that fucking amazing kiss, plus everything else." He steps towards me, but I keep retreating.

"No. Stop. Don't come any closer. Please, Mason, you need to leave. We can talk later. I just need to be alone."

"Bullshit, that's the last thing you need. Talk to me, Paige. You're shutting down on me. What the fuck's going on?"

63

I can feel the tears coming. I can't break down. He can't see me vulnerable, more than he already has. I need to come up with something to get him to go.

"Look, I'm just upset about my father, that's it. You don't know him so you can't help. Now please go. Thank you for coming, and I'm sorry I worried you. But you need to go. I'll talk to you later but please, just not now."

"I'm not leaving, Paige. None of this makes sense."

"If you don't leave, I'll call the security downstairs." I won't, but it sounds good.

"Security, what fucking security? Where were they last night when a man you were talking drunk to, convinced you to let him into your apartment? Fat good their help is to protect you, Paige." Both our voices are escalating, this is not healthy. I'm about to give him another mouthful when my phone starts ringing. It must be down here somewhere. I look over onto the table and see it flashing.

"Don't you answer that," he huffs.

"How dare you tell me what to do in my own home. Get the fuck out." The phone stops and then starts up again straight away. I move to pick it up, seeing it's Beth. Shit, can today get any worse?

"Beth," I yell down the phone. Before she even has time to speak, I immediately apologize. "Sorry, that was rude. How are you, Beth?"

Her voice tells me something's wrong. "Paigey, you need to come home. The doctor needs to see you. Your father's very sick." I knew before she even said it that he's bad. When she calls me Paigey it's when she's in grandmother mode.

"I'm on my way. Tell him I'll be there as soon as I can. How bad is he, Beth?" There's a long pause that tells me she's scared to say.

"We both know he's tough. He'll pull through. That's what he does. Be safe, and I'll see you soon." Her voice is gone, and I'm running up the stairs to grab my bag, shoes, and jacket.

"Bent, I need the car now. I need to get to my father," I tell him as soon as he picks up the phone.

"Yes, ma'am. On my way. Meet you out front." He hangs up as I'm almost to the bottom of the stairs. Heading for the elevator.

"Paige." Mason's soft voice comes from behind me. I'd totally forgotten he's here, my mind going blank as soon as Beth called.

"Mason, sorry. I need to go, my father's not well. I'm sorry, forget everything I said. Please just go, and we'll talk later." I can't wait for any explanation.

"I understand, I hope he's okay. Please let me know. I'll clean up here…" It's the last thing I hear as the elevator door closes with him still talking at me.

I've totally lost my mind. Running out leaving a guy I hardly know in my apartment, after I practically sucked his face off. Oh my god, the world is upside down and I don't know how to flip it back. It just keeps spinning faster and faster.

I tap out a text message to Mason, while the elevator's descending.

Paige: *Mason, sorry and thank you.*

Mason: *I'm here to help however you need. That's all I was trying to do. To keep you safe.*

Paige: *I know, I'm sorry.*

Mason: *Breathe, Paige. If he's anything like you, he's strong. Believe in that.*

I can't reply anymore. I just need to get to my father and find out what's really going on. I need him. He's not allowed to leave me. I'm not ready to be alone.

~

Running up the front steps of my childhood house like I used to do every afternoon doesn't feel as much fun today.

Beth's at the door waiting for me. She grabs me and takes me into a tight hug before letting me go.

"The doctor's in his bedroom with him. Go straight in." There are tears in her eyes, but I know she's holding them in for me.

Standing outside of his room, I hesitate, feeling like my heart is going to stop. Stepping through this door could change my world. If I stand here and don't enter, then nothing changes, but that's just unrealistic. My father taught me to be strong so that's what I'll be. It's what he's expecting from me.

Opening the door, I see my father lying in bed with his eyes closed, an oxygen mask on his face. I can hear the awful sound of his breathing from here. Frozen, just taking the scene in, it's Doctor Joss's voice that jolts me back to the present.

"Paige dear, please come and sit down so we can chat." My father's doctor has looked after him since I was born. He's almost as old as my father, just not quite. Daddy didn't think it was appropriate for him to look after a little girl, so I've had a female doctor since I arrived here.

Walking towards Daddy, I lean down and kiss him on the forehead. He stirs slightly. He knows I'm here. Taking his hand, I sit down on the chair next to the bed.

"How is he? What's going on, he was getting better." Looking up into the eyes of Doctor Joss, I try to gauge what he's about to say.

"The cold he's suffering has settled on his chest and developed into pneumonia. Due to his age, this needs to be treated very seriously. I wanted him admitted to the hospital this morning, but he's refusing. I know we've always discussed how he wants to be cared for at home, for anything that becomes wrong with him. Purely part of his stubbornness." He rolls his eyes at his own comment.

"What do you suggest? What should I do?" I feel like a little girl again, lost in a world I don't know how to navigate.

"I've organized for around-the-clock care with personal nurses, and I'll be here several times a day to check on him. I've given him all the medication I can, keeping him comfortable, and oxygen to make sure he's breathing as well as he can." He sighs a little. "Then we wait." He places his hand on my shoulder and gives it a little squeeze of comfort.

"I'll move home until he's better, so I'm here all the time. I'll work from here because god forbid, I take time away from his beloved business. But he can complain all he likes when he's better. I'm cancelling all travel until he's well enough. And he will get better. There's no other option. Right, Daddy?" I look at him for a response. "You'll get better so you can continue to be the grumpy retired CEO still bossing around the current CEO." I lay my head on his shoulder and pray hard that he's listening.

Beth comes in with a cup of coffee for me. My headache and breakfast have been totally forgotten. Placing the cup on the table set up next to his bed, she hugs me from behind.

"He'll pull through this, Paigey, you know he will. For once his stubbornness will be an asset. I'll get Bent to take me to your apartment and collect your things. Just give me a list and I'll bring everything home. I assume you're staying."

"Thank you, Beth. You're so good to us. Yes please, that'd be wonderful. If you can get me some paper and pen, I'll start now. I sort of ran out without much."

Panicking and being disorganized is so unlike me. Even in the toughest situation, my father taught me to stand strong, assess the problem, strategize then implement. That's no use to me here.

I feel so useless. There is nothing I can do except just sit and wait. Oh, and pray. Which I've never been very good at. Let's hope someone is listening now.

~

Beth's amazing the way she looks after both my father and me. As much as I don't feel like eating, she makes me some pasta with a tomato sauce. Plus, my favorite cheesy garlic bread. Comfort food. I insist she sit and eat with me. She looks terrible. I know how close she is to my father; even though she complains about him all the time, they'd be lost without each other.

I often wonder if there has ever been anything more between them or just an unrequited love from Beth that my father would never return because she works for him. I hope I'm wrong, otherwise that would be so sad that they've lived alongside each other for near fifty years and longed for more.

The roles we hold in this world can be so suffocating. Like chains that confine us. Whether we're there by choice or not. All the money, strength, and power, and yet you're still struggling to breathe.

I've never known what fresh air feels like.

6

Paige

Listening to the rattle of my father's lungs as he struggles to breathe is so hard. Trying to distract myself with work, it's hard to concentrate on anything. Nurses coming and going regularly, smiling at me to tell me he's still the same. I never thought that would be a good thing for a sick person, yet it's positive meaning he isn't getting worse.

I've been in contact with Tyson so he knows what's going on and he can start moving my meetings to conference calls. Speaking to Brian, he thinks we should keep it quiet how sick my father is. Investors and clients tend to get nervous if the CEO's not on the ball. Brian will fly to one important meeting, so we don't spook them.

Shit. I need to message Mason. I promised I'd call, but I can't bear talking to him. It might be the thing that brings me unstuck. He should know it's not me flying with him this week and that my dad is not doing well. Drafting the message three times, I delete it. Finally, I just type quickly before I have time to think, my finger hitting send.

Paige: *Mason, I'm sorry about last night and this morning. We'll talk later about it. Just letting you know my dad has pneumonia and I am staying with him until he recovers. I'm not traveling, instead my VP, Brian, will be with you on Tuesday. Be nice to him. Stay safe.*

Waiting for the dots after you send a message is like torture. I don't know if I want him to reply or if it'll be easier if he doesn't. Instead, my phone starts buzzing in my hand. I should have known he would call. I just can't do it. I don't have the strength. I let it go to my voicemail.

Paige: I can't talk. Maybe tomorrow.

Mason: I'm sorry to hear about your dad. I'm sure he's going to pull through this. I'm worried about you too. Are you doing okay?

This is why I can't talk to him. His message is already making tears escape. No time to be emotional.

Paige: You're kind. Thank you for asking. I'm fine. I have to be. Talk tomorrow.

Walking out of my father's room, I let Beth know I'm taking a shower upstairs.

Finally, I let my tears fall. They've been building for days, and with the sound of the water running, no one will know.

No one except me. The way it's always been.

Mason

There's that damn word again.

Fine!

She's not fucking fine. I know that, and she knows that. Yet she won't let me do anything to help her. I'm here staring out at the Chicago night, while she's out there, somewhere. On her own. Being the strong, kick-ass woman she is.

I wonder if she ever gets tired of that. Holding up the armor. I'm damn sure I would.

Mason: With everyone else, you do. With me, I want you to let yourself not be fine for once. Let me carry the weight for a little while.

No reply comes. She's gone radio silent, which is killing me. I'm waiting, but I know nothing's coming.

Lying down in bed, I wonder if sleep will come at all tonight. I send one last message.

Mason: You must know over the last twenty-four hours I've become more than just your private pilot. That kiss was so much more. When you touch your lips, know that mine feel that touch too.

It's neither the time nor the place to say this over a message, but I have no idea when she'll let me see her again. I need her to know how I'm feeling. Whether she's ready to hear it or not.

How life can change in an instant. I've felt something different from the moment I met Paige. When she shook my hand before boarding the plane that first flight. It was strong and firm, yet with a soft femininity that I felt was hiding underneath.

Today, her kiss felt exactly the same. Strong, firm, yet feminine. She sealed our path.

The fire that exploded on our lips, melted every barrier and reason in my head why I shouldn't pursue her. Nothing will stop me now.

She wants me, just as much as I want her.

No need to rush her. I'll stand and support this woman through this. Then, we're exploring what the hell that was today. Because if she kisses like that, what the hell's she like in bed.

Sleep's not coming easy. Reading's been my savior over the years, but tonight it just doesn't hold my interest. The last time I look at the clock it's just before one am. Finally, I feel my body giving in and my eyes feeling heavy. I want morning to be here so I can try to talk to Paige again

I have a real issue with feeling I can't help someone in need. I know this, and I need to be mindful I don't become obsessed with it. In my mind, I'm watching her walk up the plane stairs, slow motion. Long legs in fuck-me heels. Nice and bright. My eyes drawn to her every time. The vision getting stronger. I feel my resolve not to think of her weakening. My hand sliding down until I'm fisting my cock. The rhythm in time to her ass swaying just for me. The vision then takes me to the bath. Wishing I could just push those bubbles aside and see her breasts. Sliding into the bath and lying between her smooth legs. Feasting on her. Hearing my name screaming from her lips. Water sloshing out onto the tiles, while I'm fucking her hard. So fucking hard that she moans loud, begging me to keep going. That's what I want to dream about.

Instead, I need sleep, it will calm the brain. Maybe if I dream all about Paige just like I've imagined and that kiss. Jesus, that kiss was heaven and thinking about it will help me wake with a smile on my face. Or a problem in my pants. Either is a good result.

~

"Captain White, I've been requested to provide a pilot to take a special forces team in behind enemy lines to do an extraction of a group of women and children who have been cut off by the fighting. You will be required to do a night flight and remain on the ground while they are rescued and loaded into the bird. There is the risk of enemy fire, and I'm not overly happy with the mission. Unfortunately, the powers that be have already put the plans in motion. The pilot that had the orders for this flight has just been taken to the field hospital with a suspected heart attack. So that means they need you."

He pushes a folder towards me with the briefing enclosed. It's unusual for Major Toro to show any hesitation with a mission. "You are the best we have, so you've been assigned. Wheels up at zero-one-hundred hours. Instruct your crew and be ready."

"Yes, sir. Will that be all, sir?" I stand with the folder in my hand waiting for further instructions that don't come.

"Any questions?" He looks at me with his stern frown, and you can tell he doesn't want me to reply with a yes.

"No, sir. We will report and be ready as commanded." I stand to attention.

"Good. Dismissed." With that he goes back to his computer. I salute, turn, and start exiting the office when he calls my name.

"Captain."

"Yes, sir?"

"Safe flight." With that he continues with his work.

"Thank you, sir," I reply and close the door to his office.

Standing outside his office, I scan through the mission and take it all in. I have seven hours to have the chopper and my crew ready to head out. There is no time to waste. I need to brief them and do the preflight checks on the aircraft. Then before we head out, I need to send the usual emails I do before any risky mission. The first one to my family and then second to the boys. My family just get a brief one, with a few day-to-day pleasantries which gives me the lead-in to be able to tell them how much I love them.

For Gray, Tate, and Lex, they get the truth. Obviously, nothing classified or what I'm doing, but my thoughts and feelings. There are things I need to tell someone, and I know it will stay with them. They have my back and will never repeat what I tell them. By the time I get back from the mission, I'll have three email replies from them giving me hell about being a pussy or telling me about the latest hot girl they're sleeping with. It's exactly what I need to take away the visions of what I'm seeing and doing on a daily basis. *Especially Tate. Nothing has changed since I left home. He's still a man-whore and finding plenty of women who will put up with his huge ego.*

Several hours have passed, and I'm in the middle of my preflight checks with my flight engineer. Major Toro storms towards us at full stride. The hairs on the back on my neck are already standing up. Something is happening. I can tell by his body language.

"Wheels up in ten minutes, White. Things have turned to shit. Mission is happening now. Special forces are assembling. Get the crew on board."

Fuck.

The chopper is ready to go, but I hate when things change. It's never a good sign. I haven't written my emails home, which makes me anxious. I never miss them. Grabbing my phone, I send a quick few words in messenger to the boys. It doesn't send, but I hope it will at some stage. I skip my parents. Mom will freak out, worrying because it's unusual.

Flight suit and helmet on, I'm in my seat with the rotors going as the special forces unit starts climbing in. Their captain fills me in on the change of mission. The fighting has changed directions, and the enemy fighters are heading straight towards the trapped women and children. If we don't move now, they're going to be either caught in crossfire, or captured, and we all know the terrible things that these radicals do to the women and children.

Fuck that. Not on my watch!

Once I take the control stick into my hands, my mind focuses and nothing else enters it except for the safety of my crew and passengers, and the mission.

Being a night mission, it's always harder for me, but it helps the team get in and out easier under the cover of darkness. The radio operations room is updating me on what's happening on the ground as we get closer to the landing site.

"ETA three minutes, you have ten minutes on the ground before wheels up. Control reports that the targets are ready and assembled. Good luck, gentlemen." I see the flashes of light ahead of me. The gunfire is close to the place I'm about to set us down. My night goggles help me see the clearing in the grounds of the orphanage we're approaching. "Gunners on standby. Set down, ten, nine, eight, seven, six, five, four, three, two, touchdown. Go time." The men start scrambling from the open doors while my crew are on high alert for any movement in the shadows.

In my headset, I hear all the talk between the Zulu team. Above the shouting I also hear children crying. I block it out so not to lose my concentration.

"Wheels up in five minutes," I call into my mouthpiece to alert the team we're running out of time. My copilot reports there are soldiers running towards us carrying children. He can see women standing in the doorway with the last of the children. The first ones are being received by my crew, and the team is on their way back for the last group.

"Wheels up in two minutes," I call to the team, my senses on full alert. I need to get out of here.

"Charlie Delta Bravo three-seven-nine you have incoming insurgents. Wheels up now." I hear screaming into my ears from the control room. They have drones and satellites to see what's happening on the other side of the wall. The Zulu commander is also hearing the same call and is yelling at the women to run but there's one who is trying to give the last panicking child to the captain. All the soldiers have children in their arms, and along with the two women, are running towards us. I'm prepared to lift off as soon as the last body lands in the chopper. To my right, I hear a bang and the gate is blown up and there are bullets flying towards us. I hear the Zulu commander shouting as they're throwing all the children into the back of the chopper. He jogs towards the last woman who is slower, still carrying a child in his arms. Dragging her towards the chopper with him.

"Thirty seconds to takeoff. Come on, come on. I need wheels up." If I can't get up in the next few seconds, we are fucked.

The rapid gunfire burst explodes around us and I hear the blood-curdling scream in my ears. My gunners are now firing and my copilot signaling for wheels up. I can't focus on the picture in front of my eyes of the woman being hit and falling into the arms of the commander, just as they reach the chopper and are both dragged on board. It's my job to get everyone out of here and back to the safety of the base. I pull the joystick and lift off.

"Whiskey Sierra Lima, this is Charlie Delta Bravo three-seven-nine, we are airborne with at least one casualty on board. ETA five minutes. Over." My heart is racing, I can feel the sweat all over my body. As I bank right, away from the orphanage, I can still hear the gunfire whizzing past and praying it misses us. The sky is lit up like the fourth of July. I'm not sure I will ever be able to enjoy a firework display again.

There is screaming, crying, and confusion in the rear of the chopper as we head back to the base. My focus needs to be on flying, but I can hear it over the noise of the rotors. The medic is trying to calm her. My copilot signals that the woman has been shot in her stomach. The medic is yelling we need to get her to the hospital. I can't fly any quicker than I already am. Especially with all the weight I have on board.

73

"Whiskey Sierra Lima, this Charlie Delta Bravo three-seven-nine. ETA is three minutes. Urgent medical assistance needed for casualty, civilian woman with critical abdominal wound, over."

"Roger Charlie Delta Bravo three-seven-nine. Ambulance on standby. Over." Adrenaline pumping, I'm pushing the chopper. I need to keep them all safe so I can't do anything stupid. Hearing my medic screaming in the coms that he's losing her, crying babies and women, her voice crying to save her son. I can't do anything. Just fly. Concentrate on flying. There's the base. Almost there. Hang on. Please hang on. Save her, keep them safe…

"Keep her safe!" My eyes fly open.

Sweat running off my skin. My body rigid. Breathing like crazy. Sitting bolt upright.

Need to count. "Ten, nine, eight." Deep breath. "Seven, six… five, four." Another slow deep breath. "Three… two… one." Slow deep breath to hold in and very slowly release.

"Fuck!" I run my hands through my hair, wet from the sweat.

I haven't had a full flashback for years. I have bits of nightmares along the way. But not this one, not the whole night. I know I won't sleep now. The first light of the morning is breaking through the dark of the night. I need to get out and run. It helps burn off the pent-up adrenaline. Clear the head of the memories. Produce the good endorphins.

Loud music pumping in my ears and the sun rising on another beautiful day brings peace. Although I'm tired from just a few hours' sleep, I know today will be a good day. It's my day that I volunteer and mentor the kids at the *End of The Cycle Program.* My counselor put me in touch with them when I returned from my deployment in Afghanistan.

It's a program that helps children and families from low-economic backgrounds. The parents get help to find work and budget to improve their living conditions while I help with the kids. Mentoring them in several areas of schooling, sports, and aiming for a career path to break the poverty circle in these disadvantaged communities. Helps me just as much as it helps them. Keeps the kids off the street and safe. Helps me to feel useful.

There's been no reply from Paige after my last message. I want to reach out, but I already feel unbalanced this morning. I've told her

I'm here and how I feel. Time to leave it in her hands. Just get on with my day and hope it's a better one for her and her father.

Entering the gym at the program's main center, I feel a good vibe. The noise of the boys all playing basketball and the ribbing that goes with it is just what I need.

"Right, who's cheating here?" I yell as I'm jogging onto the court. "Because that's definitely the team I want to be on. Is it you, Leroy?"

"It's always Leroy," Jesse yells from across the court to me.

"Is that right, Jesse? Then you and I better take him down. What you say, buddy?" His smile makes my day.

"Yeah dude, Leroy, you're going down." This has all the boys splitting into teams and trash talking each other. This is the healthiest thing these boys can be doing. Working off the testosterone that's running wild in their bodies at this age, plus without realizing it, they're learning about working as a team which is a life skill.

After a few hours of playing basketball, we break for lunch that the center provides the kids. A hot meal that's better than I can cook. Some of the mentors are chefs, and they include kids who are interested in cooking, teaching them skills to get a job.

Sitting down in the mess room, Leroy places his plate down next to me.

"Okay to sit here, Mason?" I love how far he's come since starting with the program. In the beginning he wouldn't have come anywhere near me. Nor would I have gotten the manners he's showing me. It's not that his parents haven't tried hard to raise him well, he just fell into the wrong crowd and was losing his way. His mother reached out to the counselors here in hope we could do something. The young man standing in front of me should be so proud of how far he's come.

"Sure, man. You showed some hot moves on the court today. Almost got me. Better luck next time." I elbow him in the side as he rolls his eyes at me.

"You're like a foot taller than me, man. How am I supposed to get past those arms of yours? They go forever." We both laugh together.

"How did your math test go this week, man?" It's important we try to keep track of what's going on in the kids' lives. Being able to ask them a personal question rather than a generalized one shows that they're important in our lives too.

"That's what I wanted to tell you. I can't believe it. I got an A-plus. I aced it thanks to your help." I immediately place my hand up for a high five. Slapping hard, then putting my arm around his shoulder.

"So damn proud of you, Leroy. That's all you, man. You put in all the study and worked hard. See what you can do when you put your mind to it? You're a smart kid. Keep aiming high, buddy." He looks a little embarrassed at the compliments. Since the program organized for a laptop and internet access, Leroy's school marks have increased out of sight.

"Can I share something with you? I've never told anyone, but when I was little, I wanted to be a pilot. You know, those ones that rescue people with the doctors and stuff." His head's down, showing how scared he is to admit it out loud to anyone that he has a dream.

"Yeah, man, I know the ones you mean. A buddy of mine from the army is doing that out in California. Great job. Always something crazy happening in his job. What's stopping you, Leroy?" I wait for him to lift his face up from looking at the table like it's the most important thing he's ever seen.

"Kids like me don't do jobs like that. We work at the factory like my Pa." The defeat in his voice makes me feel more determined to help him make this happen.

"Leroy, what do you think we do here?" I finally lift his chin to look at me. "We help to make your dreams happen. We can't do it for you, but we can guide you and make sure you have every bit of help you need to make it. Now, I need you to tell me how badly you want this to happen. Is it just an idea, something you think about occasionally? Or is it becoming an ache that won't go away and it's getting bigger by the day?" The more I speak, the bigger his smile becomes.

"Yeah, Mason, I can't stop thinking about it. I use my computer to watch videos of rescue missions they fly, and I've found this really cool site that has flight simulators for the choppers they use." The enthusiasm in his voice is perfect.

This is why I'm here! To make a difference.

"Well, let's make this happen. Have you got your laptop with you?" He nods his head vigorously. "Go get it, man, let's start researching how you apply and what subjects and grades you need. Don't just dream it, live it!" As I slap his back, he jumps up from his seat and jogs across towards the locker room. Returning with his bag, his computer's out on the table, open and ready before I even have time to eat the rest of my lunch. Oh well, I wasn't hungry anyway.

Later, I'll message Johnno, my army buddy, and see what advice he has and any contacts he's got in Chicago I can talk to. Maybe someone who can meet with Leroy and inspire him to keep aiming for the career he wants.

Walking home, I feel lighter than when I left this morning. Watching a young mind open, the light turning on to their life, is amazing.

The weather's great this afternoon. The breeze is gentle, a perfect temperature. Sun shining, children in the fresh air playing with Mom watching from a park bench. Life here is so different to places I've been and experienced. Even though Leroy has struggled in his life, compared to kids who are growing up in a country that has an active war all around them, his life's a blessing. No part of their day is pleasant as the bombs are exploding close by, the sky is filled with bullets, and no place in their world is safe.

It's that word that gets me every time.

Safe.

I can't seem to shake that word.

Paige

"Thanks, Beth. I'll just be a little longer, I have a few things to tidy up and then I'll be down for dinner and check on Daddy."

"He was fine when I checked in a few minutes ago before bringing up your cup of tea." Beth disappears out of my father's office door as quietly as she entered. I've set myself up in his office while he isn't using it. It's easier than using one of the rooms downstairs. The only person who's allowed up here is Beth, and she's like a vault, never letting anything she overhears leave her tight lips.

Spending most of the day researching and digging through the records of the company, my brain's exhausted. Yet I need to keep going to see what I can find. I'm not sure what to even look for, I'm just hoping it'll jump out at me when I see it.

There are a few orders that look a little odd here that I need to check. The company's so big there's so much to look through. I could use help, but I just don't know who I can trust yet. Tyson offered to come over to catch up on the work from Friday and in case I need to postpone Monday or any day this week. Thanking him, I told him I'm fine and just need time with my dad.

I don't want anyone to know what I'm doing yet. Otherwise the element of surprise is gone.

Leaning back in the chair, my mind is a jumble of numbers and facts. I decide to do the only thing I can think of to get through this. I call Franco, my godfather. He will always care for my father and me. Plus, he has some of the skills and connections I may need. It's worth a chance.

"Hi, Uncle Franco," I speak into the phone.

"Paigey, how's my favorite girl? How's your father today? I'll be coming by tomorrow." His voice is comforting.

"Good thanks, Uncle Franco. He's slightly better, but just resting and still on oxygen."

"Stubborn old bastard. Now, what is it you called for, my dear?" Franco knows I wouldn't just call out of the blue.

"I need help, and you're the only one I can trust and with the skills to help," I lower my voice.

"This sounds ominous. Whatever you need, I'm here. You know that, right?" I nod even though he can't see me.

"Thank you. It's pretty serious. I have reason to believe someone is trying to sabotage the company, and I have no idea who or how. Or even why, for that matter. I just don't even know where to start, and of course I can't trust my staff to ask them for help. So, I thought of you."

"At your service, young lady. I didn't spend years in the police fraud department to forget what I'm doing. I may be retired, but I'm not old and washed up. Let's get these troublemakers and stop them in their tracks. I'll be over shortly, tell Beth I'm home for dinner. That woman's cooking is second to none."

"Sounds perfect." I hang up knowing there's one more person I still need to talk to today.

The man I can't stop thinking about but have been petrified to call.

I can't put it off any longer.

78

With sweaty palms and shaking fingers, I push the button.

"Mason." That's when my voice disappears, and I almost stop breathing.

7

Paige

"Paige, thank god. Are you okay, is your dad okay?" He sounds worried, yet it calms me. I'm trying to talk but suddenly my throat is all choked with emotions and tears are starting. "Paige, talk to me. Please don't cry. Is it your dad?" He's getting distressed, and I'm struggling to get my voice working.

"No, there's no change." The tears are really coming now.

"Is it you? Do you need me?" I can hear him getting more worried by the minute, yet I can't stop the emotion.

"Yes. No. I don't know." Fuck, what's wrong with me? I'm never emotional or not in control.

"Let me help you. Your first answer was yes. Let's go with your true feelings. My gut's telling me there's something more than your father going on. Please, Paige." He's almost begging me to let him support me.

"I can't. It's not that simple. I need to do this on my own." I'm slowly pulling myself together.

"Like fuck you do, woman! You're so damn stubborn. Stop trying to be superwoman. You don't need to do this by yourself. Yet you keep pushing me away." The frustration in his voice has me feeling it too. I wish things were different.

"You don't understand, Mason. There's so much I can't tell you. So much depends on me. Don't worry, I'll work it out. I just needed to hear your voice."

"No, you don't get to do this, Paige. You can't call me every time you're scared. Then I'm wanting to kill whoever's doing this to you, but you aren't letting me into your life. Do you realize what it's like on the other end of this phone, hearing you cry and not knowing where you are or how to get to you?" Mason's voice is full of real emotion. How has this man who's been in my life for months, turned a switch that's got every word he's saying pulling on my heart.

"I'm sorry. I'm being selfish. Not thinking about what I'm doing. Forget about it all. No more pathetic phone calls. I'm fine." I fight back the rejection, or what feels like rejection.

"*Fine!* If I hear you say fine one more time, I swear to god, Paige. No one's ever fine. Fine is a nothing word. You hear me loud and clear. When I finally have you in my bed, naked and feeling safe in my arms, holding you tight—" He pauses, hearing me gasp, then continues on, "There's going to be a little game we'll play. I'm counting the number of *fines* you give me, and I'll leave you to guess what the number will be used to count. So just think about that. The next time you try to tell me you're fine, when clearly, you're not, being able to sit down may become a luxury."

I can't help but burst out laughing. If I don't laugh, then this warm tingling that's running through my body might just overtake my emotions.

"Feeling pretty sure of yourself, are you? Who said you will have me anywhere near your bed, and naked in any way?"

His breathing is still strong and coming through the phone. "Life's short, Paige. When your heart reaches out and connects with another, you don't walk away. I. Am. Not. Walking. Away. Now stop pushing." Calm breathing and determination in his tone has me shaking.

"You have to. This can't happen. We can only be friends. You work for me." There it is. I said it. The thing we have been skirting around for a few days. Like a bucket of water onto a fire.

"Who cares! If it's a problem, I quit," Mason argues.

"No!" I scream down the phone. "You keep me safe. I need you to be my pilot. I trust you. Especially now. I need you to be the one who looks after me." We both go silent. I've said more than I should've. Finally, he understands that I need him in the only way I can allow.

"I'll be your private pilot, Paige. I'll keep you safe. Whether you like it or not. I'll protect you, even if it's from yourself. One day, you'll hopefully let me be more than that. I'll see you on your next flight.

Until then, I hope you're fine." Then he's gone. No noise on the end of the phone. Just stone, cold silence.

"Paige, you idiot what have you done?" I smack my forehead with my palm. My phone falling into my lap, I drop my head to the desk on top of my arms and cry. I've been holding it in and only letting little bits go. I need to get this out and pull my shit together.

In a minute, I'll be strong. I just need one minute. Or maybe ten.

~

"Thanks for dinner, Beth. As always, it's yummy. I'm going to put on weight if I stay here too long. Daddy better improve quickly otherwise I won't fit my clothes." She smiles at me as she clears away the dishes on the table. Uncle Franco laughs at me.

"I've seen you eat crazy amounts of ice cream even as a little girl, and you've never changed. Keep eating and forget about how you look. No matter what, you will always be beautiful to us." Passing his plate to Beth, he stands and holds out his hand to help me up.

"Let's chat about this little problem we have." Following him upstairs to the office, I feel a small amount of comfort that finally I can talk to someone about this. I'm still hurting from earlier, but I'm pushing it down and putting the company first. Just like Daddy says. The company comes first, even before me. That's what I'm doing.

"Start at the beginning, then let's get this solved." Franco sits opposite me at Daddy's desk, leaning back in the chair with his foot resting up on his opposite knee. I wish I felt as relaxed as he appears. He doesn't have the weight of the world on his shoulders.

"It's all come out of left field and the timing could not be worse with Daddy sick." I pull up the files on my computer that I've been working on today.

"I had a meeting with the government officials that we liaise with for the contracts with the defense department last week. As you know, to continue holding these contracts for the supply of technology parts, we are under constant surveillance. We knew that when we signed the deal." Franco nods his head at me to let me know he's following and to keep going.

"The meeting was a routine one, or so I thought. Tyson was sick so I was on my own. I don't know if that's why they chose to tell me that day or I would've found out anyway." I take a breath and turn the screen so we could both see the reports.

"They're finding discrepancies in the invoicing and the number of physical parts being delivered. That's bad to start with. But the problem I'm finding is the invoices going to them are for a higher amount, yet those invoices don't appear in my system. The figures in my system are for what is delivered. The payments we receive in the bank account are more than what my system has outstanding. So, on the three invoices where it has happened, there is a refund entry for overpayment. Digging further today, the refund that is going back is not to the bank account for the department we deal with." This has him sitting forward on his seat and starting to scan the screen. I can see that he's paying attention now.

"I have the bank account number, but no way of tracing whose account it is, and I'm sure it then gets transferred somewhere else anyway. It's never simple. I've loaded it all onto a thumb drive for you to take and look at. We're talking two-hundred-and-fifty thousand odd dollars over the three payments. Sure, on a thirty-seven-million-dollar contract, it's small change. Reality is, though, it's a lot of damn money, and someone is embezzling it from us and making it look like we're stealing from the government. Our reputation will be ruined if this gets out. It's also put a black mark against us for future contracts.

"I need to find this person or people fast and get the money back. I'll be transferring the money back to the government tomorrow and try to blame just an inventory problem and give a thousand apologies. Hopefully it will be enough, and it'll get buried and forgotten about before our contract comes up for renewal."

Flopping back into the chair, I'm exhausted.

"The worst thing is feeling so embarrassed that someone else found it rather than me. It slipped under my radar and I had no idea. Now I'm panicking that there are more fraudulent invoices out there with other companies and I just don't know about it yet."

"Paige, we'll find these bastards, and then I'll personally make sure they pay for what they're doing. I hate to agree, but I'm sure there'll be more invoices to be found. They usually start small to see if the system picks it up, and then the amounts escalate. I think there'll be more people involved than just one. Someone needs access to delete some of the programming on the accounting software that does the double-checking for this, plus others. The most important thing is that you tell no one about this. We need them to try again so we can grab them and follow the trail. In the meantime, I need access to your system, I'll start investigating tonight. It'll be better than the crappy crime novel I'm reading. The author has done no research and everything's just so unbelievable." He's laughing at himself now. "I know they're stories and don't have to be perfectly accurate with reality. But just a little would be nice.

"Now, you, my dear, are a very lucky lady. Not every little girl has an Uncle Franco who's a fraud investigator at her fingertips. Know this, though, princess, I won't stop until I get them. I promise we will get this sorted."

Feeling like part of the weight I've been carrying for days starts to lift off my shoulders, I stand and embrace him in a hug.

"Tell Aunt Veronica I'm sorry. I know you retired to spend more time with her," I whisper into his shoulder as he gives me the comfort hug I'm needing tonight.

"Don't be silly, Paigey. She already wants to kill me since I've retired. Apparently, I can be annoying. Go figure. Plus, she won't even know what I'm doing most of the time. She's too busy with her head in some romance book, or binge watching some show that all her friends tell her she must watch. You leave Aunt Veronica to me. Now let's get to work. The night is still young." He walks out of the office only to return a few minutes later with his bag and starts pulling out two laptops and several folders. He means business.

"Can I ask one more favor?" I look at him, hoping he sees how important this is.

"I know what you're going to say, and I agree. We don't need to tell your father until he's fully recovered. We'll have it solved by then anyway." He looks down and continues to type.

"How did you know?" I'm stunned.

"It's written all over your face. Work, my girl, time's a wasting." With that, we both get into the system and start dissecting all the major orders we've shipped in the last six months.

It's going to be a long night.

At least it'll take my mind off things.

More to the point, make my heart stop longing for what it can't have.

Mason

"For fuck's sake, damn stubborn woman!" I scream at no one as I'm pressing end on the phone.

I pace my apartment back and forth.

"Why can't she just tell me what the hell's going on? Oh no, she's some highflying businesswoman who doesn't need help. Well, I've got news for her. She's getting my help even if she doesn't want it. I might not know what the drama is, but I'll work it out." Picking up my basketball, I bounce it as I pace.

"This is why I don't do relationships. They're fucking infuriating, these women. I never know which way I'm supposed to turn. Bad luck for her that this time, I'm calling the shots. She may think we're just friends. But I know it's more than that. When she's ready to admit it too, then things will get very interesting. I'm going to fuck that stubbornness right out of her. She won't have enough energy left to say my name after the numerous times she's been screaming it all night. No one can kiss like that and not want more." The whole time I'm ranting to myself, my cock is getting hard thinking about her feistiness.

This woman has me so hot under the collar I'm talking to myself. What the hell's going on?

My counselor is going to love it when I tell her this. Will probably even laugh out loud. At least someone will get humor out of it.

My mind goes to the boys. Tate would absolutely lose it if he knew I'm yelling at the walls in my apartment and talking to myself all over a woman. I can imagine him doubled over in here laughing so hard he can't breathe. He can laugh all he likes, this'll happen to him one day too.

I had the best day with the kids, but now Paige's got me on edge again. The adrenaline's pumping, and I won't be able to settle for a while. Time to hit the gym. Work it out, or more to the point, work her out of my system. For the next few hours, anyway. I know it won't last long.

Running on the treadmill is so mind-numbing. Picking up speed, music cranked, I focus on one foot in front of the other. Thump, thump, thump. The repetitive noise of my feet hitting the machine. It reminds me of the noise of the rotors on my chopper. Their drone becomes a noise that's comforting when you're in the air. It helps keep you calm, that everything's still moving the way it should be. If the blades stop, we're down and not in a good way.

Thinking about my army days has me so off in my own little world I don't even hear or see Bent walk up next to me, until he pats me on the shoulder. I almost take him out with a fist. You don't sneak up on a trained soldier. Jumping off, I pull my ear buds out so I can talk.

"So sorry, man, didn't mean to startle you." Bent laughs as I try to slow my breathing down.

"All good. Sorry, I was thinking about something and didn't even see you. How are you doing, got the night off?" He leans against the wall next to the treadmill while he's stretching before he starts.

"Yeah, Ms. Ellen's staying at her father's taking care of him. He has a driver too. We're taking alternate shifts. Her dad's pretty sick."

"I know, she told me she's staying with him and not flying until he improves. Knew it must be serious for her to cancel meetings. Is his place near here? I haven't seen you at this gym before." I try to sound casual but want to see what he'll tell me. Which should be nothing if he's doing his job right and keeping his boss's privacy. But we have a good relationship and he knows she trusts me, so it's enough to keep him talking.

"Yeah, he has this big house close by which is awesome. It's old school, you know with the big circular drive and fountain out front but looks beautiful. I'm staying in the servants' quarters. This is the closest gym to there. I can't go a day without a good workout, so I thought I'd get one under my belt while she's all settled in for the night."

My mind's going crazy. I want to smash his face for virtually giving me her address, yet all I'm thinking is how quick I can get out of here to drive by and check it out.

"Setup looks pretty good here. You come here much?" Bent's on the treadmill now and warming up. I figure I should keep going through my workout, seeing what else I can learn about Paige from her driver. They hear and see everything, but normally never repeat it. Let's see what Bent wants to share tonight with those loose lips.

"Most days or nights. Just depends on my flight schedule or the weather. Sometimes I prefer to be running outside. I've also got some buddies I train with, so depends on when they're available." I'm back running but not at full speed and haven't bothered with the music yet.

"Happy to train with you anytime I'm here, or if you want a running partner. I ran here tonight, I'm like you and enjoy some fresh air sometimes too," he says and I tuck that fact away for later.

"Yeah, how long do you think the boss will be staying at her father's place?" I start with the first innocent question.

"Don't know, but I'm guessing at least a few days if not longer. He's on oxygen and he's eighty-one years old. Not sure how well they bounce back at that age." He's so blasé about someone that Paige is very attached to and distraught over.

"I'm sure the boss is hoping he gets better quickly. She seems close to her father." I don't know much about her family; she's never mentioned a mother so I'm guessing she has already passed away or isn't around.

"They're really close. She visits a lot. If he didn't have the heart attack a few years ago, I'm sure he'd still be running the company. He's damn stubborn, the old guy." That makes a lot of sense. Must be where his headstrong daughter gets it from.

Coming to the end of the run, we're both sweating profusely.

"That's enough for me tonight. Time to cool down." Pushing the button, the machine lowers the incline and the speed. Bent follows with his machine. I wipe the sweat off with my towel and then clean the machine.

"Hey, do you need a lift home? I've got my car so I can drop you off if you don't feel like running?" Plan A into action.

"That would be great, man. I think I've done enough for one night. You pushed me hard. Trying to keep up with you is a struggle." I laugh at him sucking in the breaths. I've always been fit, but once I joined the army, I was trained hard. I've never really stopped.

"No problem, just let me have a quick shower. I'll only be ten minutes, tops." I grab my towel and head for the locker room. Within minutes I'm walking back out and see Bent trying to chat up a woman at the counter. Yeah, good luck, buddy.

Driving out of the carpark, Bent starts to give me the directions to the Ellen family home. It's not far from the gym and again, it shows me the kind of wealth Paige's family has. I come from a family that lives comfortably and money was never an issue. But this is next-level wealthy.

When we pull up to the house, Bent explains that his room is around the back. Making an excuse that I'm just replying to a message, I sit in my car while he disappears down the side of the house.

Turning off the car, I jump out before I change my mind and walk briskly up the front stairs. Push the doorbell with force and then wait.

Waiting for surprise, anger, rejection, or if I'm lucky maybe a little happiness to see me.

The door opening has me realizing I hadn't thought this through. Paige won't be the one answering the door.

"May I help you, young man?" An elderly woman with the kindest face stands waiting for my answer.

"Good evening, madam. Sorry to interrupt your evening, but I was hoping to come in and see Paige to say hello. My name is Mason White. I'm her friend and also her pilot." A smile starts rising on her face.

"Captain White, please come in. I'll let her know you're here. I have heard her speak of you before." She gestures for me to follow her into a sitting room.

"All good, I hope," I say, trying to lighten the situation.

"So far, yes. I'm Beth, Mr. Ellen's housekeeper, pleased to meet you." She extends out her hand. "Please take a seat and I will fetch Paige for you." With that, she turns and shuffles out of the room quickly.

I hear her in the next room with Paige.

"Mason? What the hell is he doing here? Why'd you let him in?" She sounds tired and stressed. I guess I have my answer of how she'll feel about me turning up.

"I know who he is. I thought it might be nice for you to have someone to talk to rather than be stuck in this house with old people, one of which is sleeping constantly. Now hurry along, dear, and don't keep your friend waiting." Looks like I have an ally in Beth. I need to stay smiling at her, keep her on my side.

"I'm not even dressed properly. Shit, this man's such a pain. Obviously not good at taking instructions," I hear Paige mumble as she's coming down the hallway followed by Beth, who then closes the doors behind Paige as she enters the room and comes to a standstill.

"That's right, I only listen to instructions that make sense. At the moment, yours are making no sense at all."

Standing there glaring at me with her hands on her hips, she has never looked sexier. Her black yoga pants hugging every curve on her with a loose shirt hanging over the top. Her hair out and falling loosely down her back, a wave through it. No makeup on her face. They say makeup is to make a woman beautiful, yet Paige with none is the most enchanting look I've ever seen.

This is Paige. The real Paige. The one I want to get to know.

"Mason, how did you find me? What are you doing here?" There's fire in her eyes.

"Lovely to see you too, Paige. I've missed our little friendly chats. Yes, remember, friends? I thought I would check in on you to make sure you're okay and see how your father's doing." I can see my extra sweetness is driving her crazy.

"I'm so confused. How did you find out where my father lives?"

"It's a funny story of me running into Bent at the gym and thinking he may need a lift home. Especially after him mentioning he's staying here with you." My grin is spread across my face.

"You're very good at this, aren't you, Captain White. Being resourceful. I need to be careful with you." Her body language is relaxing slightly, as she's walking into the room towards me.

"Where it comes to you, Paige, I'll do whatever it takes." This time I'm not giving her any room to think. I grab hold of her face and kiss her like I've been starved without her. Her body stiffens for a moment. I'm not stopping, my tongue pushes for her to let me in. That is the last straw, and her body succumbs to her feelings. Her arms are around my neck in an instant and she's kissing me back.

I can't stop. I need air, but there is no way I want to let her go. Last time as soon as she pulled away, I lost her. This time I'm keeping hold of her. We need to talk, and I'm not leaving until she listens.

"Mason," she gasps. "We can't do this."

"Oh, we can, and we are. You can't tell me you want to walk away from the chance of what this is. The electricity in that kiss is something that's bigger than us." My hands roam over her back and drop lower towards her ass.

"It looks so bad. I'm your boss. I don't want it to be some seedy affair." Her eyes are begging me to help her make sense of every feeling running through her body right now.

"You can do whatever you want, Paige. That's the beauty of being the boss. I came here to talk to you, but I'll be honest. You in my arms, kissing me like I'm your lifeline. You have me wanting to lay you out on this couch and fuck you until you see how good we are together." My cock is rock hard, and the blush on her face tells me she's feeling it too.

"Fuck, Mason."

"Yeah, Tiger, that's what I want too."

Skimming my thumb across her cheek, I lean down, and taking it nice and slow, I show her through another kiss how much I mean everything I've just said.

8

Mason

"How long since you stepped away from your work and took five minutes for yourself, Paige?" Whispering, I pull her closer to my body, my hands on her ass. Making her feel what she's doing to me. Her body arches, pressing against my cock, a soft moan slipping from her lips.

"That's right. Imagine what this will feel like. You will be more than moaning." Running my tongue up her neck, I go back to kissing her, but this time I take it slow. Starting along her jawline until I find her lips open, taking in the sensations.

"Embrace what you're feeling. Let me in." With that, I'm kissing her relentlessly, deeply and full of everything I want her to understand, and finally acknowledge. It's like I've got one chance to get her to listen. She doesn't seem to listen to my words, but she can't ignore the feelings.

Slowly, I pull away from her lips, sensing her finally melting into my arms. Her head drops and rests on my shoulder, giving me her body weight. Such a relief. Maybe I'm getting through to her.

"Mason, we can't do this. You have my body aching for you, but my head keeps saying stop." Her voice is low and not the normal confident woman I'm used to.

"That's because your head is a stubborn pain in the ass. Ignore it, just listen to your body for once. You can't tell me this doesn't feel right." I slide my hand around her body and up her chest. Slowly, so she knows what I'm doing and giving her time to say no, I palm her breast. Lightly wrapping my hand around it, squeezing with slight pressure, just enough to have her breath racing.

"This is what your body wants. To feel, to be touched. Tell me you want this, Paige, and I promise you won't regret one second of it." She doesn't need to speak, her wandering hand on my body's the answer.

"I might want it, but it doesn't mean I can have it." Her hand glides over my cock, and I grit my teeth to stop from thrusting my hips into her hand.

"You keep touching me like that, baby, and you are going to have it all. Stop denying yourself what feels so good."

"There is *so much* here to feel." Looking down at her cheeky smile, I can see lust invading the sensible brain. Thank fuck.

"That's it, baby, stroke my ego." My hand moves down her body.

"I'm stroking more than your ego, Mason." The words on her lips have me humming while her hand's squeezing my aching cock just that little bit tighter.

"Call it what you want as long as you keep stroking."

My hand cups between her legs. Her body jumps a little with the touch, mouth dropping open and her head falling back. Oh yeah, baby, you're getting all the feels now. Deliberately, I start to rock her body so she's grinding on my hand.

"Take what you want. Tell me what you need." My head's spinning with anticipation of where this is heading.

"To forget it all." Her eyes are now closing as she slips into that land of just pure sensations.

"Now that I can do. The only thing you won't forget is that it's me making you feel this way."

She gasps as I quickly move my hands to under her ass and lift her into my arms. Her legs wrap around my waist perfectly. Backing her up against the wall, I lean into her and start grinding my cock into her. Hearing the little moans from each movement is pure bliss. Light as a feather in my hands, I release one and slide it down the front of her pants, so happy to feel her softness and the wet pussy waiting for me. I take over the stroking with my hand rather than my grinding.

"Mmm, you're so wet. All for me. Just thinking about it has you dripping, wanting more. Tell me you want more, Paige."

"More! Don't you fucking stop now. Finish what you started." Desperation from a woman on the edge of orgasming is music to my ears.

"You really are a tiger, aren't you? Just what I like, feisty and sexy as fuck." As she tries to open her mouth to argue with me, I slip my finger deep inside her. Instead of words, a low groan comes out of her mouth. My thumb pushes down on her clit and she starts riding my fingers as I'm slipping the second one in.

"So perfect, ride me, take all the pleasure you need." With a pink flush creeping up her face, I feel her muscles starting to contract around my fingers. She's so close to coming undone.

"Come for me, Paige. Show me how you let go." Her head falling against the wall, eyes closed as her breathing stops for that second before my name cries from her lips in ecstasy, her orgasm rips through her. Quickly taking her mouth in mine to swallow my name, she quivers through the tail end of her pleasure. Slowly, I slip my hand from her and allow her to just sag into my body. I'm throbbing hard all over but just want to stay right here, with her in my arms. Totally satiated.

"Oh my god," she whispers. Smiling, I don't comment and just let her have the moment to herself. Her legs unwrapping from around my waist leave me feeling a little cold. She tries to pull herself away from me, yet she can't even stand properly with her shaking body.

"What was that?" Her face raises to look at me with eyes that tell me that head of hers is taking control again.

"Pure bliss, I would say." Her hands are on my chest, pushing me off her. I want to hold my ground but know I need to give her space.

"We are in the sitting room of my father's house, and you think it's acceptable to be screwing me against the wall. Real classy, Mason." My body is now on alert to her.

"I didn't see you complaining as my name was leaving your lips." Trying to take her face in my hands again to kiss her, she ducks under my arms and scoots out behind me. Putting a couple of yards' distance between us.

"No, you can't confuse me with those lips. They have too much power." Holding her hand up at me, she signals to stay where I am.

"Still stroking my ego, I see." Yet her eyes are telling me she doesn't find me funny anymore. "Paige, stop freaking out. Talk to me. What is that persistently annoying head of yours saying on the inside?"

"To make sure you don't touch me, to start with. It tells me I don't listen when you have your hands on me." Before I can reply there's a small knock on the door and then it opens, Beth comes through holding a tray of wine with a platter of cheese and fruits.

We both freeze, and I can see the same thought going through Paige's head as mine. If Beth had been a few minutes earlier… What was I thinking? I just came here to talk to her and try to help. The next minute I'm trying to fuck her against the wall. I suppose my only saving grace is that I didn't get that far.

"Sorry to interrupt. I won't be a second. I just wanted to bring you some nibbles while you chatted. Are you staying for dinner, Mason?"

"No, he's getting ready to leave. He has somewhere to be. Thank you, Beth." Her demeanor changes completely. She maintains the control well in her role as the boss.

"That's very kind of you, Beth, apparently I have somewhere to be. Perhaps next time I visit." She smiles at me, knowing exactly what's going on here.

"I'll look forward to it." I wink at her while she's leaving the tray and disappears back out the doors, closing them behind her.

"Mason, stop flirting with my housekeeper," Paige snaps at me.

"Are you freaking serious? I just had you coming all over my hand with my lips all over you, and you think I'm flirting with your elderly housekeeper? Are you for real, woman?"

"You're doing it deliberately so she'll let you in again. You can't be here. You need to leave. I'm telling her not to let you in next time." Her stance has become more defensive and in control. Completely ignoring her, I close the distance between us.

"You can try to be all bossy here, but just remember. When you are on my plane, you are the boss. When you are coming, screaming my name, I'm the boss. The moment you leave my plane, I'm no longer your employee. So, stick that overbearing attitude wherever you like because I'm not listening. You can control your life, and sometimes you control mine too, but you can't control what I feel. What I feel is real and exhilarating and you feel it too. When you're prepared to admit that, then we'll talk. Until then, yeah, I'm going home to jerk myself off in a shower, because you don't get to control that. What you do get to do is picture that image as you lie in bed and realize what you're missing out on." Just to push her further, I lean in and kiss her mouth, running my tongue around her lips, then dragging one of my fingers coated in her juices over them.

"That's how you really feel, Paige. Just remember that taste."

Walking out the door, I know I've just been the biggest asshole, but I can't take the push and pull. If she can't work out what she wants, then how the fuck am I supposed to know?

Paige

What the hell just happened?

Sagging into the couch, curling my knees up under my chin, I try to process it. One minute I'm putting away a book in the library. The next I'm against the wall feeling sparks through my body that I haven't felt in so long I've forgotten what they're like.

No matter how hard I try to stop Mason from getting close to me, he manages to put me under his spell every time. How do I stop my body from giving in? I'm totally smitten by him, and my body is screaming for his touch. Yet I can't fuck my employee. It even sounds wrong and seedy. I'm not just his superior, but the CEO of a multibillion-dollar company. My lawyers will have a field day with this one. Imagine the possibilities of lawsuits if it goes wrong.

He thinks it's easy to just draw a line between work and life.

This can't be any further from reality if we tried. Every minute of every day, I'm still the boss and he's still my private pilot.

I need to be strong and keep pushing him away. I don't want to hurt him, but it's better this way. Stop it before it starts.

Who am I kidding?

It started the first day he stood at the bottom of the stairs welcoming me onto the plane. His touch as he shook my hand and his genuine smile. There was a buzz that awoke something in my body that day. One I keep ignoring. It's like a swarm of bees that keeps getting louder in my head. It scatters my rational thought.

Today, Mason sent them swarming, and there's no stopping them now.

I'm not sure how long I've been sitting here when the doors slowly open, alerting me to Beth poking her head in.

"Are you okay, Paige? Can I get you anything? Your dinner's been in the warmer for a while." She looks concerned at me.

"Sorry, Beth. I didn't realize the time. I'm not hungry. I think I'll just head up to my room. Is Daddy okay?" I stand gently on my numb legs that have been curled up.

"He's fine, sleeping peacefully. Head upstairs. The nurses will alert you if there's any need." She puts her hand on my forearm as I pass. I pause momentarily. "Not everything has to happen the way your father planned, Paige. You need to live, not just exist." Smiling a fake smile, I just keep moving towards the staircase. Turning back to her, I say, "I wish it was that easy, Beth." I really do.

"It can be. Only you get to make that choice," I hear her say as I keep walking.

Choice.

That word continues to spin in my head. Choice is what I don't feel I have.

I've never had.

Not even bothering to shower, I crawl into bed, and wrap the blankets around me. I don't want to wash his touch from my body. For those minutes, I just got to feel. The intensity of the touch and his words whispering on my neck. I can still hear them. His breath, hot and tingling, still has the hairs there burning.

Distance is what we need. No flights this week will help. His anger will build, and he'll see I'm not worth the bother. That's what I need. For him to see it's just not right. It won't be so hard for me if he's fighting against me instead of being drawn to me.

At the moment, he's like the tide that's washing over me. Convincing me to go with the flow. Soon he'll see I'm just like sand. The constant thing that when you come back day after day, it's still there doing the same thing. It might be in a different location for the day, but its role is still the same. The safe space away from the dangers of the tide. The solid foundation to stand on. The place you can watch from the sideline without getting wet in the craziness of the messy parts of life.

Dragging my phone in front of me, I want it to light up with a message, but I know it won't. Mason was angry and frustrated when he left. I'd done that, letting it get that far. Now I need to suck it up and move on.

I have too many other things to be worrying about. My father and the company drama. As Daddy always says, the company first before yourself. I need to keep reminding myself that as Mason tests my limits.

My next flight will be the ultimate test, I'm sure.

Mason

If there is such a thing as an exploding cock, I think mine is about to suffer from it. Trying to drive to my apartment is taking every cell in my brain to concentrate. Pretty sure all the blood from my brain has found a home in my pants, and it's pulsing like my heartbeat.

The walk from the car is awkward to say the least. Trying to avoid people. Thank god I have my gym bag to hold awkwardly in front of me. Every time I take a step it keeps banging on my manhood. Paige, you're going to pay for this. It's nasty to leave a man hanging like this. Although it's partly my fault. It wasn't exactly how I planned the night to go, nor was it the place to start that. I just couldn't help it. When my lips touch hers, my restraint seems to disappear.

Finally, the shower's running and I'm stepping under the water. I need to take care of this before I burst. The more I try and think of other things, the stronger my thoughts of Paige keep coming back. Now it's not just images; I know how her lips taste, the smoothness of her skin, and the tightness of my fingers inside her. Nothing is taking those away from me. Stroking myself with the fingers that had been buried deep inside her only a short time ago is enough to send me over the edge. My body is jerking as I finally come all over my shower floor with the force.

I want her and I want her bad.

Today just confirmed what I was thinking. We are made to piece together. Having her in my arms, legs wrapped around me, was like the puzzle locked together perfectly. She just confuses me. One minute she's falling into my arms and reciprocating everything I feel. Then she pushes me away. The thing is, although she's putting distance between us, never once has she said she doesn't want me. Just that she can't do this. For as long as she wants me, I'm not giving up. It just seems harder than I first imagined. No war worth winning is easy. This is a fight I'm in for the long haul. No matter how much I know I'm setting myself up to be hurt.

Although I know I won't sleep, I lie down on my bed not bothering with any dinner. I'd rather just lose myself in my thoughts.

~

"Where the hell is Lex? We can't start the game with just the three of us," Tate complains, looking down at his watch.

"Keep your pants on, Mr. Perfect," I say, "he's running a few minutes late. Just go warm up and see if you can manage a basket. At least that'll be better than last week's game where you didn't sink one." I throw the basketball at his chest.

This week's been the worst; I've hardly slept, and my patience is short. Tuesday, I flew Brian, Paige's vice president, to a meeting to replace her. It was not the same. I missed seeing her beautiful face, and he sure as hell didn't hold my interest checking out his ass as he walked up the stairs into the plane.

The plane's been grounded ever since. Not because there are any problems, but no flights were scheduled. Paige's been staying close to home. According to Bent when I see him at the gym, her father is finally improving. Not that I would know because I haven't heard from her since walking out on Sunday night.

I already feel sorry for Grayson being on my team for our weekly basketball match. We try to meet every Thursday at Dunbar Park. We all lead busy lives, but this has been a ritual since we left high school. There have been times where it didn't happen for periods, like when I was overseas. Although the boys sent me this ridiculous video one day of the three of them playing with Grayson's dad, and he was wearing a face mask of me and some of my clothes. I think it was their way of telling me they missed me, without getting all mushy.

I'm anxious to get playing. I haven't been able to sit still all week. Too much energy that needs using. Plus, it keeps my mind from thinking about Paige.

"Finally. Did you forget how to tell the time, Councilor Alexander Jefferson the third?" I say, bowing down to him.

"Fuck off, Mas, just get on the court. Let's see if your game is as snappy as your mouth," Lex growls at me.

"Awesome, Gray," Tate says. "We have two grumpy little boys today. Maybe we need to stop at the titty bar on the way back to work to put a smile on their faces? Is that the problem, boys? Got sore balls from no action?"

Tate and Gray start laughing as Lex and I both reply at the same time with the same words: "Fuck off, Tate." Loud and clear, he gets the message.

"I think the boys need a hard, fast game today. Let's get into it. Otherwise someone is going to lose their shit. I just can't decide which one of them it is."

Lex smacks Tate round the back of the head and the game is on.

I'm on fire today. Ten baskets and I annoyed the shit out of Tate by marking every shot he tried to take.

"Fuck, whatever your boss lady's done to piss you off, can she keep it for when you're on my team next time?" Tate puts his arm around me as we walk off the court for a break.

"What makes you think this has anything to do with Paige?" I swig on my water bottle.

"The fact you are on first-name basis now with the boss perhaps gives it away. Oh, and that you ran out of the bar last week like your ass was on fire because she called. So yeah, I think it's a pretty good guess." Tate looks pleased with his assumptions.

"Give it a rest, Tate." Grayson squirts water at him from his bottle.

I notice Lex isn't saying much either. He doesn't want Tate to move to him next.

"What, just because you have Tilly now, you're going soft on me? What is going on here? You have become a mushy girl since you got a fiancée. Lover boy number two over here is sulking like a teenage boy because his girl is ignoring him. Then, Lex, the boy behind door number three, hasn't been himself for weeks, dragging his frown around with us. Come on, guys, what's this world coming to? Lighten up, for fuck's sake, or do I have to do a group therapy session in Vegas for a weekend? Like we used to do."

We all glare at Tate and then one by one we all start to laugh.

"You're such a dick, Tate, you know that, right?" Sitting down on the bench, I'm still laughing.

"Maybe so, but it worked. About time you let go of your nuts and just chilled out. If she has you this wound up, man, is she really worth it?"

"One day you'll understand this statement. Just breathing without her near me is the hardest thing to do, because my chest is hurting too much." That's pretty much how I feel. She sucks the air out of me when she walks away.

"Fuck, not you too!" Tate runs his hands through his hair. "What, did you let him drink the same water as you, Doctor Pussy? Lex, don't you go near them. I can't afford another buddy to get struck down by the same disease. Man, we are becoming endangered, us carefree, unattached guys."

Grayson laughs at him and slaps me on the shoulder as he walks past. "Ignore him, Mas. Welcome to the club. I'd rather be a member of this one than the desperate and dateless over there. They'll work it out sooner or later. Maybe sooner for Lex than idiot Tate who seems to think every woman in Chicago can't resist his charm. Can't wait for the day that comes back and bites him in the ass." It feels good to have Gray to back me up, but I wish it was as simple as they think it is.

"I'd also love to be part of your club, Gray, but so far she's pushing me away as hard as I'm trying to pull her to me."

"I know what you mean," Lex mumbles under his breath.

I heard him, but the others were too busy laughing at me being rejected. I need to talk to Lex on his own later. There's more to his sour moods than just work, I've got a feeling.

"When you were in the army, if things got tough, did you give up and walk away?" Grayson asks.

"Not a chance, you dug deep, came up with a different tactic, and then went at it again." I answer with my shoulders pulling back and on the defense.

"So, what are you doing wasting time sulking, because she's pushing you away?" Tate says. "Dig deep, find a new tactic, and start again. Come on, soldier. If she's really the one, then stop standing back. Get up and fight for her." For the first time today, Tate's serious in what he's saying. It's almost like he can relate to it all.

"Thanks, man. I needed someone to kick me up the ass and get my head out of there. Sometimes I get stuck in that spot."

"Jesus, I don't even want to get a visual of all that. Your head stuck up your own ass. Either head is just too messed up to think about."

"Lex!" we all yell at once. What the hell has gotten into him?

The alarm on Grayson's watch starts chiming, which alerts us that it's time to get out of here. There is never enough time with the guys, but the small time we squeeze in is like gold for the soul. These boys are my family, maybe not by blood but sure as shit by soul. Sometimes I just need them to ground me and set me on the right path again. It doesn't have to be any great speech. Just being together can be enough to do it.

Goodbyes are being yelled as both the doctors are off and running together, back towards Mercy Hospital, and Lex is already jogging towards his car. He also has a tight schedule because of his court appearances. I'm left sitting on the park bench alone. I wish I had somewhere to be other than sitting at the airport on standby. There's only so much paperwork you can do before you go stir crazy. This morning was even worse because I had to put up with Aaron at the hangar while he did his regular flight simulation runs to keep up his training hours. I know it won't be long and I'll lose him as a copilot. He's almost at the required hours to gain his captain's license, and he'll be out of here and applying for jobs where he gets to be in charge of his own aircraft. For all his annoying man-whore ways, he's a good pilot, and I'm sure he'll do a great job on his own.

For the first time this week, I feel a little lighter after talking with the boys. They gave me ideas on how to approach Paige, stay focused, and don't give up.

~

Filling in the afternoon had been hard, but I managed. Finally making it home, I move through the normal routine. Dinner, shower, surfing the net, and now watching a bit of television before I head to bed with a book. Some nights I wonder if I should get myself a dog like Gray has, to keep me company. Then I shake that feeling, realizing I don't have anyone to look after it when I'm away with work. Instead, I just have to put up with the quiet nights on my own.

Shutting the television off and finally lying flat in my bed, doing my relaxation breathing exercises, I start to feel calm, ready to read a little before sleep claims me. I set my alarm for the morning even though it's not needed; it's a routine I can't break. They tell me it's good for my PTSD to keep routine. Stop's my brain from spiraling when I know what's coming.

I hit the alarm marked in my phone as weather check, set for five-thirty am. That's when I wake and log on to check the weather for my flight. Not that it's needed for tomorrow, but I'll do it anyway.

My email chimes on my phone while I'm running through the alarms that I set. Three in total.

Checking to see if it's anything important, I'm shocked to see it's from Paige. Part of me doesn't want to open it, in case she's decided to replace me with another pilot. I can't wait, though, I need to know what's going on.

Ms. Paige Ellen – CEO Ellen Corporation

Dear Mason,
We need to fly to Washington tomorrow at nine am. Please have the plane ready for this time. I will be flying with my Uncle Franco and Tyson.
It will be a day flight leaving Washington at 2 pm.
Please make arrangements accordingly.
Thank you,
Paige

What the hell is this bullshit?

My heart leaps at the news I'll get to see her tomorrow. Yet I can feel my annoyance rising at the business nature of the email. Perhaps she's forgotten that the last time we were together, I'm the man whose name was escaping her lips as she rode through the best orgasm of her life.

Okay, Ms. Ellen, two can play at this professional bullshit game.

Captain Mason White

Dear Ms. Ellen,
I will arrange your flights as per your schedule and inform the crew.
We'll be waiting on the tarmac ready for boarding at 8:45 am. Please do not be late.
I will inform my crew of the number of passengers for the flight.
Thank you,
Captain White

Hitting send, I'm laughing for the first time in days. I can imagine her face when she sees my reply asking her not to be late. There will be steam coming out of her ears. She knows I always comment on how punctual she is.

Hopefully it pisses her off and stirs the sleeping tiger.

Be ready, Paige. I'm coming for you, baby.

I hope you're up for the challenge.

9

Paige

I want to be pissed at Mason, but I know I can't.

Pushing him away, making him angry, it's what I need to do. Yet I'm sitting here wishing it didn't work. Deep down I want him fighting harder. Fighting for me.

I'm such a bitch. Mason fighting for me just leads to hurt. The kind of hurt I'm feeling. The one that won't heal, because the heart's breaking.

They say when you know, you know.

I've known from day one he's so much more. I've also known I can never do a thing about it. What I didn't know was how hard it would be, or how he feels.

His lips on mine make me lose all sense of reality. It's just us in the moment, feeling every sensation. You can't fight it. As hard as I'm trying to. He's off limits, I'm the boss.

He knows his reply to my email will annoy me. I'm never late, but maybe tomorrow I should be. Two can play at this game, Captain. Giggling a little, I know it won't happen. I don't do late and I'm not about to start now.

This week's been hard. Every time we find another piece of evidence it just makes me angrier. Who is so awful to be sabotaging everything my father worked so hard to build? Or is it someone who has a problem with me? Franco warned me to trust no one until we get more leads and can either eliminate suspects or narrow it down to possibilities. It makes me doubt every conversation, email, message I receive.

What we do know is that whoever it is must be part of my management team. They need to have high security level to pull this off. That's totally gut-wrenching. Every person that's close to me is potentially trying to sink me. I just wish I knew why.

We know the how, the where, and we're just waiting for the when. If I could work out the why then all the pieces will lead us to the answer. I've repaid every dollar back to the government from my personal accounts, so no one suspects we know as yet.

Tomorrow we fly to Washington, trying to see if we can find any more clues. Uncle Franco is accompanying me, saying he's writing a book on my father. So, he's doing research on the company. It's lame, but it'll work. I can't say he's assisting me, otherwise Tyson's likely to throw another tantrum. Worse still, he suspects something is going on and if it's him then we'll tip him off that we know about the missing money. My Aunty Veronica came up with the cover story. I think she's been watching too many mysteries on the television. She was way too excited about helping.

I feel like I'm in a glass bubble, spinning around every direction trying to see where the knives in my back are coming from. My father always said trust no one. Now I know why.

Pondering if I should reply to Mason's snarky email, I decide it's better to let it be. I know it's just as hard on him as me, so why make it any harder? Instead, closing the lid on my laptop, I lie down hoping sleep will claim me easier tonight. I don't feel like I've slept since Daddy got sick.

Closing my eyes, I'm praying. Lord give me strength tomorrow. Being near Mason, I'm going to need enough to hold back a steamroller. Because that's what he does to me. He flattens every wall I try to put up. Once he's touching me, I can't do a damn thing to resist him, and he knows it.

Oh god, it's worth it, though.

No one has ever touched me like Mason.

~

"Thank you, Bent. We'll pick Franco up on the way, please. Good morning, Tyson." I nervously slide into the car. Not that he would notice. My normal morning persona is on show as I take my coffee from him.

"Morning, Ms. Ellen. Is that Franco, as in your uncle? Why are we picking him up?" The only person I told he's coming is Mason. I don't know why. Maybe I wanted him to know who he is and that he's no threat. My mind's in a ridiculous place at the moment. I shouldn't care what he thinks, but I do.

"Yes. He's flying with us today." Leaving it at that, I feel his eyes on me, but I'm not prepared to expand any further until Franco is in the car. Everyone is on a need-to-know basis currently.

"Okay." He starts typing on his phone and is quiet for the rest of the short trip to collect Franco.

"Good morning, princess." Franco kisses my cheek as he sits next to me after Tyson moves to another seat.

"Morning," I reply, smiling for the first time today, his big warm smile making me relax a little.

"Tyson, how are you, my boy? Ready to be under the magnifying glass?" he jokes although I can tell he's watching him intently.

"Um, I suppose. Why's that?" he nervously replies.

"Oh, didn't Paige tell you? I'm an avid writer, so she has asked me to do a book on her father and his company. While he's still well enough to fill me in. Will be a great asset for the company in future years. I'll be around quite a lot just getting a feel for things and collecting research. Aren't you lucky, you get to see my ugly face every day?" He laughs at his own joke.

"Franco," I chastise him. "Ugly is harsh, distinguished is better. Tyson, please allow him access to anything he needs while he's around. Nothing is off limits. Also, get on with our day like he's not here." Tyson nods in acknowledgement, and Bent's eyes look up into the rearview mirror, telling me he's in on this conversation too.

"Wow, is distinguished the word used to mean ugly when you're old? I never knew." I shake my head at him but he's still chuckling for a few more minutes to himself.

My phone vibrates with a message from the secretary of the gentleman I'm meeting today, just confirming the time and place. My day starts falling into its normal routine. In the car working, focusing, planning, and looking forward to seeing Mason.

This morning's hello might not be as pleasant as normal, though. Keep it professional. That's what I'll do. Let's hope he does too. Who am I kidding? Of course, he will! He always has. Well, except for that moment in my father's house. That was far from professional, but hands down the best orgasm of my life.

Squirming in my seat, I'm feeling that night all over again. His fingers, his lips on my skin. The hot smooth voice that just seeps deep in my soul. Shit, I shouldn't be thinking about it. Pulling up to the plane, my heart flutters. All hot and bothered. I can't get out like this. He'll know.

Faking a call coming in, I pretend to answer my phone, rambling about some ridiculous nonsense on an order. Slowly, I'm getting myself under control. Until I look up.

Jesus. Can he get any hotter? I've never seen him in his full uniform.

Holy shit. The dark navy pilot jacket really shows off his broad shoulders. The gold strips on the sleeve look official, but what really does it for me is the hat.

Fuck me dead. Pilot's hat, aviator shades. I'm a goner.

Imagining just those and nothing else. I'm done for. There is no way I'm getting out of here without wet pants and panting like a puppy.

"Paige, are we getting out sometime today?" Franco's touching my arm trying to gain my attention.

"Sorry. I was just thinking about, um… anyway, it doesn't matter." I glance at my watch. Perfect.

"Just give me two minutes, Bent, and then I'm right." All the men in the car are looking at me strangely. Bad luck, boys. I need this point in the game.

It's time.

"Okay," is all I say.

Bent opens my door. I step out as usual, straightening my outfit, which may be just a little shorter and tighter today. Behind my glasses, I'm watching him intently. His chest's rising harder now, lips tight and body standing rigid. Oh yeah, he might be mad at me, but he can't stop wanting me. His body is showing me all the signs. Just like mine is. Nothing I do can turn it off.

His lip curls up at the sides as I stride towards him. He sees me too. There is no denying we desperately want each other.

"Morning, Captain White, eight forty-five am, exactly as requested." I smile, continuing up the stairs. Ass swaying just for him. This time it's him that just gives me the nod. Rendering him speechless is perfect. Hearing the men talking, I take my seat and start preparing for the trip. I'm not giving him an inch of what I'm thinking. Franco and Tyson take their seats and Holly's chatting to them.

Mason enters the cabin with his hat tucked under his arm.

"Enjoy your flight, all. I'll get you there safely." Nodding, he turns and heads for the cockpit, without stopping to look me in the eyes like he normally would. Disappointed at not having that moment with him, I put my head down and get stuck into work. His words repeating in my head. *'I'll get you there safely.'* That was all for me.

Hearing Tyson mumbling about Mason, Franco takes over talking to him, changing the subject. Asking all sorts of questions on the company and what his role is. Ignoring them, I make it look as normal as possible that Franco's here.

The whole flight I struggle to concentrate on work. No guessing why that is. Every time I push him, he pushes back harder. Thinking being perfectly on time would let him know what I thought of his email, then he replies with the comment about keeping me safe. He knows that's important to me. It also pisses him off that it looks like that's all I need him for.

He's wrong.

I need him to take away the ache he's created. The one I'm desperately trying to ignore.

~

Landing in Washington, I know it's time to put my business face on. This meeting is important to confirm that I run a company that can be trusted, and more importantly, that I can be trusted.

I almost make it to the car and the nerves are kicking in.

"I think I'll just use the bathroom on the plane before we leave. Won't be a moment." I turn away from the boys who both nod and take a seat in the town car to wait for me. I don't normally get nervous, but this morning something just seems different. Plus, seeing Mason just complicates my emotions.

Aaron and Holly are heading down the stairs as I get there.

"Oh, Ms. Ellen, did you need anything?" Holly stops to ask.

"I'm fine, thank you. Just using the bathroom before we leave. You continue on," I say, wanting to get up into the plane as I get more desperate to pee. I make it into the cabin as Mason is leaving the cockpit.

"Paige," he says, looking at me with concern.

"Can't stop, need the bathroom." I hope he'll just continue off the plane while I'm in here.

Closing the bathroom door in my bedroom, I breathe a little easier.

Washing my hands and checking myself in the mirror, I feel my confidence returning. It's always difficult to be a hard-ass bitch if you're busting to pee.

Opening the door, I stop dead.

The door to the bedroom is closed and Mason is right in front of me.

"Mason," my voice stumbles out.

"You say you don't want me, yet everything you say and do is telling me different." Taking the steps needed, he's so close now there's nothing separating us.

"This short, tight skirt." His hands land on my backside as he pulls me into him. "You can't tell me it's not for me. The way you walked, making sure I looked. Fuck, Paige. Feel what you do to me." Leaning down, his lips kiss softly on my neck.

My body shivering, I should be pushing him away. But I'm not. I can't. He's right. I want him desperately.

"Flirting is cruel, Tiger. You bring your uncle to keep me away, yet you draw me to you. I'm done with the games." His hand on my cheek now tilts my head up. "I want you, Paige. So. Fucking. Bad." Our lips clash together hard. Every kiss is intense. We've both been fighting to stay away, so when we connect everything explodes.

He doesn't ask, he's taking every emotion he can from me. His tongue invading my mouth. He has control, and I'm happy to let him take it.

Pulling back, looking into my eyes, I can see he's at the end of his patience with me.

"Okay," I whisper.

"Okay what?" The deep growl vibrates through me.

109

"Okay, you're right. I want you. I can't stop thinking about you. Your taste, your touch, all of it." My voice isn't much more than a whisper, still wary of all the people who are with us.

Groaning, Mason kisses me hard but short, pulling back with a beautiful smile. "Thank fuck."

"Just not here, not now. They can't know." My heart is beating so fast. I can't believe I'm doing this. It just feels right, like I can't fight it anymore.

"Tonight. I'm not waiting for you to change your mind. You message me the details." Placing his forehead on mine, we're breathing heavily.

"Just know," he says, "after tonight there's no going back. This is not a one-time thing." Shivering overtakes my whole body at the soft whisper from him.

Taking a deep breath, I give him the answer my head tells me I shouldn't. "It better not be." A little giggle escapes. I don't know the last time I giggled like a schoolgirl.

"Today's going to suck. Can you cancel the meeting? I'll turn this plane around right at once." Mason stands taller now and his arms wrap around my waist.

"We haven't even fucked yet and already he's getting needy. I've got work to do. I can't be your daytime booty call."

His hand slaps my ass. "Make no mistake, this booty will be mine day and night. You'll be the one begging for more. Now run along to your meeting. I'll just stay here with my blue balls and try not to think about you all day." He leans back and slides the door open for me.

I start to move past him, palming his cock and planting a kiss on his lips as I walk past, containing his groan from escaping. "Let me know how you do with that."

Ass swaying with emphasis, I'm walking through the plane when I hear his mumble, "Fucking prick tease. You'll pay for that, Tiger."

Oh, I hope so, Captain. I desperately want to pay for it.

I'm walking out of the plane now, like I didn't just agree to break every rule I convinced myself to follow.

For the first time ever. I don't even care.

Mason

Well, that went better than expected.

Except for my cock, who's currently in a world of pain.

Now I just need to get through today, dreaming of everything tonight will be. Hope she doesn't plan on sleeping.

Spending a few minutes getting myself under control, it's time to do my checks and file my flight logs.

"Did you look after the boss when she came back on board?" Aaron asks while passing me on the tarmac. Deciding it's not even worth an answer, I just keep walking. Smiling to myself.

Today's a good day. Back in the cabin, listening to Aaron and Holly arguing over movies isn't annoying me for once. Flicking through my social media, I jump slightly as my phone starts ringing.

"Leroy, what's up, buddy?" I ask, shocked to be receiving the call. All the kids who have my number usually text. Apparently, it's not the 'done' thing, using a phone to talk to people. Who knew?

"Hi, Mason. Sorry to call you at work. My teacher said you probably wouldn't mind. Are you busy, like, flying or something?" Nerves in his voice are coming through the phone.

"No, I'm on the ground in Washington. I'll be grounded for a few hours yet. Everything okay?" I'm feeling worried.

"Yes. Actually, really good. I just need some help if you can. You know the websites we checked out? One had a scholarship application for the flight school in California. I did what you said. I filled it in and applied."

"Good for you, man. You need to chase that dream. So how can I help?" Sitting up straighter now, I'm listening intently.

"I got an interview." His nerves have changed to excitement he's having trouble containing.

"That's awesome, Leroy. I'm so frigging proud of you. When is it? I can help you prepare." Today's turning out to be full of surprises.

"That's my problem, it's in California. I can't get there. Do you think the foundation will help? I'll pay them back, I promise. I don't want to ask my parents. I know they don't have the money and it'll make them feel bad."

"Buddy, I'm sure they will. Even if they don't, I will. There is no way you're missing this interview. Now, let's chat about all the details. Tell me everything." I walk into the cockpit to get away from the two arguing children, and Leroy starts rattling off the whole email. He's not guaranteed anything, but this is more than he ever imagined. Now to get him to believe in himself. That's the hardest part.

Sitting thinking after we hang up of ways I can help Leroy, I'm making a mental note of different questions he'll be asked. Taking the fear of the unknown out of the interview will help him. I remember how intimidating it can be in front of a panel of people. For me, who grew up in that environment of private schooling, lots of public speaking and debating, it still freaked me out. Leroy has the capability and intelligence to hold his own in the interview, it'll just be nerves.

Finally, the message I'm patiently — well, maybe not so patiently — waiting for comes through.

Tyson: Paige, Franco, and I are on route to the airport. Please have the plane ready to depart.

Mason: That's Ms. Ellen to you, I believe. Plane ready and awaiting arrival.

Tyson: Fuck off, fly boy.

Finally, he's growing some balls and standing up for himself. About time.

Mason: Appropriate language in the workplace, Tyson. I'll let this one go, but don't let it happen again.

Picturing his face holding in his anger has me almost wetting myself with laughter.

By the time they arrive back, I'm at the base of the stairs as always. They're all walking towards me, Paige's head's down, shoulders slumped. I'm guessing the meeting didn't go well. My body wants to wrap her in my arms and make it better. This is going to be torture.

I don't even get a hello, just the nod. Totally forgetting my games with Tyson on the phone, his comment catches me out. "You're such an asshole. Give up, she's never going to fuck a lowly pilot like you." Worried about Paige, I see red. Grabbing him by the throat, I push him under the plane and out of sight.

"You ever speak about Paige with such disrespect again, I'll hurt you, so badly. I don't give a shit what you think of me, but that woman inside deserves your respect. She's your boss, for god's sake. This isn't high school. Get on the fucking plane before I do something I'll regret."

His eyes are popping out of his head with fear.

"That's right, dickhead, years in the army mean I'm much more than a 'lowly pilot.'" The hairs on my neck are up, sweat pouring off me under my shirt. My pulse is running a marathon, yet I walk away holding my composure. Never let the enemy see your weaknesses.

By the time I'm coming on board, my aggression is seeping through. Aaron glares at me across the cockpit knowing I'm pissed about something. The straps on my harness are getting pulled aggressively. I need to do one more thing before we go.

Mason: Are you okay?

Paige: Not really, shit day.

Mason: I'll make it better, make you forget.

Paige: I'm counting on it. Now take me home, I've got a hot date I don't want to miss.

Mason: Yes, ma'am. Relax, so do I. Nothing is keeping me from my girl.

Paige: Far from a girl.

Mason: I'm counting on it. Show me the tiger. Got to go, the boss gets mad if I'm late.

Paige: She should. Coming late is bad manners.

Mason: Coming too early is even worse. Now stop. I've got to work.

Paige: Thank you, Mason. Just what I needed.

Mason: Always

"Can we get moving, Captain? Or are we going to sit here all day while you sort your shit out?" Seconds earlier I would've ripped into Aaron. A new calm is settling over me and instead I laugh and get the plane moving.

"Alright, since when've you been concerned with being on time?"

"Since the boss is anal about it and you've started following her around like a puppy dog. Now the pressure's on me to keep you both happy."

"Such a dick." Laughing, we both click into our roles and start taxiing to the runway while checking in with the tower. Paige might not want to tell them, but I'm guessing everyone on this plane can see what's going on. To be honest, I don't care. I just want to make sure Tyson gets the hint. Maybe then he'll stop with all the jealous shit. Then again, it could just get worse.

Landing back in Chicago safely, we go through our post-flight routine. I can still hear voices in the cabin, and I wonder why it's taking a while for them to leave today. Not that I'm complaining as I rush through my job so I can see Paige before she leaves. Aaron has already exited the cockpit and is waiting at the bottom of the stairs. I'm at the edge of the cockpit as they start departing. Franco reaches his hand out, shaking mine and thanking me for a steady flight. Not once has the other douchebag ever said a word. Instead, he's already left, even before Paige.

Approaching me, her head lowers a little, with a hint of a smile on her face. Thrusting her hand to me to shake. I take it firmly, even though she's never offered before.

"Thank you, Captain White." Our hands touching, paper slips between them. Before I've got time to say anything, she's gone, my hand clasping her note while her perfume's filling my senses. Stepping back into the privacy of the cockpit, I open the note to her handwriting so neat and beautiful.

Mason,

My apartment - 7 pm
Bring dinner
I know you don't need an address or code.
Some drunk lady already gave that away.
Paige

Even if she said be there in twenty minutes, I would've agreed. This gives me time to do a gym session, shower, order food, and still be early. If she thinks I'm waiting till seven then she's mistaken.

Paige might be a punctual person, but I'm worse. I'm impatient. She'll get used to it. Bad luck if she doesn't, because it won't change.

I didn't get a chance to ask how her father is, but if she left him today and plans to go home tonight, he must be improving.

I don't think I've ever pushed as hard through a gym session to finish early, before today. Leaving, I run into Bent who's just arriving.

"What are you doing here, man? Thought you would've moved home again already," I say, leaning on the hood of my Jeep.

"Still staying at the Ellens' property with the boss. She's home with her father now." He notices my confused look.

"Yeah, she said she'll probably move in there permanently. Old man must be about to die. Who knows? Want to join me for a workout? Could use someone to push me."

"Sorry, man, I've got somewhere to be. Gotta run." Something doesn't seem right with that whole conversation. Hope Bent's not going to start being a weirdo like Tyson. One dickhead is more than enough to deal with.

I'm not wasting time talking to him when I have my night mapped out.

Hot sexy woman.

Naked.

In my arms.

Screaming my name.

Best sex ever.

Yep, that's all I need. She wants food, I'll bring food. I'll order pasta, feeding her energy, since she's going to need it.

Riding the elevator to the penthouse tonight feels different. Nervous energy is surrounding me, not because I'm worried that she's in danger, this time. Instead, it's because being with a woman has never felt so important as it does tonight. She's not just any woman, Paige is *the* woman. The one who has finally made me stop and take notice. For once, I care more than just about tonight.

Worrying about making the right impression and letting her see the real me is a hard thing to cope with. Only my boys have ever seen the real me. My family knows me, but since the war, I shield them from a lot of what goes through my head. Mom and Dad don't need to know that I'm hurting at times. That's what the guys are there for. They listen, they talk, and most of all, they don't let me stay locked in that place. They push me to get on with it and live my life.

This is living life. In the very best way.

The doors finally open to a vision of pure beauty.

Paige is standing, waiting to greet me, for once.

Completely naked!

Every time I think I'm in control she tops me. It stops right now as she starts walking to me. Dropping the bag of dinner on the floor, I take over.

"Stop," I almost growl. "Don't move. I'm not finished looking. You want to show me your body. Then I get to take my time." Feeling my cock hardening and pushing against my pants, I slowly circle her. Using every ounce of restraint not to touch.

I want her aching for me. Her body crying out to feel my caress. When I finally give in, she'll want to come the moment I stroke her.

"Mason." Her voice is seduction at its finest. "You made a promise. Make me forget."

"One I fully intend to keep. Remember what I told you in your father's house? You get to be the boss at work. Here, this is mine. You get to listen to me." Walking behind her smooth body, I run my finger across her shoulders. As light as a feather. She knows I'm here but not enough to take away any ache.

Stepping closer, there's barely an inch between us. My front to her back. Still being fully clothed leaves her completely vulnerable and exposed in all her nakedness. Running my tongue up her neck, she's shuddering at the electricity of my touch and the breath on her skin.

Her taste is like nothing I've ever encountered. When it combines with her scent, I could be lost in her forever.

"Please, Mason. Take what you want from me." Begging is so beautiful from her lips. I knew that first night I put her to bed this is how it would be.

She needs my control.

To think.

To feel.

To finally breathe.

"There is so much I've been dreaming of. The question is where to start. You've offered me a feast. Perhaps I should feed you dinner first before I indulge." Her chest is rising sharply, trying to keep in her moans.

"How do I even know my meal is ready? Perhaps I should check first." Standing in front of her, I slowly run my finger through her pussy while she whimpers at my soft touch. "So wet for me, baby, all ready for me to taste test. You've been waiting for me, haven't you, Paige?"

"Yes," she moans slowly while I'm swiping two fingers through this time.

"Have you been touching yourself while you waited?" Her eyes widen and cheeks flush. "I'll take that as a yes." Taking her bottom lip in her mouth, she bites down on it which drives me wild. "Did it feel good, thinking of me and touching what's mine?" Her mouth opens to speak, my finger stopping it.

"While we're fucking, it's mine. Mine to touch, mine to look at, mine to eat, and mine to sink my cock into nice and deep. Have we got that straight? I promise you won't need your own hands to touch while I'm here. Unless I tell you to. I like to watch too." Her restraint breaking, her hands frantically pull at my pants.

"Uh, uh. Not yet."

"Fuck, Mason. Please." Almost there, I push her that little bit more.

"I want you to turn around and sway that delicious ass towards that table. Then bend over, keeping that ass in the air."

"What are you doing?" her voice whispers.

"Paige," is all I need to say. She turns and obeys me.

I watch that beautiful peach-shaped ass swaying naked, just for me. Shit, my restraint's breaking too.

Bending over, she hasn't quite pushed her tits into the table before I'm behind her on my knees. Spreading her with my hands. My tongue takes the first, long lick of her. Her legs are shaking and giving way. Only the table is holding her up for me.

"Pure beauty. All for me."

Continuing my assault on her pussy, she can't hold back her voice any longer.

"Oh Mason, oh fuck, …oh, …oh, …ooohh…" The words are getting jumbled and tougher for her as I suck her clit hard with all I have. Ready to send her soaring, I slide my two fingers in all at once and push as hard as I can into her, curling to find that spot.

Exploding like a rocket, her orgasm is racing through her body. I continue feasting on every drop while she quivers through the end of her high. Limp body, she's hanging onto the table like a rag doll.

I stand behind her, wiping her legs with my shirt while she murmurs. Pulling her up towards me, I see the most wonderful spacey look on her face. I slowly turn her and pick her up into my arms.

"Time for bed, baby. We have plenty more of this to enjoy."

Still in her orgasmic foggy glow, her words say it all. "Take me to bed, Mason. Make love to me."

How do I even live up to that?

Fuck, I'll be giving her the best of me.

Mind, body, and soul.

I just hope it's enough.

10

Paige

"Take me to bed, Mason. Make love to me."

The words are out of my mouth before I can stop them.

My naked body is in his arms. I should feel embarrassed and vulnerable. Instead, I'm feeling comfort and strength. I want more. He promised me the world, and I'm ready.

Softly laying me on the bed, he stands above me staring. He's ready to devour me.

"You look hungry." I giggle at him.

"You have no idea how long I've wanted you. To see the body you're hiding from me in those suits and tight short skirts." His hands are on his zipper finally.

"I can say the same. Fuck me dead, that uniform."

Smirking, his pants sit open on his hips while he's slowly unbuttoning his shirt. "When you look at me some days, it's like you want to strip my uniform off."

"Just some days, are you kidding? Every single day."

The shirt slides down his arms, and I sigh as his abs are exposed. His chest's calling me to touch it and I'm leaning up to get my hands on him.

"What do you want, baby?" His hands slide to his pants and boxers, and they're falling to the floor.

On my knees on the bed in front of him, I answer with honesty. "You, I want all of you." My hands rest on his chest, his penis at full attention between us.

Long, thick, and throbbing.

119

"Touch it, Paige, squeeze hard." My hand struggles to get around him as I slide from the base to the tip. "So perfect." His voice strains. "Now your mouth. I want to see you take it all the way in. You can do that for me, can't you, Tiger?"

A little panic is building as I lower down. Licking slowly across his tip, lapping up the pre-cum leaking from my touch. I've never been one for oral sex, but if this is what it's like with Mason, I'll take it every damn time.

With my mouth opening wide, I slowly take him inside. Mason lets out a long satisfying moan as I take it almost to the back of my throat. I feel his hand reach for my clip in my hair. Softly, my hair falls over my bare shoulders. I look up at him, taking in his cock and then drawing it out, ever so slowly. His eyes are dark and look like he's close to the edge.

"You have no idea the spectacular view from here. So beautiful. My cock sinking into you, over and over. Fuck, Tiger, you're too good at this. On your back. I'm not coming in your mouth." His hand fisting my hair, he pulls me back a little to make me stop. I want more. I shake my head and try to keep sucking, but he's having none of it.

"You deserve better than that, Paige. There'll be time for that later. Lie back and take me now. Let me show you what I've been trying to contain. What you're doing to me every single time I see you."

"Yes, oh please yes!" I push myself backwards on my bed. He's prowling over the top of me. Softly kissing up my body as he moves. Stopping now, he takes one breast into his mouth, delivering all the pleasure while his hand pinches the other nipple, contrasting with just the right level of pain. Both have me squirming and arching my body. The electricity running from my breasts straight down my body has me on fire.

"You better be sure. Like I told you, no going back. Once I'm inside you, you're mine!" Waiting for my answer, he reaches for the condom and starts rolling it on. It's so fucking hot watching him stroking himself.

"Paige!"

Oh shit, I'm supposed to be answering. I can feel his cock pressing on my opening. "Don't stop. I want you. I've never been more certain of anything." My body reacts to him like he's the puppet master, my hips raising slightly to meet his.

"So tight." Pushing into me, the sting of pain is like an aphrodisiac. Pleasure following, it just makes me want more. "So fucking good!" Mason's trying to give me a moment, but I don't want it.

"Fuck me, please, I need you."

His restraint finally breaks. His body starts pounding into me. The power and energy are heavenly. I don't need someone to treat me like glass.

I need this.

Hot, hard fucking.

A man who gives what I need and takes what he wants.

No questions asked.

He controls it all.

"That's it. Take me, baby. You're mine now, and I'm not letting you go. Ever." Mason's eyes are searing my soul on the inside.

I wish I could capture this moment

The minute I finally let go, letting him claim me.

Inner peace like I've never felt before.

Orgasms rip through us both, bringing with them the calm of happiness.

~

Hot, sweaty, and wrapped in Mason's arms, I've never felt so content.

Neither of us are speaking, just soaking in the silence and comfort. My head laying on his shoulder while my fingers are drawing circles on his chest. Watching his chest rise and fall as it slows down.

"Where've you been hiding all my life, Paige?"

I giggle a little. "Not hiding, you were just looking in the wrong place." His hand smoothing my hair is so soothing.

Leaning up and resting my chin on his chest, his hand moves to my face, softly stroking my cheek with his thumb. This Mason is different to the man who just ordered me to spread on my table so he could eat me to an orgasm. Not that I'm complaining, it was incredible.

The man lying under me has lost all the bossiness. A calmness has fallen over both of us.

"You are such a beautiful woman." The gentleness of his touch and words has me melting.

I feel my cheeks blush as I'm not used to taking such heartfelt compliments.

"Thank you," I whisper as I reach up and kiss his lips. The connection we have is evident in every kiss. Normally the kiss would get hot and heavy. Tonight, the softness is perfect.

"What made you give in, Paige?" he asks, holding my face in his hand.

"You." It's all I can answer. "The more you pushed, the more I felt you. Everywhere, all the time. You never leave my thoughts. Once you touched me, I knew I'd never contain this feeling."

My body starts to bounce on top of his chest with his deep laugh.

"So, what you're saying is, you gave up because I'm an annoying pain in the ass." He rolls his eyes playfully.

"Yes." Squealing, he kisses me like all the other times. Hard and reminding me who is in control.

"Well, maybe we can test out how big a pain in your ass I am." Raising his eyebrows and smiling, I'm slapping his chest.

"That will require more convincing, Captain."

"Now that, I'm happy to do. The night is young."

The night was exactly what he promised.

He makes me totally forget everything, including my name.

~

I wake up with Mason wrapped around me, spooning me, my butt wedged firmly in his crotch. Feeling every part of that crotch. One of his hands is on my breast while the other is on my stomach, pulling me as close to him as possible. I'm only just starting to waken, yet I can tell he's already awake.

"Morning, beautiful," he softly whispers in my ear, kisses trailing down my neck.

"Mmm morning. It can't be time to get up yet." Only half awake, I wriggle back into his warmth.

"You keep wiggling that ass and I'll definitely be up." He chews on my ear.

"Like he ever goes down. Do you ever sleep, Magic Man? Waving that wand around all last night producing countless acts of magic?" Visions of last night's fuck fest are already running in my head.

"I didn't hear you complaining, Tiger. In fact, the word 'more' was rolling off your lips quite a lot. Getting louder and louder." Mason starts moving his hands around my body, so softly with just enough pressure to know he's here. Where the pressure goes, the tingles follow.

"Complaining would've needed energy, and you fucked mine out of me." My cheekiness earns me a slap on my ass.

"Damn straight I did. Just like I promised." A soft kiss on my cheek has me turning towards his face. Rolling onto my back, he's in full view.

"Morning." I reach up and take a long and sensual kiss.

"Now that's a good morning kiss. Can I book one just like that for every morning?"

"That depends on what I've received the night before."

"We've got our boldness on this morning, have we? Be careful, I'm more than happy to spank that out of you again," he says, looking at me with the cheekiest smile.

"Challenge accepted."

"Are you feeling okay, baby? Last night was intense." Eyes full of concern are watching to see my answer.

"A little sore in all the right places. Which means I'm absolutely perfect."

Placing his kiss on my forehead, he looks a little more intense now. "I don't doubt you're sore. Absolutely perfect, that I'm doubting." I can see he's waiting for me to answer.

"I spent the night in your arms being pleasured to the point I almost passed out. Why wouldn't I be perfect?" My heart gets quicker.

"Paige, we can't ignore this. You need to tell me what upset you yesterday. Something is really worrying you. To the point you're scared."

I try to roll out from under him, but he has me trapped and he knows it.

"I'm fin…" I stop at the glare I'm getting.

"Don't. Don't even go there," he growls. Not wanting me to feel caged, he rolls off and turns me on my side to face him.

His hand on my face and his thumb gently stroking my chin, his voice is soft and full of compassion.

"Paige, let me help you. Trust me, Tiger. If you don't know who to trust, then pick me. Just like the night you were drunk. You knew I would keep you safe. I promise you now, I will always protect you."

I drop my head slightly to escape his intense analysis of me. I've been trying so hard to hold everything together for so long. Mason is the only one who gets past my walls every time. I should believe the signs. I'm coming to realize I need someone. I don't know how much more I can do on my own. I don't know why I feel so at ease with him when it's been one night. Well, one night of hot sex, but we have been flirting for months. The connection is strong, and deep down I know I trust him with my life. Which is crazy because I've never trusted anyone except my father.

"Paige, look at me, baby." His fingers lift my face to his. The immense sense of safety I feel in his arms finally breaks the dam. My tears start to fall. Not just one or two. I'm sobbing and letting it all go.

"That's it, unload everything buried deep down. Don't stop, just let it all out." He's whispering in my ear as I bury my face in his chest. His arms hold tight and his hand rubs up and down my back trying to calm me. Trying to stop the tears is hard. It's been so long since I've cried properly, not just a few tears.

"It's okay, baby, just breathe." Mason's soft kisses on my tear-streaked cheeks make me feel so warm and fuzzy. Slowly pulling it together, the tears are drying up.

Between snuffles, I'm trying to pull myself together.

"Sorry, I didn't mean to do that," I manage to say between deep breaths.

"Don't ever be sorry for showing emotion. That's what makes us human."

"Maybe, but I didn't mean to cry enough to fill Lake Michigan." I try to break the moment, but Mason's not having any of it.

"When you're finished with that lake, we'll just find another one of the Great Lakes that needs filling. You cry on my shoulder whenever you need. I want to be that person for you, Paige."

"You don't understand, I don't cry. Ever. But in the last few weeks there's been a few tears, not a lot though."

"Until today. What does that tell you?" His kiss on my forehead is so soft and gentle. I'm beginning to love these kisses.

"That I blame you," I say, smiling as best I can at him.

"Nice try. Let's start at the beginning."

Taking a deep breath, I know I need to do this.

"Maybe we should get coffee," I suggest.

He just looks at me with a smirk. "Again, nice try." Taking my hand, he brings it up to his lips, kissing it and then placing it over his heart. "Whatever it is, I will use every beat of this to help you through it."

Jesus, can this guy get any more perfect? My body melting, the words start pouring out of my mouth.

"The short version is that someone in my company is committing fraud and embezzling money. To make it worse, the way they are doing it is through the government contract we have. I'm trying to keep it hidden from them, clean up the mess, and then find the bastard who is out to hurt me. I don't understand, Mason. What have I done that would make someone want to destroy me or my father? I won't let them win. My father deserves better than to have his name dragged through the mud." Feeling the tears coming again, I take a moment and Mason can see the pain. My hand starts pushing harder against his heart, wanting to take the strength he's offered.

"My Uncle Franco, who's not really an uncle but like my family, is a retired police officer with the fraud squad of the Chicago PD. He's the only person who knows. Well, and now you. You have to promise me on your own life you will not tell a soul. Please, Mason, I shouldn't be telling you, especially because you work for…"

"It's okay, Paige, you can say it. Yes, I work for you, and I'm proud to be your pilot. You are once kick-ass boss, and I'm happy to take on any person who wants to debate me on that. It doesn't have any bearing on what this is between us."

I can't speak for a minute, needing to digest how easy he makes it all sound.

"Everything you tell me stays between you and me. The same as I wouldn't expect you to be telling everyone how exceptional sex is with me and the size of my huge cock. That will only create hysteria. Some things are best kept between us. Okay?"

I'm unable to hold back my laugh. "Thank you. I needed that."

His lips land on mine, and we kiss to relieve the tension. All it does is raise another type of tension between us.

"Now, let's continue. What's he found and who am I bashing to within an inch of his life." He's serious too.

"That's the thing, we don't know anything yet. We don't even know if it's a male or female. What we do know is that it has to be someone on my management team, or it could be more than one person. Someone who knows a lot about my movements and contracts. We're getting ready to run the next big order through the system to see if we can track them, but it also puts me at risk of the government picking up that I have an issue. Complicated, to say the least. Every time I turn a corner, it's something new." Feeling his other hand stroking my hair is so comforting.

"On top of my father being on death's door for a few days. Then some sexy-ass pilot who keeps flirting with me, I can't think straight." This woman is higher strung than normal. Now that's saying something."

"No, you don't get to blame me. If you didn't keep swaying that perfect backside in front of me, then I might have had a chance. Then you open your smart mouth, and I'm gone. I love a good challenge." I roll my eyes at him, and he laughs. "Besides, I have a great way to solve the high-strung woman problem..." he says, raising his eyebrows up and down.

"Down, boy. Give my body a recovery break. For at least an hour anyway."

"The clock starts now, lady. Fair warning."

Both laughing, he hugs me tightly.

He whispers in my ear, "I've got you, Paige. I will keep you safe. I promise." Sagging into him, I believe every word.

Giving me a moment to just get over the sharing of my life, he finally pulls back a little. Already I'm missing his warmth.

"Now that we've got all that out and the word fine has left the building never to return again, let's be serious for just a little bit longer. Paige, do you or your uncle believe you are in any physical danger?" His body tenses asking the question.

"Not at the moment as there's been no threat. But we don't know why they're doing it, so who knows. I must admit, I feel vulnerable. I hate that. I've never felt like this before. Everywhere I turn, I don't know who's watching me or listening to what I say. Yesterday I couldn't take it. By the time I was back at the plane, I felt I was going to break. It's like being under a microscope. It's freaking me out." My head hurts just thinking about it, but I'm actually feeling lighter. To be able to share this with someone other than Franco is a relief.

His face has changed and looks serious. Lines are appearing on his forehead. Feeling his body, it's getting tense.

"Mason. Are you okay?" After a few seconds, he looks at me, and I can see my Mason coming back.

"I'm good, but we need to set up a meeting with Franco. Let me be your protector, Paige. I can make sure I keep you safe even at work. My years in the military mean I'm trained to keep you safe. Besides, the rage that's inside me at the moment, that someone could be thinking about hurting my girl. That alone is enough to make me want to protect you twenty-four seven."

"Your girl," I repeat.

"Of course, that's all you took out of that sentence. Yes, Paige, my girl. Remember the conversation. There is no going back. You're mine and I'm all yours for as long as you will have me. Which better be a fucking long time because I don't plan on letting you go. Ever."

"How can you say that now? You hardly know me. I could be this really crazy-ass bitch."

"I already know you are, that's okay, I'm prepared for that." He taps my nose with his finger.

"I'm being serious. How do you know you won't get bored with me? You know nothing about me."

"See, that's where you're wrong. I know lots about you. How you are the most punctual person I know. You never wear black shoes, colorful fuck-me heels are your favorite. Mine too, just quietly, we will discuss those later." That makes me laugh, and I'm remembering that fact for a later date. "You like your coffee steaming hot. You never drink alcohol before a meeting, but a nice glass of bubbles is the preferred beverage to relax. When you're concentrating, you lightly tap your foot on the ground. You love a tight skirt and love to wear G-strings under them because there is not a line to be seen. Take it from me, I've looked. You love your father very much and have a bigger heart than you have ever let anyone see. How am I doing so far?"

"Pretty shit, really. I don't wear any underwear at all." Trying to keep the straight face, I fail after two seconds.

"Fuck me dead." Pulling me tightly to him, our mouths smash together with urgency. The tension of the situation is now coming out in our lust for each other. Hands are everywhere, and our bodies are trying to connect in every way possible. Our discussion is put to the side as Mason takes me, hard and fast, which is what we both need. It's the release that we're both longing for. It's like he's making sure I understand his claims. I'm his and he's not letting me go.

After we devour each other twice, shower through the third time, and finally make it into clothes, the morning has gotten away from us.

"You need to eat." He's standing in front of fridge yelling at me as I'm throwing things in my work bag.

"I don't have time. Your fault, so don't yell at me. I have a meeting in forty minutes in the office, and I need to prepare when I arrive. Eat what you like, I'll call you after the meeting." I run across the room to kiss him before I leave. His scowl makes me want to laugh out loud, but I know he's already struggling with no breakfast for me.

"I'll eat at the office. I promise. Stop pouting." Reaching up, I kiss him softly, taking a moment to stop. "Thank you, wherever you've come from or whoever sent you. I'm grateful. You're mine just as much as I'm yours." He tries to talk, but I kiss him again and turn to leave.

His arms grab me from behind. Burying his head in my neck, he breathes in one last time. "Stay safe," he whispers and then lets me go. I don't look back, otherwise I know I'll never leave.

The ride down the elevator is over too quickly, and I feel like I'm still rattled as I approach Bent and the car.

"Morning, Ms. Ellen. Everything okay? You look flustered," he asks, opening the door.

"Fine— Sorry, I mean it's all good." His blank look at me makes me feel warm on the inside. Mason would be proud of my change of word. Seriously, this man is going to turn my world upside down, I can just tell.

Then reality slaps me in the face again.

Tyson.

"Morning, Ms. Ellen." The sarcasm in his voice leaves me on edge slightly.

"Morning, Tyson." I decide not to take my coffee from him as I'm not really feeling like it. For some reason, coming from him this morning it just doesn't appeal.

"Thank you, but I've already had a coffee this morning. I'll dispose of it at the office." Truth be known I haven't had any caffeine, but for the first time, I don't need the rush to get me up on an adrenaline high. This morning's boost was far healthier for my body than caffeine. Maybe just not acceptable for the office, though. Smiling at my own little joke, I turn to Tyson who looks like he's frozen. His face is stunned, and he's still holding the coffee in the air.

"You never turn down a coffee. In fact, I would be fired if I didn't arrive with one. What is going on? What do you need to tell me?" I didn't realize until now how much Tyson tries to know about my life. Understandable to some degree on work time. My home life? Totally off limits.

"Don't be such a drama queen, Tyson. My routine can change, anytime I choose. I think you need to concentrate more on the work, than me personally." How did my perfect morning turn to shit so quickly?

"No! That's my job to know everything about you. Everything." His voice is raised and body language is tensing. Woah, that's creepy.

"Tyson, hold on a moment. I think we need to have a little discussion on your role. You are my PA for my work life. That is what I need in the running of the company and my workday. Not one part of my personal life or choices is any of your business. Do I make myself clear!"

"But..."

"No buts. End of discussion. Now tell me what I need to know for this meeting." I'm staring him down to shut the topic of conversation off.

His annoyance is written all over his face, but I don't care. There's a line and he is trying to cross it.

Huffing, he opens the files he needs on his laptop.

"Your meeting is at nine am with Sunshine Corp. I've proofread the proposal you wrote. There are no major changes. Then you have a meeting at twelve pm with Max about the new HR policies." He pauses and then continues with attitude, "Under the new guidelines then I guess I don't need to tell you your Brazilian waxing appointment is at three-fifteen pm."

Seriously, I'm about to let loose. I've had no coffee and he has already totally taken away my post-sex happy place. That line I thought he was crossing... he's pole-vaulted past it and is totally into the forbidden land.

"Thank you, Tyson. I think I can manage that myself." Through gritted teeth, I make a note to check my joint calendar to see what else of my private life he seems to know. I only told him I have a beautician appointment. Which could be for a variety of reasons but what the fuck. How does he even know I get a Brazilian wax? This is weird and scary. I need to talk to Franco about this. Well, not about the waxing, but about how much Tyson seems to know of my life.

Looking at him with steam coming out of my ears, I want to say 'well, you've got that wrong, I don't get a full Brazilian wax' just to shut him up, but that is so private. Plus, if I even try to speak now, I'll be screaming... loudly!

Trying to take my mind off the last conversation, I look forward and then realize Bent heard the whole thing. We may as well have a little girls' meeting on the pros and cons of waxing, full bare Brazilian or if they prefer to have some hair. I wonder what their beauty secrets are. I can't believe both these guys know something so personal about me. For fuck's sake. I just want to tell him, turn the car around and take me back to Mason and my apartment.

It's my new happy place.

No dickheads allowed.

Just one hot-as-fuck pilot who's all mine.

My man!

11

Mason

That woman makes my control issues peak at an all-time high.

I need to help get to the bottom of this with her. I might have been sent into a war-torn country to keep people safe. But we all know that in the end, it all comes back to money being the reason wars happen. People's behavior becomes irrational when money's involved. That's why I'm worried about Paige, a lot more than I let on to her. I need to talk to Franco to see how I can help.

Then the obvious question of her security needs to be discussed. She won't like it, but I don't care. It's taken me too long to feel like this about someone. I'm not letting anything happen to her.

Heading home to change and get to the airport, my mind's working on overdrive. I make lists in my head of things we need to discuss with Franco. I meant what I told Paige. I'll keep her safe. Now I just need to work out how to do that.

I'm sure this sort of thing happens in big business all the time, it just seems random to hit her company. It's not like they are aggressive players in the industry or ones to be in the media all the time. From what I can see, they operate just like any other company. The more I think during the morning, the more it seems weird. Why now, after all these years, is it happening? Is it because of the government contracts she now has? Does that mean it's more related to that, than her actual company? Or could it be a new staff member?

So many questions that just open more doors. I'm just wishing for some answers. I need to forget about that technical part of the problem. That's not where my skills lie. I'm trained to protect and that's what I'll do. My plan is forming in my head, and I'll be ready when the time comes for the meeting with Franco.

Knowing we aren't flying today, I do the basics and keep everything ready and waiting in case Paige needs to travel tomorrow. I often wonder why Paige keeps a whole crew on standby. It would be far cheaper for her to get a company-contracted crew each time she needs to fly. Not that I'm complaining. This job is the dream. For more reasons than the great salary and work conditions. Not many jobs do you get to ogle your girl while you work. Plus, now I know she's safe when she's with me, and when we're traveling, I'm never far away.

My normal routine is over with quickly. Because there's no flying today it gives me extra time to head back to the gym on my way home. I was hoping to have spoken to Paige. Since this morning, though, I've only received a few messages in between meetings. No wonder she ends up as stressed as she is. No one can ever accuse her of not working hard. She never seems to have time to stop and breathe. This eating—or more to the point, not eating—needs to stop too. That is one thing we'll lock horns over, I'm damn sure.

Pulling into the parking lot at the gym, my phone lights up with an incoming call.

"Well, if it isn't the resident man-whore, Doctor Tate. What's happening, man?"

"You should talk. Are you still dragging your bottom lip on the ground sulking over the boss lady?"

This brings a smile to my face. "You'll be pleased to know, my lip is no longer on the ground. It's too busy locking lips with my lady. Who, yes, also happens to be my boss. Now it's two each side. You single boys need to up your game, my friend." I laugh at Tate's groan.

"Fuck off. You can't leave me in the singles club on my own with Lex. You know he'll want to kill me after the first hour we're out in the bar or club. We need a solution for this and stat!"

"Well, there's an easy one. You can stop screwing every girl you meet and start looking for someone a little more permanent. It's called growing up. Not sure you've heard the term or not, but maybe google it." I'm leaning my head on the headrest, looking at myself in the rearview mirror, smiling at my own jokes.

"You're such a dick, Mason."

"Probably, but I'm okay with that. I can also confirm Paige is more than okay with my dick too."

"Just had to get that in there, didn't you, lover boy. I'll have you know, it's not like I'm not getting any. My dick is a very happy boy too, for the record." If I could see him, I'd bet he's pouting a little.

"Your own hand doesn't count. Sorry."

"I think I'll just hang up and forget I ever called," Tate huffs. He never likes when someone's humor is funnier than his.

"Get over it and stop sulking. What'd you call for, buddy?"

"I was just checking on your plans for tonight. Gray and Tilly are both off work so thought we might grab pizza at my place. Lex is good, so we just need you. Why don't you bring Paige? All jokes aside, man, we'd love to meet her. That's if you trust us not to scare her away."

I feel excitement and anxiety in my stomach. "I'll have to let you know. I'm not sure on our plans tonight. We only finally got our shit together last night, so meeting all you Neanderthals now might be a little soon. I'll talk to Paige and let you know." I'm struck by a great vision of Paige on my lap as we all sit around chatting on Tate's couch, just enjoying each other's company. I've never thought I wanted this until just now.

"I'll apologize to Gray for you, for calling his fiancée a Neanderthal. Now sort your shit out and get your ass to my place tonight. Be there around seven. Don't chicken out. We have to meet her sometime and warn her off you."

"Tell me again why we're friends. I have enemies I'm closer to than you." Tate's loud laugh echoes down the phone as we wind up the conversation and I promise to try my hardest to be there.

I have no idea how Paige will feel about this, or if we're even at that point yet. I'm sure she'll let me know. I didn't have time to really talk to her this morning. I'm aching to see her. After last night, it's almost cruel not to be able to see or talk to her all day. I hate Tyson, but maybe I'll have to make peace with him, then use him to get access to the boss lady on her busy days. Nah, it's not worth the teeth-grinding. I'll just go straight to Paige, and if she's busy I'll just have to suck it up and stop being a girl.

Jumping out of the Jeep and grabbing my bag, I see Bent walking across the lot. I thought he would still be at work if Paige is working.

"Hey, man, aren't you working, or has the boss lady clocked off for the day?" On the inside I feel a little nervous for his answer. I'm confident she would have called, but it's still early days.

"No, she's at the office in a meeting until later this afternoon, so I'm on my lunch break. Thought I'd just get a workout in." Seems weird he would drive across town to do a gym session. "You about to head inside or just finished?"

"Just arrived. Looks like you're in luck." Slapping him on the back, we both start towards the door.

"You still living at the boss's father's place?" I just remembered that he told me last time that they were still there when I knew she wasn't.

"Yeah, man, her father's still pretty sick. She's sticking close." He throws his bag into his locker without even batting an eyelid.

What the fuck?

He's flat-out lying to me. There is something going on with Bent, and I need to find out what. They say keep your friends close and your enemies closer. We are about to become as close as any two men can be without being lovers. I'm watching, man, and you better be careful.

We proceed to go through a full workout, while I'm quizzing him about his life, family friends, hobbies. All the usual stuff. Looking like I'm trying to make friends. I need to tell Paige, so she knows to be careful. I don't want to upset her, though. It's been a big few weeks for her. Maybe I'll wait until later tonight, once I've relieved her stress from today, multiple times. My cock is instantly hardening, and my balls tightening, just thinking about what's in store for them later. Down, boys, we need to get through a dinner with a different kind of pain coming... my so-called friends.

"Do you know if we're flying tomorrow?" Bent asks as we're leaving. I'm not sure what I want to tell him.

"Haven't heard from the boss, yet. So possibly not. As always, I'll be on standby. See you around."

Walking towards my Jeep, he calls out to me, "If we're not, do you want to meet again tomorrow for a workout?" What are you up to, Bent? Why are you here with me making small talk?

"Sure, message me then." Closing the door on my Jeep, I'm pondering what's going on with him.

Driving home, I've put on music to calm the mind. I need to stop thinking the worst in situations. The last thing I want to do is turn this relationship that is just beginning with Paige, into something crazy. With me overdoing it and becoming obsessive. Running through a few mind exercises, I'm feeling a little calmer when my phone starts ringing.

"Hey, beautiful. How's your day going?" I try to keep the excitement out of my voice as the grin is plastered on my face already.

"Ugh, crazy but okay. Have you missed me?" She sounds like she has really missed me.

"Like you wouldn't believe. A few times I've had to stop myself from walking into your office, putting you over my shoulder, and just walking out with you. Yelling *she's mine* over my shoulder as I exit the building." Her giggle fills my body with electricity. It's like fuel for my soul.

"All caveman style? Do you want me to wear a leopard-skin outfit to look the part? You know, and wear my hair up with a bone pushed through it as a clip. I can get my staff to beat drums as you carry me off into the sunset to your cave. How's that sound?"

"Now that's a fantasy that we are acting out. Start looking for that outfit online right now, woman. Make sure you buy me a loin cloth too. Extra-large size. We don't want any escaping serpents to scare the staff."

"Wow, that escalated quickly." I can hear the happiness in her voice to be talking to me.

"You started this one, Tiger. So, how are you really?" I ask, pulling into my parking spot at home.

"Better now I'm talking to you. I have an appointment at the beautician's in about an hour, and then I think I'll leave for the day. For once I think there's somewhere I'd rather be than here in the office. To be honest, I never thought I'd say those words. If my father could hear me, I would be crucified."

"Mmm I'm still stuck on the vision of what's happening at that appointment. Can't wait to check that out later. Okay, trying to snap out of these visions that are very distracting. Now let me guess where that place you might like to be instead of work is? Actually, I don't care where it is, as long as I'm there too."

"They don't call me a tiger for nothing. I will hunt you down if you aren't. I need you. I can't believe how much I've missed being in your arms today. What have you done to me, Mason? It's like you've put a spell on me with that magic wand of yours."

"He's magic, alright. No spell, baby. Like I told you last night. Once we cemented the connection we were fighting, I knew there would be no turning back even if we tried. Now, where are we getting naked, your place or mine? Because my cock is already protesting to having clothes on while I'm waiting for you." The skip in her breath tells me she's feeling a little discomfort too.

"You keep that up and I won't be able to wear G-string panties to work anymore." Her voice is all soft and quiet.

"Like fuck you're wearing nothing. I'm buying you big granny undies to wear when you aren't with me."

"You wish. Not a chance you will get me anywhere near them. Silk and lace all the way for this princess."

My hands are now adjusting my cock, trying to ease the pain, while the vision of her in silk and lace standing before me is flashing through my head. "Unless you plan on coming home right this minute to relieve my pain, you need to change the subject." She's laughing out loud at the discomfort in my voice.

"Now tell me where I'm fucking you, and then go do what bosses do while I count down the minutes."

"Mason, you can't say that," she exclaims.

"Oh, I can, and I did. Now, where am I seeing you and that beautiful pussy this afternoon?"

Her groan tells me she might be pretending she wants to scold me, but really, she is loving every single word.

"My place, meet me there at four. And Mason?"

"Yeah, baby?" I wait for her answer.

"Don't be late, otherwise I might have to start without you." Laughing to herself.

"Like fuck…" is all I get out before she hangs up.

A woman who drives me wild in the best possible way.

I won't be late, Tiger, let's just hope for my cock's sake you're early!

~

"I could handle that kind of afternoon meeting every day. Think I might need to block out my work calendar. Hmm, what would I list it as?" Paige looks at me, still with her blushed cheeks after one very hot sex session. Lying together on her couch, naked, is one way I'd be happy to spend my afternoons.

"Let's see, you could put 'Fuck fest with my man' or maybe 'Playing with my pilot.' No, no, I've got it. Wait for it… use the code PPP." Laughing at my own words she's already rolling her eyes.

"Do I want to know what that even stands for?" Her hands are slowly stroking my chest as she lies on top of me between my legs, her head on my chest.

"Oh, you most certainly do." Starting to run my hands on either side of her breasts, I feel her shiver.

"'Pilot Pleasuring Paige' or alternatively 'Paige Pleasuring Pilot.' They both work for me." Pulling her up my body farther, I take her lips again. I can never get enough of this woman's kisses.

"You're right. I'm totally on board with that. No denying my pilot sure knows how to pleasure me. In more ways than he realizes." Her face softens as she says it.

138

"Tell me?" I stroke her cheek and her head sinks into my hand.

"It's so much more than this pleasure. You're so much more. Today I realized it just speaking to you. You make me feel whole. It's so fast and scary but so right." Her voice isn't much more than a whisper.

"I feel it too, baby, it seems fast, but we both know it's been there all along. Now we've just set it free." Her body relaxes completely into me. "It's not just you. We are both in this one hundred percent." Lying together, we're taking it all in. Letting our souls mold into one.

"Paige, talking about things happening fast, I have to ask you something," I say, bringing her out of her quiet thinking.

"Should I be worried?"

"No, but then again I could probably answer yes to the same question. My friends are all getting together for pizza night tonight and they want us to come. They want to meet you."

"They know about me?" She looks at me like it's a shock.

"Baby, I've been pining after you for months, they sort of guessed." Giggling, she smiles.

"Well, how bad is it going to be?" Already I'm relaxing at the thought that she isn't freaking out.

"Oh, bad. They all think they're hilarious, and me having a girlfriend is going to be the aim of their jokes all night long. Don't worry, Grayson will have his fiancée Tilly with him. You will love her. She owns and runs an event planning company. She doesn't take any crap from the boys and puts them in their place, real quick. Just like I picture you doing. So, will you come?" It's like asking her on a date the amount of nerves racing around my body.

"Of course, I will. I can't wait to meet the people who make you smile. But be warned, I'm used to dealing with men on a corporate level, not as friends. This is all new to me, which is embarrassing to say."

"You'll be perfect, I have no doubt." Kissing her forehead, I reach for my phone on the coffee table. Not wanting her to move, I place my hand on her back to keep her there.

I dial Tate on speaker phone.

"Hey there, lover boy. Manage to convince your boss lady that she needs to meet me tonight to realize I'm a better option?" Smiling at Paige, I'm glad to see she isn't fazed at all.

"I haven't met you yet, but I doubt your cock has anything on Mason's, so trust me, it doesn't sound like a better option to be downsizing." I almost throw Paige off my body I'm laughing so hard.

"Welcome to the crew, boss lady, you'll fit in just fine. But fuck, Mas, you're dead to me, man, a bit of warning would've been nice. Sorry, Paige, that you've settled with my friend, but your choice, I suppose."

"Tate, you are not even close to being able to handle my girlfriend. She is so far out of your league, man."

"Far out, not another one. You and Gray are going to be painful to be around. I'm losing my wingmen, and this is a full-blown catastrophe."

"I beg to differ, actually. Perhaps it could benefit you with a whole new target group, Tate." Paige easily joins into the banter, looking very pleased with herself.

"Mason, did I tell you how much I like your girlfriend, even before I've met her?"

"Stop brown-nosing, Tate. We'll both be there tonight, try to behave yourself. Actually, no, be your normal annoying self. I'll look forward to seeing Tilly and Paige put you in your place." Paige snuggles into my chest telling me without a doubt, tonight is going to be perfect.

"For fuck's sake, Mason, you're supposed to be on my team. I'm doomed." He's laughing, knowing it's all just in fun.

"Nope, you have Lex, good luck with that. See you tonight." I hit the end button, knowing we have a little more time up our sleeve. My mind goes straight to what we will be doing to keep ourselves busy.

"I think we need to shower before we leave," I suggest, giving her the look that she totally sees straight through.

"Not sure shower sex is classified as getting clean." She pushes herself up off me to stand. "But I bet you can find a solution to this dilemma."

"Shower, now. I'm going to make you filthy and then enjoy the cleaning that comes after."

"That's right, you get to come after me." Her cheeky grin lights me up as she turns to leave. "Ouch!" she squeals, running up the stairs after me smacking her on the ass.

"That's just the beginning, Tiger, you better run a bit faster." I walk behind her, watching her naked body running up the stairs. Now that's a sight I could get used to.

I feel like the tiger chasing his prey. Ready to devour her.

Suddenly, I feel very hungry again.

~

"Are you ready for this? We can leave and go back to my place?" I ask, my hand squeezing her thigh.

"Mason, I have addressed rooms of five hundred people, chaired board meetings for thirty where I'm the only woman. I'm sure I can handle your friends." Her smile is a little less confident than her words.

"Okay then, let's do this." I don't tell her I think all of her examples were just a warmup to dinner with the guys.

Opening her door, I take her hand, pulling her into me. Kissing her within an inch of her life.

"What was that for?" She looks at me, flushed and starry eyed.

"No matter how much they tell you stupid stories about me, just remember how that feels and we will get through this." Stepping back, Paige is too busy laughing at me while we're walking to the apartment building. It helps with the nerves that she won't admit to having.

When the door opens to Tilly's face, it's a big relief.

"Hi, Mason, and you must be Paige." Leaning up to give me a kiss on the cheek and hug, Tilly turns straight to Paige to do the same. "Don't worry, I've lectured them to be on their best behavior.

Otherwise, they answer to me." As Tilly moves aside so we can enter, I hear Tate from inside.

"Only Grayson answers to you because he's whipped. Lex and I are real men." Clinking his beer bottle with Lex, they're all looking up from the couch.

"Gentlemen and Tate, this is my girlfriend, Paige Ellen, do not scare her away." I pull her into my side. "Yes, Tate, and before you say a word, she's also my boss." Standing up and coming to greet Paige, Tate is still grumbling at being excluded, while the others are laughing.

"Anyone who thinks this ugly guy is worth spending their working day with, and then back it up and see him again after hours, has to be crazy. Which means you will fit in just fine with us. Welcome, Paige." Tate leans over, kissing her on the cheek and giving her a hug. "All jokes aside, we are happy for you both. Can I get you a glass of something?" Tate nods at me to ask if I want a beer, and I give a chin lift to agree. Paige is happy drinking the same wine as Tilly.

Within twenty minutes, it's like Paige has been here all along, laughing and joining in the stories while we all devour the pizzas. Deep inside is this feeling of contentment like I've never known. To have a woman who makes me so happy and seeing her with my family. Life doesn't get much better than this.

"Seriously, Lex, you need to lighten up. You've been grumpy for weeks. You need to either spit it out or get over it," Tate throws his comment across the room to Lex who has been sitting there quietly most of the night.

"Who made you the boss? Can't I just sit here and mind my own business? I'm enjoying getting to know Paige. God help us if you aren't the center of attention for once," Lex says, throwing one of the cushions across at him.

"Tate, why are you such an edgy dick lately?" I ask. "You keep on at Lex, yet you're bounding around like you don't know where to put your feet. So, what's up your ass too? Do we need to lay you both down on the couch for a talk to Doctor Mason? Tell me all your big dark secrets." I'm trying to lighten the moment, and Lex gives me the look of thanks.

"Like I'd lay down anywhere with you. Out of all the people in this room, who actually are doctors, you aren't one of them."

"Now, now. I'm very good at listening to problems and solving them." By this stage, Gray and Tilly are trying not to laugh too much in the corner.

"Okay, what's the cure for an itch?" Tate blurts out.

"Ah well, young Tate, that's a simple one. You scratch it."

"What if you can't scratch it with the one thing you really want to." Tate's voice is a little more serious now.

"Do you mean the one *person*?" I ask. The room goes quiet for a second.

Standing, Tate starts towards the kitchen. "Who's up for another drink?" Glancing at each other, we know the conversation is over, Tate has shut it down.

"No thanks, I have some important meetings tomorrow," Paige replies.

"I'm out. Just in case I have to fly. My boss gets funny about drunk flying. Apparently, it's dangerous and hazardous to her health." I smile at Paige on my lap, who gives me a smirk.

"I would say it's just hazardous to her health being with you, full stop." Lex smiles as he gets his joke in.

"Me either, I'm on call tomorrow, so I need to be ready in case I get an early one." Grayson, the woman whisperer, as we call him. Babies and women rule his life, even more than his fiancée.

"Give me another one, who cares if I'm hungover in court tomorrow. Not like the damn jury is going to make a decision anytime soon." Lex lifts his empty beer bottle to signal another one.

"Well, I think we better feed you some dessert too," Tilly suggests. "Just to make sure there is plenty to soak up all the alcohol. Paige, do you want to give me a hand? I have some cherry pie." I give Tilly a wink to let her know how much I appreciate how she's including Paige. I knew they would hit it off.

Leaning to Paige's ear, I whisper, "I don't need any pie, my dessert is you, and you'll taste much better." Her body shivers. She's trying to stand and not show any signs of blushing.

"Stop it," she mumbles under her breath, while smacking my leg.

Disappearing into the kitchen, passing Tate on his way out with two beers, the girls are chatting away madly. It takes me back to the comments when Paige was drunk. Telling me she has no friends. No one just wants to be friends and doesn't care about her money. Maybe Tilly will be that friend she so desperately needs.

"Paige seems like a great woman." Gray light-heartedly slaps me on the shoulder. "You look happy."

"Yeah, man, I am. It was challenging getting to this point, but she is everything. I can't even explain it. It's just the beginning, but I just feel like she's always been with me. A part of me. Is that how you knew Tilly was the one for you?" Tate and Lex haven't even made one smart comment or choking sound. I should be concerned, but I have a feeling there is more going on with both of them at the moment, possibly something to do with a woman.

"Exactly that. There's no space between you. It's meant to be so easy. That's a soul mate, Mason. Paige is yours, we can all tell that." All of them nod at me, and I feel the warmth of love from my brothers.

"Thanks, let's hope I don't scare her off. She hasn't lived through one of my dreams yet. We will see how great I am after that." I should have told her about them last night. She was so satiated and looking so peaceful falling off to sleep, I just wanted to hold her. Instead, I didn't really sleep. That way I couldn't wake up in the middle of a nightmare. So, I fought it all night and just laid with her, soaking up the amazing way it felt.

Maybe I'll be lucky enough that they'll stop or when I tell her, she will understand and won't run away. I know once we get home, I'm going to need to do it. Maybe she won't want me to stay tonight. I can't assume just because I don't want to sleep another night without her in my arms that she feels the same.

"Mas, you need to stop being so hard on yourself. What you saw and had to do would change any person. Be proud of what you did for your country and all the people you saved. Just remember, like your counselor says. You can't save them all. You saved your fair share."

"I know, and my rational brain knows all the right answers. It's just the subconscious that still hasn't completely gotten the message yet. I know I'm lucky compared to what some of the guys came home with or the ones that didn't come home at all. But it still sucks I can't shake it for good. You know, to just finally be at peace."

Gray is chatting in his quiet, calming voice. He knows what I need. He was the main one to see me through trying to transition back into the normal world. It took a little bit.

"You've come so far, Mason, be proud of that. You need to believe you will get to that place of peace. Never lose sight of that."

"I know, and I'm better at seeing that now. It's just a big thing to share with someone new. It'll be okay, I'm sure," I say, unsure if I'm convincing the boys or myself with my little speech.

This dating thing sucks. Can't we just jump straight to the marriage?

Fuck!

Since when do I think about the M word.

I'm nowhere near ready for that.

Mind you, I could get her tied to me so she can't run.

Now that's an option.

12

Paige

"Don't panic, Paige, I'm not bringing you in here to grill you. The boys do enough of that on their own. I thought maybe you might need a break from all the egos in the room. They are the most caring bunch of guys I know, but they can get a bit much at times." We both start laughing, leaning against the kitchen counters.

"Thanks. They all seem nice, and I know Mason thinks the world of them otherwise he wouldn't have brought me here. Especially when we're so new." My mind is still spinning at what's happening between us.

"I hope you don't plan on going anywhere in a hurry. That man out there is totally head over heels for you. Mason doesn't let people in easily. He has his reason for that. In a few days, he already has you here with the three people he trusts most in the world. Please tell me you feel the same. I would hate to see him get hurt." Tilly seems like the most genuine person I've met in a long time. She seems a perfect match for Grayson.

Feeling the warmth of what she's saying about Mason, I can't help grinning.

"Mason is the first man who has ever broken through my barriers, the first man who I've ever let in my apartment, and the first person I've played hookie with from work. He has totally claimed me and every part of my soul. There won't be any walking away. Not for me, anyway. It just freaks me out it's all happening so fast. There are

146

so many things we haven't talked about. My life is so busy and structured on a schedule, I don't even know how to do this nothing-planned life. I know you probably don't understand." My hands fidget with nerves. I've told Tilly more in the last thirty seconds than I've shared with anyone besides Mason in years.

"Sister, you are talking to the queen of anal lists and organization. Grayson makes fun of my OCD all the time. It's fun getting around it, though. Those spontaneous moments of awesome sex, you will learn to love things that aren't planned." We both look at each other, laughing out loud, so much that I have tears in my eyes. Good tears. Fun tears.

"We are going to be great friends. I don't think the boys out there have any idea what they've done by putting us together." Tilly reaches out and grabs me in a hug. When Mason wraps me in his arms, I feel amazing and so safe and peaceful. This hug is different but just as comforting. It's a feeling of belonging and genuine friendship. Oh, Mason, you are bringing so much to my life. More than you realize.

~

Continuing our chatting about the guys, Tilly fills me in on how she and Gray met. It's the best story I've ever heard.

"How do you cope with Gray looking at naked women's vaginas all day? I mean, that's got to be hard?"

"I won't lie, it's a bit weird. It took me a little to get used to. But he tells me it's just work. They're all clinical to him. He describes it as walking through the car yard. Full of different model cars, all the same color, all capable of the same things. Then there is this one in the middle that's up on a pedestal. All shiny and sparkly, pulling him towards it. It looks, feels, and smells amazing. Then after the first test drive, he knows that's the one for him. The rest are all just the same, a dull grey. This is the perfect one, the only one that he will ever want."

"Oh my god, how did you cope with a story of comparing your vagina to a used car lot without laughing or wanting to hit him? Men seriously have no idea. Is this what I'm getting myself into?" I look at Tilly who's smiling.

"You have no idea, Paige. These four boys are ridiculous. If there's one thing I can tell you, it's that life will never be dull. Mason comes as a package deal, four nuts in the combo pack." She makes a crazy face at me.

"Or should it be the eight-nut multi pack, with four bonus bananas." I'm not sure where that comment came from, but Tilly is bringing out the naughty in me."

"Paige, that is freaking hilarious. I already love you, now I have a teammate in our war on the nuts!" Tilly gives me a high-five, then hugs me while we're laughing. We're still giggling and plating the cherry pie when I feel Mason behind me. Not touching me, I just know he's there.

"I think we've been found out." Nudging Tilly with my arm, I turn to find Mason leaning against the kitchen doorframe.

"Are you two up to no good in here? There has been way too much laughing and fun happening without me." Walking towards me, he places his hands on my waist. I have cherry pie on my fingers, so I lift one up for him.

"I'm looking for a taste test," I tell him. "The dessert's good." His eyes darken as he opens his mouth and places my finger in. His tongue makes sure my finger is totally clean.

"Mmm, best dessert ever." His voice changes to the one that makes me know I'm already in trouble.

"Well, I think that's my cue to leave the kitchen. Good luck, Paige." I'm laughing on the inside as Tilly makes a quick escape. This is one of those unplanned moments she meant.

"Are you up to your flirting tricks again, Tiger?" I shake my head for no and he smiles. He leans onto the counter either side of me, caging me in. "You know what happens when you flirt with me?" Again, I shake my head, smirking the whole time.

Tate yells from the other room, "Don't you dare fuck her on my kitchen counter, Mason. Use your own kitchen."

While it breaks the moment between us slightly, it doesn't stop Mason from taking the kiss he wants. Not just a small gentle one. He is devouring me. His tongue shows me how hungry he is for me. Coming up for air, he growls, "We're leaving now."

"No, we can't, that's rude, Mason, to leave too soon. You'll have to wait" I try not to laugh at his face.

"Nope. Hey guys, you don't mind if I take Paige home right now, do you? I believe my girlfriend has a problem that needs my attention," he yells to his friends from the kitchen.

Slapping his arm, I can feel my face turning red with embarrassment. "Mason, you can't say that."

"I just did." He's so proud of himself.

"If it means you're not fucking her on my counter, then yes, go home," Tate yells back. I hear Tilly tell him he's disgusting while the others are cheering him on.

"Welcome to the family, baby." He kisses me on the cheek and then drags me by the hand back out to the others.

"I guess we're leaving," I say with a shrug. "Thanks for having us, Tate, it was great meeting you all." I grab my bag from the table, and soon everyone is up saying goodbye. By the time I get to Tilly, she grabs her phone and shoves it in my hand.

"Give me your number. We need to catch up without these annoying ones. You can meet my friends. They're crazy too, but I think you've guessed we're all one big crazy family." Punching my number in her phone, I then send her contact to my phone. I give her a hug this time.

"That sounds wonderful; time is not my friend, but I'm sure we can make it work. Thank you, Tilly, I've really enjoyed meeting you." I whisper in her ear, "I promise not to hurt him." Pulling away, she's smiling at me.

"I have no doubt. No concerns from me. I'm so glad Mason met you. Talk soon." Tilly gives my hand a squeeze.

"Man, see what you've done. Brought another girl into the family. Now we have to put up with all this mushy stuff," Tate adds with a wink.

"Tate!" Tilly and I both shout at the same time.

"Oh lordy, what have they done?" Lex laughs, running his hand through his hair, pretending to be frustrated. On every one of the boys' faces, though, all you can see is happiness for Mason.

"Enough chit chat. I need to get Paige home. Now." Opening the door, he pulls me to him. "See you all soon. Thanks." Before I've even got time to say another goodbye, we are out the door and heading to the elevator.

"Mason, stop being a child, how old are you?" Everyone's laughing behind us.

"Thirty-five, now keep moving."

I stop in the hallway, looking at him.

"Shit, I'm older than you."

He shrugs and keeps pulling me with him.

"Oh my god, his boss *and* an older lady. This is gold!" Tate yells out.

Mason stops and turns as we all yell, "Tate."

"Seriously, you are a dick," Mason adds. "Can't wait until your time comes. Payback's a bitch, buddy." I can't help giggling at Mason now. These boys are hilarious together.

Tilly pushes them all back through the door of the apartment as the elevator doors close on us.

I'm expecting Mason to be all over me as soon as the doors are closed, but instead he's standing very stiffly in the corner.

Shit, maybe my age is a problem.

"Does it bother you?" I ask tentatively.

"What?" he snaps.

"My age, being older than you." Of all the things that I imagined would be a problem, this wasn't one of them.

"What the fuck? No." He's looking at me confused.

"Why are you over there then?" He closes the gap towards me and backs me into the corner. Running his nose up my neck, he holds his hands above me on the walls.

"Because if I touch you in here, there will be no stopping me. All I want to do is bury myself deep inside you, baby. Being caught in an elevator, I don't think that's your scene." His voice is low and he's breathing heavily on my neck. My heart rate is racing.

"No," I manage to get out just as the doors open for the foyer.

Standing straight and taking my hand, we walk out past the couple waiting like nothing was happening. Hearing the doors close behind us, we look at each other and burst out laughing. Life will never be dull with Mason, that's for sure.

~

"I wish we brought the cherry pie home with us, baby. I would be licking it off you right now. Sweet, sticky, and mixed with some ice cream, you would be the perfect delight." I can hardly contain the shivers that are racing through my body.

"Mason, please let me come. I can't take your teasing anymore. I'm aching for you. Fuck me or let me come." I'm desperate, but he controls me, so controls my pleasure.

"Oh, you will take as much as I give you. As for teasing, you had no problem with that in the kitchen at Tate's place. Sliding your sweet finger in my mouth so I could lick and suck it dry, just like I'm about to do to your pussy now. I told you we were coming home for dessert. Now let's enjoy our sweet ending."

Fuck, every time he talks dirty my heart races.

"Ohhhh Mason yesss…"

If there is one thing I'm learning about my boyfriend, it's that he always lives up to his promises.

Oh boy, does he live up to everything he promises.

~

"Do I really have to go to work today?" Mason pretends to protest, lying back on my bed, arms above his head. His abs are on show and

151

the sheet is lying across his waist. He looks like a model, ready for that perfect shot.

"You know you do. Your boss is a real bitch. She gets shitty if her pilot is not the one flying the plane. She doesn't trust anyone else." I'm watching him from my bathroom while I go through my morning routine.

"You can't be talking about my boss. She's a real sweetheart. So soft and caring. Can't imagine her being a bitch to anyone." Coming up behind me in all his naked glory, he wraps his arms around me and rests his chin on my shoulder.

"I'll always keep you safe in the air, baby. Thank you for trusting me." Leaning down and kissing my shoulder, he steps into the shower, leaving me melting into a puddle at his sweetness.

The last few days have been heaven. Having Mason in my life, in my bed, and making me smile like I haven't done in a very long time. Daddy is getting better. I have been spending time with him every day but always come home to Mason at night. Uncle Franco is slowly working through all the evidence and feels like he is getting a track on what's going on. We have arranged a meeting for over the weekend for Mason and me to get together with him and work out a plan. He knows about Mason and me, but I haven't told my father yet. This needs to happen the right way and at the right time. It'll be easier when I'm not trying to deal with the company hassles and announce a boyfriend. I know he won't be happy. Mason knows what he's up against. I just hope his charm works on Daddy, like it did on me. Well, maybe not exactly the same.

"You need to hurry that cute ass of yours up and leave," I tell him. "Otherwise you'll run into Bent and Tyson out front and that will be an issue. Imagine the outrage if your boss beats you to the plane. The captain being late." I smirk at him drying himself off behind me.

"We wouldn't want the staff to know you're sleeping with the hired help, now would we?" He's half joking, but I'm sure part of him hurts to know we're still a secret.

"Mason. You know it's nothing to do with that. I don't care who knows I'm your girlfriend and that you work for me. That's nobody's business but ours. The only reason is the fraud. We need to catch them first. I can't afford to tip them off with any major changes to my routine just now." He nods at me, but I know it's not a satisfied one.

"I'm sorry, my magic man. For so many reasons I hope it's over soon. This being the major one. I can't wait to see Tyson's face the first time I walk past you onto the plane, planting a big kiss on the lips and just keep walking." This has him smiling at me in the mirror.

"Now that I'm on board with." Tapping me on the ass, he walks out into the bedroom to get dressed.

"Of course you are, anything to piss off my PA. You just want to show him who's got the biggest dick, don't you?" I call out to him, trying to put my mascara on.

"There is no dispute on that, this will far outweigh whatever he has." He stands in the doorway, swinging around his cock, and I slip and put mascara all across my face. Normally that would have pissed me off, but I can't stop laughing.

"Such a child, you can tell who the young one is." I grab my makeup wipes to start again.

"Well, you are the cougar dating a younger man." Chuckling, he starts pulling on his boxers.

"You're going to hold the four-year age gap over my head for the rest our lives, aren't you? What are you going to do next year when you're dating a forty-year-old woman? Oh my god, that will be terrible." Even to me, I feel old saying I'm about to turn forty. "Actually, this could be good for me. They say you are only as old as the man you're feeling. I can stay younger forever." Out of the corner of my eye, I see him smirking.

"Oh yeah, baby, you can feel me up anytime you need to feel young. Even when I'm eighty, my cock will still be ready and waiting." He's full of fun this morning; I could get used to my mornings starting like this.

"Who would've thought my mild-mannered pilot is such a dirty man behind closed doors." Coming up behind me, he wraps his arms around my waist, kissing my cheek.

"Only for you, Tiger, only for you. I better get out of here. I need to have the plane ready for the very important passenger I have on board today. Have a good day at work." Giggling, I turn to give him one last kiss before he walks out.

As he's picking up his bag and heading out of my room, I call out one last thing, "No flirting with the passengers today. I have eyes watching you at work. I'll know if you start playing games with the passenger," hoping that's exactly what he'll do.

"No fair," he yells back. "My boss is so fucking hot, it's hard not to. Don't be late." Laughing to himself, I hear him heading down the stairs and eventually the elevator closing.

Leaning on the vanity, I look into the mirror. Really look at myself. How life has changed.

My eyes are sparkling with happiness. There's a glow on my cheeks and just the overall look of contentment. I thought my life was full and happy before, being the high-powered CEO. Chasing highs off winning deals and being successful. That drive is still there but now it's balancing with a whole other part of my life. Surely my work can only benefit from this. I have the perfect world. A job where I travel a lot, yet I get to have Mason with me for every single trip. Once our relationship is in the open, I can take him to functions when I'm away and we can stay together. We don't have to juggle two different jobs and still try to find time together. I just hope this can happen soon. I can't lie, this whole embezzlement is still a huge concern. Someone attacking me and the company from the inside is devastating. I'm looking forward to the weekend to see what we can piece together with Franco.

One last look and I'm happy with the results. Gray pinstriped straight skirt, a little shorter than usual. Cream silk blouse with my tailored jacket. The best part is my bright yellow heels that match my scarf. Mason is going to love this outfit. Let's see how his non-flirting at work goes today.

I have a quick conference call to do in my home office before leaving for the plane this morning. Walking downstairs and entering my office, I notice the light is already on. Mason must have been in here while I was in the shower. That man is sneaky. On my desk is a plate with fruit and yogurt, a note next to it.

My darling Paige
Every day is so much better
since you came into my life.
Please eat breakfast.
See you soon
Mason xo

How am I supposed to get on this phone call and be all businesslike, when he leaves me mushy love notes? Every day I'm falling that much harder for this man. I quickly take a selfie of me eating a strawberry dipped in the yogurt. My lips wrapped around it. He will thank me later for that image, and I'm sure it will be worth it.

~

Phone meeting done, I walk out of the elevator on my way out of the building to my car that's waiting. I notice a woman I haven't seen before in the building. She's struggling with a stroller, carrying a tiny baby girl and a toddler boy hanging on to the stroller, a coffee and shopping bags in her other hand. As she's getting closer, a strange sense of knowing her comes over me. Looking more intently at her, I know I've never seen her before, but for some reason she's familiar.

"Can I help you at all? Let me hold the elevator until you can get everything in."

Her look of surprise when I speak to her is strange. "Thank you," her timid voice says as she looks up at me.

"I haven't seen you around before, I'm Paige Ellen. Have you just moved in?"

She just nods at me as she's shuffling towards the elevator and waiting for it to return to the foyer. "A little while ago. Umm, just me and the kids. We don't get out much." The doors open, and she's quickly pushing the stroller inside, and I'm left there a little mystified at this woman and her body language. Something just isn't right.

155

"Thank you," is all I get as she pushes the button for her floor and the door closes.

What a strange moment.

Walking now to the car, my mind is drifting. Maybe she's just had a tough night with the kids, or isn't feeling well. Bent's voice pulls me from my thoughts, "Good morning, Ms. Ellen."

"Morning, Bent, thank you." I slide into my seat as usual. "Morning, Tyson. Thank you." I take my coffee from him.

"Ms. Ellen. Who was the lady you were helping?" He's looking at me weirdly.

"A neighbor, why?" I say, not giving him much.

"Just curious. She seemed a little rattled when she was heading into the building." I feel bad now for thinking he was being nosy. He was just like me and concerned she looked like life was a little hard this morning.

"Yes, she was struggling with the stroller, I don't know her, she must be new." I look at my phone to see Mason's cheeky reply to my strawberry picture.

"So, she didn't tell you her name then?"

"No, Tyson, she didn't. Why all the questions this morning?" He's starting to irritate me, and I'm thinking maybe I need to start looking for a new PA. He hasn't done anything wrong as such, he's just not the right fit for me anymore. Over the last few months, he has changed and gotten weird. Lots of questions, a little nosy into my personal affairs, and then his thing with Mason is not healthy. For some reason, he gets all weird and competitive for my attention when he's around. He's not my type at all, and the weird thing is, we got along fine until Mason started working for me. Maybe he just needs to grow up. He's only twenty-eight, so much younger than me. I'm unsure what he thinks would ever happen between us, though. I'll talk to Franco on the weekend about a change if he thinks it's possible at the moment, or I need to just put up with him for a while longer.

"Just trying to be nice. Sorry. I'll be quiet." In my head I'm thinking *yes*, that's an awesome idea. But being the boss means you have to manage your staff.

"It's okay, sorry, just got a lot on my plate at the moment. Now, let's get into work for the day." The trip then falls into the normal morning routine. In my head, though, for the first time I can ever think of, I'm thinking thank god it's Friday.

"That order for the government supply, will it be ready to ship next week?" I ask. "We can't have delays on it." Scanning across the orders planned for the month, I know the one next week is the one we're watching. It needs to go according to plan. We can't afford for any delays. Franco has put a lot of behind-the-scenes work to track every movement and login that touches this file.

"Yes, as far as I know. I'll check manufacturing to make sure. What day do you want me to let them know is the last possible date for shipping?"

"Wednesday. No excuses. I want it shipped." I add into my personal spreadsheet with Franco the details of the conversation I've just had with Tyson. We are logging every single detail. Even though we don't know who it is, I feel more confident we're getting somewhere just by trying to attack the problem head-on.

Starting on some normal work for the day, my phone starts buzzing, and smiling, I answer seeing it's Tilly.

"Hi Tilly, how are you?"

"Morning, Paige, I'm great this morning. How are you doing? Flying off to anywhere interesting today?" Her voice is always so bubbly when we speak.

"I'm just in the car on the way to the jet now with my PA and driver. Off to Boston for the day. Should be back later this afternoon. What's your day look like?" Looking out the window, I see the reflection of my smiling face.

"Okay, I get the code, no mention of names, I've got your back. Anyway, I've got a lunchtime women's small charity event, then I'm off tonight. Which is why I'm calling. We don't have any functions tonight, so Fleur is off too. We thought it a great opportunity for a girls' night out. Before you say you're busy with your man, tell him I said he can meet up with the boys at my place. They're babysitting my neighbor Hannah's little girl Daisy, so Hannah can come along. Bella, Grayson's sister, will be there too. You have to come. They are all dying to meet the newest member of the girl squad." We're both laughing now at the thought of the squad that's needed to keep the four alpha males in check. Their big egos and personalities run wild, and it looks like we have been chosen to bring them back to earth. I'm not sure what Mason has planned for tonight, but he'll have to wait. I don't think I've had a girls' night out since just after college. It's well overdue.

"I'm in. There will be complaining but nothing I can't handle. Pretty sure I know how to negotiate a deal."

"That's my girl, dangle the carrot, but only if he's a good boy does he get his treat. Told you that you would start to love the spontaneity of this life." Tilly is laughing at me now.

"We're pulling up to the jet now, so I've got to go. Just message time and place, and I'll meet you there. By myself, I promise."

"Perfect, I can't wait. You tell him from me, if I see him there, he'll be in trouble from me too. Us girls must stick together. Safe flight. See you tonight."

"Thanks, Tilly, I have the best pilot, I never have to worry. See you then." I can't help giggling a little when I mention Mason. Tilly will know exactly how safe I am.

Ending the phone call, I can't believe how excited I am for my night out. I'll miss Mason, but I'm sure he'll make up for it when I make it home. Looking out the window, I see my man standing waiting for me. All sexy in his uniform. Glasses in place. I may have let it slip how much they make me all hot and bothered. He told me they're his new favorite accessory of his uniform. As usual, we then got into a stupid debate about them not being part of the uniform. I won, and it was well worth the bet.

This is the first flight we've taken since Mason and I've become a couple. It's going to be hard being around him and not touching him. Talking and laughing as freely as we normally do. Even when we aren't hiding our relationship, I still won't be able to do big public displays of affection. I am the boss, after all. Small signs of affection will be okay. Although I know I won't be the problem, Mason will. Especially if Tyson is standing nearby. Hand holding and small kisses will be the limit. Who am I kidding, Mason doesn't do small kisses.

Bent opens my door, and I can see the small grin on Mason's face as my yellow shoes step out of the car. I don't need to know where his eyes are looking behind his glasses. They'll be firmly fixed on me. Every step I take towards him, my heart is skipping a happy beat. Trying to keep my composure.

"Morning, Captain Mason." I give him a smile, slowly walking past him.

"Morning, Paige, nice day for a flight." He gives me the usual nod.

I make sure I'm swaying nice and slowly up the stairs just for him. This is going to be fun.

Settling in for the flight while I wait for Mason to come on board, Tyson seems to be messaging rather aggressively the way he's tapping his phone.

"Everything okay there, Tyson?"

He looks up a little guilty. "Umm yes, just some stupid people in this world." Looking down again, he's back to it.

I'm not going to ruin my day with his weird shitty mood.

"Okay then." Fastening my belt, I look up to Mason as he walks into the cabin, taking his glasses off and giving me a quick wink while Tyson is preoccupied. It's as good as a kiss when we can't touch. My smile lets him know I'm thinking the same.

Once he's in the cockpit and Holly is securing the door, I know he can't come back out as he'll be going through preflight checks with Aaron. Nasty of me, but now is the perfect time to let him know about my girls' night.

Paige: Sorry I can't see you tonight. I'm busy.

That'll be enough to get him going. No clues at all.

Mason: Never too busy for me, baby. Not happening.

Paige: As the pilot, should you be texting?

Mason: No, but my girlfriend is being frustrating, so I've stopped the plane. Tell me what's going on?

Paige: I've been invited on a girls' night with Tilly and her friends. No boys allowed!

Mason: Like hell, those girls are trouble. They will corrupt you.

Paige: You aren't the boss remember.

Mason: Don't start that shit.

Mason: We need to take off. You know I'm only joking. Still need to come home to me after.

Paige: Always!

Paige: PS you won't be home. You're all babysitting Daisy.

Paige: Can we please take off sometime today? I have a meeting to get to.

Mason: You know what happens to naughty girls??

Paige: Absolutely! I'm counting on it. Now FLY!!!!

Paige: xo

Mason: Flying now with blue balls. Thanks to you!!

"What is taking so long to start moving? The engines started ages ago. Such a hopeless pilot," Tyson mumbles under his breath. Normally I would bite and defend Mason. I figure it's not worth it. Who cares what Tyson thinks!

Shooting a quick text message off to Tilly to tell her about Mason's reaction, all I get back are three laughing-crying emojis. I love this woman. Like me, her work life is busy, so those three faces let me know she thinks it's funny but no time to chat. It's a new thing for me to have a friend to share little parts of my day with. Tonight's going to be fun.

Just as I'm about to turn my phone to flight mode, her message comes through.

Tilly: Tonight – Love Street cocktail bar. 7 pm or whenever you get there if you land late

Paige: Perfect

One word is all I have time for. The plane is now moving as I switch to flight mode and get ready for my man to get us in the air. Laying my head back on the headrest, I close my eyes and think about tonight, both the early evening drinks followed by the punishment in the late evening, if I'm lucky.

Lord, I hope I'm lucky.

13

Mason

"Like fuck," I mumble under my breath but obviously not low enough.

"You all right over there, Captain?" Aaron looks at me, questioning my outburst.

"Yeah, just give me a minute." I message Paige back. There is no way I'm not seeing her tonight. I've been with her every night since we got together. I don't plan on stopping anytime soon. I know it's not logical, I just don't want to be away from her at the moment. I still haven't told her about my nightmares. The thing is, since we've been sleeping in the same bed with her wrapped in my arms, safe every night, I'm sleeping the best I have since I came home from my deployment. Maybe that's all I needed. Paige is my magic.

Shit, this can only end in tears. A girls' night with Tilly, Fleur, and Bella. Nothing good can come of this for me. The more Paige becomes friends with them, the more stories they will share. The reality of it is, though, it makes me happy she's finding friends. Women who I know are good people and spending time with her because they enjoy her company. Yes, she's my girlfriend, but that's not the reason for the invite; she and Tilly seem to have a great connection.

Messaging with Paige always seems to get off track quickly. Bringing a smile to my face, we finish with the promise of a night of

162

hot sex after her night out. I just hope she's sober enough to be able to keep her promise.

"Hey, lover boy, are we going to start taxiing anytime soon? The ground staff are about to throw their batons at the plane." Aaron tosses a ball of paper at me.

"Real grown up."

"Coming from the man who is texting his girlfriend, the same one who is sitting in the same plane as us, who we aren't supposed to know is his girlfriend." Laughing, he starts radioing the tower to let them know we are on the move as I start taxiing the jet to the runway. I don't care if they know. They're my crew and they are professional enough to keep it to themselves.

"I can neither confirm nor deny your accusations. Now let's get moving." Aaron rolls his eyes at me, and we both turn our attention to the job at hand.

Once we're at cruising altitude, I want to see Paige. Leaving Aaron with the auto pilot activated, I head to the bathroom. I pass her sitting with Tyson, deep in conversation about something on their laptops. His head is close to hers and I just want to grab him, draw a line around Paige and tell him this is her personal space. Enter it and I will hurt you. Of course I can't, but that doesn't mean I don't want to.

Instead of going into the toilet in the main part of the plane, I continue to her bedroom and the bathroom. Using the pen in my pocket, I grab a hand towel and write her another love note.

Tiger
Nice yellow heels
They did the trick, drove me wild.
The things I want to do to you in them is not for public viewing
Your beauty leaves me speechless
But your sexiness makes me ravenous
Tonight, I will feed
Magic Man

Another long day being held at a distance. She wonders why I can't keep my hands or lips off her by the end of the day. She is my stability. My calm. She just doesn't realize it.

As I walk past her, nerd boy with his head in the laptop, her face looks up me. There they are, her eyes. The center of my universe. The planets have aligned again.

I give her a flick of my head towards the bathroom and hope she gets the message.

Taking my seat back in my chair, I feel like today has a buzz about it. I just can't tell yet if it's a good one or not. The flight into Boston is perfect and the landing nice and smooth. Watching Paige leave the plane, I can tell she has her work face on. That makes me happy. I'm proud of the strong woman she is. The more I get to know her behind the mask, I see how much she cares for every person who works in her company. When she's pushing deals for the business, she wants to succeed for the company as a whole. No one else sees that, which is sad. All they see is the fearless CEO who is out there beating the best men at their own game.

With Paige's father's health improved, we don't need to be on standby the whole time we're on the ground. We're off duty for around four hours, so Aaron and Holly have headed into the city for a few hours. Holly will be shopping, and I know that will be the furthest thing from Aaron's mind. For me, I'm staying close to the plane. Even though I don't need to, I just feel better if I do.

Instead I'm now awkwardly standing in the terminals Victoria Secret store, with women all around me looking at different pieces of lingerie. I'm the only man in the shop, so of course there are lots of little giggles between women, smiles as they think how sweet it is that I'm in here. Haven't they worked out men only buy sexy lingerie because it's for their benefit? I don't need it for Paige to get my heart racing, but a little extra can make the night even more interesting for both of us.

Trying to look without really looking is turning out to be a disaster. I must appear totally out of place, and I'm sure I'm not the only guy to come in here today. You can't tell me that men traveling home to their wives or on a trip to girlfriends that they don't pop in for a little surprise for the woman in their life.

"You look like you may need a little help, sir." I'm not sure if I feel relieved or apprehensive at the woman's voice behind me. Turning, I find her standing behind me with a silly grin on her face. I decide to run with the comedy element.

"That obvious?" We both laugh.

"Relax, that's what I'm here for. Now, let's start with are we looking for silk or lace?"

"Both."

"Okay, one piece, two pieces?"

"Two." This is easier than I thought.

"Something sophisticated, sexy, or a whole lot naughty." She speaks a little bit softer this time. This is the part where it gets awkward.

"I want to say a whole lot naughty, but I think I better go with sexy." The assistant starts laughing and puts her hand on my arm. She looks in her fifties and has obviously heard it all. "Why don't we look at both and you can decide. You might like both." She heads off into the shop and I'm guessing I need to follow.

Looking over her shoulder, she asks, "What bra and panty size are we after?" There it is. The one question I haven't even thought of. Feeling stupid, I'm a bit stuck for words. I want to hold up my hands and say breast size about *this*. If I don't look stupid enough already, then that's sure to do it.

"Let me guess, no idea?" she teases.

I shrug innocently. Then have the lightbulb moment. "Just give me five minutes." Pulling my phone from my jacket pocket, I walk to the far end of the shop where there's no one standing.

"Please answer, please, universe." The ringing tone keeps going in my ears.

"Mason." Thank god.

"Tilly, I need your help," I quickly spit out.

"Hang on a minute, slow down, what's wrong, and if you say I need to call off the girls' night you are crazier than I gave you credit for."

"No, no, no, nothing like that. You have to promise to keep this to yourself. Not a word to Gray."

"Wait, hang on, now you have my attention. Okay, what's wrong?"

"No laughing, either. Never mind, I know you will anyway. I need to know what bra and panty size you think Paige might be." I hold the phone from my ear while she laughs out loud. "Are you done yet? I'm kinda in a hurry. The lady needs to know."

"Sorry, sorry. Pulling it together. But first, can I just say as funny as this is, it's so damn adorable. Good for you. Now, my guess is she would be around my size, a 32C and medium in panties. Hope that helps."

"I'm going to erase this conversation from my brain forever. Pretend you never heard from me. Got it?"

"You're too funny, Mas. Now pick something super sexy."

"Lalalalala not listening. Bye, Tilly, and thanks." Hanging up, I feel like that conversation is going to come back to bite me later.

Passing on the information to the sales lady, who is trying not to laugh, she starts pulling out things for me to look at. I want to take them all. Not sure I'll be able to hide that on the plane too easily, though. Choosing one sexy piece for Paige and the naughty one for her to wear for me, I thank the sales lady for not laughing too much.

The walk back to the plane gives me thinking time for my plan. I walk into the cabin and straight to her bedroom. Trying to choose which outfit will work, I stick with the sexy. Don't want to scare her off too early. I plant my gift under her pillows and walk in to check she got my note. I wasn't expecting to find one in return.

> *For my Magic Man,*
> *Before you, there was no laugh*
> *Before you, there was no smile*
> *Before you, I didn't look up to the sky*
> *You bring me fun*
> *You bring me happiness.*
> *You bring me the sun and the moon*
> *and the magic wand which brings me stars*

Your Tiger xo

"Holy. Fucking. Shit!" I stand staring at the note. Every time I think I have her where I want her, she tops me.

This love note is coming with me. Taking out my wallet, I slip it under my cards in the secret pocket. This paper is her giving me her heart. I intend to treasure it always.

~

Knowing they're in the car and on their way back to the plane, I put the first part of my plan into action.

Mason: How was your meeting?

Paige: A good one, productive. Feeling good about the outcome.

Mason: I'm glad. Having a good day then?

Paige: Yes, so far

Mason: That note! Thank you, made my day.

Paige: As did mine!

Mason: Want to play?

Paige: Play what?

Mason: My game

Paige: Tell me more, what's it called.

Mason: Tease me

Paige: Should I be nervous?

Mason: Anticipation is a better word

Paige: Okay, let's play.

Paige: Remembering I'm at work and so are you

Mason: Like I can forget. I hate not touching you

Paige: Ditto

Mason: Ready

Paige: Mason you are killing me!

Mason: Once you arrive, proceed to your bedroom. Under your pillow find the surprise.

Paige: Now I'm intrigued.

Mason: Message then for further instructions

Paige: Mason!

Mason: Remember the word was anticipation!

Paige: More like frustrating!

Mason: Frustrated will work too.

Paige: I have a feeling you are up to no good

Mason: That I can guarantee.

Paige: See you in ten minutes!

Mason: Can't wait!

This is working better than I planned. Who said we have to be serious at work all the time? We might not be able to touch, but that doesn't mean we can't feel each other's presence. I can just imagine her in the car with the little douchebag Tyson. Trying to look all professional while the whole time she's squirming in her seat wondering what the hell I'm up to. I'm sure she realizes it's not something innocent if she's being sent to the bedroom.

Heading down the steps of the plane, I take my normal welcoming position. I'm struggling not to look like I'm the cat that ate the canary. Although that's totally what I am. The car is pulling slowly to a stop. For the first time ever, Paige just opens her door, getting out and not waiting for the driver. Something's not right. Fuck this.

I meet her halfway. The look on her face tells me she's pissed. It's the same one that's been directed at me once or twice already. The word baby is on the tip of my tongue, but I pull it back in quickly before she directs that anger at me.

"Paige, what's wrong?" She doesn't stop, just marches past me and straight into the plane.

My first thought is to grab Tyson from the car for whatever he's done to upset her. But my need to be with her is stronger, and I can come back to deal with him. I follow her straight up the steps, into her room, and lock the door. Grabbing her from behind, I spin her then kiss her hard. Her body goes rigid and fights the kiss. It only lasts seconds before her body gives in and she falls into me. Her hands reach for my neck and pull me in tighter. Whatever she needs, I'll give. Slowly softening, Paige starts to pull away.

"Baby, what happened?" Still holding her close, I place one hand on her cheek. Her eyes look up to me. There's still a raging fire but with buried sadness.

"Franco messaged. He thinks he knows how it is all happening." She's whispering now.

"How?" I demand

"He won't tell me over message. Said we need to be sitting down together to start from the beginning to see if I feel the same. He did say he suspects it's someone close to me, but doesn't want to accuse anyone without more proof. I'm fucking furious." Her body tensing again, my thumb starts stroking her cheek trying to soothe her.

"We will get them. Don't let it get to you. That's what they want. You are stronger than that." Then the thing that always almost breaks a man: small tears pool in her eyes.

"I'm tired of being the strong one." There it is. Something I've seen from day one.

"I know, baby, I see you, I've got you." I take her in a soft, deep soul-touching kiss filled with passion, holding her tightly. "Let me take away the pain."

Her eyes open wide, a slight panic filling them. "Not here." Although the hint in her voice tells me she wants it here.

"No, Tiger, although you would like that, wouldn't you? You would love me to fuck you hard right against this wall. Have you screaming my name so they can all hear you? Knowing their boss is getting fucked hard by her pilot."

Her head's shaking no but the blush on her cheeks, the twinkle in her eyes, and the biting of her lip tells me differently.

"We're playing a game, remember? You are going to do exactly as I tell you. I'm the boss in the bedroom even though it's on the plane. Now turn around and stand in front of your bed." I can see her thoughts in turmoil, but she needs this. For me to take her out of her head. Her body slowly responds. Then, standing nice and close, I lean down, my lips almost touching her ear. In a deep whisper, while I'm running my hands up her thighs and bringing her skirt with them, I say, "I'm taking this G-string with me, and you aren't going to make a sound while I do." Her breathing hitches.

"Then you are going to strip after I leave your room. Put on the present I left you under your pillow and then make yourself presentable again. Do not touch yourself. Remember your word, anticipation. Return to your seat and let me know you are ready for me to start. The engines of course, but the vibration will remind you of what you are waiting for. The whole flight you will only be able to think of me. What my fingers feel like, how I know what you are wearing, just for me. Imagine if it was just you and me on the plane. What I would be doing to you in the little outfit. Most of all, you will sit and anticipate what tonight will bring you. No changing, that outfit stays on your scorching skin until I take it off." The faintest little moans and whimpers are now coming from her. The fine sheen of sweat on her skin and her breathing tell me she's thinking of nothing else but me.

"That's it, Tiger, remember I'm in charge. I'm the boss, they just think it's you." Slowly crouching down behind her, I use my teeth to break the strings on her G-string. Pulling it off her as her legs weaken. Just for the last seal of the deal, I drag my finger up though her wet flesh, sending her body into shivers.

Stepping back and leaving her tingling, I tap her bare ass lightly.

"Dressed just like I told you, now. You have five minutes before we fly. Don't make me wait. I hate to be late." With that, I step back, turning and leaving her in the room, ensuring no one sees anything as I open and close the door. Remaining just outside the door, I hear her groan and then there's movement. Meanwhile, I'm taking a few seconds to calm my rock-hard cock, who's groaning just as much at being left aching for the whole flight home. It gets worse, because I don't get to fulfil that pleasure until late tonight. Fuck, this is going to be a long afternoon.

Sucking my finger clean and placing her G-string in my pants pocket is not helping calm my cock. I know I'm running out of time and I need to move. Taking my jacket off and draping over my arm, I walk into the cabin.

Tyson is standing staring at me with a look of confusion but fierce anger.

"Where's Paige?" he barks. I swear, one day I will deck this guy.

"Ms. Ellen is in her room just taking a minute. She's feeling under the weather. She needed a moment on her own. Don't worry, little boy. Like I told you, I look after her in any way she needs while on my plane. She'll be out in a moment. Please be seated and tighten your seatbelt. We will be taxiing for takeoff any moment."

"You're an asshole. You know I run her life. I know every single detail about her. How could you possibly be the best person to look after her? That's my job. Stay the fuck away from her."

Breathing deeply and counting in my head, I don't want to cause an incident, but he is asking for one. I remind myself that I can't tip off any of the staff that there's anything out of the ordinary happening. Getting to ten in my count, I slowly start to speak.

"Firstly, I doubt anyone runs Paige's life except her, or knows every little detail about her. Secondly, you will never be the person to look after her. That will require a strong man, which you are not. Third and lastly, don't you ever speak to me that way again. I will do whatever I like regarding my relationship with Paige, and that is absolutely none of your fucking business. I suggest you do as I ask, sit down, shut up, belt up, before I kick your egotistical ass off my plane and leave you on the tarmac. Do I make myself perfectly clear?"

Shoving him hard into his seat as I pass, I hear Paige opening the bedroom door into the cabin. Looking over my shoulder as I'm about to enter the cockpit, I see her cheeks flushed, her lipstick all freshly applied. Her hair still neat as a pin. My heart rate returns to its normal speed—well, normal for whenever she's around. Giving her the smallest wink, I proceed into the cockpit. Behind me, I hear Tyson demanding a stiff drink from Holly. I hope she spills it in his lap.

Aaron is learning quickly how he needs to handle what's going on between Paige and me.

"Boss lady okay? Am I okay to radio the tower?"

"She will be. Yep, let's get moving. I need to get her home."

My phone vibrates.

I take a last quick look before I switch to flight mode. Three simple words.

Paige: I hate you xoxo

Just how I want her. Frustrated and thinking of me. The rest we can tackle together tomorrow. I don't reply, leaving her hanging.

Paige

Why is it when someone tells you that you can't do something, it's all you can think about doing. Mason has my body screaming for his touch even when he isn't here.

I'm trying to decide what to wear to meet the girls, standing in my lingerie, or maybe I should call it Mason's. It's just perfect, and I can't wait to see his face later tonight. Sexy, tiger-striped silk G-string. Black lace and tiger- striped silk, striped bra with a little gold heart between my breasts. I've worn plenty of high-class lingerie, but I've never felt as sexy and treasured as I do right now.

I could wear just another variation of how I dress for work, but it's time for a change. Feeling all hot and bothered, it has me looking for something that is going to tip Mason over the edge when he sees me. I've been told to meet the girls at the bar, and then we'll end up back at Tilly's to meet the boys. When I walk in with this little black dress, hugging every curve, nice and short, and these nice tall tiger-striped heels. Oh yeah, this is perfect. Probably lucky I'm not seeing him before I go out, because I'm certain I wouldn't be leaving this room.

Reaching for my ringing phone, I assume it's Mason. Instead, I groan seeing Tyson's name. I want to decline it, but I know I can't. In the back of my head, I can hear my father's voice. 'Business first, Paige, before yourself.'

"Tyson, what can I do for you on this Friday night?" I ask, trying to sound non-committal.

"Sorry, are you busy?" He sounds quiet, his words timidly spoken.

"No, I'm just getting ready to meet some girlfriends at Love Street for some drinks. What do you need me for?" I pull my shoes on as I talk.

"Oh. You don't do girls' nights. This is new. Sorry, it can wait until Monday. Sorry to disturb you." What is going on with him?

"Tyson, we've talked about this with my private life. Are you sure everything is okay? You don't normally call for nothing." There is something weird about him tonight.

"I just wanted to let you know that government order you need out by Wednesday at the latest will ship Tuesday night. That's all it was. I know the order is very important." For more reasons than Tyson can realize.

"Thank you, that's kind of you for letting me know. Now stop work for the night and enjoy your weekend. I will see you Monday. Goodnight," I say, not wanting to give him the opportunity to keep the conversation going.

"I never stop working, you used to be the same. Goodnight, Ms. Ellen." With that, he's gone.

What the fuck was that phone call? I'm starting to get a little creeped out by him now. There are too many times he either knows or says inappropriate things. But I can't let that ruin my night out.

Time to clear my head. All I want to be thinking about is having fun and meeting new friends, and a night ending with some much anticipated, mega-orgasmic relief.

My phone chimes to let me know Bent is downstairs waiting for me. Time to leave all the worries of work behind me for once. I should feel guilty. But I don't! Tomorrow will be a shit day meeting with Franco, so why worry about that now. Plenty of time for that then. I need this. More than I realized. I've never given myself the air to breathe in life before.

Tonight, that changes!

~

"Paige!" Tilly's up waving from the back of the room. Nestled in the soft pink leather benches sit the three other women. Crazily, I feel nervous all of a sudden. Walking with a little less confidence toward them, I needn't have worried. Springing from her seat, Tilly wraps me in her arms. The cocktail she's already about finished may have helped the excitement, but it's nice to feel I fit in.

"This is your girl squad. Fleur, my business partner and resident flirt, Hannah my hilarious neighbor who has the most adorable daughter Daisy and a husband who is deployed, and my future sister-in-law, Bella, who is going to make an amazing doctor just like her brother." I'm in a flurry of hugs and talking, so that when they say pick a cocktail, I just say surprise me.

That was the first mistake of the night. The second was not eating first. The third was…oh, I can't remember what I was talking about. *Shit*, the room is spinning a little bit.

"Paige, Paige, Paige. You need to tell us. Is Mason as good in bed as he looks?" Fleur leans over the table grabbing my hand for my attention.

"Oh, my fucking god. He has this magic wand dick and it puts spells on me. Like magic orgasm spells," I blurt out way more than is needed.

"Of course he does. He is one of the Fuckalicious Four, after all." Fleur laughs to herself as she says it.

"What the hell? Fuckalicious Four…I can't even deal with that. That's perfect, Fleur." Picturing the four boys, she's so right.

"But remember, my magic man is now off limits from the FF boys! Looking and no touching!" Waving my finger at them, we're all giggling like schoolgirls.

"My man is the G man. You know he knows his way around my G-spot like no other man. He is also gigantic…" Tilly is laughing as Bella yells at her.

"No, stop! We agreed no sex talk about my brother. That's just wrong." Her hands are over her ears, only with how drunk we're getting, she is completely missing her ears.

"But he is so gorgeous and…"

"Tilly!" we all yell and start giggling together while she starts pouting.

"No fair."

Bella hugs her. "Find me a man, and I will make a deal you can talk about my brother's dick all you want." Bella lays her head on Tilly's shoulder.

"Soon, baby girl, soon we will find the perfect one."

A drink is sat down in front of me. I look up puzzled at the waitress and she points to the man across the room. "For you, he said." She's walking away as I finally see who it is.

"Fuck me, it's Tyson, my PA. Why is he here buying me a drink? He doesn't listen!" My drunk brain isn't paying attention, and I get up, pissed off, and decide to make him understand.

"Paige, sit down. You look drunk," Fleur mumbles.

"Nope, I'm fine. Just going to talk work with my employee who is a major dick."

"Oh, shit's going down." Tilly laughs

I try to look super cool but honestly, I'm struggling to walk straight.

"Paige—I can call you Paige out of work time, can't I? Or is that reserved for the macho fly boy?"

"Wow, you just don't get it, do you, Tyson? I'm your boss, not your friend." He's slouching on the bar. Feeling sorry for himself, obviously.

"That's right, you're the mighty Paige Ellen. Totally untouchable, except for him." His voice is rising and people are looking; even in my drunk state I know I need to get out of here before he starts saying things he shouldn't.

"Outside now, Tyson." Taking his arm, I pull him behind me, not giving him a choice.

"What, you don't like someone answering you back?" he grumbles behind me as we make it out to the street.

"Shut the hell up, Tyson. Why are you like this? What have I done to piss you off? The last few weeks you've been acting weird, making stupid comments, stepping over personal lines. You've never done this before. What the hell is going on?" The night air and my anger are sobering me up quickly. "Plus, this stupid jealousy of Mason. What the hell is that about?" I can keep going, but I'm trying to pull myself back. My father's in the back of my head. Act professional. Don't give them any ammunition to use against you.

"You think it's all me," he starts yelling. "Our life was perfect. Until he came along. Everything was going to plan. We were a perfect team. You didn't complain or look at me different."

He's getting worked up and starts towards me. I walk backwards trying to keep my distance, feeling the building pushing into my back. He's still yelling and getting closer. Why am I so stupid to walk outside on my own?

"Tyson, you need to calm down and back away." My voice isn't as strong as usual. I try with all I have to draw up the bitch in me, but she's just not coming.

"Why? Just like you told me. This isn't work time. I don't have to listen to you!" He's close enough I can smell the bourbon on his breath.

As he's lifting his hand towards my face, I'm getting ready to shove him hard.

"You touch her, you will die. Back the fuck up before I rip you apart." My racing heart is now running to a different beat.

"Mason." His name escapes my mouth with relief.

As Mason steps between Tyson and me, my forehead drops onto his back and my hands grab his waist. I can feel his muscles shaking with restraint.

"The macho hero appears. What'd you just ride in on your horse to rescue the princess? She's more the witch, you know. Beware the poison apple."

"Go now!" His voice is deep and clear. Not to be messed with. "You're drunk and need to leave."

"So's she, but of course it's my fault." I can hear Tyson's voice starting to get quieter. He's moving down the street a little.

"Always knew you were a pathetic dick. Today you just proved it," Mason yells after him.

I'm still hiding like a coward behind Mason when everything going silent.

"Mason," I whisper.

Turning, he pulls me so tight into his chest.

"I've got you. You're safe. I will always protect you."
"Always."

14

Mason

"**W**ho's in charge of getting the drunk girls home?" Grayson asks, looking directly at me.

"Why?" Lex looks up from across the poker table.

"The messages I keep getting from Tilly tell me they've slammed too many cocktails. I can't leave because of Daisy."

Lex and Tate both sit back chuckling and tap their beer bottle together.

"Serves you both right for joining the couples' team. Off you go, Mason, go get your drunk girl and all her friends." Tate slaps me on the back, taking the cards out of my hands and swapping his hand with mine.

"That's cheating!" Lex complains, taking another sip of his beer.

"You snooze, you lose," Tate says with a smirk.

Grayson looks intently at me as I signal over the boys' heads what cards I had. Giving me the wink of acknowledgement, he slides his chips into the center, making his bet.

As I get close to the bar, my phone starts blowing up with messages from Tilly.

Tilly: You need to come. Some work guy Tyson is being a dick.

Tilly: They went outside. **Shit she's drunk. She needs you.**

There's no time to reply. I run the rest of the block. Turning the corner, I see him backing her towards the wall.

He's fucking dead, I swear I'll fucking kill him.

She's in danger.

My head is screaming voices, *'Save her, you have to save her, faster otherwise you won't save her.'*

Legs are moving even as the voices are screaming.

"You touch her, you will die. Back the fuck up before I rip you apart." I can't stop my heart from racing. My hands itch to grab him by the throat and end him. Looking into her eyes, her fear is the only thing stopping me. I never want her looking at me with that fear. Trying with every ounce of strength I have, I calmly step between them, protecting her. Now he can try hurting me, but I doubt he's brave enough.

His words are just pathetic, and I'm not even registering what he's saying. Leaving finally, I feel like I can take my first breath since I turned that corner. Turning, I pull her to me so I can feel her. My brain registering that physically she's okay.

My name whispered on her lips sends me over the edge.

"I've got you. You're safe. I will always protect you."

"Always."

It's okay, I kept her safe, I've got her. I didn't fuck it up, I promised to keep her safe. It worked. The only word in my head that's playing on repeat is *'safe.'*

I have no idea how long I'm standing here holding her. Tilly's voice is in the distance, calling my name, but I can't reply. I can't leave this bubble. Me and Paige, we are staying in the bubble.

"Mason, baby. It's Paige. Mason, come back to me, baby." Her calming voice is getting louder.

"Safe, she's safe. Keep her safe." The voices are slowing.

"Yes, Mason, I'm safe. You saved me. I'm right here." Looking into her eyes, I know I've exposed my worst secret.

Shit, I've lost it and now she'll know. I'm not whole. I can't be the man she needs.

"Are you okay to get him home? We'll get a cab," Tilly says from behind me.

"Yes, we're fine. Thanks. Talk to you later," Paige tells her and then looks up at me. "Come on, Mason, let's go home."

"Home. With you. You still want me to come home?" Feeling fragile, I don't know what to expect.

"Why wouldn't I? You have a promise to keep." Reaching up on her toes, her lips now touch mine. That tingle, my heart knows that feeling. Her calmness starts to ignite my soul again. I see her. Standing in front of me.

Still there. Strong and smiling.

My Tiger.

"I'm sorry. I should've told you." I feel ashamed.

"Nothing to be sorry for. Let's go home and talk. We've got all night." I rest my forehead on hers. How the fuck did I get so lucky?

"Bent, can you please pick me up? Yes, still at the bar. Thank you." That call will cost her something. Her secret.

"I'll get a cab. Meet you later," I say, trying to fix the situation.

"No, Mason. You're my boyfriend, you're coming with me. Fuck what they think. I'm done with hiding." Bent pulls up to the curb and jumps out to open the door.

"Everything okay, Ms. Ellen?" He gives me an inquiring look.

"Yes, thank you, Bent."

"Bent," is all I say, following her into the car.

"Mason," he replies. He's smart enough to just keep doing his job and not ask any questions.

"Home, please, Bent. I expect you will keep my guest to yourself until I have spoken to my father." Paige in full control is sexy as hell.

"Yes, ma'am," he replies and pulls out onto the road again.

Tonight has been full of surprises. Paige puts her head on my shoulder, snuggling into me. She couldn't be any more perfect if she tried.

Kissing the top of her head and wrapping her in my arm, I place my head on hers. Closing my eyes, I'm just breathing in her scent. The smell of freedom, that feeling that finally I'm going to live a life where this PTSD won't define me. Paige is the key to me moving on. If I can get through tonight, that is. Let's see when we make it upstairs how tonight pans out.

I want to tell Paige about my worries with Bent, but it just doesn't seem important tonight. The elevator reaches the penthouse, and we quietly walk in arm in arm. Guiding me to the couch, she pushes me down.

"Sit, I'll be back. Just give me a moment." Dropping her bag and flicking her shoes off, she walks around lighting candles. Turning off the lights and giving us background music, Paige settles back in my lap.

"How did you know I need you close?" I whisper into her neck.

"Because if it were me, then that's what I would need."

Sitting in silence, I know I need to start, but I just need a little longer.

"It's okay, Mason, no matter what you need to tell me. Nothing changes. We will still go upstairs, and you will make good on your promise. We will fuck like crazy and sleep in our bed together. Then tomorrow's a new day."

"Paige." I choke on her name, holding back tears. I'm supposed to be the strong one.

"This wise man told me to let it all go, that we have plenty of spare lakes that need filling."

She's done it.

What no person has been able to do since the day the world fell apart.

My tears fall and fall hard. They have been stuck for so long I can't stop. I don't know how. All I hear is Paige's soft voice repeating over and over again as she runs her hands over my body.

"I'm safe. Here with you. I'm safe. You're safe too. Together we are always going to be safe." It's like I'm back in that bubble where the calmness drifts over me, but this time I know I'm not. The bubble's gone and reality is all around me. Tears are a funny thing, they're water that you never knew you had, but as they run, they cleanse not only your thoughts but your soul. The body's release mechanism. Suddenly, it's like I need to get it all out. I want Paige to know everything before I tell her what she really needs to know.

"We were sent into an orphanage on a rescue mission. I was flying a seal team and my crew in on a night mission. It was already fucked up; we were being sent in at the last minute. We were rushing against time before the insurgents reached the compound. There were women and children stuck there." Looking up, I only see deep caring eyes full of encouragement and compassion. Willing me to continue.

"My job was to get the team on the ground, hold for ten minutes, and be out of there before all hell broke loose. There were screaming kids and chaos. The noise in a war zone is like nothing you will ever know.

"I'm yelling time frames at the team, and it was getting harder and harder to hear above the rotors, the approaching gunfire, the seal team working, and the kids screaming. There was one woman and two children left to get to the chopper. I'm watching and yelling as they're running for the doors. Then the explosion happens, gunfire starts, and my gunners are trying to keep them at a distance. Getting the last kids into the chopper, I'm getting ready to take off and I hear through the headset the worst scream of pain I have ever heard. I'm trying to work out what the hell is going on and get my chopper off the ground as my team are signaling to go. The screaming doesn't stop, just gets louder. It never goes away.

"My medic yells we have a woman with gunshots to the abdomen and we need to get to the field hospital. Everyone is crying, screaming, and the soldiers are trying to calm them. One little boy is crying. *Please help my mom, keep her safe, she needs to keep safe.* He kept chanting it over and over again. It was coming through my headset the whole flight. I pushed that chopper to its limits, but I was already overloaded. I had to be careful. I had to back off on speed, for fear of something breaking. She was running out of time. My medic was calling for me to go quicker, her son was crying for me to keep her safe." I stop when the noise in my head is too loud. I close my eyes and breathe. Focusing and trying to slow my breathing down.

"Take your time, Mason. I've got you. I'm not going anywhere." The feeling of her lips on mine has me opening my eyes again. Bringing me back to her.

"I lost her, Paige. I couldn't keep her safe. It's my fault she wasn't safe. I should have flown faster. Gotten her off the ground earlier. I couldn't save his mom. I'll regret that until the day I die."

"Mason, did you shoot her?"

"Fuck no, those bastards did."

"Then you didn't kill her. They did. It's that simple. Do you understand?"

"But it was my job to get her out of there safely."

"No, your job was to rescue as many children and women as you could. You did that. You got them all out. It was a war zone. Nothing is normal or sticks to a plan. You said yourself the plans changed last minute. More people than just you were involved in the mission. Every person did their best to get them out. If you didn't go in and try, they would all be dead. You did the best job you could. As a mother, don't you think she would have happily given up her life knowing you saved her son? Have you ever thought of it that way?"

It's like everything she's saying slows down. My brain is trying to absorb it all… that woman giving up her life for another. I have never looked at it like that. There are people I know I would give my life for. My family, my guys, their families, and now this amazing woman in my lap. The one who, through everything I've just told her, still sees me. The real me. The man I buried deep down and only let part of out.

"No one has ever said that before. Not the counselors, my family, or friends. No one… until you. My beautiful girl."

"That's because they didn't know what you needed to hear. You need to know that her life meant something. No matter what happened, her life mattered. To that little boy she was the world and that was her gift."

"Why are you so smart? You totally get me. You understand me better than I understand myself, how?" She giggles. The sound of heaven after such a somber discussion.

"That's a chat for another night."

"Why not now?"

Slowly standing from my lap, her hands drop to the bottom of her dress. Pulling it up and over her head.

I can't help the low groan she brings out of me.

"Because you promised to make me scream. You touched me, dressed me, and promised to fuck me hard."

"Tiger, just like I pictured. So. Fucking. Sexy." The vision takes away my fuzzy head. All I can think of is taking control. I need to be in control.

"You think you get to decide what happens tonight?" Pushing to the edge of the couch, my hands reach out and pull her by the hips closer.

"Just perfect." I run my nose up her silk G-string covering her sweet mound.

There's that shiver she gets when I touch her.

"Mmm, that sweet scent tells me you've been waiting for me, haven't you?" Her hands are in my hair and hanging on.

"Yes, all day," she says, sounding tortured.

"Did you obey me? Did you touch what's mine?" I look up to see her shaking her head madly. Words are becoming harder for her.

"Good girl, Paige, maybe I should reward you now."

"Please," she moans, her nails digging into my scalp.

My fingers now slip down the thin silk that has been hiding the promised land. Stepping out of them, she spreads her legs apart; she knows what she wants.

"Now your bra, Tiger, nice and slowly. I want to see those tits that taunt me all day." I watch her slide the straps down her arms and drop it to the floor. Her sensual breasts sit there, calling me.

"Tell me, baby, what did you fantasize I'd do to you? Was it my fingers that you imagined, wiping through your folds just like this? Making you quiver and arch your back just like that. When I touch just right here, and you want more. Is this what you were thinking as the vibration of the plane drove you crazy?" She's trying to stay upright, biting her bottom lip to hold in her moans.

"Or was it my tongue that will lick up all that cream that was weeping while you thought about me. Remembering how I touched you in your bedroom."

Not waiting, I lean in and swipe up to her clit, taking my first taste. No longer can she hold her voice. She cries out loudly.

"Argh, so we have our answer. I told you I would feast tonight. Hold on tight, baby. Enjoy the ride."

Through all my emotions of the night, the only thing that's clear are my feelings for this woman. My tongue laps up her wet pussy as she moans and breathes through every sensation. Fucking her in and out with my tongue, I work her swollen clit with my thumb. I know that she is so close, the shortness of breath, her thrusting against my face, and the moaning of my name. No sound is more beautiful than that.

Ready to let her fall over the edge she has been hanging off all day, I drag my other thumb up to her beautiful puckered rose bud. The unexplored treasure. Slowly rimming it, her eyes widen. Her hands pull my hair harder and her body explodes with all she has been saving for me as I push my thumb into her ass for the first time.

"Fuck, fuck, oh god, fuck Mason." Her legs wobble. I pull her into my lap, straddling my cock that is begging to be set free. Not giving her any reprieve from her high, I take one nipple into my mouth, sucking hard. Her breath is shortening again.

"Mason, I can't, I can't again."

"You can and you will. Breathe, baby, you'll be wanting more. See?" Taking the other breast in my mouth, I pinch the first breast. Biting and licking, she can't decide if she wants the pain or the pleasure.

"I can't, oh god more, yes more. Mason, I don't know if I can…" She barrels through another big orgasm that's still shuddering through her body.

Throwing my shirt across the room, I'm desperate to be naked with her.

"Now it's my turn. Strip me, Paige. Get on your knees." Fire in her eyes shows how she loves this. She needs me to take away her thoughts too. Tonight, she's giving me what I need in a totally different way. Letting me be the man I need to find again. The protector, the one who keeps her safe mentally and physically.

"Like what you see, baby? That's it, taste me too. Take me just how you know I like it." Looking to the windows of her apartment facing the city of Chicago, the reflections of the candle flames flicker on the glass, offering a soft glow of Paige from behind. Naked on her knees in front of me. Showing me all the pleasure, she's been waiting to release all day. Her beautiful ass and curved body shimmering in the candlelight.

I want more. I want her body.

"Baby, stand up. Come to me." In tune with me, she reacts, and I pull her to me. Lifting her by her ass into my arms, her legs wrap around my waist, squeezing tight.

"Tell me you want me. That you need me." I'm almost begging her to confirm her acceptance of me as her man.

"Make me yours, Mason, take me bare and claim me. For the rest of my life, I need you to keep me safe."

Not stopping, I lay her down with me on her couch, taking one last look at her face to make sure she's still with me.

"I want you so badly."

With those words, I push all the way home. Being inside her with nothing in between us is just that, I'm home and don't plan on moving ever again.

"Mason, you need to move. Please, make love to me, my Magic Man." The last straw. Her words have me giving her exactly what she wants. Thrusting as deep as I can and then withdrawing until she's moaning at the loss. Keeping her hanging on for release is the most beautiful sight. Her body chasing mine, full of lust and greed of taking what she wants to satisfy her needs. We are as desperate as each other to reach the pinnacle.

"Come with me, Paige, come now." Pushing hard so she feels every part of me, I fill her full of my come. Branding her as mine. All mine.

Balancing above her so I don't squash her, I can't wait. I take her mouth and share every emotion I'm feeling. I need to tell her. I can't hold it anymore.

Taking her face between my hands and looking deep into her soul. "I love you, Paige. I can't wait a minute longer. You need to know. This is it for me. You're my forever girl." Her face gives me everything I need to know. I'm not on my own.

187

"I love you so much, Mason, every single piece of you, even the ones you hide. I've never loved before, but I know why now. It's you, I've been waiting for you."

Rolling to our sides our bodies entwining together, we continue to love each other for the rest of the night, right here in the candlelight, in the space where I'm finally letting go and starting to live again.

~

"Daddy, I'm fine. I've been taking care of myself." Watching her face as she talks to her dad on speaker phone is hilarious.

"Paige, you've been taking a lot of time off work since I was sick. Beth told me you were staying here and then visiting every day or couple of days. You cannot leave the business to look after itself." Her father's voice does sound elderly and like he's still getting over his illness.

"I'm still working even though I've been looking after you. Now stop worrying about me and the business and just keep getting better, okay? Now I need to go because there's another work call coming in. I'll see you soon. Love you." I can see the love in her eyes as she says it.

"Love you, Paige. Goodbye."

"That man will be the death of me with his nagging one day."

"Well, he is right about looking after yourself. Baby, you need to eat something. I know you're anxious about seeing Franco, but food will give you the energy to get through the day."

"What is it with you and eating, Mason?" She looks at me like I'm a weirdo.

"It's my job to look after you when you aren't doing it yourself. Now eat, woman!" Pretending to get all bossy with her, she just pokes her tongue out at me.

"Seriously, I'm the one in the relationship who's supposed to act like a child." I throw my napkin at her.

"Something you excel at." I open my mouth to catch the grape she throws at me.

Taking a few more bites of her breakfast, she looks up at me a few times in between. There is something else going on with her. This is more than the talk we're about to have with Franco. If she doesn't know how to tell me, then I'll take matters into my own hands.

Standing and shoving the chair back, I walk around to her side of the table, pulling her up out of her chair.

"What's going on, Mason?" She squeals as I'm putting her over my shoulder, walking to the couch.

"This is the truth couch now. I've renamed it. Last night you had me here telling you everything. Now it's your turn. You have something you've been trying to say to me all morning and just don't know where to start." Her eyes give her away, I know I'm right.

"No matter what it is, it can't top mine."

"It'll be close. I want to tell you… it just never seems like the right time."

I can't work out the emotion in her voice. "Well, now it is. Take it from me, it will feel better out in the open. Last night was the best night's sleep I've had in a very long time."

"Umm, it's because you tired us both out. I'm sure you could describe it as being fucked within an inch of my life. Exhaustion usually brings solid sleep."

"Shit, so that's all I needed all these years then?"

Slapping my arm, she smiles. "No, because it wouldn't have been with me."

"Paige, stop with the diversion tactics. You are talking to the gold medal winner at changing topic to avoid hard discussions."

Taking her face in my hands, I kiss her forehead then her lips. "I love you, nothing you say is going to change that. Now spill it, woman."

I give her a few minutes to sort her thoughts, then pick her up and place her in my lap, just like last night. Finally, the words start coming.

"I'm not who you think I am."

My heart stops. What the fuck does she mean? I'm trying not to freak out.

"Sorry, that came out all wrong. It's nothing like you're thinking," she clarifies, obviously feeling my body tensing.

"What I need to tell you is… Daddy is not my real father. I have no idea who my real mother or father are. I was abandoned on his front doorstep with a note giving details of my date of birth and asking for a better life for me. He tried really hard to find my mother but had no luck. So, he adopted me, and I became Paige Ellen. I was just a few days old. He took me in and loved me with all his heart. Not many people know, but I wanted you to know…" As she pauses, I want to tell her it's okay, but I know I need to let her mind process her thoughts and get it out. Me interrupting is not what she needs. Rubbing my hand on her back, I hope it lets her know it's okay.

"I need you to know… I don't really know who I am. The frightening thing is, I never will."

I can't let her go through this on her own. "Paige, I know exactly who you are. A strong, independent, kick-ass woman on the outside, and on the inside, a caring, loving and beautiful soul. Someone who loves her dad unconditionally. Just because he isn't your blood doesn't mean he isn't your father. We all have family connections that are stronger than blood. Look at my guys who are my brothers. I would die for them. That's family, baby."

She nods slowly. "But I have no medical history, no idea of nationality, nothing."

"Well, you better keep healthy then, eating properly will help." I poke her in the side with my finger which brings a little smile. "The rest, well, has it made any difference in your thirty-nine years so far?"

"Not really," she answers, looking out the window. Slowly, I pull her face back to me.

"Tiger, none of us know who we are when we're born. Life molds who we become. No amount of background makes you a good or a bad person. You choose that. You are Paige Ellen, the woman you have chosen to be. Someone who I think's pretty amazing, and I'm so damn happy I've found her. I love you just the way you are."

I slowly kiss her lips, her nose, her cheeks damp from the little tears escaping, and finally her forehead.

"Now I can really show you how much I love you, but I'm not sure you want to meet up with your uncle smelling like sex?"

Her gorgeous giggles escape. "Nope, you keep the magic stick away. Understand me?" Pulling out of my lap, she sits on the couch beside me. "Keep your distance."

"You're so mean."

"No, I'm not, you just distract me, and the next thing I know I'm naked and moaning under your spell." She holds her fingers up at me in the symbol of a cross. "Stay back, you are too powerful."

"I don't hear you complaining when I'm touching you. Just like I could do right now." I put up my hands and lean towards her.

"Don't you touch me." She makes the fatal mistake of trying to get away from me and falling backwards onto the couch. Taking my chance, I'm on her, while she's screaming.

"Now what're you going to do, baby? You're trapped and I'm horny. Bad combination for you, I would say." Pretending to ravage her neck like a hungry animal, my hand tickles her side and she's in a fit of laughter, her body finally relaxing.

"Stop, that's unfair."

Now that she's relaxed a bit, I stop the tickling and wait for her to look at me. "Paige, we may have laughed it off, but I want you to know I understand how hard that was for you to tell me. Like I said, you are who you are. Be proud of that. Thank you for sharing something so personal. I will keep your secret safe in here." I place her hand on my heart. "Promise."

"Thank you, Mason. Everything you said means the world. My Uncle Franco and Beth know all about it because they were here at the time. But other than that, no one knows anything except I was raised by my father as a single parent. He is very protective of my privacy and paid for all the right paperwork to exist when he adopted me, so there are no questions in relation to my parents. I wanted you to know before we see Franco, but more importantly, I don't want anything between us, no secrets. I feel we crossed that line last night, so it's important for me to be as open as you were. I didn't think I could love you anymore, but last night my heart exploded with love and pride. You were so brave. So open and raw. Now we both have no baggage to drag around."

"See, this is why you're so successful. You know all the right words. Now kiss me before I put you over my shoulder again and whisk you upstairs to have my way with you." Before I have time to finish, her lips are on mine. Sharing all the emotion she had stored up inside.

"Hmm, not sure that's a good enough kiss to stop me. You might need more practice." Before she protests, I lean in and kiss her again, making sure she knows all I care about is her, no matter her name, or where she came from.

I love Paige Ellen and that's all she needs to know.

"Now, can you go and make yourself presentable to meet Uncle Franco? I don't want him thinking I've deflowered his little girl. I'm a respectable pilot, you know, with a professional image to uphold. I can't be walking around smelling like I've just been mauled by my girlfriend."

"Wow, I've just realized your ego is as big as Tate's and Grayson's. Please tell me Lex missed out and at least one of you is normal."

I roll off the couch and onto the floor, I'm laughing so hard. "Not a chance. You should see him in action in the courtroom. His ego is bigger than all ours combined."

"Impossible. Absolutely impossible."

"Aren't you lucky our egos are as big as our..."

"Stop, Mason. Don't you dare finish that sentence. I do not want to be thinking about your friends' dicks. That's wrong in so many ways." She jumps off the couch and heads towards the stairs.

"You dirty little thing, I was going to say hearts."

"Liar!" is all I hear from the top of the stairs along with her laughing as she heads to her room.

Today is going to be hard enough. She doesn't need to be carrying any extra stress into it. The laughing and joking means mission accomplished.

Now on to the next war we must conquer.

This time, though, we are entering as a united strength. Bring it on!

15

Paige

"This is like taking my first boyfriend home to meet my father, except Franco isn't even my father. That day is going to be hell, just warning you." Dropping my head onto Mason's shoulder, I cuddle into his arm, his hand on my thigh. It's not often that I'm in a car traveling around Chicago that's not being driven by Bent. Mason was adamant there's no need now. I have him to take me wherever I need when we aren't working. I have to admit, I'm loving this feeling of being a girlfriend, him fussing and at times, bossy. Not that I'm telling him how much I love when he's bossy and in control. Oh boy, do I love him in control.

"What! I'm not the first boy coming home to meet the family? I'm shattered." He thinks he's so funny.

"No, believe it or not, in my thirty-nine years I've actually dated others. Just none have survived the family," I say, trying so hard to keep a straight face. "They run scared. My father's pretty intense."

"Tiger, I'm sure he is, he raised you. But understand this: Nothing will ever scare me away from loving you. Understand? No matter what he says or how he tries to chase me off, I'm not letting you go. I told you yesterday. You're my forever girl. If he doesn't like it, well, then he'd better learn how to change his attitude real quick."

I can feel him getting a little tense. "Breathe, Mason, I was joking. Although it's kinda hot when you go all alpha over me."

"Well, I'm not joking. I mean it. Plus, just for the record, I'm happy to go all 'alpha' over you anytime, baby. You know that. Now can we not talk dirty anymore? I don't want to walk in to see Franco, while sporting a raging hard-on, which seems to happen a lot around you, gorgeous."

"I can help with that if you like."

"No! Hands off," he yells instantly.

"Oh, not so funny now the shoe's on the other foot, is it, Magic Man." I lean back to my side of the car giving him time to concentrate.

"Not sure you've worked out the punishment game for that sassy mouth of yours yet." His sly grin is adorable.

"Oopsie, my bad. I'm sorry, Captain Mason. Am I a naughty girl?" My sweet and innocent voice completely changes his facial expression.

"Fuck, Tiger. Can you just sit there and not say a word until we get there? You're killing me here. I'm going to have to drive around the block until my cock settles. Now behave or I'll spank you. But it will be on the hood of my Jeep out front of your uncle's house."

"You wouldn't!"

"Keep talking like that and just watch me."

I'm not sure if he's joking or not, but I'm not game to test the theory.

The last ten minutes, we're driving in silence while listening to music. A few times, I want to sing along, but I don't want to embarrass myself, more than I already have, apparently. According to Mason, my rendition of Eye of the Tiger that night left a lot to be desired. I doubt that's the case, but I'm not arguing.

"It's the red-brick house up here on the left. With the beautiful gardens. My Aunt Veronica loves to garden, and she used to let me help plant the flowers in the spring. I remember every year waiting to see whose patch would flower first. I've been very blessed with the people who helped raise me."

"I think you were a gift to them, too. I can't wait to see photos of you as a little girl with dirty hands and knees. A little hard to imagine, little miss perfect playing in the dirt."

"You have no idea. You better behave or you may never see those photos."

"I don't need photos to prove you are a dirty little girl, Tiger." Jumping out of the Jeep, he's laughing at his own joke as he comes around to my door.

Taking his hand, I slide out.

"Alongside that huge ego in your head is a big fan club for your own jokes, isn't there? Wow, it must get crowded in there. Not sure you can fit me in your world, Mason." I walk past him smiling.

"And the sass just keeps coming, tonight is going to be very interesting."

My head has been spinning since I got the message from Franco yesterday, yet with everything that's happened since, and Mason trying his hardest, I've managed to get through without letting my thoughts consume me.

The front door swings open and Aunt Veronica is racing down the stairs towards us.

"Christ, woman, let them get inside first," Franco yells from the door.

"Hush, you," she calls over her shoulder as she continues barreling straight for me.

"My Paigey, how is my beautiful girl?" This woman is the closest I have to a mother, and I'm reminded of how great she is. I need to make more time to visit.

"Hi, Aunt Veronica, it's so good to see you. You look fantastic."

"Now you're lying, but I'll take it anyway. Now who is this handsome man here? You might have passed the Uncle Franco test, but the Aunt Veronica test is much harder," she teases, already giggling at her own joke. The rest of us know she's too soft to hurt a fly.

"Ignore her, Mason my boy," Franco says. "She's just trying to get a hug from a young man who is way better-looking than me. Get in here, woman, we have work to do."

Mason, laughing, leans down and kisses her on the cheek, taking her in a big hug. It puts a big smile and a little blush on her face.

"Lovely to meet you, Veronica. Paige was just telling me about growing up with you. You are just like I imagined."

"Oh, I like this one, sweetie, we might keep him." She wraps her arm around his waist and walks inside.

"Umm, I guess I'm on my own then," I call out from behind them.

"Yep," she calls back and keeps steering Mason towards the steps.

He looks over his shoulder, winking at me and just checking I'm okay.

"I see how it is. Just remember, you were my aunt first, you traitor." All of us are laughing as we enter the house. Mason stands holding the door for me. He gives me a quick kiss on the cheek as I pass and closes the door behind me.

The smells of my childhood envelop my senses. They take me back to a time of feeling carefree and loved. I wasn't worrying about running a huge company and caring for an aging father whose health isn't the best. Nor was I fighting against an asshole who is embezzling money from me. Take me back to the times of baking cookies, glasses of milk, and playing princess dress-up in the garden. Oh, how I have forgotten all of these memories. It's sad that my life has gotten so crazy that I've left so much behind. I didn't realize until this moment what I've been neglecting in my life, or more to the point, *who* I've been neglecting. I need to make some changes in my life. Mason's hand on my lower back snaps me out of my thoughts.

"You okay, baby?" he whispers in my ear.

"Yeah, just realized what I've been missing. Time to make some hard decisions and take more time for me, whether my father likes it or not."

"You're the boss. You do what you need to do. Including penciling on the calendar your afternoon PPP meetings. They are vitally important to your sanity."

"Argh yes, to relieve the stress of my boyfriend who is slowly sending me insane."

"Can you two stop making googly eyes at each other and get into the kitchen? I have food, and Paige, you look like you need a good feed."

Mason rolls his eyes at me and we both laugh and walk down the hallway towards the amazing aroma that is making my mouth water.

"There better be chocolate chip cookies or I'm going to drop to the ground and throw a tantrum." I kiss Uncle Franco on the cheek as I sit down next to him on the seat Mason pulls out for me.

"Now there's a story for you, son. This one was the best little tantrum thrower I've ever seen. All over these chocolate chip cookies and not being allowed to eat a plateful." Franco is getting ready to start the stories.

"If you want me to keep all your secrets, I suggest you keep mine. Now, where's my glass of milk and that plate of cookies with my name on it?" Everyone starts laughing and the conversation continues on stories of me growing up and the part of my life spent in this house with them.

After my Aunt Veronica finished filling me full of her food and both she and Uncle Franco reveal way too much about my childhood, I have to face the music.

"We should get started on work... give me the bad news." Mason's hand sitting on my leg gives a squeeze to let me know he's right here with me.

"That's my cue to leave you people to the serious discussion. I'll be out on the deck reading, if anyone needs me." With that she's up and clearing the table.

"Let's head into my office. I have everything set up in there." I feel like I'm heading into war. Mason sits on the chair next to mine and pulls it close. He can feel the tension coming off me.

"Paige, relax," my uncle says. "Everyone in this room is on your team. We are going to get this bastard and then you can move on, not having to worry. Now, I'm going to give you everything I've found and let you see how I've drawn my conclusions and see if we agree on the answer."

Nodding and grabbing my notepad and pen, Mason looks just as tense as me. I know the business part won't interest him, but the who and my safety will be what he wants to know.

"About twelve months ago, there were a few transactions on the account that were very minor. They were paying for some invoices for office supplies. Two hundred and twenty-nine dollars and the other for four hundred and fifty dollars. Like I said, minor, but they did get paid to the mystery bank account we're chasing. These were what we call their test transactions. Checking if any questions get raised. Getting the bank account details into the system, so when they need it for the larger transactions it's already linked and verified." Clicking away on the computer, he brings up the transactions and invoices for me to see.

"Bastard!" I can already feel the muscles in my neck and shoulders tightening.

"When you are a multibillion-dollar company, these are never going to be questioned. Stop blaming yourself. I can see it on your face already." Franco is giving me the caring uncle look, not the police investigator look.

"Let's keep moving." I don't want to agree with him. I should've found this earlier.

Franco continues, giving us the background of all the invoices that have happened, slowly increasing in value, and an overall view of where we're at.

"Now it's time to get into the details behind the invoice that I've been able to find, which wouldn't be obvious to the normal person. I have had my best computer hacker working on this, and they have signed all the non-disclosure and privacy documents needed. This woman could tell you today what you ate for breakfast and the color of your underwear, she's that good. Don't ask me her name or how she knows. I don't want to know the answer."

I can't stop my sassy inner voice from sneaking through, as I think to myself, *what if I'm not wearing any underwear?* Then I realize who I'm sitting across from. Shit. Mason raises his eyebrows at me. Suspecting he's thinking the same thing as I am, I feel a little heat from his stare.

"What are you two smiling at?" Franco looks at the both of us.

"Nothing," we both say in chorus.

"You don't have to tell me. I know how much trouble you are on your own Paige, mix Mason in and I'm guessing you two are trouble together." Franco laughs at us, and it breaks the tension. Franco now opens up a log of different computer accesses to our system.

"As you can see, the first set-ups were done by an employee who is listed as working in the IT department. The records say he has since left, but the truth is he doesn't even exist, never did. All the records of this 'fake' employee were created online somehow after they hacked into the computer server. So, the reality of it is that these invoices were not done in the building but through hacking into the system. We're still trying to find out how. Now comes the interesting part." Franco's whole demeanor changes.

"The large invoices to the government contract were all edited to the new suspicious figures under Tyson's employee login. The refund credit payments were authorized by an employee number for someone who doesn't seem to exist, and Tyson second-authorized them. Here's the thing, though. This wasn't done at the office or through his company-issued laptop. The login has come from a remote computer that my hacker is still trying to track down. She does know, though, it is in the Chicago area."

"What. The. Fuck." I'm slowly trying to digest what Franco has just revealed. "Why would he do that? This makes no sense."

"I should have fucking killed him last night while I had the chance. I told you he was a dick." While I'm confused, Mason is angry. He hasn't liked Tyson from the start, but I don't think any of us imagined he'd be capable of anything like this.

"Are you sure it's him? I just can't imagine he has the knowledge or skills on how to do this. He's an efficient PA but not someone I would think is smart enough to pull off something like this." My nerves are all over the place. I don't know if I should scream or cry. I can't sit still. I need to pace. Mason reaches out to grab my hand as I stand, but I pull away. I just need to digest this.

"We have worked so close together for over a year now. He has been the best PA I've had. Was that all an act, has he just been playing me the whole time? I can't believe I'm so fucking stupid. I knew something was different lately. I just thought he was jealous of Mason. Even last night it was all about Mason."

"This is not your fault, Paige." Mason's forceful voice shows his anger.

"What are you both talking about last night? I need to know everything." Franco grabs his notepad and starts scribbling down everything we say. Both of us are talking at once.

"By the time I arrived, he was about to assault her. I should have killed the bastard.

"No, Mason, you did what was the right thing. You controlled your temper. Protected me and he ran off. I don't want to be visiting you in jail." This time I go to him because I know that's what he needs. He's doubting himself in his head again. Placing my hands on his shoulders, I let him know I'm here.

"Shit, have you talked to him today? This is bad. We don't want him running off now. He needs to take the bait and complete this last transaction. Paige, you need to call him and make up whatever is needed to get him to work on Monday."

Mason stands and bangs the desk with his fist, showing how unhappy he is about the whole thing.

"No fucking way is he going to be alone with Paige. Never again!" Now Mason is pacing the room, and it's my turn to try to calm him.

"Look, we need him. I will make sure I'm with her at all times. That way it won't be awkward between them. I can keep an eye on when he is on and off the computer and match with the login records. We have built-in programming hidden that triggers us every time there's movement from his login and what it's accessing."

Franco stands and walks towards me, putting his arm around my shoulder. "We are so close, we can't let him get away. You can do this, sweetheart. I know you can. Call him now and make peace. I will not leave your side, plus Mason will never be far. We can post him somewhere in your building with the live security camera feed. He's trained in this, I'm guessing?" I nod. "Okay, and when we travel, Mason's with us anyway. What do you say?"

I want to say no way. I'm not spending another moment with him, but I have to listen to Franco. He knows what he's doing.

"I don't like this, Tiger, something feels off about it. I'm not sure what, but it just doesn't sit well with me. I've been in enough situations that turned to shit, and my gut has always told me it was going to happen." I can tell in his voice it's really worrying him.

"Mason, it's okay. I understand, but we have no other choice. We have to get him and make him pay for what he's done. I know I won't get the money back, it's probably long gone. I need to get justice, though. Do you understand that?"

"Of course, but it doesn't mean I have to like it. You are not to leave Franco's side if you aren't with me. I know Tyson is weak and probably no physical threat, but just so you both know, I will be wearing my gun when I'm not flying. I'm not risking losing you, baby. I told you. I will keep you safe."

"Son, I don't think that's necessary, and we can talk about it later. For now, let's just get him back on board. We have the shipment ready to go Tuesday night, so we need him around." Franco sits back at his desk tapping away into his laptop. "Okay, I've got my hacker tracking this call, so ready when you are, Paige."

Mason worries me. He's really struggling with Tyson being anywhere near me. I understand his PTSD will make this harder with his need to keep me safe.

"He touches her, I will shoot him dead. No regrets." He walks over and stands with his arm up resting against the wall next to the window. He's staring out at the yard, and I'm sure just trying to keep himself in check. His breathing's deep and he's trying to slow it down.

"Paige, call Tyson and smooth it over. Have it on speakerphone, though. I need to hear every word. Mason, are you going to be able to keep quiet, not a sound? Or do you need to leave the room?" Franco is in charge of this case and Mason has to take orders from him. He doesn't like it, but he's doing it.

Taking a deep breath, I sit with my phone and dial Tyson. Not knowing what's about to happen, I feel anxious.

"Ms. Ellen." Tyson's voice is flat, not showing any sign of emotion. Pulling myself together, I imagine a boardroom of men I'm trying to convince to go with my idea. Put the charm on and do what is needed to win the deal.

"Good Morning, Tyson. I thought it best we talked about last night before work on Monday morning." Keep the bitch voice on. Straight to the point and no emotion involved.

"I assumed I no longer had a job," he mumbles.

"That is why I'm calling now. You still have a job as you're valuable to me. I think we both had too much to drink last night and said things we didn't mean or were out of line."

"Yes, that's true." His voice is perking up at the chance he may not have blown his cover for stealing from me.

"I'm sorry, Ms. Ellen. I was out of line, and I apologize for the whole thing. I had drunk way too much and not eaten. In fact, I don't remember much of it, to be honest." I know that's bullshit, but I'm going with it. He may have been drinking, but he wasn't drunk. If anything, I was worse than he was.

"Thank you, Tyson. Yes, I had more than I should have too. I'm sorry for what I said. I thought maybe we could just start Monday with a clean slate. Does that sound okay?" Franco is giving me the keep going signal. I need to find something we might have in common.

"Is everything okay? You've been acting different, and then you looked like you were drowning your sorrows. Is there anything I can help with at work, as your boss?"

I hear him have a little giggle to himself. "No, thank you. I'm fine, and I think we need to keep it purely work. That's what you complained about before." Little shit. He's trying to give me attitude when he should already be out the door. He's very cocky.

"Yes, that's true. Let's just forget I asked that. Do you need to talk to me about anything else before I go?" Finally, Franco gives me the thumbs-up that he has the trace.

"You need to talk to your boyfriend and tell him to stay away from me. Workplace harassment is a thing, and I would already have a good case against him." Oh, fuck he did not just say that. Mason has turned and is glaring at me with a look that says he's ready to fire the gun and shoot him dead. Holding up my palm so he stops, I watch him standing there like a bull, steam coming out of his nostrils.

"I can speak to him. You also need to show him some respect. It is a two-way street," I say, biting my tongue so hard.

"Understood. But just so you know, I would have been a better option. That's the last I'll say on it." He sounds all confident like he's back in control. He is so far from reality that I can't wait to make sure he pays for everything.

"Thank you. I will see you Monday morning. As per the schedule, we're flying. Email me if there is anything I need to know. Otherwise, thank you for making time for me."

"Thank you for letting last night go, Ms. Ellen. I promise I'll work hard for you every day."

"I expect nothing less, Tyson. See you Monday."

Pushing the button to end the call, I stare at my phone, making sure the phone call is definitely over. I put it down like it's got germs. He will pay for this, I'll make sure of it.

"Great job, kiddo. We're working on the trace now. Excuse me for a moment." As he walks out of the room, I know it's to leave us so we can talk this through.

There's no talking, though.

Mason needs to remind me that I'm all his. He walks straight to me, wrapping me in his arms and kissing me like it's the last kiss on earth. My fear, anger, and confusion has me joining him in the intensity.

I pull back briefly.

"You were never going to be his. Ever." He takes me again, and I'm just melting into him. This is what I love about him. He never holds back. I'll never wonder how he's feeling.

"Not for one second did I ever want him. Only you, always only you." Laying my head on his shoulder, we just breathe each other in. Slowly we part slightly.

"Are you going to be able to do this, Mason? I mean, keep control plus be able to concentrate on flying while I'm in the cabin with Tyson?"

"And Franco!" he forcefully reminds me.

"Yes, and Franco. But are you going to be able to do this? I know you're already holding back from leaving the house right now, finding him, and giving him what he deserves."

"Damn right, I'm ready to kill him. I'm a better man than him, though, Paige. I will get him, and it will be through all the right channels. Then one day I'll visit him in jail, showing him pictures of my wife, pregnant with our child and tell him what a fantastic life we're living. Because if I can't kill him, I will want to torture him."

"A wife and child, congratulations. I'm sure you'll be very happy," I say, trying to pull away a little farther.

"We will be very happy, you, me, and our family. I'm going to marry you one day, Paige. You can be sure of that."

"Wow, what a romantic proposal."

"It's not a proposal. You'll know when it is. I meant it when I said you're my forever girl."

"Mason, you have me, just breathe and let's get through this shit. Then we can relax and start living a normal life as boyfriend and girlfriend. You know, like normal people do. Where they actually slowly build a relationship."

"Mmm, you keep thinking that. In the meantime, let's bury this little shit."

"Not literally, I hope."

"Again, you keep thinking that." We both start to laugh a little. It's one of those situations where it's so stressful you need to laugh to release some tension.

I know deep down Mason would never do any of the things he said. His bark is worse than his bite. But I also know that if it did come to it, he would lay down his life for me. For that reason, among others, I know he is my forever man too.

"Right, are you two on the same page now? Can we get a plan of attack happening?" Franco walks in, sitting down at this desk again and looking at us like children.

"Yes," we both murmur at the same time. Mason gives me a wink, holding my hand and sitting down together.

"Okay then, we have a trace on the tower the call was pinging off and a rough location. It's not near Tyson's house, but that doesn't mean anything. What we need to do is wait until Monday, and when we start getting notices of his logging in and where the location is, we can start matching things and piecing it all together." We all nod and start working out what the logistics of next week will be and how we will continue to push Tyson into a corner until we have him.

We spend another hour making sure we have everything covered and everyone is happy with it. Finally, it's time to leave and try to forget about this and just enjoy the weekend. I have so much work I should be doing, but I just don't feel like it. All I want to do is be with Mason and pretend I'm not a CEO but just his girlfriend who has a nine-to-five job that I leave at work when I walk out on a Friday afternoon.

Back in the car, Mason won't tell me where we're heading. All he says is it's a surprise and it'll make me smile. When I try to joke that it involves wearing no clothes, he bursts out laughing and says that would be very awkward for me. For others, there would be a lot of cheering. That just confuses me totally.

We made a deal that when we got in the car there was to be no work talk and Tyson's name wasn't to be mentioned. It doesn't mean I'm not still thinking about it. It's hard not to. I'm sure Mason is too. We're both just hiding it.

I was busy asking Mason how he's going to cope around Tyson, while the whole time I have no idea how I'm going to do this. I can't show any emotion or drop any hints, and I have to pretend to trust him, and the whole time still try to run my business so it's not suffering while I'm caught up with all this.

If I can get through Monday, then maybe it'll get easier from there. That's if Tyson survives the day around Mason.

This whole thing is shit. There is no other way to describe it.

The one person I want to tell is my father, and I can't because I can't risk his health.

When he finally finds out, my life will be hell.

And then there will be the Mason bombshell.

Fuck, that day is going to suck!

16

Mason

Her eyes are wide and looking around trying to work out where we are. I can put her out of her misery, but I won't. It's too much fun watching her. The building doesn't have many markings on it. The families who are supported by the *End of the Cycle* program are proud people. They don't need to have it rubbed in their faces with big bold signs every time they walk through the door, that they need help. It takes enough courage to ask for help. That should be the hardest step. After that, this place should just feel like home and like we're all one big family.

Opening her door, I can't help but laugh.

"Paige, nothing in this building is going to bite you. I promise. Don't look so terrified."

"Okay, let me see, my life at the moment is all about someone wanting to destroy me. Now you want me to walk into a building, without a clue what or who is in there." There's an element of fear in her eyes.

"Yes, baby, it's called trust. Do you trust me to keep you safe?" I ask, holding both her hands in mine.

"Totally!" she answers passionately.

"Then what are you worrying about?" Putting my arm around her shoulders, we start walking to the front door. "I promise you will love this."

The moment we're through the door, the noise of the kids starts to fill the air, laughing, chatting, and of course some yelling. That would be from my department, the basketball court. We continue until just inside the gym door and the court is in front of us. Full of my kids in the middle of a game.

"Mason?" I can tell she's confused, but the fear has disappeared.

"Welcome to *End of the Cycle* charity foundation. I'm a mentor here for the kids and some parents. I started volunteering here to help my PTSD and to see if I could give something to the community. To make a difference. The joy they have given me in return far outweighs anything I've done. The role of the charity is to help parents and kids break the poverty cycle. We do it by helping the parents to gain employment or upskill to get better jobs. We give them financial counselling and any other help they may need. For the kids, we help them with schooling, mentor them in life skills, and just try to keep them from making bad decisions. Giving them a choice, allowing them to dream." I know I sound like I'm selling her the charity, but it's something I'm very proud of and passionate about.

"I had no idea. Mason, this is amazing. I'm so proud that you're here to help all these people. More than you know. I don't know where my mom came from or why she gave me up, or my birth father for that matter. Her choice can't have been easy. So, to help people who need you, it speaks volumes about the kind of man you really are. That super tough alpha male you try to show everyone doesn't fool me. I know deep down what a huge kind heart you have." Standing on her tippy toes, she kisses me as her hands hang on around my neck. I'm thankful today she chose to dress casual in jeans, sneakers, and a tight fitted shirt. Paige on her tippy toes in her usual attire in front of a group of teenage boys would cause even more problems than I've already got.

A chorus of wolf whistles and catcalls ring out across the court. I should have warned her. Giggling to herself, she knows she just created a spectacle and I'm about to be roasted for it.

"Ready to face the music?" Kissing her forehead, I turn and walk with my arm around her towards the game that is now stopped because of us.

"What's your problem? Haven't you seen a man kiss his girlfriend before?" They all start laughing and carrying on.

"We're more shocked you even have a girlfriend," one of the boys yells.

"Or why such a pretty lady would go out with you," another continues, which of course creates another uproar.

"Well, aren't you all comedians today. Now if you're finished being smartasses, I'd like to introduce you to my beautiful girlfriend, Paige. Be nice to her or you answer to me, alright? Now, who's winning?"

"Leroy's team as per usual," one of the girls says from the back of the crowd.

"Is that right? Well, maybe we need to do something about that. You okay, baby?" I look back at Paige and see the biggest smile on her face.

"Absolutely."

"But that makes the teams uneven, then you're cheating." Leroy dribbles the ball in front of me with his cheeky grin.

"I'll even up the numbers. Leroy, can I join your team?" Paige steps forward towards him, steals the ball from him and takes off across the court with it. Heading towards the basket, she shoots the ball and sinks it perfectly, nothing but net.

Holy. Fucking. Shit.

"Hell yeah, you can be on my team." Leroy starts cheering as he heads off towards Paige who's looking all innocent.

"Wait just a minute. Ms. Ellen, get your cute ass over here. Since when have you been able to play basketball like that?" I yell out at her.

"Since high school, Captain White." She pokes her tongue out as she stands next to Leroy, arms folded, leaning like she's trying to look cool.

"What's wrong, Mason, scared your girlfriend is better than you?" Leroy knows exactly what he's doing.

"Oh, not at all. Bring it on, baby. This is going to be good. We are taking you down." All the kids are cheering and clapping.

Both teams are in a huddle, talking tactics or really just trying to psych the other team out.

"Okay, this is what we're going to do. Leave Paige to me, there is no way she's getting past me. You guys be ready for the pass once I get the ball off her. No matter what, we just have to get as many hoops as we can and take that cocky grin off Leroy and Paige's face. Got it, team?" Placing our hands in the middle, the cheer goes up and we take to the court.

"Well, well, well, look who we have here." I stand in front of Paige, bouncing around like an idiot.

"What's your problem, Mason, scared you'll get shown up by a girl?" She tries to look all tough, flexing her biceps.

"Pfft, not at all, Tiger. Bring it on." I grab her around the waist, lifting her off the ground and planting a kiss on her lips. Placing her down, she's giggling like one of the kids on the team.

"Hey, boss man, get your hands off my player, that's cheating," Leroy yells out to me.

I turn to see him with the ball, dribbling towards me.

"That's what happens when I'm so handsome, she can't keep her hands off me. What's your excuse for acting like a girl?" With the banter as distraction, I make a steal and have the ball, running away from both of them down the court and passing to one of the young girls on my team who shoots it perfectly through the hoop.

"Like you were saying, tough guy?" I taunt, pointing at Leroy as I'm high-fiving my teammate.

"Oh, I see how it is," Paige interjects. "Dirty tactics are your game, are they, Captain? Well, bring it. I've got plenty of those up my sleeve too." Paige wiggles her ass at me, and it's game on.

The points are coming, thick and fast, the game going from end to end. The crowd is getting bigger, and I think every person who's at the center is now in the stands and has picked a side to cheer for.

At one stage, Paige is trying to get past me and we're dancing around each other. Her back to my front. She dribbles the ball with one hand and tries to push into me with her ass to get past. I'm laughing at how our bodies are rubbing together until she slides her free hand behind her body and grabs my cock, giving it a squeeze.

Catching me totally off guard, I jump backwards. Laughing, she's past me and down the court performing a pretty perfect jump shot.

How did I get so lucky?

As I'm running down the court, the buzzer goes off and we've lost by one point. Shit, I'm going to pay for this. Not stopping, I grab her and lift her over my shoulder, smacking her ass and carrying her off the court. The kids are going crazy and the joy in the room is so electric.

Slowly lowering her down, I hug her and quietly whisper in her ear, "You thought you were already going to be punished. You have no idea what's in store for you tonight, my little cheating Tiger. Revenge is sweet." We break apart, and the kids are chanting that Paige is the new champion of the court.

I get overrun with Paige's teammates lifting her on their shoulders, and she's paraded around the court like some superhero.

"Same time next week, Ms. Ellen, in this same place, there's a rematch and we'll beat your cheating ass. You can count on that! Won't we, team!" My kids are all cheering and high-fiving me.

Paige winks at me as she's carried away like a Greek goddess.

After she's basked in her glory of being the hero, we're all sitting in the mess room, chatting while we grab an afternoon snack, dissecting the game and complaining about how Leroy and Paige only won because they cheated.

"How did we cheat?" Leroy asks innocently

"Yeah, Mason, tell the kids how we cheated." My Tiger thinks she's hilarious.

"Do you really want me to share that, Paige, hmmm?" The kids start to work out it's something a bit naughty. There's laughing and cheering. I grab her and land a kiss on her lips, then lean to her ear. "Tonight, you pay for that, baby." Her giggle tells me she is more than happy to pay up.

"Leroy, tell me, did you hear back from the charity yet? Will they pay your airfare?" I put my hand on his shoulder to give him the confidence to talk about it in front of Paige.

His smile drops a little. "They said they'll pay for half. I have to come up with the other half. I'm not sure I can do that, but I'm trying to find a second job somewhere."

"Buddy, I told you, if they wouldn't pay it then I would. You are flying to that interview. You'll be giving this scholarship your best shot. Why didn't you just tell me?"

"I can't take your money. It's not right, Mason."

"Leroy, you didn't ask, I offered a gift. You have the drive to become a pilot, and I will do everything in my power to help you get there." Putting my arm around his shoulder, I pull him to me.

"Leroy, what sort of interview is it?" Paige is looking at him with eyes full of tenderness and compassion. I'm so glad she didn't ask about the money. She's thoughtful enough to know it's a tough subject.

"I want to become a rescue helicopter pilot. Mason helped me research and apply for some scholarships to different training facilities. I have an interview for one in California, but I need to fly out there at my own expense. My parents don't have the money, so Mason suggested we ask the foundation. They can give me half, so I need to work to find the rest. I'm just not sure I have enough time to get it. It's next week." His head drops slightly, feeling the disappointment.

"Leroy, you are going, I'm paying, and we need to start preparing for the interview." This kid has come such a long way. Passion like that is what makes a great rescue pilot.

"I have a better solution." Paige looks at me with a subtle wink. "Mason, you know how we were flying for that meeting in California in two weeks' time. Why don't I see if I can move it forward, and Leroy just comes on the flight with us? You can take him to the interview while I'm working, and then we fly home after that. Will that work for you two?" Her beautiful voice, so calm like nothing is a problem like she's just driving a car five minutes across town to drop him off somewhere.

Leroy's jaw is on the table, and I can see he's trying to understand what she's saying. He doesn't understand she's my boss and the plane's a private jet.

I know there are no planned trip to California. She thinks I hide a big heart, but this woman is nothing like the world sees her. Her heart is beautiful and so giving.

"Leroy, Paige is my boss. She owns the private jet I fly every day. So, what do you say, want to take a trip in her jet, with the best pilot ever flying? You can sit up in the cockpit with me and learn a few things." The light shining in his eyes is an image I will never forget. To know someone cares about him and wants to help. Yes, he's over the moon about it all. But it's more that Paige wants to help him, someone who doesn't even know him.

"I...I don't...Oh God, thank you. I just... Man. I can't even compute this. You own a plane, like a big plane, like a fancy plane." His words are all jumbled, and he's like a five-year-old vibrating with excitement.

"Yes, Leroy. I do. I have been very blessed and worked hard. Mason flies me all over the country to meetings I need to attend. I'm lucky to have such a great pilot. He keeps me safe, and he doesn't look too bad in a uniform either. Just think about how the girls are going to go crazy over you in a flight suit. Take it from me, get yourself some aviator sunglasses. You'll thank me later."

He's blushing, and I thump him lightly on the arm.

"She's right about the glasses, man, gets them every time." We all start laughing.

"Paige, I don't know what to say, I can work to pay you back."

"Leroy, you owe me nothing. We're flying there anyway, there are spare seats, so why not fill up the plane. It doesn't change the cost of the flight that I'm paying for anyway. Now let's talk about this interview and what you need to do. Mason can help you with all the technical parts, but I might know a thing or two about the interview process and what I look for when I hire someone. We also need to get you an outfit. Fly boy here is hopeless, so why don't we organize for my guys to give Mason some suits in your size. He can take them to you and help you pick one. Then we'll be organized for Friday. It is on Friday, right?"

"Yes, ma'am. Friday this week. My school gave me the day off if I could get myself there."

"Well, you can tell them it's all organized and you won't be at school. Now we need to make sure it's okay with your parents. I mean, I'm not sure how I would feel about some random weirdo flying my son across the country."

I don't even know what to say to her. Her kindness has floored me. Leroy has no idea what she's doing for him. The time, the money just to get him to the interview. All just because she cares. My love for her is absolute, but this just took it to the next level if that was even possible. One day, when Leroy is graduating, I'll explain to him how much this woman did for him.

We need to get out of here. I desperately want some alone time with her. I want to say just to enjoy each other's company, but we both know that's not the only reason. She needs to know how much it means to me, what she's doing.

As I stand and pull her with me, her grin tells me she's reading my body language perfectly.

"Buddy, we have to get going. Talk to your parents. I'll give them a call tomorrow and we can sort out some details. In the meantime, I want you to go home and research every single fact you can find on this company, down to what color underwear you need to wear as part of the uniform, understand me?"

Paige slaps my arm. "Don't be ridiculous. Yes, Leroy, research everything you can find. Scrap the underwear idea, though, Mason's being a dick."

I hold my chest, mocking her. "Me? How can you even insinuate that? I'm an angel and so perfect."

Pretending to cough, Paige puts her arm around Leroy and under her breath and in the middle of the cough, tries to mask her reply. *Cough.* "Bullshit." *Cough.*

"Get over here, woman, before I make you pay for that comment."

Leroy is laughing at our banter. I'm not sure he's seen anything like it before.

"Mmm, whatever." She turns and kisses Leroy on the cheek. "Study hard and we'll talk soon. Now, come on, my supposed perfect angel. Let's head home."

Walking out of the room, all the kids start to call out their goodbyes to both of us, which I can tell makes Paige happy. I don't say anything until we make it to the Jeep. I open the door so she can jump in. Passing her the seatbelt, I close the door and walk around to my side.

When I turn to look at her, she's staring at me, smiling.

"What?" I ask, starting the engine and heading for the road.

"Why didn't you tell me what you do here? What an amazing gift you give to kids like Leroy." Her hand lands on my thigh.

"Baby, I just give up my time. What you offered Leroy today is more than I could ever give him. We both know there was never a California meeting planned. We don't even normally fly to California. Let's talk about that for a moment, shall we?"

Blushing a little, she turns to look out the window.

"Mason, can you introduce me to the organizers of the foundation, please? I would like to get involved like you do. I don't want to just throw money at them, which I could easily do and then walk away. I can see what a difference you're making in these kids' lives. You see it in their eyes, what it means just to have you turning up for them. Every kid on that court today thinks the world of you. With good reason. I want that too. I want to give back. Life handed me a pretty good deal with where I ended up. But it could have been so different. I know that and never take it for granted. This is a perfect way for me to show how grateful I am in life. Plus, I get to do it alongside you. What more can anyone ask for?"

"Baby, I would love you to help me. You have so much to give. Not only in knowledge but in understanding of life. At the end of the day, all these kids and families need is to know someone cares and doesn't think they're a lost cause. It's not a choice to be where they are, and instead they are choosing to try to change that. We're the help they need to get there."

Turning from looking at where I'm driving, I see Paige has tears running down her cheeks. I try to lighten the moment. "Baby, I thought you said you don't cry. You know what it does to me to see your tears."

215

"It's your fault. Before I met you, I don't think I'd cried since I was a teenager. When Shorten Olsen told everyone I kiss like a fish." She's laughing, but I feel like I just want to find Shorten Olsen and make him pay for that.

"Well, from plenty of firsthand experience, I can tell the world he was very wrong. Bad luck, Shorten, you missed out on the best woman in the world at kissing. Especially when those lips are wrapped around my cock giving me special kisses. We know who the fish was, and it wasn't you." Stopping at the traffic lights, I lean over and kiss her, swiping away the tears.

"Thank you." Her smile is enough to let me know she's fine.

Both Paige and I jump a little at the phone ringing though the Bluetooth. Seeing it's Grayson, I know what he's calling for.

"Hey, Gray. I'm just in the car with Paige."

"Hi to both of you. I've got Tilly with me too on speaker. You know why we're calling, don't you?"

"Yep, and I can assure you I'm great. The best I've been in a very long time. Paige and I had a really big talk, she knows everything now. But thanks for checking. I can always count on you, buddy."

"Damn straight you can." Gray is always sure to let me know that he's there for me.

"Paige, how are you? That was intense last night, and I'm sure it got worse when you got home." Tilly's soft voice comes through the phone speaker.

"It was a big night, that's for sure, but we made it through it. Thank you for messaging Mason. I was feeling threatened just before he arrived. All good now." I can tell Paige doesn't want to dwell on it too long. "What are you two up to today?"

"Anytime Paige, I've got your back," Tilly replies.

"We've just been out walking Memphis, Gray's dog. You'll have to meet him. He's so adorable. Actually, I should say our dog. I think he loves me more than Gray, now."

"That's harsh! Memphis knows who his boss is. Well, most of the time," Gray objects.

"Okay, you just keep telling yourself that." Tilly starts laughing which sets us all off.

"How about you guys. What exciting things has Saturday brought you?" If only Tilly knew the half of it.

"Mason just took me to the foundation, and we met the kids. What an awesome place that is. I had the best time. Even managed to beat him in a basketball game." She looks at me, very proud of herself.

"Hang on, what did you say? Mason, is that right? You got beaten by your girl in a game of basketball? I'm not sure you can be part of our boy pack anymore. We might have to take your man card off you."

"Fuck off, Gray. Next time we play I'm bringing Paige and she's on my team. Then let's see what you say. She's like the ultimate pool shark. You wait," I tell him while the girls are laughing at me.

"Whatever" Gray says, "I'll wait to make judgement on the man card. We're about to take Daisy for an ice cream and play in the park. Want to meet us there?"

Looking across at Paige, I see the same look there that I have inside. "Thanks for the offer, but we're heading home. We have a few things to do there."

"I bet you do," he says. Tilly giggles.

"Do you want details?"

They both scream the answer at the same time. "No!"

"Mason, you are shocking. Too much of an oversharer at times." Paige says, now running her hand up the inside of my leg, watching me squirm, and I try not to make a sound every time she runs over the top of cock.

"No way. Tate takes the prize for that one. You just wait. Sometimes we just shove a sock in him," Gray replies as my mouth is hanging open while Paige is now stroking me through my pants. Thank god I can see the building ahead, and I head to the garage to park the jeep.

"We're home now, gotta run. Bye, guys."

"Don't get that cock caught in the elevator door in your hurry to get it out, Mas. See you both soon," Gray calls through the phone.

Hitting the end button on the call, Paige is now rubbing nice and firm.

"You going to continue that upstairs, or am I lying back right here and letting you ride me until your screams echo around the garage?"

"Oh, I intend to continue this but with my mouth and not here. I'm not sure you want my neighbors seeing me naked and on my knees in front of you while you fuck my mouth... nice and... hard." Her voice is sexy as sin coming out of her mouth.

"Baby, there are two things you can guarantee. First, no one ever gets to see you naked except me!" My voice is almost a growl as she keeps stroking. "Secondly, I'll be fucking more than your mouth hard, Tiger." Taking her hand in mine, I kiss her palm. "Hold that thought until we make it upstairs. I have plans for you."

As she opens her door, I don't even wait for her to get out. Turning her to face me, I slip my hands around her ass, pulling her toward me. I lift her into my arms, her legs wrapping around my waist perfectly. I press her up against the side of the car, kissing her hard, and close the door. Letting her know the kind of afternoon she has in store.

Not letting her go, I continue my assault with my lips in the elevator while grinding into her.

"You created this problem, sweetheart, so now you feel the same tension I'm struggling with," I whisper in her ear. "One day, I am going to fuck you against this mirror. Taking you from the ground floor to screaming an orgasm by your penthouse. You won't have time to even breathe." I nibble on her ear then start down her neck, listening to her tiny whimpers.

"Would you like that, Paige? The risk of being caught, the chance there's someone watching the security feed. Seeing you falling apart, just for me." My cock is getting to the point where I'm about to lose control.

"Oh god yes!" The words fall from her on the end of a moan.

"That's it, baby, feel everything you're doing to me. You have no idea all the bad things I want to do to you."

"Bad." She shivers as I slide one hand down the back of her pants.

"Yes, bad, but oh so good. I like naughty little girls, and you, Paige, have been very naughty today." Hearing the elevator slow, I know it's close. Both the penthouse and her orgasm. But she doesn't get to find that peak just yet.

"Please, Mason, please." She continues to grind hard against me as I stop. She's trying to get that last little stimulation she needs.

The elevator doors open and I take just one step out where I stop to make her wait that little bit longer.

"Not yet. You're being punished for being so shameless today. You need to be begging before I let you come and find that release you're chasing. Now walk over to the windows and strip naked, giving me a show while you drop to your knees. Remember, I'm the boss." Slowly letting her slide down my body, both of us enjoy a kiss full of heat. Paige pulls back, slowly turning, as we both look up at the same time.

"No man will ever be the boss of my Paige. Not in my lifetime."

"Daddy!" Paige jumps in shock and pure embarrassment to what he's just heard and seen. Me on the other hand know I'm totally fucked. First impressions are priceless, and this one will be worth a million dollars in that rating.

With her frozen, I'm not backing down one bit. Pulling her back into my body, I snake one arm around her waist and lean to her ear.

"Breathe, baby, I've got this." I can feel her body shaking.

Walking us both forward together, I put my hand out to shake Mr. Ellen's.

"Hello, sir, I'm Mason White, Paige's boyfriend. I've heard a lot about you. Paige didn't want to overwhelm you while you were sick, but we were going to come and have me meet you in the next few days if you were well enough."

"You expect me to believe that, Paige? I may be old, but I'm not stupid. How long have you been carrying on like a harlot and soiling your image with this disgusting man? Why in god's name would you let him speak to you like that."

I don't give a fuck who he is, no one speaks about Paige like that.

"Mr. Ellen, I don't care what you think of me and I don't care who you are. Nothing gives you the right to speak to Paige like you just did. This woman beside me is the kindest, most loving and genuine woman I know. So, I suggest you apologize or plan on leaving now."

Paige's body still quivering, she's just staring at him and can't speak.

"You can't kick me out of my own building, young man. Nice try." Her father tries to stand tall and exert his authority.

"No, but I can kick you out of my girlfriend's home and the woman I'm going to marry. So, would you like to try that again or shall we start escorting you to the elevator."

Fuck him. I'm not backing down, the old bastard.

"Married, pfft. Paige will never marry. She is married to the business. That was decided years ago. Isn't that right, Paige?"

Her mouth is moving but there's nothing coming out.

Then it happens.

She pulls away and heads towards her father.

The only man who will compete for her heart.

17

Paige

This is what I've needed all day.

Mason to take me and make me forget everything that's happening around us and stopping me from thinking. Being in his arms, listening to him talk dirty is my stress release. I don't know what I had before him, but nothing can compare to my Magic Man.

Fuck, looking up and seeing my father and his voice has me shivering. Hearing him breaks any fun that was about to happen.

Seeing my father standing in front of us, his look of disapproval and disappointment, and then the words he says, feels like my world is crumbling around me. Never did I ever think I would hear my father describe me as a prostitute. My heart feels like a knife is being pushed into it each time he speaks. I'm frozen and don't know how to function.

Mason takes control. I've never felt so loved. To have a man stand up to my father without hesitation is truly the best feeling. My father is intimidating, but Mason does not back down. He somehow still speaks to him respectfully, not taking any crap but not disregarding that this is still my father.

Then... the final blow to my heart. I knew this wouldn't be easy, but I never thought it would be this hard to hear.

"Married, pfft. Paige will never marry. She is married to the business. That was decided years ago. Isn't that right, Paige?" My father is waiting for an answer. I know I need to dig deep and use the strength that has always been there; I've just never needed it until now.

Walking away from Mason, I feel the loss of his strength. I see the doubt settling in as he's wondering why I'm walking away from him.

I need to do this on my own.

It's been a long time coming.

"Daddy. We need to talk about this. Why are you here?" Leaning in, I kiss him on the cheek.

"Paige, answer the question." I was hoping to do this softly, but he's pushing to make sure that doesn't happen.

"You want my answer? Just like that! No talking or explanation." I stand in front of him, my shoulders back.

"There should be no hesitation on the answer, Paige. We have always known what your life would be."

"No, Daddy, *you* knew what my life would be. You want my answer? You're right, it needs no thought." I take a deep breath and relax my shoulders. This is my life. I need to live it my way. "I'm marrying Mason. Not a doubt in my mind. I love him with a love I've never known. One day we will walk down the aisle in a big white wedding, like little princess girls dream of. We may even have a child or two. Who knows, but what I do know is that this is my decision. Not yours, not Mason's, but mine. I choose to marry the man I love, not be married to my work. That doesn't mean anything has to change with the business, nor will it. So, there's your answer, Daddy. Are you happy now that you pushed when you should have listened and worked through this? There is so much more to tell you; now you get to choose whether or not you will stop being stubborn and sit here and listen, if you will bother to get to know Mason like I do."

This is like being in a boardroom. My nerves are going crazy on the inside, yet on the outside I'm not giving anything away. It's like a standoff. Neither of us is prepared to give in. My father looks a little shocked at everything I've just said and the fact that I haven't backed down yet.

I reach out the olive branch.

"Please, Daddy, you need to hear what I have to say. Then if you still don't like it, you can leave and start whatever actions you need to remove me from the company."

Storming to the table, he mumbles to himself under his breath, "That's not happening. No one run's my company except my daughter. So, we need to sort this farce quickly." Taking his seat, he clasps his hands together on the table.

Shit, I'm not prepared for this. I wanted time to get straight what I wanted to say. He has taken that choice away from me.

Feeling Mason's hand on my lower back, a sense of calm comes over me.

"You've got this, baby, I'm here with you the whole way." His quiet whisper is enough to let me know I'm not alone. Although determined to do this myself, it's good to know he has my back.

I sit down opposite my father in the chair Mason pulls out for me.

"Daddy, I will always love you more than anything, and I'm so eternally grateful for you taking care of me. Being my father and giving me the gift of being your daughter. No matter what happens in my life, that will never change." I take a little breath.

"I know it's only ever been the two of us. You shared your love and all the knowledge and skills I needed to be your successor. I've loved every minute of it. But there is a part of me that yearns for more. The last few weeks with Mason have shown me a life I never knew. Laughter, fun, being crazy and reckless but in a good way."

"Hmmm," he growls at the thought of me being crazy and reckless.

"I know you have wanted only the best for me all my life and made my decisions for me. To protect me. I'm not that little girl anymore. I don't need you to make my decisions. I will always want you there for advice and guidance, but I've got this, Daddy. This life thing, I can do it on my own."

"You make your own decisions and look what happens," he snarls. "You have a boyfriend who wants to boss you around and punish you. He better not be a man like that movie that everyone talked about. You know, with that Grey man." Both Mason and I burst out laughing. I can't help myself. My dad looks angry at our reaction, but I can't help it. I quickly get myself back under control.

"No, Daddy, Mason is nothing like that. I'm also concerned why an eighty-one-year-old man knows anything about BDSM, but let's leave that alone, shall we." Mason is choking next to me. "Mason is my pilot, that's how we met."

"Oh, good lord, so he's after your money. Well, bad luck, I have it all tied up."

"Not one single dollar. I don't need your money nor want any of it. I'm in love with your daughter, not her money," Mason booms. "I take offence to that, sir."

"That's enough, both of you." This is going to take forever if they keep butting in.

"He captains my plane and keeps me safe every time we are in the air. We've had a connection for many months, but we both tried to keep our distance because of the working environment. It just got too hard. We have a good relationship and need to be together."

I wait for a comment from him, but he stays quiet.

"Being with Mason does not affect my working life for one single moment. You can drop that line of thought before you even start. We are both professionals and can keep our work and personal lives separate."

"Gee, look how well that worked, keeping things separate, when you're here together like this. How separate did you keep it?"

"Oh, for god's sake, Daddy. You aren't even listening." My frustration is rising rapidly. Mason puts his hand on my leg under the table to help ground me.

"I'm listening, but all I'm hearing is waffling, Paige."

"Sir, with all due respect, this is really hard for Paige. What she's asking you to do is listen, not only to the words she's saying but also the ones she's not. Please let her finish." My heart leaps at the support he's giving me. He's not trying to step in but instead gives me the confidence and space to do this on my own.

"Daddy, what I'm telling you is I'm in love with Mason. I love my career and the company. I'm not giving any of them up. I can live a life and have them all. I know you don't think I can, but for the first time in my life, I'm making the decision on this. You don't control the company anymore. I do. You trusted me to run it, so you need to continue to do that." The look on his face is actually one of shock right now. He's not used to me laying down the rules.

"Paige," he says, his voice softening a little.

"I know you were never lucky enough to find your love, and you replaced that void with me. For that I'm grateful. But didn't you do all this so I would be happy?"

He nods.

"Well, Mason makes me so happy. He protects me and makes me feel safe and secure." I lean across the table to takes his hands in mine. "Do you think you can at least try to get to know Mason and see how amazing he is? Please, it's important to me." I see the moment his fight breaks a little, and my whole body feels the tension start to dissipate.

"Mr. Ellen, I love your daughter more than I ever thought it possible to love another person. I promise you right now that I will lay down my life to protect her, love her until the day I die, and try never to hurt her. What you heard as we came in was just a little fun between two adults who are madly in love, and with that comes..."

"Son, I'm struggling here, I suggest you don't finish that sentence. All I'm going to say to you is this. I'm not happy about it, but I will try to tolerate it, just for my Paige. But know this, I may be an old man. But if I find out you have hurt her in any way, I will kill you. Finishing my life in jail won't be a problem if it means I have killed the man who hurt my daughter."

Mason leans over the table to shake his hand.

"That's a deal, sir, and I totally respect that." They give each other the chin lift. Like a bro code.

"Oh my god! Daddy, you did not just say that. You can't go around threatening to kill people just because you're old. Seriously! I'm thirty-nine years old. I'm not a little girl anymore. Stop with the melodrama. Now, can I get you a drink so we can talk about what you're doing here on a Saturday afternoon unannounced?"

"Let me do that, baby. What can I get you, sir?" Mason stands and rests his hand on my shoulder.

"Jonathon, although I enjoy the sir, Paige will yell at me. Please call me Jonathon. I'll have a soda water with a wedge of lemon. The stupid doctor won't let me have alcohol yet. So damn Beth has locked up the liquor. That woman is so bossy."

Mason and I share a look. I know we're both thinking the same thing. Maybe he *has* known love.

"She's just looking after you, which I appreciate. I love Beth and will always be grateful how caring she is in everything she's done for us. You can't deny you love her too." His eyes pop a little wider, then mumbles something and ends the discussion as Mason places his drink in front of him.

"Can I get you a wine, baby?"

It's been a long day. After thinking for a moment, I say, "A vodka. Wine just won't cut it this afternoon." Smiling and rising his eyebrows, I know what he's thinking. A tipsy Paige is a fun Paige, or so he tells me.

Trying to keep the conversation light for a moment, we talk about the weather and how he's feeling. Once he's settled in then I want to know what is going on.

"Daddy, why did you come to see me this afternoon and not call? What's going on?" He sits back in his chair looking at us both. Back and forwards.

"One of the staff may have let it slip you have a man that you were seeing. I wanted to know what was going on. Why you hadn't told me. I don't like secrets, Paige, or finding out private things from the staff."

I can feel the hair on my neck raising.

"Who told you?"

"That doesn't matter now. I just would have liked to hear it from you."

"I'm sorry, it all happened quickly, and you were very sick. I knew initially when I told you that I would get the negative reaction, just like I did today. I couldn't risk that with your health."

My head is torn about sharing everything else that is happening in the company. I've always hated keeping things from him, but I just don't know if it's a risk to what we have already planned to try to catch out Tyson.

Mason reaches over and puts his arm around me. This man reads me like a book, even when my pages are blank.

"It's time, Paige, you need to share it all. He deserves to know."

I know he's right. Just how do you tell your father the business he has worked so hard to build is being attacked from the inside? It's going to be the biggest kick in the guts.

"God, Paige, don't tell me you're pregnant. I'm not sure how much more I can handle today. I'm an old man, or so you have reminded me."

Mason and I look at each other and smile a stupid grin. I mean, it's not impossible. I'm on the pill, but with the amount we've been having sex, there is only so much modern medicine can hold back.

"No, I can confirm that's not the case. Although it would be far better than what I'm about to tell you." His face drops a little, showing me how old he really is. While his mind is still active and strong, his body is starting to fail him.

"I don't like the sound of this."

"No, you won't, but just let me tell you everything before you let loose, okay?"

"I can't guarantee that, but I'll try."

I proceed to tell him the whole story and what we know so far. How Uncle Franco is involved and helping me with the investigation. That we made the decision together, not to tell him until he was strong enough to cope with it. True to his promise, he doesn't say anything. Just sits there showing all the emotions; anger, shock, hurt, and confusion. All of which I have been feeling from the moment I first found out.

"I know how you feel. It's eating me up alive too. I just don't understand why Tyson is doing this and why us?"

Finally, my father speaks in his calm and quiet voice. "I wish you had told me earlier, but I understand why you didn't. The hurt in my heart is intense. What have we ever done to him that deserves what he is doing to the company? I've always operated my business by not attacking others. Been ethical and never underhanded. I just don't understand." He looks every one of his eighty-one years, sitting at my table.

Mason walks away and pours him a small scotch. "No matter what the doctor said, I think this will do you more good than harm right now." Looking up at Mason, my father for the first time since we walked in really sees him. The kind man he is.

"Thank you, Mason, I think you may be right."

Taking a sip, he closes his eyes as it slides down his throat. I can tell he's struggling with everything that has happened today.

"Daddy, you have to promise me you won't talk to anyone about this or try to do anything. We are close to this plan being implemented so you need to leave it to us."

After another sip of his scotch, he looks across at me.

"Paige, I hate to admit this, but I have to let you handle this. I'm actually too old to cope with this. To digest it all and handle the stress." He laughs to himself. "I bet you never thought you would hear that from me, did you?"

My heart is in my throat. The worry I've had for the last few weeks while he was sick are finally coming true. My father is an old man. He needs to be cared for and enjoy his old age. Although he can still be part of the business on a general level, he can't be part of the stress that goes with it.

"I should be doing a happy dance that you are finally realizing your limits and letting me run things how I need to. But Daddy, you have always been part of every element of this business. I don't know how to do this without you." Until this minute, I didn't realize the fear of being completely on my own.

"I didn't raise you to be weak, Paige. You are a strong woman and the most accomplished and admired business owner I know. You don't need me, you haven't for the last ten years. It was me that needed you. I wasn't ready for the scrap pile or to feel useless. So, I kept pushing you to live a life that didn't allow anyone else into it, except me. I made you need me. I'm sorry, Paigey. That was wrong of me. Who am I to deny you love? Just watching Mason and you together, I know I need to step aside and let another man take the reins of being your man to lean on."

Tears are flowing fast down my cheeks again. This is becoming an annoying habit. Mason's arm is tight around me. I feel his love, and in my father's eyes I see his. With all the bad things that are happening, there is so much love around me, and I'm blessed in this life. Standing, I walk to my father and wrap my arms around him, hugging with all my might. One day he won't be able to hug me back, so I will cherish every day he still can.

"We will get them, Daddy. I promise. These bastards won't get away with it."

I hear Mason move behind me.

"I promise I will keep her safe through all this too, Jonathon. You have my word. I will kill him before I let him touch her."

My father laughs at Mason. "You did good, Paigey. He knows the most important asset in his life. You!"

"Damn straight she is."

As I pull away from Dad and stand, Mason wraps me into his arms, comforting me.

"Enough of this mushy stuff," I huff. "You're both supposed to be these hard-ass men, yet here you are making me cry. Time for a subject change." Giving myself space to breathe and collect my thoughts, I walk into the kitchen to get some water. Behind me, I can hear Mason talking to my father about sports. Finding out what he follows and who his favorite teams are.

Leaning on the counter, I take in everything that's just happened. I knew eventually he would accept a boyfriend. I forgot, though, that Mason—who can charm anyone instantly—would have my dad wrapped around his little finger within ten minutes.

Thank god. I don't know what I would've done if that hadn't happened.

Now to concentrate on catching Tyson and fixing this mess once and for all.

~

"Do you think your father will object to a wedding next week?"

"Not a chance, Mason. You haven't even proposed. Plus, I want the big white fairytale wedding. Not happening in a week."

I'm lying on his chest in bed late after my father finally left. It was like he knew we were going to have sex as soon as he left.

He was right.

He hung around for what seemed like forever.

We'd been wound up since we arrived at home, so as soon as the elevator door closed, Mason was on me. My hands were stripping him, while he was taking what he could from under my clothes.

We couldn't wait. Mason needed to fuck me and reinforce that he is my man. I needed to just feel him and nothing else. I just wanted to be taken away to that place where he makes my body sing.

"Why are you worrying what my father will want? You're not marrying my dad."

"Thank god, because it would be weird to be marrying Jonathon while I'm fucking his daughter." He's laughing at his own jokes again.

"Oh my god, what a visual that just gave me. Not one I ever want to see again. You need to give me something else to think about." I flutter my eyelids at him.

"The next thing you're thinking about is food. You need to feed me, woman. I need recharging, you drained every bit of energy out of me."

"Literally." I giggle.

"Yes, Tiger. Literally. Now, let's order some food, and then I can test out this bath of yours. With bubbles. It looked very inviting the last time I saw it," he says with a smirk.

"It wasn't the bath that was inviting to you. It was the drunk naked girl in it." I roll my eyes at him.

"Drunk? I didn't notice. I just thought she deliberately fell out of the bath to get my attention."

"Yep, let's go with that answer, shall we." Laughing, I reach for my phone.

"What do you feel like eating?" Opening the app, we scroll through the choices.

"I could really go for some pasta, you know, good energy food. I have a busy late night scheduled tonight." His hands slowly slide up the outside of my thigh.

"Hmm what makes you think that?" I pretend not to be affected by the sensation creeping up my legs.

"This."

Squealing, I drop my phone as he rolls on top of me, growling like an animal as he takes my breast in his mouth, and at the same time, his fingers are on my folds. He swipes one finger from bottom to top while I moan out load.

"You can't deny you don't want to play some more. You can try to trick me with your words, but your body never lies to me, Paige." What words, I can't even think.

"Mmm... play now, eat later," I mumble

"That's what I thought. I'll just use my reserve energy. I'm not missing out on another chance to hear you scream my name."

"Mason!" is already screaming from my mouth as he pinches my sensitive clit and sucks hard on my breast at the same time, making me combust into an instant orgasm racing through my body.

He may have the extra energy, but he's killing me with love tonight.

~

"Remind me again why you thought we were the right people to be shopping for suits for Leroy. You said you would get your guy to sort it out." Mason is grumbling about shopping on a Sunday.

"Yes, you are my guy. Plus, I wanted to personally pick it. It needs to be just right. Give the impression they're looking for. Someone who took the time to prepare and cares about the interview. But not too out there or expensive-looking that they don't think he deserves the scholarship."

"Sweetheart, you're overthinking this. Leroy will be happy if he just doesn't have to turn up in his jeans and hoodie. Now just pick one and let's get moving. Everyone is meeting for brunch and then to the park to give Gray's dog Memphis and Daisy have a run around and play while we all lay back and do nothing." He's looking at this watch.

"Is this what a normal Sunday is like for you?" I'm curious, still learning new things about him.

"Not all the time, but yes, most of the time Sunday is for just chilling out and getting together with friends or doing something for myself. You need to get used to this, Paige. I'm not letting you work on a Sunday unless it's urgent. Before you even say anything, I also get to determine what's urgent."

My hands go to my hips instantly.

"Let's get one thing straight. You will not tell me how to run my life or what is urgent or not in my business. I might want to change things in my life, but I make those decisions, not you. Remember the rule, you're the boss in the bedroom, mister, not the boardroom."

As I stare him down, his shoulders are shaking a little until he can't hold it in anymore. The laughter escapes as he puts his hands on mine and pulls them off my hips.

"Steady there, Tiger. Was just checking I hadn't completely fucked you into submission. I still want my feisty girl...most of the time." He kisses my forehead then steps back to the suit rack.

"You're an ass, you know that, right?" He turns his head to the side and winks at me and then keeps going. He's lucky I love him.

Although it was all a joke to him, I'm secretly glad I got to say my piece about my work. I don't want it to become an issue. I'm not stopping working as hard as I do, just choosing the times I'm working.

I must have been in my own little world when I feel his arms wrap around me.

"Paige, stop thinking. I know nothing is changing in your life. I know there are times work will come first. I'm a big boy, I can cope with that. I don't want you to change who you are because you're with me. I just want to make your life easier with me in it, not harder. Relax and take a breath." His lips land on mine, softly kissing me to take away any worry I was feeling.

"Argh, what was I doing again?" His kisses have a habit of doing that to me. Damn, Magic Man.

~

"Thank god that job is done. Remind me never to shop with you again." Mason is still complaining as we walk into the café for brunch with his friends. Before I even get close, a little girl comes running at us and launches into my arms. Which causes laughter from all around.

"Hello, Paige, I'm Daisy. Hannah is my mom and my dad is off fighting the bad guys. You are sitting next to me. Do you like pancakes? Because I love pancakes." She's not even drawing a breath.

"Um excuse me, where's my hug, kiddo? I'm the favorite around here, how come Paige got one first?" Mason ruffles her hair and leans in to kiss her cheek.

"Because she's the pretty lady and you're just a stinky boy." Her body wriggles in my arms, laughing at her joke. I can see why she and Mason get along.

"Besides, you're not the favorite. Memphis is." With that, she's squirming to get down and off across the café again.

"Well, Mason, beaten in the favorites ranking by a dog. Now, that's priceless," I lean up on my toes to whisper in his ear. "You'll always be top of my list, especially the one labelled sexy hot lover." I walk away to the table, leaving him there puffing his chest at his quiet compliment.

Men, it's so easy to make them happy.

The café must cringe when these guys walk in. There's no quiet brunch happening. Besides, we take up half the tables when we join them all together. It's funny how I've gone from meeting Mason to being included as part of his 'family.' It's not just the Fuckalicious Four in this family, although they like to think the world revolves around their egos. Having the girls' squad here too makes it one crazy bunch, everyone talking over the top of each other.

Normally I would hate this type of chaos.

But I've never been happier in my life.

Watching Daisy eating her pancakes is hilarious. At first, I didn't realize what she was doing. Then it all clicked when I felt something wet on my hand that was sitting on Mason's knee. Memphis is introducing himself with a lick on the hand. I've never had a pet, but this damn dog is so adorable. Loving him up under the table, Daisy then tells him to sit as she feeds him. Which he does straight away, and then she continues one mouthful for her, then one for Memphis. I'm not sure who this dog loves more, Grayson, Tilly, or Daisy.

Can't wait to see the two of them at the park in action. A small part of me is yearning to see Mason playing with this little girl and her puppy.

For the first time ever, I feel my ovaries twitching.

Goddammit.

That's a challenge I'm certainly not ready for.

18

Mason

"Say it again."

"Mason is the favorite fruncle." I can listen to Daisy giggle all day as I tickle her. That and when she calls me a fruncle. Her way of saying we're a friend that's like an uncle. It's so damn cute. Memphis is jumping around barking next to me, wanting to protect Daisy but also wanting to be part of the game.

"If she wets her pants from laughing so hard, Mason White, it's all your fault. You won't get ice cream either."

Daisy and I both stop and look at each other.

"Ice cream," we both squeal at once. I jump up and throw her on my back for a piggyback ride, and we gallop over to the picnic table.

"Ice cream, Mommy, we've been good. Haven't we, Fruncle Mason?" she shrieks, bouncing up and down on my back.

"Of course we have, kiddo. We are never naughty. So come on, Hannah, spill the beans. Where's the ice cream you've been hiding?" I'm standing next to Paige at the table who has this strange look in her eye. She's smiling, but it's just more than that.

"Yeah right, Mason," Grayson laughs at me. "Hannah just has the ice cream sitting around in the sun waiting to give you one when you're ready."

"Sounds like a good idea to me, what do you think, Daisy?" She's too busy trying to make me move her up and down like a horse ride.

I don't think she's listening, but she sure shows me. "You're so silly, Mason, they would melt if she just let them sit there. That's just dumb. Maybe you aren't my favorite anymore." Wriggling and sliding down my back, she's off over to Tate to see how she does there.

"Fruncle Tate is my favorite now because he isn't silly like you, Mason." Everyone is laughing at her except me.

"Well, that means Tate is the person who has to go and get the ice creams for everyone then. Because he's *so* special. He always says he's the awesome guy who gets all the women. So now he has you too, Daisy. He is super lucky. Now let's make a list of all the ice cream he needs to get. Fruncle Tate is so amazing, he's also paying for ice cream for everyone." We all cheer—except Tate, who's trying to give me the evil eye. Which of course just makes me laugh harder.

"How do you suppose I carry all this ice cream, genius?" Tate glares at me.

"I'm sure Bella will help you. Isn't that what interns get to do, be bossed around by their Doctor-in-Charge?" Tilly raises her eyebrows across at Bella who looks like she wants to kill her. Hmm, wonder what that's all about.

"Yeah, when we're in surgery. Out here he can go suck a d…"

"Bella!" Tilly, Gray, Hannah, and Paige all scream.

"Sorry, well, you know what I was saying," she grumbles.

"As long as it's not you sucking it, then there's no problem," Grayson pipes up, and all the boys are fist pumping.

"Yeah right." Fleur laughs. "Bella is not stooping that low. We are on the hunt for a very distinguished gentleman, not a hairy Neanderthal."

"Seriously, did you all leave home this morning deciding it was going to be pick-on-Tate day? I get enough of this shit at work."

Gray smacks his shoulder and says, "That's because you've pissed off half the staff, but at least the other half still think you're a nice guy."

"Mommy, Fruncle Tate said some naughty words," Daisy breaks into the conversation.

"Yes, he did, and his punishment is he gets to take you and Memphis for a walk over to the ice cream van and get us all an ice cream. Maybe you can go with him and help him," Hannah suggests, I'm sure to give herself five minutes of peace and quiet.

"Plus, Bella, because she nearly said dick when you yelled at her," Daisy says. Everyone stops dead and look at Daisy and Hannah. We don't know if we should laugh or try to stand still like statues with no expression

"Oh, Daisy Waisy," Tilly says, trying so hard to keep a straight face, "you are so funny. Of course Bella wasn't going to be naughty like Tate."

"Like hell she wasn't," Tate yells, and none of us can hold it in anymore. Including Hannah.

"Tate, seriously," Lex says, "I don't think you should ever become a father. Your children will know every swear word by the time they're three." Lex throws Memphis's ball at him, which has the dog going crazy.

"Won't be from me, more like their mother."

"What the..." Now it's my time to catch my words. "Got something you need to share with the group, Doctor?" I look at him, trying to watch any body language that will give me a hint.

"Nope. Now, what ice creams am I getting? And Bella, you're coming too. You got me in trouble."

Daisy is jumping up and down with Memphis dancing at her feet. As we give our orders to Tate for him to put in his phone, Bella is watching him the whole time. She's obviously not impressed with him for dragging her along. Although she's a far bit younger than all of us, Bella fits in perfectly. She's a little sister to us all. When Gray wasn't around to protect her, then it was up to one of us to step in. Pretty sure she has wanted to kill us all on multiple occasions growing up, but she also knows how much we care.

"Hey Bella, need help with controlling Tate at the ice cream shop? He throws tantrums when he doesn't get his way, if they don't have his favorite flavor," I call out to her to snap her out of whatever little thought she's lost in.

"I can handle Tate, let me assure you." Smiling at me, she takes Daisy's hand and is already heading across the park.

"What's the deal with those two?" Paige snuggles into my side and whispers in my ear.

"Before today, I would have said nothing. Now I'm not so sure. Bella is currently working under Tate for her rotation at the hospital. Maybe it's just a tough situation. Working for your almost brother." Paige smiles and looks a little skeptical at my answer. To be honest, I'm not fully believing it either.

After ice creams and plenty more banter, it's time to head home and spend the afternoon getting ready for tomorrow. I know my primary objective will be to keep Paige calm. It's going to be a tough day.

"Not sure I'll make basketball this Thursday. This week is a little busy, plus I'm prepping Leroy for his interview. So, you might have to find a substitute," I tell the boys as I'm putting all our trash in the bin.

"Not like we'll even notice you missing. Hey Bella, want to fill in for Mason? You'll be a better addition to the game anyway," Lex throws in.

"Better-looking," Tate mumbles under his breath.

"Depends if I'm stuck at the hospital," Bella replies before kissing Daisy.

"It's okay, we know the boss there, I'm sure he'll let you out for a lunch break. That's what he does to get to the basketball court."

"I'll see, I can't promise anything," Bella says as she's hugging Daisy goodbye.

Daisy comes towards us, a little slower this time. I think all the running around with Memphis has tired her out. Just what Hannah was praying for.

"Bye Fruncle Mason and bye Paige." Her little hands are raising for hug. "Is Paige going to be my Fraunty too like Tilly?" Her innocent little face looks with love at Paige, waiting for the answer along with a hug. It's one of her things. Daisy is big on hugs. Grayson told me it comes from her dad Trent being deployed overseas. She misses him and hugs make her feel loved and close to her special people.

"I have to wait and see, Daisy. Mason might not want to marry me. Maybe if we wish hard it might come true." Both of the girls look up at me with love in their eyes.

"Maybe soon, sweetheart, send a big wish up to the sky. Be good for Mommy, won't you?" I give her a big squeeze.

"I'm always good, well, most of the time. Bye." With that she moves onto the next Fruncle. Before Daisy came into my life, I hadn't really thought much about children. It's not that I didn't want them, I just never really thought about them. Now I know I want them. More than one. Today I've even been picturing Paige lying naked on our bed with a beautiful rounded stomach carrying our baby. If I didn't know before today, then that thought alone tells me she's the one for me.

Looking at Paige standing next to me, she looks a little taken aback.

"Baby, you don't need to waste a perfectly good wishe. There is no doubt we will be getting married. You just tell me when, and I'll be there in full uniform, glasses and all, if that's what you want." This brings a smile to her face.

"What about just the glasses and no uniform. That would be perfect."

"Oh yes, I'm sure the guests would love that. Especially your father." I sweep her into my arms and lift her off the ground.

"One day soon, baby, I'll be on my knee for you. So, you better start working out your answer. You're mine, and I'm not letting you go. Even if we aren't married, I don't care. Forever is our end date. Nothing is going to change that. Actually, living in sin does sound kind of hot." Loosening my grip, I let her slowly slide down my body until her mouth is level with mine. "Love you, Tiger, so damn much." As I kiss her lips, softly and gently, I find myself full of the sensations she brings me.

We break apart after hearing all the crap from the boys. We ignore them and still stand in our bubble.

"I didn't know love could be like this. Thank you, Mason, for opening my eyes to what I've been missing." I place her on the ground, taking her face in my hands as I kiss her forehead. Holding my lips there just that little bit longer, taking in all I'm feeling, I hope she's feeling it too.

"Can you two go find a room, or even a car? Seriously, is this what it's going to be like every time we're together?" Tate says, half laughing and half complaining.

"Absolutely, so get used to it!" Letting go of Paige, I run towards Tate.

"Do you want a kiss too, lover boy? Are you feeling jealous?" He's off running.

"Don't you dare come near me. I don't want your germs contaminating this fine manly specimen." Too busy watching me, he doesn't realize Gray and Lex have come around the front of him. They tackle him as he's passing, holding him down.

"Come on, lover boy, do you want some lessons on how it's done?" Making loud kissy noises, I lean down towards him.

"How old are you boys?" Tilly yells out "Stop picking on the little boy in the playground."

"But it's so easy, Miss Tilly," I call out.

"Mason, do not get Tate germs on those lips and expect to be allowed to kiss me again," Paige yells to me.

I laugh and play slap him on the cheek.

"Saved by the girls." Before I get to move, he's caught me off guard and I'm on the ground with him.

All four of us wrestling.

Yes, Tilly is right.

We are still kids at heart.

I hope that never changes.

~

Spending the day with the 'family' yesterday was just what Paige needed. What started as brunch dragged well into the afternoon. Then we picked up some takeout on the way home and sat on the floor in front of the television just watching some trashy movies.

Paige fell asleep in my arms for a while, and then we finished the night with the bubble bath and some soft and passionate sex. I wasn't expecting her to fall asleep as easily as she did. Maybe I wore her out.

I'm lying awake now as the dawn is breaking, just watching her breathe and looking so peaceful like she doesn't have a care in the world. That's what makes her successful. Her poker face, but more than that, her poker personality. The ability to have her personality show how calm she is when really on the inside she's freaking out.

No matter what occurs over the next few days, I'm not letting anything happen to her. I would rather sit in jail after I kill Tyson than let anything happen to her. I'm just not convinced he's working on his own. It seems too high-tech for Tyson, but then maybe it's all a big act. I'm usually good at reading people, and I just don't get that vibe from him. Yet all the fingers are pointing to him. Something seems a little off with Brian the VP for the company. Although he has offered to help her out, he didn't try very hard, only traveling once to take her place. The day I met him and flew him to a meeting, he looked at me with a suspicious eye. Then when he was heading to the town car at the airport, he kept looking back at me like he was worried I knew whatever he was feeling guilty for.

"I'm the one who's supposed to be stressed," she murmurs, still with her eyes closed.

"Morning, Tiger," I say, kissing her lips, cheeks, and finishing with the forehead.

"Morning, Magic Man." She pauses a moment. "You were successful." Her eyes slowly flutter open to see me.

"That's good to know. Do you want to fill me in, though, successful in what?" I run my hand over her hair and smooth it off her face.

"Fucking me to sleep. Literally." Laughing out loud, I pull her to me so she's lying on top of me.

"Happy to be of service. I aim to please." I softly kiss her lips. So soft and smooth and a taste I'll never get sick of.

"Mmm, well you pleased every muscle in my body, just so you know." Her hands slide up under my arms so she can hug me tight as she lays her head on my chest. "Today is going to be crappy, isn't it?"

"I'm not going to lie to you and say it's going to be all rainbows and unicorns. But you'll be fine and get through it. You're my Tiger. No one can touch you." My hands drop to her ass. "Except me, of course. I get to touch you everywhere."

"Something you take advantage of often, mister."

"Well, I can't have you thinking I don't love you. That would be devastating. I figure if I show you often then you won't forget." I'm trying to pass it off as a joke but what I'm saying is how I feel. I don't want to lose her now that I've found her.

"Stop being so sweet. If I have to channel my inner bitch today, it's a bit hard when you say things like that to make me melt."

"Baby, I want to use more than words to make you melt this morning." I kiss the top of her head softly.

"I know, but we can't. You make me all mushy after sex. How am I supposed to get into the car all boss-like with Tyson after that?" Lifting her head up to show me her big eyes, I can see she's now a little more awake than before.

"Because I'm not going to make love to you. I'm going to fuck you. Hard! Your adrenaline is going to be rushing so hard you won't even need coffee this morning. Now get on all fours on the bed facing the mirror. I want you to see what I'm doing to you. How hard I'm going to be pounding into you." She can feel the tingles on her body the more I talk. "Now, Paige! I don't have time for you to think about it. You will do as I ask." Her eyes light up as I take control over her emotions and her body.

She moves from on top of my body to the position I told her. On my knees behind her, I grab hold of her hips.

"This is going to be hard and fast. Just like you want it, isn't it, Paige?"

She moans as soon as I ask her. "God yes."

"First, we're going to make sure you're ready for me." Taking one hand, I slowly swipe through her wet pussy, and her back arches from the sensation.

"Does that feel nice, Paige?"

"Yes," she pants her reply.

"But we don't want nice this morning, do we?" I move my hand away from her clitoris that I've been circling nice and slowly, up onto her ass cheek.

"Fuck no." Her voice is starting to get more urgent.

"That's right, because I told you it would be hard, which means hot and dirty. Just like you're craving." I bring my hand down and spank her ass cheek.

Screaming out in pain and pleasure, I know she wants more.

"You like that don't you, Tiger. You want me in control. I'm the boss here, remember." Her skin against my hand makes that loud slap that has her trying to hold her place and not give anything away.

"Are you going to be a nice sweet lady today?"

"Yes," she moans.

Whack, I smack her again, her ass pinking up nicely.

"Wrong answer, Tiger. Who are you going to be today?"

"A bitch, a hard-ass bitch," she yells to make sure I understand.

"Yes, you are. You're going to think about this moment all day. When you're doubting who you are or need confidence, remember this." *Smack*. "Be the hard woman you are." *Smack*. "The one who is here on her knees taking this." Hearing her moan and pant, I sink my cock into her as far as I can.

"Mason," she screams. "Yes, Mason!"

"Take it, baby, you're tough, now take it."

Both my hands grip her hips as I'm pounding with my balls slapping against her skin each time. Feeling her clenching my cock, I know she's so close to letting go.

"Tell me. Who's the tough woman?" I'm holding back with everything I have. I can feel the orgasm coming, but I need to finish this.

"Me," she murmurs.

"Not good enough. You're not coming until I'm convinced. Who's the hard-ass boss?" I lean forward to get my arm around her.

"Me!" she screams as I pinch her nipple, and she explodes around my cock. I can't hold back any longer and let go, releasing inside her as I pound her three more times. Then slumping forward on to her back. I wrap my arms around her waist and roll us both on to our sides.

"Remember that today. You, Paige Ellen, are the same strong businesswoman you were before all this happened. Don't let them get to you. You've got this and I've got you."

"Thank you, it means the world."

We continue to lay wrapped in each other for a few moments, the comfort and calm what we both need.

The alarm on my phone breaks the silence, and we both groan, knowing that's the end of our tranquility.

"Sorry, baby, I need to do my weather checks. Why don't you shower, and I'll make you some breakfast," I ask, expecting her to say she's not hungry, her standard answer when she's stressed.

"That sounds great. Thank you. I'm starving, and I blame you for it. I need to refuel my body." She moves on to her back next to me then leans up and kisses me, with all the passion that she has. "I love you, Mason. For everything you are and for all you do for me."

She was complaining about making her melt before.

Fuck, woman, that just tugged on my heart.

Hard.

I need to break this seriousness and keep her on the upbeat.

"Thank the lord, finally she gets the idea of breakfast. Energy to get you through the day. If you're hungry, I'm making a feast. Now go and wash that ass with my nice piece of handprint artwork on it."

Groaning, she sits up on the bed. "The ego is back. I'm out of here. Get to the kitchen, slave." Waving her hand over her shoulder at me, she heads into the bathroom.

The next time I see that wiggling ass it will be walking up the stairs of my plane and flirting like crazy with me.

I can get used to this life.

Paige

I watch Mason get into the elevator to head to the airport, the doors closing. I can feel my anxiety start to rise. The look on his face was telling me he didn't want to leave me alone. But it's important we keep to the routine as much as possible. They all know he's my boyfriend now, but we still have to work like we normally would. Him at the airport doing his preflight checks and me in the car with Bent, Tyson, and Uncle Franco. Mason insisted that Franco meet me here, so we get into the car together. He doesn't want me alone with Tyson at all.

It's still early so I wander into my office to pass the time. Before Mason and all this fraud craziness, I never had a problem focusing. Already today it's difficult, and I haven't even left the apartment. Mason's words keep replaying in my head. *'You've got this, and I've got you.'* Most men would feel threatened by a woman who has a high-profile life and wealth. They would try to take over and assert power, jumping and overtaking my life. Mason just guides me, supports and makes sure I know he's always right beside me if I need him. Not once has he tried to take over. A huge reason to love him and his ego. Off in my Mason bubble, the chime on my phone makes me jump a little.

Franco has arrived downstairs and so has Bent. I need to get moving and meet him in the foyer. Grabbing my work bag, I stop for one last look in the mirror.

Pull the shoulders back, chin up, and smile like a normal workday. Forget everything that's going on. Wipe from my mind Friday night with Tyson.

I walk into the elevator, turn to the doors, and take a deep breath.

"I'm the hard-ass bitch. I've got this."

By the time I reach the foyer, walking out of the elevator, Paige the businesswoman is ready to go. Bring it on, boys.

"Morning, Franco. Hope you're ready for a fun week." I kiss him on the cheek and then walk out the open door he's holding for me.

"I can't wait to spend the week with you. Keeps me out of Aunt Veronica's hair." We keep walking towards the car, not saying any more. There's no need. Everything was sorted on Saturday, and the plans were gone over many times.

"Morning, Bent. Thank you." He's standing holding the car door.

"Morning, Ms. Ellen, Franco. You're traveling with us again today. I didn't realize. I could have picked you up." Sliding into the car, the hairs on my neck are standing up and my heart is beating fast. Sitting there holding my coffee is Tyson looking very sheepish.

"Yes, I'm going to be with Paige every day this week doing research," Franco replies to Bent as he sits next to me.

Tyson and I are still sitting and not saying a word.

Franco gives me a subtle nudge to snap me out of it. "Are you going to take your coffee, Paige, before it gets cold? We all know you hate cold coffee."

"Good morning, Tyson. Thank you." I reach out and he hands it over, not wanting to touch me in the slightest.

"Good morning, Ms. Ellen. You're welcome. I hope it's how you like it." He's trying to appear confident, but I can see he's a little nervous. I'm feeling the opposite. The longer I'm in the car, the more the anger is starting to build.

"I'm sure it will be. Now let's get working. I need the numbers on that shipment leaving tomorrow on the government contract. Also, can you get me the advertising budget on the new security chip? Plus, I need to see the revised contract for today's meeting." The best thing I can do if I'm nervous or angry is to work. If this fucktard is going to try to deceive me, he's got another thing coming. He is not going to have time to even think of ways to screw me, I'll have him working that hard.

"Umm okay, hold on a moment. I'll pull all that information and send it to your email for you to check." Giving me a confused look, he starts typing on his laptop, doing as I asked. We normally work in the car, just not quite like this where I'm throwing several things at him at once. Turning to Franco, he gives me a look telling me to calm down. I'm grinding my teeth trying not to say anything. I just want to let loose on what I think of him, as well as for everything that happened at the bar where he made me feel vulnerable.

No one has the right to make another person vulnerable in any way, shape, or form.

The hard-ass bitch definitely has kicked in now. I'm taking control.

While Tyson is working on his computer, I can see Franco watching his every move, while pretending to read the morning paper on his tablet. I need to work too. Besides trying to keep calm, I actually have a business to run. Opening my emails, I start replying and delegating work for the day to different people. The information from Tyson is popping up on my screen, and I open the order for the shipment going out tomorrow night. So far, it's still sitting at the correct order quantities and value.

Franco tries to break the tension in the car and starts asking questions of Bent and his role in the company.

"My job is simple. To be ready to drive Ms. Ellen anywhere she needs me to. She calls, I come. It's that simple. I mean, she is a very wealthy woman, so that's how it works in her world. She works while I drive," Bent replies. His answer intrigues me a little. Referring to me as wealthy. I've never treated him like I'm any different than he is. I must admit, it hurts a little that's how he thinks of me.

"Oh, I know how busy she is," Franco chuckles, "never gets time to visit us anymore. I have to come to work to spend time with her," he jokes around, trying to keep it light. "What do you do while you're waiting for her? Like today, while we fly off for meetings?"

"When you're away on the jet, I'll go and get a gym session in. Get the car detailed. Things like that. I'm always done before I'm needed just in case you get back early. I like to play games, so I've usually got my computer or tablet to amuse myself."

"You must get bored at times?" Franco asks.

"No, it's okay, the games keep me distracted."

Not even thinking as we pull into the airport and start across the tarmac, my words just come out. "I'll be needing you less now, Bent. Mason likes to do all the driving on the weekend unless we plan on drinking while we're out. We can talk about that later." I see both the shocked look on Bent's face in the rear-view mirror and Franco's because I'm saying random things to the staff.

"Oh okay, sure, Ms. Ellen. Whatever suits you," he mumbles in an irritated tone.

Nothing else is important now.

I can see him.

My private pilot, standing waiting for me just like he always does.

Not quite as still while he waits today, but I can guess why.

As the car pulls to a stop, he's next to my door with it open and his hand there for me to take.

His touch makes everything right. The calmness flows through me, and his smile looking down at me with those damn glasses on just makes me relax.

The groan from Tyson behind me under his breath and the pissed-off look on Bent's face tells me the boys aren't happy, and to be honest, I don't give a fuck.

My hand is in his and I feel safe.

Just like he promised.

"Good morning, Captain," I say quite confidently as I stand, smoothing my suit before I leave the car. Just like usual.

"Good morning, Paige. We're all ready for you. Let's get you on board."

For a second I think about my next move and don't care what they say.

Leaning up, I kiss him on the cheek then continue to walk to the jet.

His look of absolute satisfaction that everyone knows I belong to him makes it worthwhile.

"Thank you, that sounds like a good idea. Let's get started with our day," I say over my shoulder.

I hear him behind me, mumbling and laughing loud enough for only me to hear him. "Yeah, I love how my day started, you hard-ass bitch."

This just makes me sway my hips that little bit more as I walk up the steps.

Too right I'm a hard-ass bitch.
But I'm *your* hard-ass bitch, Captain.

19

Paige

As I take my seat on the plane, everyone else gets settled in. Mason is already in the cockpit, and Holly is closing the door. My phone buzzes in my hand, and I try not to react and make it too obvious. On the inside, I'm smiling from ear to ear.

Mason: How's my girl?

Three simple words that mean the world. All he sees in this mess is me. Not the money, not the business reputation, just how it's affecting me.

Paige: Better now I'm here with you.

Mason: You look stunning. I'm going to need bigger pants if you keep swaying your hips like that.

Paige: Don't you dare. Those are the perfect size.

Mason: Like what you see, baby?

Paige: Very much so. What I see, feel, lick, and suck.

Mason: You are in trouble, Tiger. Obviously, this morning wasn't enough.

Paige: Never. Now get flying please, Captain. I have a meeting to attend.

Mason: Yes, boss!

Paige: Don't you even start that shit, mister!

Mason: But it's fun.

Paige: So is sleeping alone at your place

Mason: Playing hard ball. Okay, your wish is my command.

I hear the plane engine grow louder.

Mason: Love you. Sit back and relax. I'll keep you safe xoxo

Paige: Love you, and I'm counting on it xoxo

The plane starts moving, and I know that's the end of the messages and switch to flight mode.

Obviously, Tyson hasn't learned from his mistakes.

"Who were you messaging? You should have had your phone switched over to airplane mode."

Jesus! Just breathe in and out. I want to react and scream at him to back off. Maybe if I tell him the truth then he'll shut up.

"My boyfriend. Not that it's any of your business. Tyson, please don't slip into old habits. My personal life is off limits. Have we got this straight this time?" Nodding, he looks at me. No look of being sorry, though.

Franco just rolls his eyes at him.

"Tyson, I need to get some background on you for the book, if that's okay?" Franco sounds lighthearted like it's just part of the research he's doing. "Can you describe your role in the organization, what you actually do on a day-to-day basis for Paige?" Franco has his pen and paper ready to take notes, while I press record on my voice recorder when Tyson isn't looking.

"I'm sure Ms. Ellen could tell you." Tyson looks over at me.

Franco answers before I have to. "Tyson, we all know she's the boss. She has no idea how much you do for her. That's why it's better for me to talk to you about it." I have to give it to my Uncle Franco. He is good at this. I can see why he worked so long for the department.

"You're probably right there. I doubt Ms. Ellen knows at all how much I do for her, over and above my paid duties." He glares at me with his smartass look.

"Well, why don't you tell us then. Maybe it might get you a pay rise." Franco laughs while I'm seething on the inside.

"I don't need more money. I have enough of that," Tyson replies straight-faced. I can't stand to listen to this. I'm about scream. Standing, I walk to my room and close the door. It looks like I'm using the bathroom, but I need to just breathe and take a minute to cool down.

No, he doesn't need fucking money, he has mine, and plenty of it. Bastard has the balls to sit there and throw that in my face, thinking he's funny. I'll give him funny when I send his ass to jail. I want to talk to Mason, but I know I can't. This whole situation is shit.

Just sitting on the bed for a few minutes, I channel my strength, stand up, smooth myself out again, and walk straight to my seat. Sitting down as the boys are still talking, my phone still silently records away.

"So, we've covered what you do on the administration side. Do you work on the finance side at all with invoicing, ordering, or only with getting the information for Paige?" Interested to hear how Tyson answers Franco's question, I snap back into the moment with my full attention.

"No, I'd only ever look at invoices for Paige or for research into suppliers we are negotiating with or new tenders we're seeking, and she needs background information."

"Yeah, that's what I thought. Leave all that for those finance geeks, hey. So, what sorts of extra things are you working on outside office hours that Paige should probably be paying you extra for?" Franco keeps prying but not making it sound invasive.

"Well, up until a certain captain came onto the scene, I was handling her personal diary and keeping Bent informed, so he knew where to be and when. The two of us work closely together. Apparently, that service is no longer needed, or so I've been informed recently. And as you heard this morning, Bent's duties are being scaled back as well." He's looking directly at me although answering Franco.

"Paige is a big girl. I'm sure she can look after her own personal diary." Franco laughs, trying to break the moment. "The work you do at home, is it just things you don't get time to do at work?"

"Some of it, yes, or work that's needed for the next day that comes up after we've finished. Basically, there are times Paige and I can be talking or messaging at eleven pm at night, trying to make sure something is right for the morning. That's when we would have a good laugh or chat over a wine. Or, she has me coordinating with Brian, our VP. Sometimes I'm working with Brian late at night too, for things he's contacted me directly about."

I'm a little taken back by what Tyson has just said. I don't think I realized how much I've been working and how that impacts the people who work for me. If Tyson wasn't robbing me blind, I would actually feel bad right now for not appreciating him more. I also didn't know that he was doing extra work for Brian, either. Which doesn't make sense as he has his own PA and team of staff. I've been so busy running the company and making sure we're continuing to grow, that I've placed my trust in people who I thought had the same vision as myself. Ones who I thought had my back. Now I'm not so sure, and I'm a bit confused as to what else has been going on that I don't know about. I know in my role as CEO that I can't know everything all the time. My job is to focus on the big picture, however I feel like there are things happening that I'm missing. It's not a comfortable feeling.

"Is it okay if we do more of this later?" Tyson asks. "I have work to do before we get to the meeting. I'm happy to fill in any gaps on the return flight or later." Part of me wants Franco to keep going with the questioning, but I know what Tyson is saying is right. We both have work to do before we get there.

"Of course, young man. Sorry, I could talk all day, just ask my wife. She complains I never shut up. Get your work done and we can talk later. I'll be around for weeks. This won't be a quick process. There's so much to learn." With that, Tyson puts his head down and starts tapping away on his keyboard. I discreetly turn off my phone from recording. Then start with the work I need to get done. It helps to take my mind off everything we just learned from Tyson.

~

The thump as we hit the ground upon landing is always a jerk through your body, but a good one. Knowing you made it safely through another flight and are on the ground. Collecting my bags, I hear Franco suggest to Tyson they head out to the town car and wait for me. I'm thankful he's giving me a minute with Mason before I leave the plane. Holly and Aaron seem to get the same memo, heading out before me with just a quiet smile on their faces.

I'm standing in the cabin watching as he comes out of the cockpit towards me. His face says he's concentrating on work, until he looks up and sees me standing there.

"Hello, my beautiful lady, did you enjoy the flight?" Placing his arms around my waist, he kisses me quickly on the lips, then pulls back to check on my expression.

"The flight was lovely and smooth, the captain did an excellent job," I reply, giving him another kiss.

"You're good for my ego. But..."

"The company was shit. Can you organize better passengers next time? These ones leave a lot to be desired."

Mason starts laughing at me.

"You survived, though. He didn't do anything to upset you?"

"No, it's okay. Anyway, I better get to my meeting." I didn't want to worry Mason with the things Tyson said. It would just get him angry, which I don't need at this stage.

"Knock 'em dead at the meeting and then hurry your cute little ass back to me. I'm just on the end of the phone if you need me. Even if it's just to vent because you're spending the day with your dickhead assistant." Mason strokes his finger down my cheek.

"Don't make me feel all mushy. Love you and will see you soon." Kissing him quickly, I grab my bag and start walking out. I need to keep my tough shield up, and every time, Mason manages to make it melt away.

He's laughing behind me as I walk away.

"Love you too, my Tiger."

~

Arriving back in Chicago, Mason checks on me again, telling me he won't be too long and will meet me at my place. Traveling back with Bent, Franco, and Tyson, I'm quiet and lost in my own thoughts. It's been a long day trying to be upbeat like nothing is wrong, concentrating on work and the meeting while not able to really talk with Mason and holding everything in my head. I'm just tired. The thought of backing it up and doing it all again tomorrow is exhausting just thinking about it.

Bent drops us off at my apartment, and Franco and I are standing on the sidewalk waiting for his Uber to take him home.

"Interesting day. Send that recording to me so I can relisten tonight and see what else I pick up. Did you know how closely Tyson and Brian were working together?"

"No, not at all. I was surprised by that. Brian has his own PA and team under him. Sure, there's the occasional time he would need information from Tyson, but not a lot. He should be working directly with me." Feeling the strain of the day, I just want to head upstairs, take my shoes off and pour a glass of wine and wait for Mason.

"Well, that's something we need to add to our investigation then. I've had a message from Madam Hacker — or maybe we should just call her Miss H. Anyway, there have been no changes or opening of the invoice for the shipment, as yet. I don't imagine it will happen until after the initial shipment has left, and then it will be quickly changed before the next morning when the invoice would be emailed by the accounts department. So, tomorrow night will be the one to watch. I need you to stay out of the system tomorrow night, so we know if anyone is using your login for anything also. I'll let you know when you can go back in. So have the night off. Go on a date. Do something other than sit and worry about this. There is nothing you can do until he plays his hand."

Franco puts his arm around my shoulder, giving me a squeeze.

"Doubt I'll be able not to worry. I can't get it out of my head, no matter how much I try or Mason tells me to relax. I'll just be glad when it's over." I sigh as his Uber pulls up to the curb.

"Not long, sweetheart. We are so close. Just hang in there." Kissing me on the cheek, he releases me.

"I'm okay. He doesn't get to win this. I do. Give Aunt Veronica a kiss for me. I'll see you in the morning."

We part ways, and I head into my building.

Waiting for the elevator, it seems to be taking forever. I'm just thinking about tonight and what dinner I should organize for Mason before he gets home.

The ding of the elevator's arrival brings me back to the present.

As the doors open, I get a shock to see the little boy from a few days ago standing in there on his own, looking a little timid. I doubt his mother knows where he is or that he should be down here on his own.

I think the best course of action would be to just keep him here in the foyer for a few minutes to see if his mom turns up. If not, then I'll start trying to work out what apartment he comes from.

I crouch down so I'm at his level.

"Hello. What's your name?"

He looks at me, unsure if he should talk to me.

"It's okay, I'm a friend. I'm going to get you back to Mommy." With that, he looks a little relieved.

"Jack. I want Mommy." The doors on the elevator are trying to close at this stage, so I hold them back.

"I know, little man, come out here and we'll find Mommy for you, Jack." Holding out my hand to him, he looks at it for a moment and then takes it and walks towards me.

"Good boy. Now let's just wait here and see if Mommy comes down." He looks at me funny.

"Mommy's crying." Oh god, she might not even know he's gone.

"Is she hurt, Jack?"

"Mommy's sad, the man made her sad." Shit, there's something weird about all of this. I need to call Mason.

"I'm just going to call my friend Mason while we wait, okay, Jack?" He nods at me and I don't even know if he understands.

"Hi, baby, I'm almost home. Are you okay?"

"Yes, but I just have a slight problem. A little boy who's lost his mom is in my building. There's something weird about it. He said his mom is crying and the man made her sad. I'm waiting in the foyer to see if she comes down."

"Don't leave the foyer until I get there. Do you understand me? You don't know what you're walking into. I'll be five minutes, just stay there." His voice is stern, and I know it's to make sure I'm listening and paying attention.

"I'm not silly, I won't. That's why I called you." Jack is looking at me, and his little lip is starting to quiver a bit. "I need to go. Jack is getting worried. I'll be here waiting."

"You better be," Mason yells as I hang up. I know he will now be driving like an idiot to get here. Now to keep Jack from panicking.

"How old are you, Jack?" I watch him trying to get his fingers together.

"I'm four," he says as only a four-year-old can say, proud and with three fingers in the air.

"Wow, you are a big boy then. What's your mommy's name?" He looks at me like I'm stupid.

"Mommy," he answers straight away. Oh god, this is going to be hard

"Yes it is, good answer. But what do the other big people call her? Like, my name is Paige, so does Mommy have another name like that?" He's thinking hard now.

"The lady at the shop says Mia, but the mean man calls her bitch." Fuck, this doesn't sound good, I think she's in a dangerous situation.

"Is the mean man your daddy?" He shakes his head no.

"Does your daddy live with you?"

"No, he's a cranky man too. I don't like him."

Fuck, what is going on here?

While I keep him talking, I'm watching the elevator to see when it finally lights up, what floor it starts on.

I need to start a new conversation that isn't something scary.

"What's your favorite toy, Jack?"

His little face lights up. "I have this truck that's red. It's my favorite. But I like cars and planes and dinosaurs." He starts to get wound up to tell me more.

"That sounds really cool. My boyfriend, he's a pilot, and he flies a plane. A big one that people go on." Out of the corner of my eye, I see the elevator coming down from the eighth floor. I wonder if it's his mom.

"Can I go on his plane? With the big people? I've never been on a plane. Is it big?" Just as I go to answer, the doors for the elevator open and his mom comes rushing out with the baby girl on her hip. She races and grabs Jack into her arms and hugs him tight. Behind me, I hear the foyer door open, and Mason comes storming through it.

I hold my hand up behind me to signal for him to slow down and be quiet, hoping he'll get what I mean.

Softly, I start to speak. "Jack, is this your mom Mia?" He nods his head excitedly.

Her head jerks up from his neck where she had it buried.

"How do you know my name?" She looks terrified.

"It's okay, Jack and I were just chatting until you came. I didn't want him to wander off and get lost. He told me. My name's Paige, by the way."

"What have I told you about talking to strangers, Jack? You can't tell them our names. We have to go." She stands, taking his hand.

"Wait, please, let me help you. I think you're in trouble and need some help." Again, just like last time, I'm feeling this indescribable pull that I know her. "If you're in danger, we can help to keep you safe. My boyfriend is ex-army, we can help you." She keeps hitting the button for the elevator, hoping it'll open for her. "Please, Mia, is someone hurting you?" I'm almost begging her.

The doors open, and she quickly drags Jack into the elevator.

"You can't save me from you," she mumbles as the doors close.

"What the fuck?" I turn to look at Mason. "What did she mean?" He's behind me by now with his arms around me.

"I don't know. I'm just glad you're okay. What the hell is going on here?" Turning me to him, he takes my face in his hand.

"You make life a damn roller coaster, don't you, Tiger," he says, kissing my forehead softly.

"I'm worried about them, Mas, something is going on. Dad is a cranky man who doesn't live there, and the mean man makes mommy cry. What the hell is all that?" I look at him for reassurance of what we can do.

"Unfortunately, she doesn't look like she wants our help. You offered it to her, but she ran. Let me talk to Lex and see what he suggests we do. He'll know, having seen this sort of thing all the time in his work." Mason squeezes me a little tighter and then picks up my bag that had been dropped on the floor. He pushes the button for the elevator.

"There is something weird about that woman. I can't tell you what, but it's just a funny feeling I get when she's here. Maybe it's just the fear or sense of being lost I'm picking up on."

"Maybe it's something completely different, like a mental health situation. Which would explain the weird comment before. Come on,

259

we need to get you upstairs and pour a stiff drink. It's been a hell of a day." He leads me into the elevator through the open doors.

"I need more than a drink. I'm almost at the stage that shots seem like a good option." He laughs at what I've said.

"Not on a school night, missy. How about I compromise, a straight scotch and a bath with bubbledubles in it." I can see he's trying to hold in his laugh.

"You're so funny, Mason. I'm not drunk now, well, not yet anyway. For trying to be funny, you get to run the bubble bath for me." We enter the vacant elevator, but Jack and his mom and sister are still in my mind.

"Cool, as long as I get to watch."

"Nope, you get to organize food. I'm hungry, and make sure there's chocolate. Lots of it," I demand. Feeling frightened for Jack and his family, it's pushing me over the edge of manners.

"Oh, angry anxious Paige has arrived. Any woman demanding chocolate is feeling stressed."

"Damn right, I'm stressed. My company is a mess, my PA is cheating on me, or better described as stealing money from me. There is a lady and her kids in my building in danger and I don't know what to do about it. Plus, my boyfriend is picking on me. I deserve lots of chocolate, alcohol, and perhaps a good back massage for that." To be honest, one drink and I'll be asleep.

"Okay, baby, I can arrange all that. I can even arrange the back massage with a happy ending," he says, wiggling his eyebrows at me.

I smack him on the arm and then fall into his body for a hug.

He shrugs. "What? It always makes me feel better if I'm stressed."

I look up at him horrified. "A massage with a happy ending? What the hell, Mason."

"No, crazy lady, calm down, I just mean the happy ending. Better known as sex with my girlfriend. Are we good now?"

"Maybe, it's yet to be seen." Walking into my apartment, I still feel shaken. "Mason, should we go and try to find Mia, just to check on her?"

"No, baby, but let me see what I can find out from Lex while you're in the bath, okay?" I agree but reluctantly. I'm worried for her and the kids. I have to trust Mason, though. Hopefully he can find something out.

"Okay. I don't like it, but okay."

"Right, let's get you in that bath, and I'll bring the glass of scotch. Notice I said glass and not bottle."

"Haha, very funny. Always the comedian. It better be a big glass is all I can say."

Walking upstairs, I can't believe the day it's been.

How did things get so hard?

Life is supposed to get easier when you find the man of your dreams, but I keep finding drama to complicate life.

I hope his love for me will stand through it all.

It feels like I'm drowning and the only thing keeping me above the water is Mason.

Mason

I get Paige settled in the bath which will keep her busy while I make some calls. Whoever that dirtbag is threatening Mia and her kids is going to pay for it. There is no way in hell I will stand by and let that happen. I can't tell Paige some of the army contacts I still have because they're special forces. I need to call Ashton and see if he's in the country. He will have a contact here for me to help keep an eye on Mia. Meanwhile, I call Franco to see if his contacts can find out who this Mia is and why she thinks Paige is a threat to her.

There is definitely something not fucking right about this whole thing. I can feel it in my bones, and that's never a good thing.

"Franco, it's Mason. I need help on something without Paige knowing."

"Okay, let's go then. Tell me what you need."

"Information on a woman and her two kids living in this building and the possible men who are hanging around her."

"Okay, I don't like the sound of this, but continue." I have Franco's full attention now. So, I continue to tell him everything that has happened and what I know about her.

"I'll see if I can get anything from the surveillance cameras in the building and work out what apartment she's in. Then I'll see what douchebag comes visiting. Also, where she gets the money to afford to stay there. Leave it with me and I'll send anything I find to your phone as soon as I get it."

"Thanks, man. I'm calling an army buddy to get a contact who can keep an eye on her without her knowing, until we can get her safe from whoever this dick is."

"Mason, why are you so invested in this?" Franco questions me.

"Nobody should have to live in fear. I've seen enough of it to last me a lifetime. Plus, Paige has some weird feeling about this and so do I. I just want to keep Mia safe. By doing that, I keep Paige safe, because I have a feeling she's not going to rest until she knows what's going on. You know what women are like, they can't leave things alone once they start on something." We both laugh.

"Jesus, don't even get me started about Veronica. She never lets go of things like that."

"I better go so I can make this call before she comes looking for me."

"Okay, I'll be in touch, but whatever you do, don't approach this guy on your own. I don't want to have to bail you out of jail for this too."

"I'll try my best but can't guarantee anything."

Our call finished, I dial Ashton, hoping he's currently in the country.

"Mason, how the hell are you, man? Long time, no hear," Ashton's deep voice booms down the line.

"Yeah, I'm good, man. Finally living the dream life. How about you? You still playing hide and seek with the bad guys?" We both chuckle.

"Nah man, got out just last month. It was time, plus I ended up with a few too many bullet holes. They don't like damaged goods in our line of work."

"Shit, I didn't hear. Everything okay?" I feel bad that I didn't know he'd been injured on duty, and I haven't been in contact.

"All good, man. Touch and go for a while. Bullet through the lung, among other things. Figured it was time to become one of the soft cocks of the world like you, brother."

"Welcome to the club then, you big soft cock." I can't stop laughing at him. He's one of the toughest guys I know, but also frigging hilarious. He was one of the guys who kept me sane on deployment, because he reminded me so much of my boys.

"I'm guessing you aren't calling to check on my soft cock, though."

"Ashton, I can assure you, your cock is the last thing on the list of things that I worry about. Unfortunately, though, I do need some help. It's a long story, but I need a favor." I proceed to tell him everything in point form, and he listens without interrupting. "So, I just need someone who's around who can keep an eye on Mia until I can find out who this guy is and get the police involved. I'd do it myself, but this shit with Paige has me protecting her. But there is no way I can stand back and let a woman and her children get hurt on my watch."

"Fuck no. I'll do it myself. I'm in Chicago, man. Just settled here a week ago. Just haven't had time to look you up."

"Seriously, that's the best news I've had all day."

"Send me everything you find out from the uncle, and I'll get on it. We can talk and catch up after this. Don't want to be seen with you until we work this out."

"Awesome. Look forward to it. I'll pay you for it, just let me know what you need, and I'll make it happen." Ashton is one of the only guys I'd trust to protect Paige so I can rest easy, knowing he's on the job.

"Like fuck you will. I don't need your money. You can buy me a beer when we're finished."

"That's a deal. I'll be in touch. Thanks, man, I really appreciate it."

"You're one of my brothers, man. You know the code, anything for a brother." I feel that deep sense of belonging that only someone who has served will understand.

"Yeah, man, anything for a brother. Talk soon."

I feel anxious, standing in the living room and staring out at the city.

I don't like it, and I hate that it involves Paige.

That word is racing in my head again.

It won't leave me.

Safe.

I need to keep her safe.

20

Mason

Last night was intense trying to keep Paige calm. All the scotch did was give her extra courage to storm downstairs and find Mia, to take on whoever the guy is and then save the world. This woman has a heart of gold, but for Christ's sake, do not get in her way when she wants to use it to save someone.

I had to tell her about Franco looking into it and the friend I have watching over Mia and the kids. There is no way I will ever be able to keep a secret from her. She's like a hound dog and can sniff out anything. Although she was more settled once she knew that Mia was safe for the moment.

Franco found out she's a single mother who rented the apartment a month ago. Mia Walker, thirty-eight years old. Mother of two children: Jack, four years old, and Kayla, nine months old. Married to an Edward Walker who lives in Bellevue, Illinois and works in a mechanical shop. In debt with no assets. Several credit cards with transactions mostly at the local bars. He's obviously the cranky daddy who isn't living with them. What we don't know is why Mia is now living in this expensive apartment block when she and her husband are in debt up to their eyeballs. The rent is paid each week in cash over the counter at a bank down the block from the apartments.

We're still waiting on the surveillance tapes from the building to find who's visiting her here. Ashton has the images of her and the kids. He's in place outside the building in case she leaves and is watching every person who enters the building. Until we know who's going in to see her, it'll be hard for him to know when she's in danger. But we should have that by the end of today hopefully.

So much is happening it's hard to keep your head around it all. I'm thankful that Ashton is in charge of the Mia situation so I can be fully focused on my girl. While she's showering, I prepare her breakfast and make sure everything is in place with Franco. We aren't flying today, so after she arrives at work, I'll be entering her building through the service elevator to monitor the security footage of her office and floor. That way I can be the eyes on Tyson if Franco gets caught up anywhere else and can't be with her. Not that I think he'll do anything to hurt her at work where there are witnesses, but I'm not prepared to take the risk. Paige is also getting a little edgy about all the weird things going on around her. So, she feels safer if she knows I'm close by.

"What are you thinking about?" Her arms wrap around me from behind as I'm looking out the window in the kitchen. Her voice startles me a little, but her touch takes away any tenseness it caused.

"You, baby, wondering what outfit you're going to torture me with today." Pushing off the counter, I turn so I can check her out.

"Mmm, I approve. Love you in black with red shoes. Pity you aren't on my plane today. Maybe we might have to test out the mile-high club." I wink at her, while she rolls her eyes at me.

"Who would be flying the plane while this is happening, you wild man? I'm not sure I trust Aaron to keep us in the air." She walks away from me to fill her coffee cup. A great view to start the day.

"That's what the auto pilot is for. Plus, I'm pretty clever. I can do two things at once," I say, laughing at my own joke.

"If you ever try to have sex with me and something else at the same time, it'll be the only time you ever try it, that I can guarantee. Now what's for breakfast, master chef?" She's snarky this morning. The stress is building, and she's trying to hold it together, but it's getting more difficult.

"Well, on this morning's menu we have a ham-and-cheese omelet on Turkish bread with avocado and tomato. Does that suit my lady?" I bow in front of her to try to get her laughing. I get a small smile, but that's about it.

"Thank you, Mason, but I won't be able to eat all of that. You know I struggle with breakfast. Maybe just the toast and the avocado." She sits and starts to pull apart her food.

"Not a chance, you need to eat. I know you aren't good at it, but we're getting better each morning with how much you have. There's so much stress on you, your body needs fuel to keep it going."

"But not this much fuel," she complains.

"With the amount of energy we burn at night, you should be eating twice that. Now see how you do, and I'll eat the rest before I leave for the office too." She groans and starts on her food.

After a few minutes of silence while eating, I decide to see what she thinks of my thoughts for later.

"Tonight, you aren't allowed to be doing any work, so I was thinking, why don't we see if the 'family' wants to do dinner out somewhere. It'll take your mind off waiting for Tyson to take the bait with the invoice. Franco can keep us in the loop with everything as it happens. What do you say?" I can see her thinking it over.

"I'm not sure I want to go out. Maybe they could come here, and we order in, how does that sound?" She's quiet this morning, her voice flat.

"Sure, if that's what you want. I'll see who can make it and arrange for some Thai to be delivered. Is that okay?"

She nods with a mouthful.

"Paige, be honest with me. Are you staying home to be close in case something happens with Mia?" She looks down, avoiding eye contact when she answers.

"Maybe. I just can't stop thinking about her and little Jack. He's so adorable, and we had a real connection. Jack and Kayla can't defend themselves if someone's hurting them." She looks up slightly, and I see water welling in her eyes.

"Ashton will keep them safe. He's in contact with me all the time. Trust me, sweetheart. We won't let this guy get to them again." She nods and takes another mouthful. I'm not convinced she believes me.

"I'm just going to finish getting ready, and I'll be down in a minute." Paige stands and leaves her breakfast half-eaten. She's not her normal self. I don't want to push her. Having everyone here tonight will help her to get through another tough night.

Cleaning up the kitchen and waiting for her to come back down, I send a message in the 'crazy fam' group message.

Mason: Dinner at Paige's apartment.
7 pm just let me know who can make it.
Need your help to distract Paige from work stress.

"Bent is downstairs," her voice comes from the stairs as she's walking back down.

I meet her at the bottom. "Do you want me to come down with you?"

"No, don't be silly. Tyson won't be in the car today. It's just me. I'll see you tonight." There's no way I'm letting her leave like this.

"Come here."

"I need to go," she complains.

"Paige, come here." This time she knows I mean it, my voice stern. Walking the few steps to me, I take her work bag out of her hand then wrap her up in my arms.

"You need to breathe, baby. You can do this. I'll be watching you all day. Nothing will happen, except you giving me a hard-on every time you bend over in that skirt. You'll kill me having to watch your ass in that tight outfit all day while I can't touch. This is like torture, you know." Finally, a smile comes onto her face.

"Maybe I'll need lots of files from the bottom drawers today then." She giggles a half-laugh.

"You're evil. Just think of the blue balls I'll have by the time I get home. So be ready to fix that situation for me tonight."

"In front of all your friends? Dream on, Mason. I'm sure that's not the kind of dinner party they're expecting. I don't share my dessert. I'm greedy like that."

"Now there's an idea, chocolate for dessert. I can work on that. Prepare for things to get sticky."

"You're crazy, you know that." She smiles the first genuine smile I've seen this morning.

"This is true, it's a well-documented fact. But you know what? I'm *your* crazy, so sorry, you'll just have to learn to deal with it." I kiss her firmly on the lips.

"Now get to work, you don't want to keep everyone waiting." Turning her and tapping her on the butt, she's laughing at me as she enters the elevator.

"Love you." I hear the tiredness in her voice.

"Me too, baby. See you soon."

As the doors close, I feel her pain radiating to me. I want to take it all on for her, but I know it's not possible nor what she needs. Paige is the sort of woman who needs to be in control of her own life yet have me by her side. Any man who tried to tame my tiger would be in for a rude shock.

Checking my phone, I see that everyone can make dinner although both the doctors are on call, so who knows who we'll end up seeing. I need to call Lex and talk to him about Mia. Last night I needed to know more about her and get things in place to get her safe. Now I need to know what avenues are out there for her if she wants to seek legal help. It's important to give anyone who has been controlled by someone else, the power to help themselves. It's part of the healing process to feel empowered.

I finish off my breakfast and clean up. I just want to get to the office so I can be close to Paige. I hate being far from her. Jumping into the Jeep, I call Lex so I can be doing two things at once. Contrary to Paige's belief, I'm good at multitasking.

"Mason, what's happening?" Lex's voice comes through the speakers in the car.

"Hey Lex, glad you can make it tonight. Just wanted to talk to you about something, though, quickly if I can."

"Sure, man, what's up?" I hear noise around him so he's likely already in the office or the courthouse.

"It's a bit of a long story, but here's the short version. I need your help with a lady in Paige's building that we think may be in trouble in a domestic violence situation." I go on to explain everything with

Mia that we know, and briefly tell him what's going on with Paige and her business. I know I can trust him to keep it all to himself.

"Shit, Mason, no wonder you need us over there to distract Paige tonight. She's having a shit time. She seems like such a great woman, it sucks this is happening to her."

"Yeah, buddy, she is one in a million. So, if you can give us any information that will help us if we can get Mia to listen, it would be appreciated."

"I'll email you a list of some organizations that can help her, and I'm happy to assist her with anything legal if needed." Lex is now talking to someone in the background at the same time.

"Perfect, thanks, Lex. I'll let you go. I can hear you're busy. See you tonight."

"No problems, yeah, in court today. I'll see you tonight."

With that he's gone, and I'm pulling into the carpark down the road from Paige's office. I can't park in her building just in case Tyson sees my car there. I walk down the street with my cap pulled down low over my eyes and keep my head down. It feels ridiculous, like we're living in a spy movie. Who lives a life like this anyway? I thought this kind of shit was just made up in books and movies, but obviously not.

Let's see what today will bring. I slip into the service elevator with the security pass Franco gave me, and I'm on my way to the security room we've set up.

~

After the first few minutes of Paige flirting with the camera, knowing I'm watching and then sending me dirty text messages, she's settled into work and I think almost forgotten I'm there. Tyson seems to come and go from her office, along with Brian her VP, often during the day. Along with other managers and staff. She's just sent me a message to say she's having lunch with Franco, so I don't need to worry about her for the next hour. That gives me time to watch what Tyson—and Brian, for that matter—are up to while she's not around.

Brian seems to be doing what I would expect. In his office, working, eating lunch, taking phone calls, and a quick visit from his wife to drop off a suit to him. They must be going somewhere after work.

Tyson is at his desk, working on his computer and dealing with phone calls. I'm starting to think this is a waste of time until he gets up and looks around suspiciously. He then walks quickly into Paige's office and closes the door. Bingo!

I quickly message Franco to tell him to make sure they don't come back until I give them the okay. I don't want Tyson disturbed so I can see what he's up to.

The first thing he does is walk to her coat stand and lift her jacket to his face. Smelling it. Now that is fucking weird and freaks me out. There is no way she is ever to be alone for one second with this guy. Now he's walking to her desk and looking it over.

Initially, he's just searching through papers on her desk, like he's looking for something. Then he starts in her drawers; there's one that's locked. Good girl, at least he can't get to your personal things. His face is getting more frustrated.

He quickly sits at her desk, typing on her computer. This could be a good sign that he's up to something if he can access her machine. The typing is getting more frantic, and he doesn't seem to be getting anywhere. That's very interesting since he would need her password to access the invoices that were approved by her, supposedly. Maybe he has some software that does it for him when he's not on his work computer. I don't know enough about that side of things.

Picking up the tablet off her desk, he tries his luck with that, and the satisfied look tells me he has what he needs. Pulling his phone out, he starts snapping photos of something and then keeps scrolling up the tablet so he can take more pictures. What the hell is he doing? I can't see clearly enough what's on the screen to see what he's up to.

Then there's a noise or something outside her door that startles him. Straightening her desk and turning off the tablet, he quickly heads back to his own desk situated outside her office and goes straight back into work like nothing just happened.

I message Franco to tell him we need to know what's open on Paige's tablet as soon as she gets back in her office and that they're clear to head back upnow. Tyson is now looking through his phone at the photos he took until he sees Franco and Paige walking towards him. Franco stops to talk to him so that Paige can go into her office and not be disturbed. Closing the door behind her, I see her take her phone and push it. My phone on the desk starts vibrating.

"Mason." Her voice sounds a little panicked.

"Just breathe, baby, nothing is wrong, I just need you to open your tablet and tell me what page is open."

"What was he doing in my office, what did he touch?"

"It's okay, nothing, just papers on your desk, and he was looking through your drawers. He couldn't get into your locked one."

"Thank god. That's the one with all my private files and my handbag." Her voice is talking fast, still quaking with nervous energy.

"Paige, slow down and concentrate. What's on the tablet?" I say again, trying to get her to focus.

Watching her open it up, she looks a little confused. "What is it?"

"Just my personal diary. The one he no longer has access to. Why would he want that? That won't help him steal money from me."

No, you're right, Paige, but it lets him know where you are twenty-four hours a day, and that worries me.

"Have you put tonight's dinner in there yet?"

"No, there's no need, it's at home."

"Good, so he only knows future events which we can now change if we need to. Thanks, baby, it's not anything big so you can get on with your day now. Everything is falling into place. You're safe, and Tyson is giving us evidence to get him charged. It'll all be over soon. Now just relax and think about tonight, a nice wine, good food, and laughs. Oh, and of course dessert. Which is becoming my favorite meal."

"Really, Mason. At a time like this you're thinking about sex?" She sounds frustrated.

"Fuck, yeah. With a hot girlfriend like you, I'm always thinking about sex with you. Past sex, future sex, and the sex I would have with you right now if I were in that office with you." I can feel my balls tightening while the vision is building in my head. "Paige, go and lock your office door," I tell her sternly

"Mason, I can't." Her voice is just above a whisper.

"You can and you will. Lock the door now and stand in front of your desk where I can see you." I can see her hesitating, and then finally her body moves towards the door. "That's it, baby, let me relax you."

"What are you doing, Mason?" A little quiver has the hairs on my body standing up; she's trying to show she doesn't want to do anything she shouldn't, but already her voice and her body language tell me she does. Knowing that this security feed only comes to my computer and nobody knows it's there, I don't have to worry about this falling into the wrong hands.

"I'm making my girl relax and feel better. Now lean against your desk and slowly run your free hand over your body. Touching those perfect tits. Give them a squeeze." Now it's me groaning into the phone. "That's it, just like that. Does it feel good?"

"Mmm," she whispers into the phone.

"Close your eyes, no thinking, just listening to my voice and imagine the touch is my hand. Now run it down your thigh and slowly drag the skirt up your legs so I can see my pussy." I can see her hand hesitating. "Now Paige, I'm in control."

Her hand then moves automatically.

"Good girl. Now, because you've done as you were told, I want you to leave your G-string on and slide your hand over your pussy and rub it up and down, so you feel the pressure. Like when you like to ride my leg. That's it, baby, just like that." Seeing her open her mouth, I know a moan is about to escape.

"Remember, you can't make a sound, Paige. Close that mouth and swallow that moan." This is the hottest thing I've seen. Rubbing my hand over my cock, I want more than anything to let him free too. But this isn't about me, it's about Paige.

"If I were there, I'd be on my knees in front of you, slipping those panties down your legs and placing my hands on your mound. Opening you up and licking you from bottom to top. Tasting you and getting myself off on it. I want you to slip your finger under your panties, Paige. Swiping up and down. Feel how wet you are. That's all for me, Tiger. You're getting close, aren't you, baby."

She's biting her bottom lip and nodding her head to keep quiet. It's the most divine sight.

"Do you want to come, Paige, or should I make you wait until tonight?" Her head starts shaking no like crazy. Oh yeah, she's ready to explode. She needs this release. Fuck, so do I.

"I want you to really start to rub your clit now, baby. How you need to get you there." Her body starts rocking back and forward on her desk as she fucks herself with her fingers.

"You're so close, harder, yes, really ride that hand. Take it, take the good feeling." Her head is starting to drop back, and her body stiffens.

"Now, Paige, come for me now!" I growl through the phone at her.

Then her orgasm shatters through her body. Leaning back with her mouth open but no words coming out, her body shakes as it rides the waves of the orgasm. I can tell her legs feel like jelly as she's slumped on her desk.

"Fuck. That was so fucking hot, Tiger. Watching you like that is next level." My breathing is strained just like my pants. "How do you feel now, sweetheart?"

"Mmmmmm," is all she murmurs.

"Open your eyes for me, Paige. I need to see that mushy look I love on you. Knowing it's me that put it there."

"Bastard, how am I supposed to work?" she whispers, looking at the camera with the hint of a smile.

"Well, you can always call a PPP meeting out of the office this afternoon. I'm all for that."

"You're a bad influence, Mason. One that's like a drug. I can't get enough."

"Music to my ears, Tiger. Now go into the bathroom and clean yourself up. Bring back out the hard-ass bitch and finish the afternoon. But just know tonight you have a debt that needs paying. My cock is screaming right now. Throwing his own tantrum."

"Poor little thing. I'll see what I can do."

"Love you, Tiger. Now stop being a dirty little boss and go and make yourself respectable."

"Love you, Mason, but fuck off and leave me alone. Otherwise, get that cock down here and fuck me on this desk." Laughing, she walks to the bathroom door.

"That's cruel. Be careful what you wish for, Paige. You might want to keep that door locked so it keeps me out. Now, behave." Hanging up the phone, I lean back in the chair and groan out load.

That woman is going to kill me.

Or more specifically, my balls.

~

Finally, today is over, and Paige and Franco have just left for the ride home with Bent. Shutting down my computer and locking up the office I'm in, I'll be glad to get home to my girl. While she's home with me, I can relax and know that all is under control.

Walking to my car, my phone lights up with Ashton's name.

"Hey, just checking in quickly with my findings for today. Mia and the kids left the apartment briefly this morning to walk to the supermarket down the road, getting some basic supplies. They all seemed happy enough, although Mia is definitely frightened. She's watching everywhere, looking for someone. But I saw something else today that I thought strange and wanted to let you know."

"Thanks, I appreciate you keeping your eyes on her. What else did you see?" Almost at my car, I stop to hear what he says.

"Thought it was a little strange that Paige's driver was at the apartment block, entering through the front door with a key. He was there for about 30 minutes, and then he left again. Not sure what that's about," he says.

"Me either. Thanks, I need to find out more about that. This whole thing is fucked up. Paige is on her way there now, and I'm not far behind her. Talk soon." Cutting off the call, I need to get to my car and home. What the hell is Bent doing there during the day? Why has he got a key? Thank god Franco is with her this afternoon. I'm starting to think Bent is involved with Tyson, and somehow, they're doing this together. It would make sense in that they are two of the people who are closest to her all the time.

I need to fill Franco in and get his hacker to look for Bent on the security surveillance. He shouldn't be able to get to the penthouse, but I'm not certain of anything with this anymore, the code being her dad's birthday makes it pretty easy. If he's been in her apartment, I'll rip him to shreds. I don't want Paige with Franco when I call him, so instead, I'm driving home quicker than I should be while all the information we have is piecing together in my head. Like a jigsaw, but some of the edges don't match the other side. So far it looks like this is a joint thing with Tyson and Bent, but there are a few things that don't fit with Tyson either. We're just going to have to wait until tonight for the login to the invoice and see if we can work it out from there. Nail them and put an end to this.

Pulling into the parking at the apartment, I know I need to calm down before heading upstairs. I've done my best to distract Paige these last few days so I can't fuck that up now. A quick call to Franco before heading up the elevator, and he tells me Miss H should have the tapes analyzed by tonight. Thank god.

Riding the elevator gives me time to pull myself together. I've always wondered how Paige puts up her wall to take on the world. The last few days I feel like I'm doing the same thing with Paige. Showing her that everything is under control as much as it can be and for her to just remain calm. Whereas on the inside, my brain is going nuts the whole time trying to piece it all together. Then there's the whole side situation with Mia in the mix. My main priority is Paige, though, so as the elevator slows, I feel a little calmer knowing she's with me. Looking at my watch, I see it's only six pm. Plenty of time before everyone is arriving for dinner. I have a debt to collect and now feels like the perfect time.

The doors are opening and there she is, perfect as always.

She's read my mind, knowing we both need this.

Still in her red heels and just black lace underwear.

"Are you the debt collector?" she asks in the sweetest voice.

"Too fucking right, I am." I stalk towards her.

"You like to be watched, Tiger, I've learned. Well, I'm going to fuck you for the world to see." I reach for her and pick her up in my arms. Her legs and heels wrap around my waist, so she's rubbing against my rock-hard cock. Walking quickly to the big glass windows of the living room, I back her against them.

"Just here, I'm going to fuck you hard for everyone to see. That's for teasing me at work today and having all the fun without me." Not giving her time to talk, my mouth comes down on hers. Both opening and tongues dueling for control, the kiss is hot and consuming. I grind against her, trying to find some relief already.

"Oh god please, fuck me, I need you. I need this," she pleads, pulling from the kiss.

"We both need this." Leaning down and pulling one side of her bra back with my teeth, I take her breast in my mouth, sucking until she's moaning loudly. Just as I back off a bit and she starts to relax, I bite down on her nipple that's hard and waiting for attention.

"Fuck!" Paige screams.

"Yes, that's what I'm about to do to you."

Holding her against the window with one hand and my body, I'm racing to undo my pants. My cock is already peeking out the top of my boxers, too impatient to wait. I pull it out and push her lace to the side, slamming home and just staying still to savor the moment.

"All. Fucking. Day. This is all I could think about. Being inside you." My voice is strained, trying to hold on before I totally lose myself in her.

"Mason, please," she purrs.

"Yeah, baby, hold on. This won't take long."

I take her over and over again as we both let the confusion in our lives go. Her nails are digging into my shoulders the harder I fuck her. The pain is just what I need. To feel every part of her here with me.

I can't hold on any longer.

"You're mine, all fucking mine," I yell as the orgasm takes over.

"Yours," she screams too and then slumps forward into my body.

That's right, mine, and he can't have you.

21

Paige

"How do you do that?" I ask as I try to shift my head off his chest.

"Do what?" Mason asks as he lifts me off the window. Letting me slowly lower my legs.

"Fuck me until I'm like jelly and all mushy." I'm still draped on his body to hold me up, my arms around his neck.

"Just talented. You know, my big…"

"Ego," I say before he can say cock.

"Baby, that was cruel." We're both laughing.

"You know what's cruel? Making my legs like jelly and now I've got to walk up the stairs to my room." In one swift movement, I'm in his arms again and being carried.

"I'm loving this slave thing I've got going on with you. I think I could live like this forever." As we're getting to the top of the stairs, Mason stops.

"Are you asking me to move in?" His face looks serious. I wasn't, but the feeling of him being anywhere else than with me just feels wrong.

"I thought you already had. When was the last time you stayed at your place?" We both look at each other.

"I guess it's settled then. Are you sure you want a roomie?" he asks timidly.

"No." His face drops. "I want my boyfriend living with me. In our home. Together."

He cheers loudly, running towards the bedroom still carrying me. "You're going to regret this, but too late now. You're stuck with me. Smelly socks and all." He throws me onto the bed where I bounce and can't stop giggling.

"Tilly's right. You act like you're five sometimes."

"You have no idea what you're in for. The child in me loves to come out to play."

"So I'm learning, now get in the shower. Your family will be here shortly. I would like to smell clean, not like hot dirty sex," I demand, pointing to the bathroom.

"What makes you think after we shower together you still won't smell like hot dirty sex?"

"You're insatiable. You, in the shower, now. I'm going after you." Getting up off the bed, I take off my shoes and walk into the closet to put them away. Mason is behind me and wraps me in a cuddle.

Quietly in my ear he whispers, "I love you, Paige. Thank you for being my home. I'd live in a shack with you. No walls, furniture, or money mean anything to me. You are my home. That's all I need." Closing my eyes, I lean my head back on his shoulder and sink my body against him.

"Me too, Mason, me too. I know I can't be without you anymore. I need you with me, but more than that, I want you with me all the time. It would hurt too much for you to be anywhere else." We stand there for a minute or so just soaking up the moment, and then he breaks away, walking straight into the shower. I've got a feeling the emotion was overwhelming, because I know it is for me too. The speed at which this has happened is crazy, but it's right. Not a doubt in my mind.

~

"Paige, you have no idea what a pathetic singer this guy is. Has he showed you the karaoke video yet?" Lex yells above all the noise of everyone at the table.

"Don't you dare." Mason points at him with a mouthful of food.

The uproar starts from all the boys.

"I can't judge, Mason tells me mine is pretty bad too."

"No way can it be as bad as his, have you heard it? See these windows here? They'd all be cracked." Tate's pulling out his phone. "You have to see this."

"Just remember, Tate, revenge is sweet. You press play on that, and it's coming back to bite you one day, asshole." Mason is trying so hard to stop him.

"What's wrong, Mason?" I tease. "I'm already better at basketball than you; now even though I'm bad at singing, apparently I'm still better than you. It's okay that you come second all the time." Not realizing what I'm saying, the boys lose it. They're all laughing, and Mason has spat his drink out of his mouth.

"Baby, I'm a gentleman, I'll always be coming second." Mason kisses the side of my cheek, while the boys are all still carrying on.

"Seriously, one day maybe they'll grow up," Tilly says to me from down the table.

"Nope, doubt it. If it hasn't happened by thirty-five, it's not happening at all," Grayson announces.

The boys all fist bump across the table.

"For god's sake," Fleur groans and rolls her eyes. "I need to find me a serious man, not a boy like you idiots." She and Bella put their arms around each other. "Bella and I are on the lookout for real men, so if you girls see any, be sure to point them in our direction."

"Not happening," Tate growls quietly next to me. Before I can say anything, he's pressed play on his phone and all I can hear is a wall of noise. Drunken singing that sounds really bad.

"Oh Mason, is that you?" Reaching for the phone off Tate, I see my man on the stage, very drunk. But very fucking hot in his army uniform. Holy shit. I thought the pilot uniform was good. But oh my god. The terrible singing disappears, and all I can focus on is the sexy guy singing. As the video zooms in for a close up, his eyes catch me.

He looks lost. It's not from the drinking. His soul is lost. I see how bad he really was when he came home. I look up at him now, into his eyes, and all I see is happiness and brightness. Such a change. I'm so proud of him, seeing where he's come from. I'm not sure anyone else will notice it, but I see him. The whole him.

"Come on, Paige, you have to agree how bad that is," Lex is asking.

"All I see is a sexy soldier on the stage whose got some moves," I declare to the table.

"Yeah, that's my girl." Mason grabs me and pulls me in for a kiss.

"You two are disgusting, you know that. There's just too much happiness happening between you two." Tate waves his hand at us.

"You're just jealous. See, true love means she doesn't even hear how bad I am. If you're really lucky, one night if we're drunk enough, we'll both sing together for you. Now that'll be a treat." Mason's laughing.

"I thought you liked your friends? Why would you want to punish them like that?" I ask while everyone starts laughing at us.

"That's what friends do," Lex cuts in. "They punish each other. That's part of the fun. I mean, we're punished every day just having Mason as part of the group." Lex grins at me with a bit of cheek.

"You're all crazy, that's all I know," Fleur declares. "I think we need another girls' night out again without all the crazy boys. We can be ladies and all sophisticated."

"Because that worked so well for us last time. Fleur, you were trashed on cocktails. What part of sophisticated is that?" Tilly throws a napkin at her.

"Hey, I wasn't as bad as Bella. She was crying on my shoulder about how we needed to find her a different man because the one she wants isn't available."

"Excuse me," Bella yells. "What happens on girls' night stays on girls' night, or shall I repeat the conversation about the FF's."

"No!" all the girls scream at once. Which just winds up the boys, and before long, there are more voices than you can follow in any one conversation.

Mason's phone starts ringing, and I see it's Franco. He jumps up from the table.

"Excuse me, I need to take this." They're too busy still yelling and laughing as Mason quickly moves out of the room for quiet into the gym that's downstairs.

"Franco, what's happening?" He puts it on speaker phone because I followed him in. I want to know what's going on too. "Paige is with me and you're on speaker."

"Hi, princess. Okay, we have news. There has not been any movement on the invoice as yet, but the shipment has just left the factory and the invoice has been actioned at the factory to be dispatched in the morning. I expect any moment there will be a login from somewhere, because they'll be seeing what we are, they'll know it's been shipped. But there is some disturbing news from the surveillance tapes." He takes a breath and continues straight on. "Bent is the man who moved Mia and the kids into the apartment in your building. He has been coming and going when you're on an interstate flight during the day. I can't believe it all myself, but I have a feeling he's the man that Jack described as the angry man who calls Mia a bitch. He looks very aggressive on some of the tapes as he leaves."

"What the fuck?" I can't hold it in. "This can't be happening. Why is he with Mia, how can he even afford an apartment here? How the hell does he know a single mom from the middle of nowhere?" My mind is racing. I'm so confused.

"There's something that has been niggling at me about him, and I just couldn't put my finger on it," Mason says. "He was trying too hard to be my friend and lied to me about still staying at Paige's father's house. This shit has gone on long enough. We need to find out if he's hurting Mia. If I find he is, I'll make him hurt more than he could ever have imagined possible. It'll be long and slow. Bastard! He was right under our noses. That explains why Ashton saw him here today, during the day."

Looking at Mason, I can see how livid he is. Normally I would try to calm him, but there's nothing I can do to calm myself, let alone him.

"You need to tell Ashton," I say to Mason.

"Already done," Uncle Franco says. "He's outside watching. The moment Bent arrives at the building he'll follow him in. That bastard will never lay another hand on her. God help him if he's touched either of the kids. I'll kill him myself."

Mason starts to pace the room. The nervous energy is beginning to build and peak for him. Stopping dead in his tracks, he looks down at his phone, and I see his whole face turn red.

"Ashton just messaged. He's in the building waiting for the elevator. He has a bag over his shoulder. He's waiting with him and is going to follow him up to that floor. I'm going too."

I grab his arm. "No, Mason, let Ashton handle it. You're too close to this. You can't distance yourself." Now my anger has turned to being so frightened.

"She's right, son, let Ashton handle him. We don't want you hurt," Franco says through the phone.

"Like fuck I'm letting a brother enter a battle on his own. Paige, stay here." I can't hold his arm any longer, he's gone and out of the room.

I run after him screaming, "Mason, please, no, just stop. Don't go. I can't lose you." At the elevator, he's banging hard on the button, waiting. Turning to face me, he puts his hands on my shoulders, holding me at arm's length.

"Paige, this is an order. You stay with the guys, they'll keep you safe." By this stage, everyone is behind me trying to work out what the hell is going on. "Lex, it's Mia, she's in trouble. I need to go down. Protect her." He shoves me into Lex's arms as the doors open.

"No," I yell, stomping on Lex's foot and lunging out to put my hand in the door to stop it from closing. "You need me to help with the kids, Jack will trust me. Please, Mason, I need to do this too." I'm almost begging. "I'll help. We'll keep her safe once we get the kids. We're a team, Mason, you're not on your own." Lex shoves me forward into the elevator before Mason has time to disagree. Stumbling into him, I feel the three boys behind me as the doors are closing. Peering up at Mason, he looks torn.

"I can't lose you, baby. I just can't. I won't recover. I need you safe," he whispers to me and softly kisses my forehead.

"Your family has got your back; they'll keep me safe. I promise. Don't do anything stupid because I can't lose you either." He pulls me as tight as he can into his body while the elevator descends.

I listen as Lex quickly explains to Tate and Gray what's going on, and the two of them are as irate as everyone else. Just as the elevator starts to slow, Mason's phone vibrates again.

"It's him. Bastard, it's fucking him," Mason growls.

"Who, what are you talking about?" I grab his phone.

"Oh, my fucking god. How the hell did he do this?"

I reread the text message on the phone.

Franco: The invoice has just been changed.

The login used was Paige's ID

It's coming from her building.

It's Bent. It has to be.

Get the bastard.

Get the computer, it's evidence!

"Mason," I say as I grab him. "Don't kill him. I mean it. I don't want you hurt or in jail. Just stop him, and we call the police. Promise me, Mason. Promise me!" The doors of the elevator open to a big guy dressed in dark clothes, with his finger on his lips to make sure we're quiet.

I've never been so scared but so determined in my life.

Mason and Ashton are talking to each other in hand signals and codes. He then turns to me, whispering in the lowest possible voice.

"Stay outside the door. Wait. We will send Mia and the kids to you, and then you get them out of here safe. Back home. Do not, under any circumstances, enter that apartment. Do you understand?" By the look on his face, I know not to cross him. This is his expertise. I'm not good at taking instructions, but today I listen. Nodding, he looks up to the other guys who also nod their understanding. He then leans to Lex and whispers something to him who then passes it to the boys. I want to know, but I'm guessing it's Mason's way of trying to keep me safe.

Grayson pulls me back against him and holds me tight. Tate stands in front of me. Lex is on the side of me so that effectively I'm surrounded by them all. Ashton walks up to the door. Mason flattens himself against the wall next to the door.

Ashton checks that everyone is set, then he lifts his hand to the door, banging a couple of times.

"Maintenance, checking the smoke alarms, as per the email we sent."

I hear noise but can't hear what's being said.

"Won't take long, ma'am. We'll be in and out in five minutes. Otherwise the fire department has to come in and do a thorough inspection." Ashton remains calm and signals to Mason that they're coming to the door.

Slowly the door opens, and I hear Mia's very timid and scared voice. "My husband's not home. I'm not allowed to let people in when he's not here."

"That's okay, ma'am, it will take five minutes and we will be out the door again. If you would feel more comfortable, you can wait outside with your kids while I'm inside. Here's my ID card." He holds something up.

There's quiet where she must be hesitating a little and doesn't know what to do.

"Okay, but I'm leaving the door open and only five minutes. Don't touch anything." You can tell in her voice she's trying to sound tough, but there's very little fight left.

Mason

Ashton walks in casually. Listening, I try to quietly follow him.

"Who are you?" Mia asks me, looking at me scared.

"His assistant. Looks like you have children here. Where are they, asleep?" Mason asks.

"Umm, yes umm sleeping in there. You can't go into that room." She stands in front of the door.

Ashton goes about pretending to look at the fire alarm on the ceiling, when we hear a little voice from behind the door. "Ouch that hurt." Then there's a noise.

We both move at the same time. Not waiting any longer. Ashton grabs Mia as I charge through the door.

Sitting on the bed is Bent, typing madly on his laptop while trying to hold onto Jack.

"You can stop now, Bent, and let the boy go, it's all over," I calmly say to him.

"What, do you think I'm as stupid as that? These kids are my insurance policy. If I hand them over, then I'm screwed." He doesn't look panicked at all.

"No matter what, you are not leaving this room without handcuffs or in a body bag. You choose." You can't get any plainer than that.

"Always the hero, aren't you, Captain. Come in and sweep her off her feet so she thinks you love her. We all know you're after her money. Well, guess what? I have my fair share from her too. So, you won't get it all."

"Bent, let the boy go and then we can talk about this." Ashton is beside me now, carrying the baby girl who he managed to grab while Bent was distracted with me. He passes her behind me to Mia.

"Go, Mia, now," he instructs her.

"No, not without Jack. I can't leave my baby. Not like she did." She's starting to get worked up which is the last thing we need.

"Mia, we've got him. Go."

Hearing her crying behind me, I know she won't leave.

"She's dumb, my sister, she never listens. She wasn't supposed to talk to anyone, but of course she opened her big mouth. Talking to her and letting her find out their names." Bent says. Behind me I hear Mia gasp.

"If she's your sister, why are you treating her like this? Why are you scaring her and hurting your nephew?" I try to keep his attention and am thankful Jack is standing still and not making a fuss.

"She's just my half-sister. She's not worthy of any attention. That's why Mom got rid of her."

"You're a liar. She was protecting me," Mia yells. My head is now spinning at how this all links in.

"You're such a stupid bitch, just like that other stupid sister of ours, your dad didn't want you. You were girls. The weaker sex," he yells loudly.

"Fucking asshole, why would you say that?" I shout at him. Then Bent starts yelling his story at me.

"So, Mom got rid of them. She finally got it right and left their dad and got remarried, then had a baby. Me, the perfect male. Just what my dad wanted. He was so proud of me. He didn't need or want any more children."

Ashton is like a ghost in the night. He has managed to take Jack from Bent while he's busy yelling at me and Mia. As Mia comes around to the side of me, I see she doesn't have the baby any longer. First two safe out of this nightmare. I put my arm out and stop her from going any farther.

Then my worst nightmare. *Her* voice behind me.

"Bent... are you my brother?" Paige is holding firm and calm. My heart is racing. I don't want her in here. She must have heard what he said from the hall. Damn the guys not stopping her.

"Paige and Mia, out now," I demand.

"What's wrong, lover boy, don't want your meal ticket getting hurt? Well, it's too late. She took what should have been mine, so I took it from her." I know she hasn't listened to me. I can feel her presence behind me.

"Bent, please, I need to know, are we all related?" I just want to get her and shove her out the door, slamming it behind her and locking it.

"Don't you listen? Christ, you run a big company with all that money, and you're just as dumb as her. We all have the same mom, but your dad was a dick and didn't want a girl. He used to bash our mother. So, she got rid of you before he had a chance to hurt you. The perfect mother protecting her kids." Bent is now standing, getting more agitated. I need to shut this down.

288

"So why are you stealing from one sister and holding the other one here and hurting her?" I ask to get his attention back on me.

"Fuck off. I'm just taking back what is mine that she stole from me. My father died years ago. Everything was left to Mom. But instead of leaving it all to me when she died, no, she wanted to leave her precious girls something."

Both the girls gasp behind me at finding out the mother they never met has already died.

"Girls I didn't even know existed, until I found the scrapbook on the ever-successful Paige Ellen in her will. With a letter explaining about two baby girls she had and what happened to them. But here's the kicker. Until I found you both, nothing from the will would be distributed. But imagine the jackpot I found with one of my sisters and her wealth. So, for years I was living with no money until I managed to get the job driving little miss precious here wherever she wanted. To be at her beck and call. Listen to her order me around like trash. But all the time I was working out how to get to her."

"I'm going to take you down for this," I say, looking directly into his eyes so he can see the anger in mine. "You don't realize what you've done and who you're up against. These women are strong. You might think you've played them, but it looks to me like that's reversed now."

"Bent, why? Why didn't you just come to me? I would have given you the money, to both of you. As much as you needed. I'd have taken care of you. All I wanted all my life was a family. To know where I came from. You don't understand what that feels like." Paige's voice is starting to break. I want to tell them both to get out of here, but I know that the girls need this closure. To know why he betrayed them.

"I do." Mia's broken voice follows Paige's. "I didn't get the happy family, Bent. Or the money and good life. No one wanted me. I ended up in foster care. I got a family who didn't really want me but felt sorry for me. They tried but had other mouths to feed. Lying awake at night, all I ever dreamed of was a family of my own. Look where that got me. Married to an asshole and then blackmailed by a brother I didn't even know who was going to give me up to the abusive man I was hiding from. Once you found me Bent, you could have saved me and the kids, but instead you continued our hell. I'll never forgive you for that. " Mia is crying now, and Paige is broken.

Time to end this now.

"Ashton, now. It's time." He knows exactly what I mean. Get the girls out and leave me with this piece of shit. I know my family will take care of them. Get them safely upstairs. I can hear Paige crying and screaming outside that she doesn't want to leave me. They'll take her anyway. They know the score.

"Is this where the big bad boyfriend kills the thief? I bet that'll make you her hero. Then she gets it all, doesn't she? The happy life, the money, the whole deal." Bent is standing defensively, and I've still got no idea if he has a weapon or not.

"You'd like that, wouldn't you, Bent. The easy way out. Well guess what, I'm not that nice. I want you to suffer for everything you've put your family through. That's right, they were your family and you betrayed them. Just like the lowlife you are. Then you went and dragged others into your little game. Tyson, who doesn't have a backbone and can't stand up to you." My fingers are itching to grab hold of him, but I promised Paige I wouldn't.

"Are you for real? That pathetic little boy was so easy to manipulate. His biggest problem is that he's in love with his boss, but then you'd know about that, wouldn't you. Like a woman who pushes you around, do you?"

I hear Paige's voice in my head. *'Promise me, Mason. Promise'*. I need to keep breathing, otherwise I'll kill him.

"You just pretend to be tough but really she wears the pants. See, that was Tyson's problem. He wasn't strong enough for her either. She didn't even give him a second look, but it didn't stop him from trying. Then you came along. Really fucked up his plans, didn't you. Made him very helpful with information for me, though. That and the secret cameras in my car. It's easy to see their passwords when they type them in. They're all so gullible." Bent stands there telling me everything and how proud he is of what he did.

"See, here's the thing, Bent. Where you thought you were so smart, in fact you're just fucking dumb. You could have had all you already took and more. That woman you tried to punish for something she couldn't control has the biggest heart and is the strongest person I know. It's a powerful combination. But you already knew that, didn't you? You felt threatened by her strength. You didn't want to play baby brother to your older sisters. So instead of getting to know them, you just wanted to destroy them. Epic fail, man. You see, we've been watching you for weeks, compiling evidence, and have a whole case on you and your fraud. Now we have Mia's blackmail case too. You will be living in a place with plenty of male cell mates who will be happy to get close to you and play big brother."

"I'm not going there. I'll kill you and run before I go to jail," Bent says and starts to move his hand.

"Wouldn't try that if I were you." Ashton says, his gun now at the side of Bent's skull, cocked and ready. Leaning behind Bent, he pulls the gun from the back of his pants and then sticks it in his own. "See, it's like this. I have this rule about my family. Both by blood and my brothers in arms. I look out for them. No one gets to hurt them. You would never have the gun out before I got the shot off. I'd be happy to kill you. But we made a promise to that beautiful lady out there. We promised we wouldn't hurt you. And that was before she even knew you were her family."

I walk closer now that Ashton has him.

"Bent, that's where we're all different to you. Life is about the people you share it with, not the money it brings you." All the violence that had been building in my body has now settled. I don't want to even waste my energy on him. "Pity you didn't work that out. But don't worry, I'll enjoy living the rest of my life with your sister, as well as getting to know your other sister and the kids. I'll look after them and keep them safe. That's what I do. I value people's lives. Enjoy jail." I know I'm done now. I need to get to Paige. She needs me. Walking out of the bedroom, the policemen that Ashton and Lex would have organized are standing there waiting.

"He's all yours. Don't play nice, he doesn't deserve it."

Standing outside the door just breathing in, I know I need a moment before I go upstairs. If tonight had happened a few years ago, I don't know how I would have handled it. I'm not a violent man, but I've seen a lot and had to do things that aren't nice, for the good of my country. I struggled to get over the feeling of not saving someone, so if there were a threat against anyone I loved, I probably would have reacted first and thought about it later.

Paige has changed all of that.

She's changed me.

Helped to release me from my nightmare.

Taught me what love is.

Real love.

The kind you can't live without.

You need it to breathe.

Ashton walks out and places his hand on my shoulder, checking on me, to see if I'm okay. I realize for the first time in a long time… I am.

Standing here, I'm breathing perfectly and know I'm strong enough to go and be the one that Paige needs.

It's my turn to be that person for her. Just like she was for me.

22

Paige

Holding my breath, I hear all the yelling.

Mason telling Mia to get out with Kayla, and of course she's refusing. I want to run in there and take Kayla from her so at least she's out, but I know I can't. She doesn't trust me.

Oh my god. Bent is her sister.

Ashton comes quickly out the door with the two kids. Passing Kayla to Tate, he then shoves Jack towards me. Just as he does, I hear Bent say something I will never forget for as long as I live.

"You're such a stupid bitch, just like that other stupid sister of ours, your dad didn't want you. You were girls. The weaker sex."

I push Jack into Grayson's arms which makes Grayson let go of me. I'm through the door before the boys can stop me. I need to know. Is that why I feel so much when she's near me? Do I have a brother and a sister? I have to ask.

"Bent…are you my brother?" I feel calm because I'm in the room with Mason. Waiting for Bent's answer, I look from him to Mia and back again. My mouth is dry and my mind is on overdrive.

Mason orders us out, but I need to know more. I want to hear him say it.

So many words are coming out of his mouth, but the only ones that seem to stick with me are, "We all have the same mom…" Bent's voice drifts off and becomes a blur to me.

I have a brother and sister. I have a family. They know where I come from. But wait, why has he done all this to us? He was the only one who knew we were family.

That's when I hear the word. That evil word that brings out the worst in people.

Money. I should have guessed. The fraud. He was after money.

"Bent, why? Why didn't you just come to me? I would have given you the money, to both of you. As much as you needed. I'd have taken care of you. All I wanted all my life was a family. To know where I came from. You don't understand what that feels like." I'm trying so hard to hold it together, but I'm quickly losing the strength.

Then she breaks me. Mia's pain in her voice totally rips my heart apart. Her life was not like mine. She has been hurt, never felt love, been betrayed yet managed to still protect her babies. She never knew the love of a family, so she created her own and has done her best to keep them safe.

I do the only thing I feel I can. I reach out and grab her, show her that I care. I'm the one person she wasn't expecting in her life, yet I'm the one who has cared from the moment I saw her.

Everything is becoming loud, and the words aren't making sense. Ashton grabs both of us and starts pulling us outside to the kids. Mia breaks from me to grab them both as tight as she can. She's looking at all of us and feeling very threatened. I'm trying to talk and make it okay. Just the words aren't coming out. Tate has hold of me and is talking calmly, trying to get my attention.

As soon as he says the words, "We're taking you all upstairs. To get you safe," I snap out of my haze.

"No!" I yell at him. I try to pull out of his grip. "No, I'm not leaving Mason. Let me go. I'm going back to Mason!" They all ignore me, and both Gray and Tate have me and are dragging me to the elevator. The more I yell, the tighter their grips get on me. Lex is already holding the doors open with Mia and the kids inside. Jack is crying and has buried his head against his mom's leg.

"Paige, that's enough. You're scaring the kids. Stop now." Tate is right in my face, totally shocking me that he would speak to me like that. But it's sinking in as I look at poor Jack who now looks scared of me.

"Ashton has his back. He'll be okay," Gray says quietly to me and then pushes me forward into the elevator. The doors close and the movement upwards makes my heart hurt that I'm leaving my love with a madman who's here because of me. If anything happens to Mason, it will be my fault.

Arriving home, the girls are all waiting, and the boys deliver me into Tilly's arms as I break down and cry, sobbing on her.

Until I hear the small voice behind me. "Paige?"

I pull myself together. Oh god, she'll be so confused and scared. I'm supposed to be the big sister.

"Mia, I'm so sorry. I didn't know. Did he hurt you? Are the kids okay? Oh, my sister Mia, whatever he told you, I had no idea."

We both fall into each other's arms. I'm sobbing so hard I can feel my body heaving. We're both full of distress, yet there's a connection that I felt from the moment I saw her.

Mia keeps trying to say something, and it's all mumbled in the crying. I pull back to look at her so she can get it out.

"I'm...so...so...sorry." Then more tears are coming. This poor woman, all she has felt—all her life by the sounds of it—is that things are her fault.

"Mia, no, you didn't do anything. It was all Bent." Hearing her so scared, my strong angry feelings are starting to come to life.

"I believed him, but I should have asked you." Her face is a mess with red blotchy skin and swollen eyes.

"No, no, no. We can talk about this later. But don't take any blame for anything. You're here with me. You and the kids are safe, and nobody will ever hurt you again." I'm holding her by the shoulders so she's looking at me.

"You can't say that. My life is always like that." Before I can say a word, Lex is beside us.

"Not anymore. Now that you have Paige it means you have family. We're all here to protect you. That's what we do." Mia looks up at him, confused that a complete stranger would say anything like that. I see the girls have the kids in the kitchen, feeding Jack chocolate and Bella is rocking Kayla to sleep. Grayson, Tate, and Lex are all standing around us now.

"Mia, these are my friends...actually, sorry, they're *framily*... friends who are family. They will protect us all. You're safe here, I can promise you that. Once Mason gets here, he'll make sure of it." The tears are coming back into my eyes as the panic is still just under the surface.

I look at Tate. "You promised me. Where is he?" I'm struggling to be brave for Mia.

"Keep breathing, he'll be up soon. We all know there's no way he'll leave you alone with us handsome single studs for very long," he says, trying to make me laugh, but it doesn't work. All I can see is Mason standing in front of Bent.

"Speak for yourself, I'm far from single. The rock on Tilly's hand says so." Grayson looks towards her while she's waving her hand in the air.

"Okay, smartass. Just me and Lex then. That's enough to make Mason feel threatened anyway." His arm wraps around my shoulder, and he guides me to the living room. Everyone is trying to cheer up Jack and explain to Mia who they are. Nowhere is quiet when we're all together I've learned.

"Get your arm off my woman," is all I hear before I turn and run straight into Mason's arms. I jump and wrap myself around him as he buries his face in my neck.

"Mason," I whisper as the tears are flowing again.

"My Paige, you're safe," he says into my neck. Lifting his head, he kisses me like the world is ending. Like we've been close to danger but have come through the other side.

Before we break the kiss, I hear the boys all cheering and wolf whistling. Which sets Kayla off crying, and that leads to the girls all yelling at the boys.

Pulling back from his devouring lips, I take his face in my hands.

"Welcome home, Mason, I want you to come and meet my family and let you introduce your framily." The smile on his face at my name for his friends tells me everything is going to be okay. We have a lot to work out and deep wounds to heal. But together we can get through this.

As he slowly puts me down but not letting me go, I hear a throat clearing behind us.

"Fuck, sorry, man. Ashton, this is my girlfriend Paige. Paige, Ashton, who is one of the best men I know. Someone who will always have my back and yours."

Without a word, I launch out of Mason's arms and hug Ashton tightly. "Thank you, for everything. For keeping Mia and the kids safe, and for bringing Mason back alive. Who knows what he would have done if you weren't there?" Pulling back, Ashton starts laughing.

"I know exactly what he would have done, but that's not a story you need to hear. You're welcome. I've talked to the police downstairs, and they're taking Bent to the station. They'll need to take statements from you all, but I convinced them to give you tonight together." Ashton takes a step back from me at the same time Mason wraps his arms around me again. My man is feeling very territorial tonight. I can't blame him, and to be honest, I don't want him far away from me either.

"I should leave you to it." Ashton puts his hand out to Mason.

"No please, stay," I offer. "I know Mason wants you here. I'm sure you'd like something to eat, or wait, I know... a stiff drink. I think everyone needs a stiff drink. Please, Ashton." He looks across at everyone, his eyes lingering on Fleur, and I can see he's trying to decide.

"Come on, man, I owe you a beer at least, and I need to debrief before tomorrow. That was intense. Besides, take it from me, Paige doesn't take no for an answer."

Chuckling, Ashton nods, and we head over to the others.

I notice Lex talking to Mia who now has Kayla in her arms and looks exhausted. I need to go to her. She needs me, and I need her too.

"I need to sit with Mia," I whisper to Mason, and he smiles and lets me go as he takes Ashton to meet the others.

"Please come and sit with me. You must be exhausted, and I'm sure Kayla's getting heavy." Putting my hand on her elbow, I help her lower herself into the couch.

"Paige, I was just saying to Mia, I'm going to go downstairs and see if the police will give me the baby port-a-crib. If not, I'll go to the nearest Walmart and grab one and some diapers. The rest we can figure out tomorrow." Lex is speaking in a quiet calming tone. Not like the man I see when he's around his friends.

"That's awesome, thanks Lex. I can't even think clearly, and to be honest, I know nothing about kids." I kiss him on the cheek as I sit next to Mia. "I guess I'm about to learn. You do know I want you to stay here with me, Mia, for as long as it takes to sort this mess out and get you somewhere to live on your own."

It's just the two of us now with Lex slipping away.

"Thank you, but I don't have any money or any way of getting any. I can't have anything in my name. I ran away, Paige, from my husband. He threatened if I ever left and took his meal tickets with him that he would hunt me down. I can't stay here for long, just tonight. I don't want you in danger. Plus, I don't know if Bent told him where I am. He threatened to so often that I'm scared he did." The fear in her eyes is real, mixed with sheer exhaustion that's from more than tonight's ordeal.

"Mia, look around you. Every person in this room is now on your team. No one will let him hurt you or the kids again. Lex is a lawyer, and he already knows your story and said he'll help you. If there's one thing I'm certain of, it's that Mason will sort your ex-husband out, I promise you that."

"Damn straight I will," Mason says, joining us. "Mia, you're safe with us. He will never get near you, and by the time I'm finished with him, he'll wish he never met you, or your family. That's more than a promise, it's a fact." Mason sits on the armrest of the couch next to me with his arm around me. The weight of it is a comfort to know he's near.

Mia nods, trying to hold back the tears.

"I'm so sorry you've had a hard life, Mia. I feel guilty for all I've had, but I can assure you from now on, life will be full of love, happiness, and comfort for you and the kids." I reach for her.

"And family?" She looks at me with hope.

"Forever. You are my family forever." We both sit leaning into each other with our heads on each other's shoulders. Quiet tears run down our faces. I look down at my niece, sleeping peacefully, unaware of tonight's craziness. That will take some getting used to. I'm now an aunty to two adorable little ones.

"Baby, I spoke to Franco on the phone when I was downstairs and let him know everyone's okay. I suggested that we see him tomorrow. I haven't told him about Mia being your sister. I figured you might want to tell him that one." Mason runs his hand over my head softly.

"Thank you. Yes, that's a conversation I need to have in person and not tonight."

"I'm going to leave you two to talk. There's so much you need to work out. I'll send all this rowdy bunch home, so you can get some quiet time. Plus, I think Jack needs some quiet time otherwise getting him to sleep is going to be interesting." Mason gets up and leaves us alone.

"They do exist," Mia whispers.

"Who?" I ask, confused.

"Real men, kind ones." Her eyes follow Mason across the room.

"They sure do. The ones in this room are some of the best." I want to reassure her that she's safe with every single one of them.

"I've only just found Mason, and I'm very grateful. One day, you'll find your real man. He's out there tonight waiting for you. We'll both make sure this little one never knows any different than what a real man is." I run my finger over Kayla's cheek.

"Sounds nice, but it's not in my story, I don't think. I'm just happy with my little ones and raising them right. That will be enough for me."

Today has been too unbelievable, and I hardly know Mia, so I let the comment go for now. It'll be my job as her sister to build that self-confidence and sense of self-worth back up again until she's standing on her own.

By the time everyone has gone around in circles saying their goodbyes and offering support, it seems to take at least thirty minutes. As they're waiting for the elevator, the doors open to Lex who has so many bags, I'm not sure how he got them all in there with him.

"Lex, what the hell have you done?" I ask, stepping in to help carry some of them for him.

"I just grabbed a few things that Mia and the kids will need. I figured new things would be better, you know, fresh start." Looking a little flustered, he tries to get it all out so the others can get in. I keep waiting for everyone else to give him hell about it, but no one says a word. Mason steps forward to help him, and everyone else just proceeds to say goodbye and leave.

"Lex, I can't pay for this." Mia looks frightened.

"What? No, I don't expect anything. This is a gift for you and the kids. You needed them tonight, and I got them. It's that simple."

"You're very kind, I don't know how I can repay you for all this."

"Just seeing you smile once tonight will be payment enough. Now let's get this set up so you can get these little ones to sleep, and you and Paige can finally talk. I'm guessing it'll go long into the night."

I look at Mason who smiles with a little wink.

"Let's go, Lex, I'll show you the guest room where we can set them up. They can sleep in there with Mia. I doubt she wants her kids too far away at the moment."

"Thank you, for everything, all of you. It means more than you know."

"This is just the beginning, Mia. Welcome to the family," I say as I kiss her and pick up Jack who's now getting tired. I tuck his head into my shoulder and kiss his forehead.

What a difference a day makes.

~

Driving in the car with Mason, Mia, and the kids towards my father's house is terrifying but exciting at the same time. Last night lasted into the early hours of the morning. Once we got the kids to bed, we stayed up talking and trying to make sense of everything that had happened yesterday, the events leading up to yesterday, and both our pasts.

Mia told us how Bent made me out to be a woman who has stolen all our mother's money and they needed to get it back. He put her in the building so he could keep an eye on her and so she could help spy on me. But he was angry at her for not doing very well at it. She said she felt funny about the whole thing, it just wasn't adding up once she met me.

Piecing together what we'd both found out, it was hard to imagine the pain our mother must have felt giving up not only one baby girl, but to have to do it again a year later. She must have lived in true fear all the time. I wish we knew more.

Of course, there were tears over Bent and the loss of a brother we didn't even know, yet a sorrow for the chance lost to get to know him.

It was so late that Lex ended up staying and sleeping on the couch because he wanted Mia to feel safe that no one could get in. If the elevator opened, he would hear it and they would never get past him. It horrified me that he wouldn't take one of the beds, but I have to admit, I thought it was a bit cute.

Mason organized for the police sergeant handling the case to come to the apartment to do the statements instead of us going down to the station. It was much easier with the kids. It was perfect that Lex was there so he could support us all and will represent Mia and the kids in everything she has to now go through.

Franco was also there and delivered all the evidence he had, along with all the computer records he took off Bent's computer this morning. There was no disputing he was the mastermind behind everything. Tyson, it turns out, was just a misguided infatuated man who Bent took advantage of. I will have HR deal with him. Although he lost his way towards the end, his work is excellent; it's just he started stepping over that very fine line into my personal life.

Brian, although his role with the company is a little blurred, had nothing to do with this mess. It was actually Tyson who used to contact him late at night, which Brian just put up with because he thought I really needed Tyson to help me. We'll talk more about that and give him more responsibility so I can step back a little to get to know my family.

Now the hard part.

For all my life, my father has been the only family I've known. Along with Beth, Uncle Franco, and Aunt Veronica. They were all I needed. Although I yearned for more, I never expressed that to them.

I don't want my father to feel anything has changed now that I know more about my biological parents or that I have a sister and niece and nephew.

Pulling up into the circle driveway of the house, I sit and take a deep breath.

"Let me go in for a few minutes on my own first."

"Sure, baby, we'll be right here if you need us." Mason leans over and kisses my cheek. Mia reaches between the seats and puts her hand on my shoulder, giving it a squeeze for support.

Walking into the house, I head for the sunroom where I know Daddy will be having his morning tea with Beth, reading the paper while she reads a book.

"Paigey, we weren't expecting you." Beth jumps up to come to me. "I'll get you another cup and plate for you."

"No, please sit, Beth, there's something I need to tell you both, and it's important." I walk to my father and lean down, kissing him on the forehead. "Hi, Daddy, how are you feeling this morning?"

"Fine until you just said that. Spit it out, Paige, no crap. Is it the business? The fraud? Has something happened?"

"You could say that. We caught the person responsible last night. However, you're never going to guess who it was or what followed. It was Bent." My father's face registers shock and sadness. He sits for a moment digesting what I said and then eventually speaking up. "I

302

trusted that man with my baby, and he betrayed me. I put you in danger, Paige. I will never forgive myself for that."

"Daddy, don't be silly, you could never have known. He was very clever. I'll leave it to Franco to sit with you and explain the ins and outs one day as to how he did it. There was more to it, though. The reason he did it all was one of greed and jealousy of me." Both Daddy and Beth are looking at me waiting.

"It turns out he's my half-brother, and I have a sister who is a mother to two little ones, so I'm also an aunty." I stop, waiting for a reaction.

"Well, fuck me." The words out of my father's mouth shock me more than the last few days' events. Beth and I, both in shock, react together.

"Daddy!"

"Sweetheart!"

I turn to look at Beth, who's red, and her hand is over her mouth.

I start to giggle. I can't help it. "Well, it looks like today is full of surprises."

"Jonathon, I'm sorry."

"Oh, stop it, my love. I'm sure Paige guessed years ago. Why else would you put up with my moods and grumpy nature?"

He puts his hand out to her to come and sit with him.

"If you two have love and happiness, I could not be more pleased. Why didn't you tell me, though? Why have you kept it a secret?"

"Your father is old school, Paige. Plus, early on we didn't want to give the adoption agency a reason to take you away. I mean, I'm the housekeeper and he's my boss."

"Forty years ago, but not now. Daddy, you are a stubborn man sometimes."

"Never going to change, you know that."

"Beth, you are a saint." I get up and hug them both.

"Now, can we go back to the bombshell you just dropped about a secret family?"

I proceed to tell them everything that happened and about Mia and the kids.

"They're in the car with Mason, do you want to meet them?"

"Of course, of course," Beth starts chatting. "Bring them in. I have grandbabies—well, sort of—to spoil. Oh goodness, I need to find cookies."

"Sit still, woman, so we can meet them first. Then you can go fuss all you like."

I stand, looking at them both.

"None of this will ever change how I feel about either of you or change our relationship. You do know that, right?"

"Of course, we do. Now stop stalling, child, and go get them." My father, always the bossy one.

Mia walks in shyly, Mason with Kayla in his arms, which is so hot. and Jack's holding my hand.

"Daddy and Beth, this is my sister Mia, my nephew Jack, and my niece Kayla. This is my father Jonathon and his partner Beth." Mason looks at me, trying not to laugh.

My father walks straight to Mia and takes her in a hug.

"I'm sorry your mom didn't bring you to me, I would have loved and taken care of you too. Please call me Daddy if you like. I don't have long left in my life, but with what's left I would love to make up for what you've missed." Mia bursts into tears, and he wraps her up in one the hugs that I so vividly remember from when I was a child and scared.

Within minutes, Jack is sitting on my father's lap, and Beth is cuddling Kayla while we all chat together. I don't know what I expected, but this far outweighs anything I could have imagined.

From such a horrible deed comes such a beautiful new life for us all. We all have a long way to go to heal, but as a family, we can get there with each other to lean on.

~

"You okay, baby?" I feel Mason behind me starting to wake.

304

"Yeah, I think I am. I'm not sure how much I slept, but it's not a lot."

I'm still getting over the news from the DNA test that said Bent wasn't even related to me or Mia. That must be why I never got the same tingling around him as I did when I first met Mia. Then thinking of him befriending our mother in her dying years makes me sick. It's awful that people prey on the old and vulnerable. He can rot in jail for all I care, for everything he's done, including to my mom. Mason kisses me on the cheek, rolls me onto my back and lifts me onto his chest. One of my favorite cuddling positions.

"Yeah, I agree. I don't think you've slept all week since Mia and the kids have arrived. You need to remember, Mia has been raising them for four years on her own. I think she's all right to get through the night without your help."

"But she needs rest, and I can help. She doesn't need to do it on her own anymore."

He starts laughing at me.

"Paige, she told me last night that she loves you dearly, but if you sneak into her room one more time in the middle of the night and freak her out, she's finding somewhere else to live."

I smack him on the chest, unsure if he's joking or not. We lay in silence for a little longer until I get the courage to ask the question that has been worrying me the last few days.

"Mason?"

"Yeah, Tiger?"

"Kids, do you want them?" His hand that's been rubbing up and down my back stops still.

"Why do you ask, baby?"

"That's not an answer." I lift my head up to look at him.

"When I was in the army, I never thought about it, or even when I came home. Then I met Daisy and thought she was pretty cool." Leaning forward, he gives me a quick kiss on the lips and then continues. "Then you came smashing into my life, and thinking of you carrying my child and having a mini Paige running around fills me with a happiness I never imagined. So yeah, baby, I want kids with you. Why are you asking? Oh god, you're not pregnant, are you?" I can't help but giggle at the fear on his face. I want to string it out a little longer, but that's just cruel.

"No, I'm not, although it wouldn't surprise me. I'm not sure how much the protection of the pill is supposed to take with the amount we have sex." His face relaxes a little. "I just never thought about kids," I admit. "My life plan never even included you, so kids were something that wasn't even in my head. Over the last few weeks, though, I'll be honest, it's one of the things that keeps going around my thoughts. Now with Jack and Kayla here and watching you with them, my ovaries are doing one hell of a dance and trying to make me take notice." I pause and think about saying the next part, and my heart tells me it's the right thing to do. "I'm thirty-nine and not getting any younger, so if I'm going to have kids, I need to do it now. I know that's scary, and we haven't been together that long. I understand if that freaks you out and you want to walk away."

Looking at him, his face lights up. "Marry me," he says.

"What?" I gasp in shock.

"You heard me. Marry me, Paige, let's make beautiful babies together. I heard the practicing is pretty awesome too."

The words won't come out of my mouth.

"Well? What do you say, Tiger? I told you from the beginning, you're my forever girl. Let me be your forever boy." I can't help it. I start giggling just looking at him. He's like a little boy begging.

"Yes, Mason. Yes!" I squeal as he rolls over on top of me and kisses me all over my body.

"I love you, my fiancée. Now, can we start practicing?" He wiggles his eyebrows.

"Like you and your magic cock need practice."

We both hold still for a minute and stare into each other's eyes. Savoring the moment.

"I love you, my Magic Man. You will always be my pilot, flying me safely through this crazy life."

"Always and forever I'll be keeping you safe. That's what my love is, baby, your safety net, never letting you fall. You be my bossy Tiger, and I will always be your Private Pilot."

"Deal."

Which we sealed with passionate kissing and a hot, hard fuck.

EPILOGUE

Paige

"Can you see him yet, Mommy?" John Jr. asks from the top of Mason's shoulders.

"Not yet, little man, keep looking." My eyes are straining like everyone else's to the other side of the parade ground.

"I see him, back row in the first group." Mason points for Johnny so he can find him.

"Lewoy, Lewoy, here I am!" Johnny starts calling.

We both laugh at our little boy.

Leroy has become part of our framily. Like a much older big brother to Johnny and little Maisy. I look down at my beautiful girl all wrapped up sleeping in my arms.

Being the man he is, Mason did everything possible to get Leroy through the interview for the scholarship and accepted into the flight school. He knew that Leroy didn't need him to step in and get him a position. It was more important for Leroy to work hard and get his dream all on his own.

I couldn't make the flight to California for the interview at the time, what with everything that unfolded finding my family that week. But Mason never let Leroy down and took the jet with my blessing and made sure he got his chance.

Down below us in the stands, I see Leroy's parents and sister standing so proudly. His mom is crying and his dad with his shoulders squared with the emotions we're all feeling today. It has taken five years, but finally Leroy is graduating as a helicopter pilot in the air rescue division, taking top honors of his graduating class. We flew his family out with us so they could see him, and it was the first time they'd been on a plane. Not sure it was the experience they were expecting, having Johnny running around telling them everything he knows about the plane, and I think about a hundred times that his daddy is the pilot and his mommy is the boss on this plane.

I laugh at that statement. His father has tried so hard to convince him that he's the boss, but still to this day the same applies. On our plane, I'm in charge, and in our bedroom, he's the bossy controlling husband. Which I am more than happy to be on board with.

"Mommy, why isn't he waving back? I'm his buddy." Johnny has his little pout on that looks just like his father when he doesn't get what he wants.

Mason gives Johnny a little bounce on his shoulders. "You are his buddy, but remember what I told you, son? Leroy isn't allowed to wave to us because he'll get into trouble. See how no one else is waving? They're all concentrating on marching and not making a mistake." Mason tries to explain it to him, although I can see he still doesn't really get it.

"He looks so handsome in his dress uniform." I elbow Jacinta, our nanny, who giggles with a little blush on her cheeks. There is definitely something going on between her and Leroy. I don't ask, and to be honest I'd be thrilled if there was. Jacinta has been a godsend to us. I still get to work, and Mason still flies me everywhere I need to go. Then he helps Jacinta with the kids if they're with us while I'm in meetings. Cutting back a little was just what I needed, but it was never an option to stop working for me. I need the buzz of the corporate world. Now I get the joy of coming home to the family I always longed for.

Having Mia working with me is amazing too. She has trained up and is now my PA. To be honest, the best damn PA I've ever had, but I'm biased. Watching her blossom into the beautiful woman she is today still brings me happy tears.

"Hey, Tiger, I'm the only person you're allowed to say is handsome in a uniform." Winking at me, Mason still makes me melt. Picturing him in uniform — then the vision of no uniform — still makes me flush. My man is one hot pilot.

I thought I could only have one type of life when I became the CEO of the business. Only living for work.

Then came Mason.

He showed me love, compassion, but also how to never lose my strength and drive. Mason has allowed me to have it all.

The perfect life…so they say. I would call it my perfectly crazy life.

The only one I want.

Mason

There are many moments in your life that are tattooed on your heart.

The day I met Paige, kissed her, made love to her, told her I loved her, and the day she became my wife. My kids have tattooed me black-and-blue since the day they were born. They totally own my heart and soul.

Then there are other days that you always remember, and today is one of them. I've mentored many kids over the years, but none have become as special to me as Leroy. Seeing him in front of me, standing to attention as he is presented his wings, is one of my most proud moments. It's even more special that he got here on his own. I've guided him but never stepped in and taken over. His hard work and determination to better himself have achieved his dream. Nothing is more amazing than seeing a boy become a man.

"Daddy." Johnny is tugging on my hand and bouncing up and down next to me. "Can I go yet, can I?" Standing next to the parade ground as they throw their hats into the air, he's dying to run to Leroy — or Lewoy as he pronounces it. I've got a feeling he'll be twenty and still calling him that.

"Not yet, nearly. Just a little patience."

"Mommy says I don't have that big word, just like you." I laugh out loud at him.

"I think Mommy could be right, buddy."

Spotting Leroy coming towards us, I hold back my wild-child son so his parents and sister can see him first. After all, they're the family, and we are just the framily.

"Okay, off you go." Letting Johnny's hand go, he races to Leroy and almost climbs him like a monkey up a tree.

Feeling Paige's hand on my arm, she still gives me that tingle every time.

"You did good, Mason. Look at your boys." I try not to let anyone see the small tears in my eyes.

"We did good, baby. Both of us." I lean down to kiss her, and my little Maisy too.

"Just like we've always said. Family is more than blood. It's who you choose to love and keep safe."

I wrap my arm around her shoulders.

"Every day I'm grateful for the love for every person in our lives. But you hold my heart, Paige, and you always will."

"My heart is yours, Mason. You took it a long time ago."

Looking up at me with her beautiful eyes, I say the only words that suit.

"And I'm keeping it safe with me, my forever girl."

THE END

Continue reading for Chapter 1 of Naughty Neuro

KAREN DEEN

1

Tate

You're a prick, you know that?" she yelled as I closed the door behind me.

I always tell them how it is, straight up before the clothes come off. They agree, I'm all about consent, and it's great.

Then... we finished.

The look in her eyes told me she hadn't listened to a word I said.

Her body language telling me it's time for me to move. She was snuggling in for the cuddle and then the words would follow. *'Stay the night with me.'*

I tell them and *tell* them.

I don't do sleepovers!

Why can't they just see it for what it is. A good time. No strings attached, no commitment. We both get what we want or need. It feels great, relieves stress. No one gets hurt.

But no, they always want more.

If they thought about it before the post-orgasm glow, they would realize I'm not boyfriend material. Not even close.

I'm a player. I can't deny that.

I don't always want to be this way. My life isn't currently cut out for the ties that come with being in a relationship. That's not to say I don't want one. For the right person things would be different, I'd be different. I don't even need to search for *her*, because she's so close it hurts, yet I know I can never touch her. Instead, I bury my torture by sleeping around.

Working as a neurosurgeon at Mercy Hospital, my life is not always my own. A negative that comes from being one of the best in the business, or so they keep telling me.

I'm in demand and not in a good way. I get the cases that others won't attempt.

Others say I have a big ego, but I need to be cocky to even brave some of the surgeries I do. My success rate speaks for itself.

Climbing into my Porsche, I sit for a moment leaning against the head rest, contemplating why women chase me.

Is it my job and the prestige, or my money? I know my reputation of being good in bed is well-known and totally true. It just comes from years of experience. But what is it that has them all wanting more?

Do any of them even bother to look past my big cock, the way I can use it, and then the lifestyle that can go with it?

Starting the car, I shift into gear and pull out of the parking spot. Imagining Clarissa inside messaging her friends, telling them what an ass I am. Nothing I don't already know.

Time to head home to sleep. I never know what tomorrow brings in my world. I always need to plan for the best and be prepared for the worst.

~

My morning hasn't been too bad. Besides the death stare from Clarissa as I walk onto the unit to do my rounds.

It's nothing new. I've dodged plenty of daggers before now. Best way to handle it is to put on the charm and further piss them off. They move on quickly enough.

I don't go out of my way to hurt them, totally the opposite. By making them understand I'm not worth it, it saves them from feeling any pain.

"Morning, ladies." I give them the charismatic Tate smile and wink as I pass.

As expected, I hear the '*love*' from the three female nurses huddled around Clarissa, two of whom I have previously slept with and the third one is gay so she's happy to join the *Hate Tate* party today. Kevin, my only male nurse ally on the unit today, falls into step beside me to help with my rounds.

"Wow, you're popular here again this morning, Doctor M. Feeling the love, are we?" Kevin laughs as we enter the first room.

"Oh, definitely. I'm sure they're all comparing notes as we speak. Now, let's get onto some more interesting things, like how Mrs. Spinelli's brain is feeling this morning, shall we?"

Picking up her chart, we both switch into professional mode. We can all joke and carry on between each other, but when it comes to my patients, I'm deadly serious. Even if Clarissa had to assist me today, I know without a doubt she too would be professional the whole time until we walk out of the room.

"I'm really pleased with your progress, Mrs. Spinelli. If things continue like this, we'll have you home in no time, cooking for the family and all the bambini grandchildren."

She smiles up at me through tears at the mention of her family, and I see her husband, who never leaves her side, squeeze her hand with all the love he has. He doesn't say much, but I know his life would stop if something happened to his wife of fifty-three years.

"Just no dancing on the tables yet, okay?"

"You didn't say anything about the chairs, though." She laughs with her cheeky smile.

"I have to watch you, don't I? Keep an eye on her, Kevin, otherwise she'll be having a dance party in here tonight."

We all have a laugh as I move on to the next room.

"Thanks, Kevin, I'll be back later to check on Mr. Chester, but page me if there's any change in his temperature." I leave the unit to head to my office and wink at the ladies again just to keep my asshole status going. Sitting at my desk, I open my laptop. So far, today has been a normal day — well, as normal as it can be.

Until...

That one email that turns my day to shit with just two words! It's the rotation roster for my next group of interns. Six future doctors who think they've got what it takes to become a specialist doctor or a neurosurgeon, which are at the top of the doctor chain, in my eyes.

We are the ones that all junior doctors, at one point, want to be. We work on the brain, for god's sake. How damn cool is that? Every day I pinch myself that this is my life. Saving people's lives by operating on one of the most important organs in their body.

The heart specialists will argue that point... but they've got nothing on the brain. My eyes start skimming down the list. Six interns in total for me to torture over their six months of trying to impress me.

John Bricker – that's an unfortunate name to grow up with. Too close to dick or prick. I hope he doesn't live up to that name.

Scott Lowen – I'd heard about this guy in the hospital. Thinks he's a hot shot. Well, this'll be fun. I'll take that chip off his shoulder.

Molly Hollo – This is her last rotation before she graduates, so she should be full of knowledge. Let's see if she has the edge she needs for this specialty. I love to see the passion in new doctors.

Andy Lawson – First time in rotation. Will either want to impress or fly under the radar. Remains to be seen.

Stuart Finn – Another know-it-all. Plus, from what the ladies tell me, he is trying to work his way through the female nurses, without much success. There are only a few of us who have that talent.

Arabella Garrett – Fuck! Just fuck!

Those two words!
They are bound to cause me a world of pain.
My best friend's little sister.
I knew this day might come, but I'd hoped she would be teamed with one of my colleagues.
Grayson's going to kill me!
I've known Arabella since she was just older than a baby. Watching her toddling after Gray and us boys when we all became friends in high school. She was a super cute little sister to us all. Then when their mom died, we all stepped in to protect her from the outside world of hurt. She had been through enough, and we made a pact ensuring she would never be so broken again.

Gray warned Lex, Mason, and me the day she turned eighteen. Arabella wasn't the little girl we left behind when we were all away at college or forging our careers. She was off limits for anything except being his sister. No looking, touching, kissing, flirting, and definitely no fucking.

Taking one look at her in the skintight white dress she wore to her eighteenth birthday party was enough to know that fulfilling Gray's rules was going to be hard. Hard being the word of the day! I remember that night like it was yesterday. It was the first time I thought about her in ways you should never think about a sister. Even if she is a pretend sister!

Now, staring at my email, I know it's too late to have her swapped to another doctor without offending her. Bella would have her notification email already. If I tell her I don't want her under me, I know what she'll think.

Shit! That's not a vision I need to be thinking about. Snap out of it, you horn dog. By assigning another doctor, she'll think I have no confidence in her. Which is totally the opposite of how I feel. She is doing amazing as an intern. All the reports I've seen show what natural talent she has. I know neurology is not where she wants to focus her career, but it's such an important part of any doctor's training. Knowing how the brain affects the body can help a diagnosis.

Bella is a born pediatrics specialist. I've seen her with children on the unit, talking and treating from teenagers down to the little ones. They respond to her, and you can see the light in her eyes while she's with them. I need to discuss this with her and see if she's okay working with me. Maybe it's not my decision to change this. The thought of her changing actually worries me more than putting up with seeing her every day.

The more I think about it, I actually don't want her working with my colleague. Because if she's not with me then she ends up on Dr. Zoran's list, and that's not an option. He considers his female interns' *fair game* to seduce. I might be a man-whore, but I never abuse my power in a relationship or any work position.

There have been times I've felt I needed to report what I suspected, then he changes his tactics at the last minute and I have to back out. He runs a fine line between what is acceptable and what's not. It just seems too much of a coincidence that every night shift he works, he rosters on a single female intern to work with him, on her own. Why it is never a male is just a little obvious to me.

I have other emails to sort through, trying to push my thoughts of Arabella aside, I know full well it won't leave my mind until I deal with it.

My phone rings. I look at the name lighting up the screen.

Well, can the day get any better?

"Hey, you in your office?" Gray's voice booms down the phone.

"Yeah, why?" I'm still distracted by my emails and want to avoid the topic of the one I keep going back to.

"Just letting you know I'm off this afternoon so won't be running to the court with you. Meet you there."

"Okay, man. You're obviously just afraid I'll show you up. At least I won't have to take it easy on you by slow jogging so you can keep pace." I can't help but chuckle.

"Whatever, you idiot. Got to go. About to get busy, you know, helping bring a human into the world. The most important thing in this hospital. Being a real doctor." I hear him laughing as he hangs up the phone.

He *has* to be kidding. Sure, being a Gynecologist/Obstetrician is impressive, it just doesn't compete with operating on brains.

Grayson is one of my best friends, and although we give each other shit, every day all day, I couldn't live this life without him, Mason, or Lex. It's just the way it is. We function as a unit. There's something about your friends, you can't put it in words easily. Well, I can't. I just know that they have my back and I have theirs. It's that simple.

Looking at the time, I need to get some work done before I head out for our weekly Thursday lunchtime basketball game. Or should I call it our weekly hour of giving each other hell about whatever is going on in our lives. We started doing it as a way to see each other as our lives and careers moved us in different directions. We can't always make it each week, but regardless, the game goes on. I'll move heaven and earth to be there, it's that important.

There's been times in our life where it was hard, like when Mason was deployed overseas in the army. We missed him like crazy, and although no one said it, we were worried he may not come home. His role as a chopper pilot was dangerous. Our Thursday game was like our prayer vigil talking shit about him and sending him stupid videos and pictures. It helped us, but we didn't know how much it helped him to get through the horror he was living, until he came home and finally shared it with us.

Now it's just our weekly game full of stupidity and stress relief.

The morning flew past with different consults and discussions with other staff on diagnoses they needed help with. I've changed clothes and am walking to the elevator to head down to ground level. Then I'll run down Michigan Avenue to meet the guys at the court. It's hot as hell outside, so I'm wearing a loose muscle tank top and shorts. Probably not appropriate for the hospital, but hey, it's not like I'm doing rounds in them. No different to some of the Lycra shorts the chief of staff turns up in when he rides his bike to work. Man, those shorts should be outlawed. The bulges they show are disgusting, clinging so tight to the body, there's nowhere to hide anything. There is no good place to look when he walks towards you. It's dick and balls on show for the world to see. I mean, I love to show off my assets, but that is just gross.

Waiting for the elevator, my favorite nurse of the day walks past, and if I didn't know better, I'd swear I feel the imaginary dagger being shoved hard between my shoulder blades. Some days, working in this place is like being back in high school and playing on the football team. Everyone wants to sleep with the quarterback, but they can't take the rejection when they don't get to be my girlfriend and wear my letterman jacket.

The ding alerting the doors opening breaks me from my daydream.

"Bella," slips from my mouth. I try to get my body to move but it feels like I have weights on my legs. The look on her face tells me what I need to know. She got her email. What it doesn't tell me is how she feels about it. Now to battle my better judgement and ask that very question.

Fuck, today is my lucky day!

Arabella

If I can just have a few hours to myself for a shower and some sleep, I will be in blissful heaven. I know I have just six months of residence to complete, but I'm not sure I will survive it. I look at my brother who is now living the good life. An established doctor and choosing his hours of work. Not the shit shifts the resident interns get, and if we're lucky, it's just one graveyard shift and not back-to-back, which seems to happen a lot. I know I was blessed to get my position here in Chicago at Mercy Hospital and still be close to my family, but some days I wonder how much of a blessing it was being in the same hospital as my big brother.

Grayson and Tate laugh at me when I complain about the long hours. Telling me we all have to be punished, it's what makes us better doctors.

Yeah, right.

They only say that now because it's not them in the middle of it. Plus, they don't have two big brothers who are doctors. One a brother by blood and the other a brother just acting the pain-in-the-ass like we're related. I know my mother made Gray promise to look after me before she died, but being twenty-five now, I'm sure I can adult all on my own. He made that promise when I was five years old and hasn't given me a breath of space since.

Then there are the boys.

My *'extra brothers'* as I call them.

It's like I can't even sneeze without at least one of them replying with a *'bless you'* out of nowhere. I love them all dearly but enough is enough. Mason and Lex aren't too bad, but Tate...

Where do I even start with Tate.

It's like he tries to play the cool older brother. He has the worst jokes—even worse than my father, and that's saying something. Tate doesn't have a serious bone in his body in everyday life. Yet put the doctor's coat on and it's like his twin brother comes out to shine. His talent as a neurosurgeon is not even in doubt. There are a lot of people who are alive because of his skills and intelligence.

His reputation precedes him in the hospital, and it's not just his surgical one I'm talking about. If I believe all the gossip, he has slept with two thirds of the single females on staff at Mercy. Hell, he's probably slept with half the single women in Chicago. Well, I hope he's only with the single women. It makes me want to gag every time someone talks about him and the supposed superhero cock he has. I mean, really, I don't want to think about him with another woman. It's just hell!

Then they use me as the messenger in getting him to call them back or give them his number. It's annoying. The crazy thing with Tate, though, is he's super protective of me. At times even worse than Grayson which is a little peculiar. Any guy who has even tried getting close to me since I grew boobs has been warned off by my brothers. Who makes it to twenty-five and is still a virgin?

No one would believe it if I told them.

I try to joke about how I meet men the boys don't know. Grayson shuts down like he doesn't want to hear it, but Tate's reaction always makes me curious. He fires up and threatens to find them and scare them away from ever going near me again. Of course, he then tries to laugh it off that he's joking, but I never believe that.

I lay my head on the bed in the doctors' rest room. I don't have the time to go home to sleep. A few hours here will be better than nothing and enough to recharge the batteries. Picking up my phone to set an alarm, I notice an email notification. It's probably important as I only have my work emails on my phone, not my personal address.

Lying back staring at the words in front of me, I feel the adrenaline surging through me.

Shit, I have my new doctor assigned for the next six months.

Doctor Tate McIntyre!

I thought life was painful with having two doctors in the hospital who are overprotective and constantly checking on me. Now I have to train under one. This is going to be a nightmare! As soon as the other interns find out who I am, they'll turn against me and think I'm getting special treatment.

How am I going to put up with Tate being my boss?

Will he even trust me?

Acknowledge my skills?

Stop seeing me as his little sister and instead as the doctor I am?

There's no way I'm sleeping now.

My mind is too busy trying to work out how the hell I'm going to cope with this.

After I try calming my thoughts about work, my real fear takes control. How do I hide how I really feel about Tate when I have to see him every day, for hours on end? Although it's been hard over the years, I've managed to keep everything to myself. Not that I've had anyone to share it with. My brother would totally lose his shit with both me and Tate, even though he has no idea. My friends are all from either medical school or from work at the hospital. That's a big no to share anything with them.

Dad and I are close, but this isn't a conversation to be had between a father and daughter. I can't just turn up at his house for a coffee and say, *'By the way, Dad, I've had a major crush on Tate since I was sixteen. Also, I'm a virgin and all I dream about at night is him being the one to change that.'*

My poor father would have a stroke and it would be all my fault. Instead, I keep it to myself. It's not like anything can come of it anyway. Now I just have to be punished for six months and ignore those eyes that dance every time he looks at me, and that cheeky smile he wears when he puts his arm around my shoulder and squeezes me close, which would be a whole different story if it weren't done in fun. I've never had to try so hard to stop my body from shivering when he touches me. A few times he has asked if I'm cold and I end up wearing his jacket even on a sixty degrees

Fahrenheit day. Men... they are so stupid. Why would I be cold on a hot day?

I keep telling myself I shouldn't even be thinking about Tate like this. He is the biggest man-whore in the hospital, which I am constantly reminded of. He's not even someone I should want to settle down with. Yet, I can't think of anything I want more.

There's no way he is the one you dream about growing old with. The Prince Charming, who rides in and sweeps you off your feet and takes you to the castle. Marries you in the big white puffy dress and makes you his princess. You have the perfect family together, two children, a boy and a girl. Then you live happily ever after.

I giggle out loud in the sleep quarters. Luckily there are no other doctors in here with me. Just trying to picture Tate anywhere in that story is just comical. He would be the guy who hangs out in the local tavern, with all the town wenches hanging off him begging for their turn tonight, almost scratching each other's eyes out to be picked. Imagining describing that story to Tate, he would take great delight in being the center of attention. As always, it's all about Tate.

Trying to sleep is becoming a waste of time. There's no way to switch off my brain. Why do I have to be the one who has the big imagination in the family? Or, as Dad tries to tell me, the overthinker. Apparently, I'm like my mom in that department. Thanks, Mom, couldn't I have gotten a better trait than that one?

I sit up on the bed then rise to my feet. I know the only way I'll make it through the next part of my shift is to start the caffeine loading. Although the cafeteria has shit coffee, it's as potent as rocket fuel which is what I'm going to need.

"Hey, Lozzie, I'm just heading down to grab some black tar, better known as the cafeteria coffee. Do you want one?" I ask my head nurse who is old enough to be my mom, and at times has given me the hug I needed to suck it up and keep going through a tough shift.

"No way, sweetie. I'll stick to my herbal tea. If I'm going to die, I would rather it be from something good like an overdose of chocolate. Not poisoned by that stuff you try to say is coffee." She waves me on as she sticks her concentration back in the file she's reviewing on the computer.

I know she's being funny, but it's partly true. Yet, being a doctor, and although we know the health issues, we all need that black tar to get through our days or nights, or both.

"On my death certificate, can you make sure they put, 'death by cafeteria coffee'?" I call over my shoulder as she chuckles, and the elevator opens for me. Walking in and turning to lean against the back wall, I'm still thinking about my email.

Grayson is going to go crazy when he finds out. To be honest, that pisses me off. This shouldn't even involve him. Yet it does and it will, you can bet money on it. Hands in the pockets of my coat, my head leaning back on the wall, I close my eyes for a moment to digest everything. I can feel the elevator slowing to stop on the neurology unit, which will be my new home for the next six months. The doors start to open, and I take in a deep breath, letting it out while slowly opening my eyes.

Shit!

"Bella." That voice.

Christ, I can't take my eyes off what he's wearing — or the lack of, more to the point. I can see his muscly arms and a peek of his chest through the open sides of his tank top. Why does he have to be so damn good-looking? Couldn't he be ugly, have big thick glasses, a bear belly, and a receding hairline like some of the other senior doctors here?

"Tate," is all I can say standing there staring at him. Neither of us move.

The doors start to close, but he lunges forward to stop them until he now shares the elevator with me. I need to pull myself together. There is no way I'm going to show any weakness here.

"Or should I say Doctor McIntyre, my new boss."

"Hmm, so you got that memo too," he says, coming to stand beside me and leaning against the back wall. "How do you feel about it?" he asks a little tentatively, which is not at all like Tate.

Oh, no you don't. You do not get to treat me any differently than the other interns.

"The same as I do with every rotation change, nervous but excited about learning new things and from a new doctor. Why do you ask?"

"Come on, Bella, cut the tough bullshit. It's just you and me in here for the next thirty seconds. Are you going to be able to work with me as your boss, and it not be an issue?" He's now turned and facing me, his stare burning into my soul.

"Get over yourself, Tate. You're just another arrogant doctor who will push me, try to make me cry, and tell me how hopeless I am, all in the 'interest' of making me a better doctor. What, don't you think I'm up for the challenge? Not one of the boys like you're used to?" I see the frustration building in his body language.

"Bella, that's not what I mean, and you know it." As he's waiting for me to speak, I make him sweat. His glare grows more intense, trying to work out what I'm thinking before he finally relents. "What's up your ass today, Miss Tinkerbella?" he asks with a cheeky grin.

"Don't you dare. You know that name is off-limits at work, Tate. Don't you dare disrespect me in the hospital. I may not be the top neurosurgeon here, but I'm a doctor and should be treated just like all the others." He backs away, holding his hands up in surrender. "So, to answer your question, if I'm okay with you being my boss. Absolutely, bring it on. I'll show you how good a doctor I am. By the time the six months are over, you will not only be eating your words of doubt, but you will be trying to hire me to become the next wonder child of neurology. Which, by the way, will be a waste of time, I don't have the ego for that job. I prefer to just quietly go about my role of saving the vulnerable children in the world without the need to share it around the hospital." I have no idea where that whole speech came from, but it's out there now, so I need to own it. I can feel the elevator slowing down so I can make my escape shortly.

"What the fuck was all that shit that just came out of your mouth, Bella? All I asked was are you okay working with me. You know, one of your big brothers and the crap the interns will give you?" I've pissed him off and I don't care.

"They don't worry me in the slightest. I only care what Doctor McIntyre thinks of my skills and that he grades me accordingly. Do you think you can manage to treat me objectively and just like any normal intern?"

Running his hand through his hair, I see he's ready to start giving me a big brother lecture but is trying to rein it in as the doors open.

"Yeah, Bella, you want normal intern treatment? You've got it. But when you hate me by the end of this, don't come complaining to me or Gray." He gestures for me to leave the elevator first.

"Bring it on, Doctor McIntyre. I look forward to working under you." I storm past him, and I'm totally heading in the wrong direction for the cafeteria, but I need to escape before I lose all the cockiness I'm feigning.

The only time I want to be working under him has nothing to do with this hospital.

Damn. This is going to be hell.

LIST OF TITLES

The Complete TIME FOR LOVE Series is now available:

LOVE'S WALL #1
LOVE'S DANCE #2
LOVE'S HIDING #3
LOVE'S FUN #4
LOVE'S HOT #5

Standalones:
GORGEOUS GYNO
PRIVATE PILOT
NAUGHTY NEURO

Coming Soon
LOVABLE LAWYER

ACKNOWLEDGEMENTS

They say it takes a village to raise a child.

It takes a tribe to write a book. Thank you to all my tribe. I'm so grateful for each and everyone of you.

To my beta readers who pushed me with Private Pilot to bring you the best book I possibly could. Vicki, Linda, Nicole, Shelbie and Di. I love you girls. I couldn't write without you keeping it real, telling me what needs improvement and pushing me to write faster, in the nicest possible way of course.

Linda Russell and the team at Foreword PR & Marketing. Thank you just doesn't seem enough for the help you give me. For the laughing and crying you get from the other side of the world and the random questions at weird times of the day. Linda you have a big heart and I am grateful we have connected. Plus, I need a late-night mother who yells at me from the US to go to bed. Love you lots

Contagious Edits are my savior. Lindsay thank you for making my jumbled words make sense and adding the many commas that are always missing. You are amazing for looking after me and always doing the edit as quick as possible for which I am extremely grateful. I would be lost without you.

Opium House Creatives and Sarah Paige. You make my covers look hot, teasers sizzle and read all my words to format them and make them look pretty. Thank you for always doing your best for me and nothing is ever a pain. Even if I change something ten times. So grateful to have had you on this journey.

To all the bloggers, book groups, promoters, and book lovers who share our posts, talk about our books and makes us smile every day. The indie world wouldn't survive without you. Thank you for everything you do for us.

My readers. You are AMAZING! When I write I want to share the world that's in my head. You beautiful people allow me to do that and then shock me with your amazing reviews and messages. Grateful for the love you share with me.

My mentor, blessed and grateful for you in my life and the guidance you give.

To my family and friends – I promise you will see me out of my office sometime this year. Just keep hanging in there.

My husband Michael, children Josh, Caitlin and Aimee. Thank you for your love and patience. You are my world and reason for breathing.
Grateful.
Karen xoxoxo

Printed in Great Britain
by Amazon

25773894R00192